THE BUCKET SHOP

BY

Vernon Phillpot

©

'It's all guess work'

(cover Jo Ross)

CHAPTER 1

RAY

When someone tells me that something is true, my initial reaction is invariably an unspoken 'Oh yes, says who?' I don't mediate the feeling; it's entirely spontaneous and arrives fully formed. My face, thank goodness, gives nothing away. It is totally non-judgemental and presents an attentive picture of equanimity. But inside the alarm's gone off and I'm on suspect-fact-alert.

I guess you would say, if you were kind, that I have a pathological mistrust that anything I'm asked to believe is actually true, and therefore - a bona fide fact.

It started, or at least I became aware of this irritating mental tick, when I was told on more than one occasion as a child to drink at least five pints of water a day or else. 'Or else what?' I said; a reply which was received with either shocked silence or angry bluster. But I soon discovered that no one actually knew what the *'or else'* was;

they guessed: dehydration, death or some crippling illness connected to my kidneys, which at that time in my life were little more than rumours. I was ten and not impressed. I doubted it. Why five pints and not six or more? And who had measured them, because I'd never been asked? Most importantly: what happened in the end when those questioned popped their clogs? Did the 'five-pinters' actually live longer than those who had pleased themselves? Again, no one knew. Most facts, I therefore concluded, were fickle and not to be trusted.

Take Vikings; as a ten year old I was very keen on the Vikings, and Vikings as everybody knew had horned helmets or, if they were very important, helmets to which raven's wings had been attached. I'd seen pictures in my school books of hirsute, burly men standing on the prows of Vikings ships with fine helmets thus adorned above their bushy, massive beards. We were taught that this was a fact. I doubted it, and my suspicion was based upon personal experience. When my brother and I played Vikings, we fought each other with wooden swords and wore helmets made of cardboard to which we had attached cardboard cut-out wings or horns fashioned from toilet rolls. In both cases, swift chops to the skull always resulted in the wings or horns being dislodged. They were absolutely *not* battle worthy. No self-respecting Viking bent upon rapine and slaughter would have worn a helmet that got in the way of his sword play.

Only later were my childhood intuitions confirmed, when as an adult I read in a Sunday colour supplement that Vikings had never worn horns or wings, and that the belief was entirely due to the romantic fantasies of a nineteenth century, Wagnerian, costume designer.

I'm saying all of this now because of what Ed had said to me earlier when we were drinking our coffee in his aquatics shop.

'Over seven hundred varieties of them, mate.'

This was in response to my looking at a tank of startlingly bright little fish with blood red bellies and iridescent stripes along the edge of their blue and white spines. As soon as I had heard him my internal inquisitor had arisen with the unspoken 'Oh yes, says who?'

'Nice colours.'

'Grand little fish,' he said, tapping the aquarium affectionately. 'Kids love them.'

He hadn't answered by unspoken question, but I let it pass. 'Sell many?'

'Oh aye, them, guppies and zebras. The big three, all cheap and cheerful.'

We've been friends ever since the seventies when we were teenage art students at Lincoln Collage of Art and later at Chelsea.

'Never kept a fish,' I said, straightening up. 'My mother had had a bad experience with a goldfish when she was pregnant, so wouldn't let fish into the house.'

'Most popular pet in the country is fish.'

I raised my eyebrows, the visual equivalent of 'says who?'

As if reading my mind, he said, 'That's more than all of your dogs, cats, rabbits, hamsters and guinea pigs put together.'

I let that pass as well, because I thought it was in essence true, since fish are usually kept in bunches, which means that there are always more of them than most pets. It was not what I would call a real fact; it was more of a guesstimate, since who in their right mind would go to the trouble of getting all the available data on pet ownership and then adding it up?

Ed's fascination with fish is long standing. When we lived together as students, he had a small tank beside his bed, which he kept going right up until his graduation party, when some bloody conceptualist deliberately emptied a full glass of vodka into the tank and they all went belly up.

He keeps them partly because he loves fish and likes to look at them and partly because his business: 'Fin Aquatics' bolsters the modest income he gets from his painting. Guppies and the others might only be worth a quid or two, but some of his collector's fish are worth anything from a hundred to a thousand pounds each. The sign above the shop was a joint effort; I did the lettering and layout, and he painted the two impressionistic clown fish at either end. Some arty people have been a bit sniffy about him dividing his time between fine art and shop keeping, but there's no real conflict between the two, because he opens when he likes, lives above the shop and paints in one of the outbuildings. There are not many places in London where you can still do that, but Walthamstow, in east London, is one of them, although not for long, property prices are rising even there.

I had walked from Millfields in Hackney, near where Angie and I live, up the River Lea to the marina at Springfield, and had then headed up Copper Mill Lane past the reservoirs to the bottom of Walthamstow market, which is in fact the High Street. Nearly half way up, off to the left, is Buxton Road, and on the corner is 'Fin Aquatics'.

'Longest market in Europe, this: a mile from top to bottom,' he had said, not long after he'd moved in.

I doubted that, and found out later that it was only reputed to be the longest. It was in fact approximately one kilometre. I should have said something at the time, but I didn't, which is a pity, because he still repeats that untruth as a fact.

Being no longer employed allows me to visit Ed whenever I wish. And once the morning rush hour is over and there are no more cyclists tearing past, I can bimble across the marsh quietly listening to the bird song, and Geordie, our border terrier, can sniff about without fear of being sliced in half.

He's actually Angie's dog, but as she's never home for long, and I am officially retired, most of the exercising falls to me, not that I really mind. She's a British Sign Language interpreter and today was interpreting at a conference at the British

Library. Actually, just to get things right, I should restate my employment position as: *offensively retired*, since I was made redundant last year from my job at the Ordinance Survey, against my wishes. Despite what the flash monkey from Human Resources said, at fifty eight, not many alternative doors to employment open to you. But I keep busy with my own private cartography; I take commissions, making maps for all sorts of organizations and individuals. At present I'm working on a historic study of all of the tributaries of the River Lea, where they rise, the origins of their names, past uses, that sort of thing.

My visit had nothing to do with any of that. In August, I'm fifty nine, which means that from then on I shall be taking my first tentative steps towards the killing fields of oblivion, in other words, entering *'the shadow of the valley of death'*. From sixty onwards people you know start to drop off the planet in ever increasing numbers, and who's to say that you won't be next? As God's creations we've been allotted three score years and ten in which to do what has to be done, but the ten bit often seems a bit unstable, as if the Almighty had tagged it on as an afterthought. It is certainly not a fact, and not necessarily even an average. I've already lost friends and relations, most of whom were far younger than me. This sixty niggle is nothing to do with death itself; I've no worries about that. We all die, that's a certainty, a genuine fact that you could take a hammer to, and a fact you learn at a very early age. Having two sets of grandparents is Nature's way of giving you a foretaste of your own demise. Their phased exit is to soften you up for your own death sometime in what you hope will be the distant adult future. But when friends die in their thirties, forties and fifties, it's harder to reconcile, scarier in fact, since it wakes you up to the continual presence of the grim reaper lurking somewhere behind you; at sixty, he's close enough to smell his breath.

Ed and I, when we're together, spend most of the time drinking coffee in the shop, if it's open. Walthamstow market is not the sort of place to leave the door open and hop upstairs for a brew, too many odds and sods around. A real fact about the market is that it is a long street containing every variety of new Briton you can think of. Ed likes it.

He comes from Boston, on the Lincolnshire side of the Wash, went south as a student and never really went back. Although he did try once when he was looking for a cheap studio space, but his then wife, the long-gone Meg, couldn't stand it; she threatened to shoot herself rather than stay any longer in the company of what she called 'web-footed, potato heads', which insults their agricultural origins, and repeats the ancient slander that Bostonians evolved webs to help them keep afloat in the ague infested swamps of the Fens.

All very dramatic, but when in the end Ed wouldn't budge, she followed the age old route down the neck of a bottle and relied on drink to dull the ache of being in a town whose only claim to fame was that the Pilgrim Fathers were so disenchanted by what they saw that they sailed away as soon as they could to try their luck amongst the native heathens of North America. Whether Ed should have persevered despite Meg's developing drink problem is debatable; artists can be selfish bastards. What changed his mind in the end was realizing that as far as the small coterie of gallerists and art critics who controlled the London art scene was concerned, nothing beyond the North Circular, or the M25 if you were lucky, was worth the expense of traveling to see it. In their eyes, Ed was the mountain and they were Mohammed, and if he wanted to be taken seriously as an artist, he needed to get himself back down to London sharpish.

The one thing you can rely on Ed for is the quality of his coffee. As far as I can remember he's always drunk coffee. As a student, he was the first of our gang to regularly drink real coffee, and the first to own one of those Italian, aluminium, stove top coffee makers that have become universal style icons. His original one, a much blackened Bialetti Moka Express is still in his studio, but is now used only to hold his brushes.

I'd brought some shortbread biscuits and we were sitting comfortably in the shop talking of this and that. Geordie was curled up in a corner beneath a sunbeam.

'You know people go on about bucket lists, don't you?'

His eyebrows rose as if expecting some hideous revelation. 'Yes.'

'Listing things you want to do before you die?' I said to make it absolutely clear.

'Yes. Usually done by people who are still too young to worry about it.'

'Ah, Ed, now that's where I'd beg to differ. Waking up in the morning is only an assumption. Death comes when it comes, so thinking about it is not a waste of time. In fact it's a useful preparation; it gets you to focus on the important things in your life while you've still got the time.'

'Oh god, this is not a sixty thing, again, is it?' he said. 'Ange told me you were getting morbid.'

Ed has the face of someone who knows a lot about life through the misadventures of youth, and when he says things like that you are half convinced that what you're listening to contains wisdom. He wasn't always so physically characterful. As a student he was quite handsome, in a son of the soil sort of way. He's thickened out since those days, of course, but he was stocky even then, and his right painting arm and shoulder have muscled up through constant use. Never fat, he's kept his figure, but robust. His cap of unkempt short hair is the one thing that hasn't changed. There are no silver threads amongst the brown, which looks odd when seen above a face aged by his early indulgences. According to Angie, who's known him almost as long as I have, 'It's the sort of face that louche woman are drawn to.'

'If you mean my concern with the passing of time, then yes.'

'*And yonder all before us lie deserts of vast eternity.*'

6

'That exactly.'

'Kicking the bucket?'

His flat Bostonian vowels made what he said sound vaguely sordid.

'Yes. If it was you, what would you put on your list?'

'Nothing. I've done it all, already.'

I looked into his watery blue eyes, at his stubbly chin, and at his posture of belligerent contentment. He was lying, especially as he was always going on about wanting a major show in a good London gallery before he died.

'Supposing you hadn't done it all, though? Do you think it's a good idea to clarify the mind and write down what's important still to do - before it's too late?'

He scrunched his mouth and did his usual little rocking of the head; at least he was considering it.

'If you mean bouncing up and down from the end of a fucking bungee or sky diving – no. That's fucking nonsense. That's sensation seeking. Hardly a fitting thing for a man approaching death, is it?'

When he's being obtuse I sometimes want to punch him in the mouth, but unfortunately he would punch me back, and he's stronger. So I hit him where it hurts.

'Like having a London show in a good gallery.'

The scrunching stopped and his mouth and lips had begun to wriggle around instead, so I knew I'd riled him.

'That's not an item on a fucking adolescent wish list, Raymondo, that's recognition. That's holding your head up amongst your peers. You can't wish it to happen. It's conferred. Like a fucking knighthood. Totally different.'

A customer came in and glided effortlessly around the tanks trying not to attract Ed's attention, but his presence silenced us both.

He calls me Raymondo when he's being sarky. But he was wrong. You can create your own recognition. All sorts of people do it through a bit of palm greasing or networking. They make an effort. Ed never puts himself about more than he has to. I put this down to a lack of real drive and the fact that stuck out in this Edwardian suburb he'd become complacent. He gets by. But what would he do if he was not alone and there were others who were working to make his wish come true? What then?

'Ant eggs and snails, please.' There was a hint of the steppes in the customer's face and voice.

'Freshwater or tropical?' said Ed, all smiles.

I put my coffee mug down on the counter, mouthed 'See you later', and slid out.

7

CHAPTER 2

ED

Have you noticed that when a fish makes a sudden turn, it leaves a pure line drawn in the water? They're almost too brief to see. They exist in the mind only as an afterthought. I've always thought that Ray is drawn to these ogees in the water more than to the amazing colours of tropical fish.

When we were at the Chelsea School of Art in the seventies, he was always banging on about the acuity of the line, pursuing it like a mad Zen monk wherever it led him. One minute he'd be raving about the clarity of ancient Assyrian wall plaques and the next going into ecstasies about a Picasso black and white print. It didn't matter where he found it. He said that the best artists held chaos at bay by the precision of their marks.

'Look at this, Ed, look at that line! Cuts like a sword.'

I wasn't at all surprised when later he went from being an illustrator to being a cartographer. Although I think he'd also have made a good Zen artist; one of those blokes who make lightning quick daubs on great sheets of rice paper with fat, well inked brushes. Not me though, I couldn't survive without colour *and* form, and despite what he thinks, fish and water are a perfect combination of both. That's where the same battle lines are drawn.

I don't do too badly selling my art, but it sells in fits and starts, and bills still have to be paid, so alongside the fine art and selling live fish, I've developed a moderately lucrative side-line making and selling fish prints using the traditional Japanese gyotaku method. It's the ultimate in recycling. If one of my more colourful fish die, which sadly they sometimes do, instead of bunging it in the bin, I use it to print with. And if there are no handy bodies available, I raid the Turkish fishmongers up the market for interesting looking exotics.

As an art form, gyotaku began hundreds of years ago when Japanese fishermen wanted a pictorial record of their best catches before selling them in the market; the modern equivalent would be some bloke having his photograph taken for a fishing mag while cradling his catch.

The first print I made was from one of my own clown fishes. Being so small, it probably wasn't the best subject to start with for a cack-handed beginner like me, because when I pressed down on its belly to make the image, its guts popped out of its arse. I didn't really get the hang of it until I'd moved on to bigger, fishmonger sized, fish like red snappers and red mullet.

First you clean the fish, stuff all its vents with cotton wool to stop any leakage, dry it off with a hair dryer and then dab it all over with black, nontoxic, acrylic paint. After that you wipe most of it off again, cover it in good quality rice paper and *gently* press the paper down to make the actual contact. Remove the rice paper carefully and voila - a ghost like impression of a fish complete in every detail. You can usually get a couple or more prints out of the same pressing, which is great if you want to do them side by side to give the impression of a shoal. The skill comes with what happens next: adding the colour and painting the eyes, which don't leave a good enough impression on their own. Using fishmonger fish gives you an added bonus: when the job is done, you can clean off all the gunge and its fish for tea!

When Ray popped in the other day, I knew at a glance that he hadn't come to buy more of my work for his modest collection. I guessed it was his current hang up about approaching sixty: approaching as in *sometime next year*! I'm not dismissing that. Thoughts of mortality come to us all. Five years ago, when I turned fifty, I had a mild flirtation with the Grim Reaper, so I know how scary it can feel, but being told you might have lung cancer is not the same thing as having it. I was lucky and so relieved when the doctor gave me the all clear that I went straight out side and lit up again - to celebrate.

That's not Ray's way, though; warning lights started flashing in his head. And believe you me, he loved his tobacco, but he sussed the whole thing out and stopped it dead, just like that. There were no ifs or buts, he said he was a slave no more and knocked it on the head. We were both heavy smokers, preferring the strong French classics like *Gauloises* and *Gitanes*, the real coffin nails. You've got to admire him, not an easy thing, heroic even, but bloody disconcerting, because it revealed a less familiar Ray, one given to the same strong minded gestures you might find in serial killers and religious nutters.

He's not religious, though, thank god, but if he were I guess you'd call him a 'hide-and-seek' Deist, someone who believes that God has hidden the answer to the riddle of the universe in the world around us, and that it's our duty to find out what it is by hard work and diligence, one step at a time, much like completing a dot-to-dot picture book.

Me, I'm more a *what-the-fuck-am-I-supposed-to-do-today?* sort of bloke. If I wake up then I'm alive, which means the day already exists, so from then on it's down to me how I spend my allotted time in the great existential dance of being. But in the end what does it all matter? You've got hardly any say in it. When your time is up both *the hide-and-seekers* and *the what-the-fuckers* like me are taken out as and when, *que sera sera*, and no amount of philosophical fretting will alter that. The clock is ticking when you are born and will end more or less when your genes decide that it will.

I swear that Ray actually sees his allotted time like a great big egg timer, and every grain of sand escaping is a day lost or a thing undone. I know he's already hunted in the alphabet of his DNA for his origins, which is taking his dot-to-dot concept back through time. He said it was to jump history and start from scratch, since only the aristocracy has any real proof of their historical pedigree. They can show you who they are descended from by unrolling ancient, illuminated, vellum rolls and pointing to registered armorial bearings. The rest of us of us poor sods get ours unrolled from the expert examination of our spit.

The august university to which he sent his spit says he's a Celt, but considering his nervousness about his death, I'm surprised he didn't take the opportunity to ask the real question that's bugging him: 'How long have I got till they pull the plug and I exit from planet Earth?'

In my case, I dread to think what my DNA would reveal. Apart from me, we Farrows never left Boston in Lincolnshire, as far as I know, although it being a port, god knows what riff raff has ended up stranded on its mud banks. I wouldn't be surprised if it revealed we were the missing link between humans and the fish that walked out of the sea on their fins.

What lies behind his fretting is a feeling that life's disappearing so rapidly that unless he's quick about it he'll die with too many things left undone. A touch of the *'We have left undone those things which we ought to have done; And we have done those things which we ought not to have done; And there is no health in us'*. Although I'm not sure he's much bothered about the *'ought not to have done'*. Not me, though, I do what I've always done – paint. My dot-to-dots, if I had them, are my paintings. They go backwards in time, each painting leading off from the one before it right the way back to my earliest childish daubs, which is less metaphysical and more to do with just sticking at it.

His unwanted redundancy probably didn't help his pessimistic outlook, that was brutal and broke the anchor chain too early before he was ready to go, but you'd have to add into the mix, how he was before the chop; the bits he was responsible for. And if you were being honest, him never having had a very active sex life with Angie must have made him a tad restless. It's hard to think straight when you're yearning for something you're never going to get. Not that that is unusual, from what I've heard, for as far as sex is concerned, once the babies are born and raised that's the job done. Long lasting marriages are less hot beds of lust and more three-legged endurance races. At least with my ex, the delectable Megan, she only kept the fires going for as long as she did to compensate for the remarkable joylessness of the countryside around Boston. It was fornication as an aesthetic act, a defiant gesture against the acres and acres of surrounding cabbage fields. No mean feat, because although there's plenty of lust, there's not much passion generated in the Fens, or then again, if it wasn't that, then keeping me quiet was to disguise her real intention, which was to fuck off home to her mother in Sleaford as soon as she could. Not that I hold that against her.

Ray, Meg and me, met at Lincoln Collage of Art on the foundation course, but she very wisely gave it all up at the end of the summer and went to work in a florists. Being with me, she cottoned on fast that an artist is more of a wanker than one half of a pantomime horse. We are not romantic souls; we're introverted and pre-occupied. The artist as a light hearted, careless, urban vagabond is a product of the last century and inherited wealth. I only just made enough in Boston to keep the mortgage paid on our squalid terrace house in Worm Gate, a damp little runnel just off the Haven.

That's why I admired Ray's eventual switch from graphic design to a paid existence in the Ordinance Survey. Unless they are mentally lopsided, most art students should shuffle off the nonsense of 'being an artist', recognize their limitations, get a job and paint at weekends.

As I said, when he came through the shop door I knew what he wanted to talk about: the latest dots he'd discovered in his dot-to-dot book. These new dotes concern his burial, and whether it's important to search out the actual site of our final resting place? This stems from a half-wit idea he's got hold of that we all carry inside us an ancestral knowledge that draws us like a magnet to our final resting place.

To me, that's a load of old hippie bollocks. He may have been born seventy-odd metres up on the dizzy heights of the Lincoln Edge, but I was born only two metres above sea level on the silt lined banks of the Haven, or thereabouts, on land God created as an afterthought. My ancestors had the cosmic vision of fish and could not imagine life beyond the Wash and Boston's muddy fingers. Me, I was off early down south where hot life coalesced around the Thames, and as a consequence, when I die they can plant me where ever they like. My cockle-headed ancestors can whistle for me from the watery hell where I've no doubt many of them remain.

The trouble with Ray and lot of other Sunday supplement liberals is that they want their cosmic revelations to be open to all comers as a kind of transcendental democracy. He still thinks spiritual knowledge is transferable like some new age credit note. If he has a 'final thing' to do before he kicks the bucket then, he assumes, so does everyone else, and making a bucket-list should be looked upon as the first hesitant step towards spiritual curiosity. But bungee jumping and skydiving, the most common items on many lists, are not signs of a metaphysical yearning, but a media goaded prod to sensation seekers.

But Ray being Ray, he's gone one step further, he wants to open a spiritual one-stop-bucket-shop where likeminded folk can gather for support, recommendation and solace as they lay bare their seriously weird or transcendental desires.

'We could vet them,' he said, 'weed out the nutters and the ones who simply want to get excited, and then work as a team, each one helping whosoever appears first on the list'.

'Musketeers of the soul,' I said factiously, to his deaf ear.

As it happens, I have the key and use of a lock-up off my backyard, and in a fit of comradely solidarity I told him he could deck it out and use it. It was in truth a way of letting him burble on, but now he assumes I'll join the club and give him a hand.

'There's nothing I want to do, mate, before I die that I'm not doing every day.'

'Ah, but to complete the circle, your painting needs display. Before you pop your clogs, Ed, we've got to get you the retrospective that assures your reputation. That way, all of your paintings that I own will increase in value. Win, win, win all round.'

That was dirty; because he knows what he says is true, although the increase in value bit is incidental. To painters like me, essentially somewhere between impressionism and naturalism, our oeuvre, our stuff, is not the current flavour. My paintings are neither witty nor humorous asides; they are created from hard won mark making. So being the sap I am, I said yes, and that, I guess, is what he wanted to talk about.

CHAPTER 3

RAY

It pains me that Ed still smokes, especially since it did for his dad. All the time I was with him he had a fag on. He doesn't always smoke it to the end, but it's there on the side slowly burning away. And that is not just the pious thoughts of a convert; it's a real concern for my friend. As an ex-smoker, I can't say I don't enjoy snuffing a bit of his second hand smoke up the nostrils, from time to time, but I feel awful about it because I know what it's doing to him. He's so blasé about the whole thing. In the end, I suppose, the main difference between us is that he's just a smoker, and I was both a smoker and a collector of smoking paraphernalia.

I became absolutely obsessed with all of the tackle that goes with smoking. It was never enough to simply light a cigarette or load a pipe. Oh no! The lighter had to be right, and for me that always meant a Zippo. My first one was absolutely bog standard steel, but later, thanks to e-Bay, I bagged my pride and joy, a genuine, US military, Zippo from Vietnam, complete with 'Nam 71-72' and a peace sign incised on the cap, and on the base section a crudely engraved inscription that summed up the average grunt's view of the war: 'We the unwilling led by the unqualified to kill the unfortunate die for the ungrateful'. It was battered and the underlying brass was coming through the coating, but I loved it.

I was a nicotine addict; I confess that, but I never sunk so low that I would smoke any old shit. I've always had a sense of propriety – that there is a right and wrong way of being in the world. I also believe in beauty, and despise ugliness.

Now being an addict might make you think that it ruled out what I've just said, since in the public imagination we addicts are little better than slavering robots who will do almost anything to satisfy our various addictions. Not so me. Right from the start I found the mass produced fags sold on the High Street lacking in both quality and taste, and one other thing: romance. They were the equivalent of the awful keg beers that the brewers tried to palm us off with: all fizz and no soul. Ordinary fags smelt awful, and they still do. Catching a face full of someone else's smoke leaves your eyes sore and your lungs heaving.

Had Ed and I never discovered French cigarettes, I'm not sure that either of us would have become addicted, so strong was our shared loathing for the standard brands. I can almost remember the first time that I caught a lung full of exotic French tobacco; it was heady stuff. I'd always liked the smell of cigars and pipes and had never worked out why cigarettes couldn't smell equally delicious. When I smelt my first *Gauloise* I knew they could. If they were not available then I'd smoke *Gitanes*. Both came in beautiful evocative packets, design classics. The *Gauloise* packet was blue and soft and bore a drawing of a Gaulish helmet, while *Gitanes* came in fabulous darker blue packet showing a stylized gypsy dancer. Then there were the real stars of the French tobacco experience: *Boyards*, nothing compared to their dark pungent raw taste or smell. You couldn't get them everywhere; we'd have to beg them from someone who'd been to France on holiday. They were truly exotic. They looked like sticks of yellow chalk since the tobacco was rolled in yellow maize leaves. By god they were wonderful, and as carcinogenic as they come, real killers.

As I said, getting French cigarettes wasn't always easy, so in time I moved away from shop bought cigs and began my love affair with rolling your own or, on occasions, smoking a pipe. This is when finding the best tobacco I could afford became important. I would search it out in those little, bespoke tobacco shops that used to exist in most cities. I was also never a common or garden finger roller; I could do it and admired the dexterity of the best of them, but pathetic looking smokes that looked like a cross between weasel shit and a fat spliff had no place in my smoking history; my productions were as good as tailor-made because they were produced from an ancient, second hand, 'Zig Zag' rolling machine. It was cheap when I bought it, and cheap when it was first made. Its surface had been worn smooth by constant use and, I like to think, by a little love, which I swear I could feel through the palm of my hand. An added bonus was that it was made by the original French company and therefore predates all of the cheap Chinese copies that have since flooded the market. I can't swear to it, but I've a strong suspicion that it was made in the original factory at Mantes-la-Jolie in the Île-de-France before that facility was destroyed in the war.

When I was sat smoking, I would sometimes catch myself fondling the Zippo, or become aware that I'd put my hand into my jacket pocket and was letting my finger's trace the two words: 'Zig Zag' on the rolling machine's lid.

I still have them both, they're in my collections' cabinet, although I've not used them in anger for nearly five years now, not since Ed had his scare and I went to see my doctor, who suggested I should give up the evil weed. It wasn't that I was on the verge of death or anything. He said if I carried on as I was I would end up *'drastically incapacitated'*, that's medical speak for 'totally fucked'. Angela, as you might expect, added her two penn'orth to his recommendation and - *Shazam!* - by amazing strength of character, I gave up, not even resorting to chewing gum or hypnosis. Bang, clean break. It wasn't easy, but I always knew that I could, because I've always prided myself on having a disciplined mind. I couldn't have done my job if I hadn't. But even so, tobacco going from being central to my life to nothing was quite a step. Suddenly my collection of pipes, tobacco pouches, cleaners and stampers was not a thing of beauty and a joy forever, it was a scarlet woman constantly reminding me of the joys I'd lost. I got rid of practically the lot; the best went on e-bay and the rest got sent off to the charity shop or the bin.

One thing I have kept, since it's useful for storing things like paper clips and pencil sharpeners, is my favourite ashtray, now completely cleansed of all ash and tarry residues. It was a present from my sister on my fifty-ninth birthday. It's more or less square, has an outer rim of mottled brown and an inner sunken bit that is essentially stone coloured but marked at the four corners and at the centre with intricate, indigo blue, Zen like squiggles. Turn it over and you'll find scrawled decorously across its base the letters: FG, the maker's initials, and a little stamp with a G in a circle. It's nothing; it's an ashtray. I like it, of course, but in the grand scheme of things making an ashtray isn't the hardest or the most creative thing in the world to do, and yet the maker, the potter, felt compelled to own it and to embellish it. That's ego; isn't it? That's what most skilled, artistic people do – they proclaim their individuality and their works' origins. But a maker of ashtrays is no more skilful than me. In my work precision was all. You can't mess about with maps. They either are representations of what you say they are or they are fantasies. And yet I believe that a cartographer is also an artist, that our work has beauty and has style and grandeur. The difference is that unless your work is bespoke you go unnoticed and unknown. We're like those medieval craftsmen who built some of our most beautiful and enduring artefacts but whose names are lost in time. The work speaks for you but doesn't say your name.

Up until my redundancy this never bothered me particularly, but then it did. After all of those years of toil I suddenly realized that nothing that I had achieved would ever be attributable to me. My professional life would pass unnoticed. That's when I decided to leave my signature on my last piece of work. I wasn't the first one to have done that, others in the office had already added their initials or full names onto maps, losing the script in some of the coastal detail. God help us if we had been discovered. It would have been a sacking event. But I thought I'm already being sacked in all but name, so what the hell.

I was working on an OS Land Ranger map of the Isle of Arran, just off the west coast of Scotland, when I slipped '*Ray Brook*' into the hatching of one of the more rugged stretches of the coast. I won't say where, all I'll say is that it was a bloody deft bit of penmanship, and lies somewhere south of a line drawn between Drumadoon Point in the west and Holy Island in the east

You hear about the replacement of jobs and services by computers, but unless it's you being replaced, you let the news slide over you and disappear into the slop bucket of constant information. But let me tell you, being bested by technology sucks! I'd given umpteen years of my life to perfecting my cartographic skills, only to be told that all the time I had been heading down a cul-de-sac marked 'obsolete technology'. That was a kick in the guts.

I'm more or less over the pain and despair of it, but not the feeling of being the walking wounded in the on-going wars of progress. My pedigree now stretches back in time to include the handloom weavers, the spinners, the Luddites and the agricultural followers of the mythical Captain Swing. We are all the left overs, the footnotes in the history of technology; and our reward? Time on our hands, and it's that that concerns me, considering that at fifty-nine there's a lot less of it than there used to be. But, and it's a big but, empty time is not time on your hands, its virgin time, and therefore I'm more or less free to use it to put in place the final building blocks of the edifice I've come to know as me, Raymond Brooks. People tell you when you are young to find out who you are, which sounds complete nonsense to a child. 'I know who I am. I've got a name. I'm your son or daughter.' In adolescence you understand the question, but only later as a mature adult do you realize that you don't know who you are, that you are a shape-changer, a work in progress; as someone on the brink of doom, you have the chance to put the final touches to the whole edifice, to present to the world the finished article.

'Oh that's who he was.'

I know that both Angie and Ed think my interest in finding my final resting place is bizarre verging on lunacy. I can accept that, to someone who doesn't share my head my thoughts and desires are always going to be odd. We are different people. Our swan songs will therefore be different.

I can't deny that having a magnetic pull to some region or place sounds closer to the fantasy world of the scientifically disposed, but it's not. Facts are like ice cubes, they are solid until heat is applied, and then they change their nature. Why, for instance, do we humans like one person rather than another? Apparently, we are drawn to each other by a weak ability to respond to each other's pheromones. It's still unproved, but maybe a new fact is being formed from the melting of the old ice block that said that pheromones had no power over us.

When it was first postulated that birds and other animals had some special component in their make-up that enabled them to migrate long distances, it was unclear what it was and where it could lie. Navigating using visual landmarks, the position of the Sun and stars and the smell of particular places is part of it, but it doesn't explain it all. How is it that the Artic Tern, which weighs a mere eighty to a hundred and ten grams, can fly from somewhere like the Farne Islands off the Northumberland coast all the way to Antarctica and back again to breed, or the leatherback turtle go from Asia to the west coast of the US, a distance of over ten thousand miles, in its hunt for jelly fish?

Some scientists have suggested that these animals have inside them an iron-containing molecule called magnetite, which works like a compass in response to the Earth's magnetic field, or, more recently, that some birds and other creatures use photo-sensitive molecules that alter their state depending on the direction of the Earth's weak magnetic field, which in some way they can access.

That is not *'hippy bollocks'* Eddy bloody Farrow. No mate, it's at the cutting edge of science, where facts are born. And all that I'm suggesting is that it's within the realms of possibility that some of us have a weak internal location mechanism that is accessible to some, but not all, people. I am drawn to East Anglia, fact, and I suggest, since this is a long term attraction, it could be based on some form of genetic inheritance, since I have an arse-about-turn reaction when it comes to anything west of the Greenwich Meridian Line. The west is foreign, alien territory. So my quest to investigate this phenomenon is science not bloody witchcraft. I want to track across the region taking internal readings of my reactions until I feel I can zero in on a significant place. It's going to take time, but think of the reward! To feel like the round peg feels as it slips effortlessly into a perfectly fitting round hole. That is a quest worthy of a Parsifal, and that role falls to me and to me alone, since it relates solely to me, Raymond Brook.

CHAPTER 4

GEORDIE

'If you can't endure then you'll never make much of a dog'.

I'd like to think that I inherited that maxim from my father, but sadly, like most dogs, I've never met him. I was told by my mother, of distant memory, that I was his spitting image, but since we're both border terriers and our family have been that way from time immemorial, it's not surprising. No, I got that pithy observation from an old Labrador I met in Millfields Park, in Hackney. I was quite young, little more than a pup, and was being given grief by Raymondo, the Alpha male in my small ménage. He'd been shouting at me for not bringing his stupid ball back to him, and I'd been acting up; you know, just ignoring him and sniffing about. Well, that's when I met the Lab; he had totted up while I was otherwise engaged and, like most affable dogs, had begun to sniff my arse.

'You're a fool to yourself, mate. Play their bloody game. Chasing a few balls now and again is nothing, is it? Especially if you can't win. Keep the Alpha happy and you'll be living in clover for the rest of your life.'

I turned round to sniff him. 'Every time I get his sodding ball he bungs it away again,' I said between sniffs. 'That's rubbish. There's no pleasing him.'

'Listen, sunshine, that pretty little thing round your neck is not a decoration; it's a collar and on that collar is a ring, and through that ring they fasten your lead. Dogs are not free, period. You, my hairy little mutt, are a pet, which is a slave by another name. So lump it. We're all slaves; every one you can see running about now is a slave. Every one, that big black dog over there, the one they call Arthur, those whippets, the cockapoo, me and you. But most of us live well. It's not much of a trade is it: swapping your hypothetical freedom for a life of luxury and a few moments every day pleasing one of the naked apes? In any case, it's all hypothetical, because if you can't learn to put up with all of their vagaries you'll end up at the vets with a needle in your neck - the big sleep.' He said, closing his eyes and wagging his dewlap.

That set me thinking, but as thinking takes time, and I was young, I took his warning at face value and did what he said; I ran all over the place chasing balls and sticks and anything else that Raymondo threw for me. But I did think about it eventually, and time and circumstances have proved that the old lab was right, life as a slave is a damn sight less demanding than going feral and a life on the run.

My pack, for want of a better name, consists of Ray, the one doing the bunging, and his wife, whose name is Angela, but who is normally called Angie, and Ed, Ray's best friend. Because I'm a Border terrier, they called me, rather unimaginatively, Geordie, but most dogs around here know me as Skrart, with a rolling r and the accent on the a.

As you've no doubt noticed, one of the great differences between us and humans is their insatiable appetite for hoarding. My possessions are few, a couple of well gnawed lumps of antler, a few manky, threadbare toys from a cut-price store, and a few anonymous looking, but succulent lumps of pig skin marinating nicely buried somewhere in the garden. I am content, but them?

Ed's shop is a fish shop, fine, the well-organized ranks and ranks of tanks, and all of the gear make sense, but his home and studio, madness; cluttered beyond belief. It smells nice, I'll give him that, even rank in places, but stuff clutters every surface. The bedroom, my favourite place, since I often get to lie there unmolested amongst his daily cast offs when he's supposed to be looking after me, is marginally clearer than his living room. I like it best when he's not alone, when he's active in the pit, and by God that man can certainly make the bed talk. He bangs away like a creaky floorboard. And the aroma! Oh, when naked apes couple – heaven, and so exciting, although in my case also a bit depressing, since when it comes to a sex life I don't have one.

I've watched it lots of times of course, right from start to finish, and it's the finish that's another difference between them and us. In my experience, which, if

I'm honest, is essentially limited to Ray and Ed, when humans have done the business they roll apart onto their backs, giggle or mumble incoherently and, in Ed's case, reach for their cigarettes. Very occasionally, and full marks for adaptability, Ed tries something he's obviously learnt from watching us, and mounts his partner in what he generously calls doggy style. But there the similarity ends, because when they've finished they still collapse in a heap and he reaches for the fags, but we, and god knows how we do it, since I've never actually done it, end up locked together, backside to backside, unable to pull apart even if we wanted to. And the big question is - where do the tails go, because I have absolutely no idea?

The nearest I've ever come to real sex was when I was young and tried to shag Angie's leg. I loved it, she didn't, and as soon as she'd noticed she'd hop about on one leg trying to shake me off. Not long after that she took me for a visit to the vet and, for no apparent reason, I no longer felt so attracted to bitches of any kind.

Being petted or stroked is about as close as I've come to stimulation since then. I can't reciprocate easily, since I'm too small; it's only when they bend down to take their shoes off that I can usually get in a few quick licks to their faces. But their hands are magic. Ray's more of an ears and coat man; it's nice, but too quick and his fingers rarely get through to the good bits. Ed, who has very square ended, stubby fingers, is good for itches; he takes his time, and with a bit of subtle manoeuvring I can usually get his fingers to delve right down to the skin itself. It's Angie who really gets to the places that dog's dream about. When I was younger, she was brilliant and often tickled my tummy while she was watching a movie. I'd just lay there, legs in the air, and let her have her way with me. If the film was good and she got deeply involved, her lovely fingers moved up and down my stomach so quickly that my pointy red pepper used to pop out in appreciation. The trick was to keep still and not attract her attention, because one look and she'd see my cock vibrating like a demented wagtail.

According to them, my six dog years is roughly equivalent to forty-two of theirs. Angie is fifty-five, and some might say she's a bit old for me, but my word what a cracker, and what a smell. Licking her skin is unbearably beautiful, especially her ankles. They are delicious. If I could, believe me, I would, but as I only come up to her knees I can't. It does happen, cross-species love, but not often. I knew an Alsatian who had had his mistress, or said he had. Big dog, so I wouldn't put it past him.

But on that day when Ray and I left the shop, I had nothing on my mind but food. Walthamstow market is one of my favourite destinations, because the journey up and down the High Street is filled with odours of delight. The whole of the world's cuisine wafts up my nose, and if I'm quick, some of it goes down my throat.

Wherever apes swarm together there'll be food. I wasn't given a first class nose for nothing. I'm a terrier and the market is designed for terrier action, not the where's-the-fox type action that we Borders were bred for, but stomach work. Food rains down from these stalls all the way from the top of the street to the bottom, and so it's dive in, snatch, bolt and move on before whoever you're with gets aggravated. If it's Ray, the yank on the lead nearly snaps your head off; if it's Ed, it's more of a drag. He pulls on it as though he's disappointed, and he's telling me to 'leave it out mate', which is fine, but far too weak and slow to stop me. It's all in the shoulders and terriers are built for action.

Another good thing about being walked by Angie is that she is fun. She doesn't mean to be. Instead of running after every ball she throws, I get the chance to make her dance about a bit and to give her canine education a gentle nudge in the right direction.

I am totally aware that when it comes to smell humans are about as receptive as jellyfish and that if they do smell something then that is about as far as it goes – they register *a* smell. But for us *a* smell doesn't exist. Smells are compounds, they talk. They have a range and texture that humans are just unable to comprehend. For them a fart is nothing but an embarrassment. They sniff, are disgusted, and move away in different directions. When we fart it draws us together. We can tease it so far apart that we can detect its individual molecules in all of their symphonic complexity. We can know the nature of all the food that's been eaten and when it was consumed. We can tell the farter's sex, age and emotional state. Damn it, we can even detect the presence of diseases that they are totally oblivious to.

Humans might think that compared to the rest of the animal world they are intellectual giants, but that assumption is based upon two things: words and what goes on in their heads. Words are sounds, and even earwigs make sounds. They're not special. We dogs make sounds, not many, it's true, because we save them for specific purposes: to communicate over a long distance; like the beautiful haunting howl of the wolf, or to communicate with humans and puppies. Words are simply organized grunts. And one is hardly ever enough; to make themselves understood the naked apes need hundreds of them, thousands of them, so many in fact that they store them in books. We sniff and we understand.

That being the case you might wonder why we've ever tried to educate mankind and aid its evolution. Self-preservation, simple as that: naked apes are killers, and with their limited ability to comprehend the subtleties that float around them in the air, they are forced to respond to life's vicissitudes with violence. We were once, long ago in *The Wolf Days*, all praise to our prick-eared ancestors, competitors with them. We stalked the same pray. Sadly for us, their restless heads produced more than their usual damaging response to their surroundings: they had an idea, which is their customary response to everything: they invented weapons, and invented countless way to give our ancestors constant, belligerent and murderous grief. Had we not worked out an antidote to this we would have all vanished from the world long ago. They might have invented weapons, but we reinvented *them*. It's not over: this is the ongoing and sometimes painful enterprise that all dogs are involved in, but so far it has brought dividends and has allowed us to coexist on the same planet.

Angie has the most expressive hands of any ape I have ever met. Her signs are poetic; they float in the air like silk flags. I can watch her for ages. She's good, but her skill has also made her a tad conceited. She believes that she has an inherent understanding of the physical gestures that we dogs use when communicating to each other, and believes, listen to this, that we use our growls and noises in a vain attempt at speech! The conceit! We use simple stuff because they're too thick to understand what we want without making it obvious.

I'm not saying she hasn't got an understanding, but I am saying it's pretty basic: curled lips mean 'don't touch' could get bitten; roll over means 'you're the boss' tickle my tummy. It's at that level. Recently she's announced to everyone that she'd read in a magazine that scientists have discovered that when we are happy we wag our tails to the left, that's looking at us from the front, and when we're unhappy we wag them to the right. Hello! We've been at their education for millennia and they've only cottoned on to that *now*, in the twenty-first century!

The other day she and I were doing our usual morning walk across Millfields towards the River Lee Navigation canal and the old Middlesex Filter Beds nature reserve. She walked on ahead lost in her head, and I trotted along enjoying the wonderful scents of summer. Somewhere between the entrance and the canal she had an idea; I'm guessing it was to test the tail wagging evidence. I saw her stop and turn back to look at me. I ignored her; I was too busy teasing the news from around the base of one of the plane trees. Then she called my name. I deliberately went round the back of the tree. She called again and began clacking the dreadful signal clicker she carries to gain my attention. It's not offensive but it is annoying. In the end I gave in and trotted towards her. Overjoyed that I understood what she had been trying to communicate, she rubbed my ears and handed me a treat. I insist on that; failure to award me something for my troubles in their education and the clicker is scrap.

'Good boy, Geordie, good boy.'

I wagged appreciatively.

'You're happy,' she said, looking at me.

You have just given me a treat, sweetheart, of course I'm happy, and you playing lady bountiful show that my efforts at modifying your behaviour are working. Then I noticed that she was looking knowingly at my stern and the way that it was wagging to the right. Before I could do anything else she bent down and began scruffling my ears.

'There's a good boy.'

I look up, big eyes, treat? None. But she hadn't finished. She took out the manky tennis ball from the 'dog bag' and gibbering around in front of me made a half decent effort at throwing it further into the grass.

'Fetch, fetch.' I looked keen, but was reluctant. 'Geor-die - fetch.'

Never a 'please' or a 'will you fetch? Just 'fetch'. I skipped off after the ball and brought it back wagging effusively. She noticed the tail and was delighted. I scoffed the treat.

'You two have such a rapport,' said a young woman packing a small child on the back of her bike. She dismounted and they air kissed.

Angie accepted the complement with a little grin. 'I think doing what I do for a living has meant I've become more sensitive to non-vocal communication.' Her friend accepted that without demure. 'So how's the basement going?' she said, raising her eyes on the word basement. The woman rocked her head.

While they chatted about their houses, I slipped off towards the rubbish bin.

'Skrart, my old son.'

The voice came from a stocky Jack Russel, who came up to me wagging his tail in greeting.

'Narrick, long time no see,' I said, looking him in the eye. 'By heck, you look trim. You had a haircut?'

'Last week. Good isn't it?'

'Well you smell good.'

'Am good, am good.'

'That your man over there, the bloke with the phone?'

'Never off it, still, while ever he's occupied, I get to crap where I like,' he said smiling. 'Don't you hate it when they hang around your arse with those stupid little poo bags?'

'Tell me about it.'

'Whoops, he's looking. Stay well, Skrart, better get back or he'll start shouting.'

When I turned back to Angie, she and her chum were looking at me with quizzical eyes, never a good thing. I sidled over and looked up.

'See! See how it's waving to the left? That's positive. Means he's happy.'

'Not to the right then?'

'Yes to the right if you are the dog, but to the left if you are us.'

'Unless standing behind.'

Angie nodded.

'And he's happy?'

'Yes.'

I don't know what made me do it, but I instantly stopped my tail at half-mast and dead centre.

They both peered down at me looking puzzled.

'What does that mean?' said the mother.

'Geordie fetch!' Angie threw the ball belligerently straight down the path, and I went haring off after it, much to the distress of an approaching cyclist. 'Sorry! Fetch Geordie!'

I picked the ball up in my mouth and stood stock still. Non-verbal communication eh? I wagged fiercely to the left so that the message was unmistakable.

'Not too happy about that is he?' said the yummy mummy.

'Fetch!'

I relented and wagged to the right equally fiercely. 'No it's fine, just needed time to process the call.'

With that I raced off with the ball, dropped it out of sight in the grass and hid. 'Process that one, princess.'

CHAPTER 5

ANGIE

'God, Greta, I ache all over. That last Salute to the Sun nearly did my back in. It was wonderful.'

I lied, of course; it was excruciating. An hour in a sports-bra bending and stretching in yoga is never absolutely wonderful. It is a grey experience, bits are fabulous and bits are bloody awful, especially if I've had a busy week, but you don't tell that to your best friend if she also happens to be your teacher.

'It sets me up for the day.' Or it makes me hobble about like a cripple for a few hours afterwards.

'I worry about you, darlin',' she said, clipping the g off with a continental disregard for concord. 'You stand for too long in your job.'

'Yes, no, but not always, sweetie. Although the seminar this morning went on for hours. Thankfully, I shared it with Martin, who's really good, which isn't always the case. Some of the so-called professionals I get to work with are absolute tossers.'

'What was it about?'

'*Conflicts in style and register caused by divergent nominals.*'

She looked at me as if I was speaking Martian.

'It was my client's PhD dissertation.'

While she rolled her mat and sorted out the room, I explained, without conviction, what little I'd understood about the role of divergent nominals, but she had lost interest and, not being English, changed the subject without any verbal amelioration to what was really on her mind.

'So, is Raymond going ahead with his crazy 'bucket list' idea?'

I recalled an earlier conversation with our son, Max. I'd asked him to have a word with his dad to persuade him to shelf the whole idea, but he wouldn't have any of it. He said that Ray should be encouraged, and that I should stop being so negative. But he lives in Brighton, and anything weird sounds perfectly normal in Brighton.

'The alternative, mother dear, is for you both to moulder away being hip in Hackney doing nothing. And I mean hip as in your arthritis.'

He can be very cutting.

'Yes he is, Greta. He's going to put an advert in the local papers asking for interested people to meet him at Ed's place next week.

'My god, all of the nation's nutters in one place.'

'It's only the Hackney Gazette.'

'Yeah, that's what I mean.'

Was I just being negative? Was Max right? Nobody likes to be thought a kill joy. I do see his point a bit: none of us lives forever, and it would be easy to vegetate; not that I think for a moment that I do: yoga, choir, occasional performance and plenty of work isn't exactly vegetating. And in the autumn I occasionally do pottery, Tai chi and life drawing. For god's sake, I'm only fifty-five, hardly got started. But in Ray's case, I'm not so sure. He's always busy with his map things, of course, but the redundancy certainly hit him hard. Maybe I should be a bit less critical, embrace what he's doing and think of it as just another evening class. Thankfully, Ed will be there, he's sensible.

That afternoon, while Ray was off somewhere up the Lee, I walked across the marshes to see Ed. The three of us go back so far that there's nothing I wouldn't run past him first. I'm trying to remember exactly when it was that we first met. I know where it was: 'The Roebuck' on the Kings Road in Chelsea. I was a barmaid and they were both at the Collage of Art on Manresa Road. This was the early 80's and the road was roaring. That's when I fell pregnant, and that's when Ray and I shacked up permanently. Somehow that moment is forever in my memory associated with *The Muppets*, not the show itself, but a repeat of Kris Kristofferson's duet with Miss Piggy. I had the words of *'Help Me Make It Through The Night'* going through my head for ages, especially the line: *'Let the devil take tomorrow'*, because it more or less summed up my attitude to getting pregnant, and was the belligerent attitude I took when confronting my mother back down in Paddock Wood. But she liked the song and was overjoyed that she was going to be a grandma. I put that down to having been a widow for so long.

What worries me about the whole idea is that Ray will get morbid. It's good to think about one's own death, but not for long, now and again is fine, and sixty these days is nothing; it's the new forty, which makes me somewhere in my late thirties.

I put my continuing mental youthfulness down to a good diet, yoga, Pilates and meditation. Not forgetting my regular walks with Geordie. It says on my IPhone that I walk between three and six miles a day, when I'm not working; it would be even more if you added the miles I clock up on the bike. Because of all that I'm pretty confident that I've created a cordon sanitaire around me that will keep me more or less death free for a bit yet.

Work helps too, especially as I'm self-employed. It keeps me mentally alert, and can be so various that there is no time to get complacent. I went to Bristol Old Vic a couple of times last month, where I was interpreting for a performance and I'm off to Edinburgh with them next month; they're taking the show to the Fringe, which will be fabulous. And last week, I did two sessions at University College, one for a deaf client presenting her thesis and one for a deaf academic friend who is part of a research group. It can be bloody hard and not just the physical side. Trying to work out the meaning of what's being said and interpreting it at the same time is draining. At the end of the day I'm shattered. I'm like someone with two brains, neither of which is communicating properly with the other.

When I get to Ed's it's always the same routine, daft I know, but I really look forward to it after all of the bustle and confusion of work. Routine allows space for the brain to coast. If the shop's open, I make sure he hasn't seen me, and then sneak in, duck down and hide between the tanks. The fun bit is that he knows I'm coming over, so he's expecting me to do just what I'm doing, but what he doesn't know is when it will be, so he's constantly slipping in and out trying to catch me before I can spring out on him.

'Boo!'

He jumped, which was brilliant, but not that brilliant, because I nearly got hot coffee spilled all me.

Once the greetings were over he closed the shop and we went upstairs; I left Geordie down stairs, much as I love him, three really is a crowd.

The routine continues but without the giggles, or with them if we've not seen each other for some time. And as I'd seen him only the other day, we both sat on the bed side by side. I took off my sandals; he was already barefooted.

'Good walk?'

'Great. There were kids pond-dipping in the ditches.'

He leant across and kissed my ear and I snuggled up against him.

'I've missed you,' I said, 'and it's been a busy week.'

We don't have a lot of time together and so we don't like to waste it, so we normally undress ourselves. It's quicker. That sounds like we're a couple of tired old gits, but we're not, we're both excited and expectant; there's nothing languid about our love making, and never has been. Just because we've been lovers for so long hasn't jaded us. We're still hot to trot and can't wait to embrace and get down to the business. Taking our clothes off independently is simply to speed up the flesh part, the wonderful and endlessly joyful love making that Ed and I have enjoyed almost ever since we first met all those years ago.

We have shared so many wonderful times both in Walthamstow and all around the country, since Ed often follows me to where ever I'm working. We click. We know what delights and we love to offer it to each other. I guess that's why we've been together for so long, and not living together helps; there's no time to get blasé. And if I'm honest, short intense times are more conducive to good health than constantly being in each other's company. Ed is also not the most tidy and organized of people. That would drive me crackers after a while, and I have an awful feeling that I would become a bit of a nag.

Our relationship reminds me sometimes of a cowboy movie. I'm the trim, uptight church woman in a border town where my husband runs a small hardware store and spends day after day toiling with the accounts. To compensate, I go riding to a cabin in the hills where a rough-necked John Wain type tends the cattle and drinks whisky. Now, in principal, I can't stand scruffy, smelly men, I'm far too organized and particular for that, but every so often I get an urge to be treated roughly and held close to a John Wain like character. Ed is he, and sometimes his chin can get very rough, but in small doses it's absolutely wonderful, erotic even. I have to make sure that I don't get a beard rash. He's is always very careful of my neck and face, but when it comes to my buttocks there's no stopping him. His chin's like sand paper and my poor cheeks are on fire when I leave, which makes walking both exciting and difficult at the same time.

I never set out to create a ménage-a-trois. It just happened. We were always together, and at first we sort of shared our affections. The college film society once screened Francois Truffaut's sixties film *'Jules & Jim'* , which was about Jim, a French Bohemian, and Jules, a shy Austrian, who both fall in love with Catherine, in the film the wonderful Jeanne Moreau. It's set at the time of the First World War. She marries Jules, they have a daughter Sabine, Catherine is serially unfaithful, the war ends, both men live, she has the hots for Jim, he rebuffs her and it all gets mixed up and in the end she lures Jim into a car and drives it off a bridge while being watched by the horrified Jules. I totally identified with Catherine, because I loved both Ray and Ed. I used to go to work humming the soundtrack, and even thought of naming my baby Oscar after the film's Austrian star, Oskar Werner. That might have been a bit difficult so I chose Max, which sounds German, as an homage.

I can't absolutely swear that Max is Ray's child. I'm pretty certain that he is, since Ed was still heavily into his first wife Megan, and I've got a feeling that they had both gone home to Lincolnshire at or around the time I think that I became pregnant, and Ed and I weren't seeing each other all that often. It was only really just before and after his divorce that we continued where we had left off.

When we had had sex Ed grabbed his fags and lit up. Instead lying where I was enjoying the last seismic aftershocks of my orgasm, which is what I would once have done, I got up and opened the window to let in some fresh air. We're so used to this part of the routine that neither of us takes it as an unvoiced criticism.

'Fancy a cuppa, sweetheart?' I said, after all I was up and a cup of tea does wonders for me after a good seeing to.

'Love one.'

Living on his own means that Ed has what he needs where he needs it, and so there's always a kettle nearby, so I sorted out the makings and watched him lying back happily while the kettle boiled.

'Have you had your blood pressure checked yet, darling?' I said, seeing how red his face had become.

'I'm going to once I get a bit of time.'

'Here,' I handed him a mug. 'The last thing I want is to explain to Ray that I fucked you to death.'

'I've just done the equivalent of a two hundred meter sprint, woman, what do you expect? I'm rubicund by nature, in any case. It's a healthy glow. And there's nothing wrong with my heart, sweet pea, or anything else,' he said, stroking his flaccid penis lovingly.

'Good, because I hate wearing black.'

When he had finished his fag I got back on the bed and we sat propped up side by side. This is one of my favourite times. I'm feeling relaxed, my juices have flowed, my head is calm and I'm ready to talk.

'*The Bucket Club!*' I said.

'*The One-Stop Bucket Shop*'.

'Oh?' I said.

'He was worried it would get confused with a hardware shop.'

'So it is going to happen then?'

He leant over to the floor and retrieved a copy of the '*Waltham Forest Guardian*', already open at the small ads.

'*Need help to achieve a secret aspiration before you die? Joins us at the 'One-Stop Bucket Shop', where you'll find a sympathetic ear and friends eager to help you realize your final ambition. 7.30pm, Tuesday 12th June, corner of Buxton Road, E17 7EH, next to Fin Aquatics.*'

Proof positive. It was no longer an idea stuck in his head, and June 12th was less than two weeks away.

'Oh.'

What else could I say? It meant I would lose them both on Tuesday evenings? But then again, it did mean I'd get a chance to watch 'EastEnders' without any interruption.

'Life is a shipwreck but we must not forget to sing in the lifeboats.'

My mother had an endless trove of pithy quotations, like this one of Voltaire's, and as a child I believed that she was almost a genius. It was intellectual camouflage, as I realized later. She was an education snob, and it was just her way of obscuring the fact that she went to the Brighton Municipal Training College *before* it became part of the new University of Sussex.

I really believed as I walked back down the river, parrots screaming overhead, common terns quartering the water and cormorants heading back to the islands in the reservoir that I lacked for nothing. I had a son, who although unmarried, kept in touch regularly; a husband who was a friend and could mend things; a friend who was a lover and made beautiful art works, and a hoard of good women friends. That's it, isn't it? There is nothing else, especially as we had been lucky enough to buy our house in Hackney before the house prices went barmy. Life didn't get much better.

I then got the fright of my life. A huge bird flew over my shoulder and landed in the bull rushes in front of me. I screamed; it was so unexpected. Birds don't usually come anywhere near you when there's a dog. Then I saw that it was a huge grey heron.

'Oh my god!' I said to myself. 'It's only eating something.'

Sticking out of its beak and already half way down its gullet was a great, big, fat rat! Impossible! Heron's eat – fish? Rats are mammals. That's almost cannibalism. I was witnessing a wild life phenomenon. I took out my *IPhone* and scrambled to get some shots off.

'No, no, video, video!' I shouted out loud, almost dropping the phone as I came to my senses. '*YouTube*!

By the time I'd found the camera and had slid it across to video the rat had disappeared, swallowed whole. I was blown away. The bird took off and for a moment my mind went blank, and then I remembered. There was always *Facebook*.

CHAPTER 6

ANGIE

I wasn't going to go, which made it worse, and sat on the train in a state of anxiety. Surely someone must have arrived for the meeting by now; it was getting late. I wasn't going to but in the end I sent Ed a text: *'Anyone there yet?'*

'Three.'

'Are they - all right?'

'Um.'

'Oh! How's Ray?

'Fine.' There was a pause followed by a new text. *'-ish'*

Up until the slightly delayed extra text, I had felt more or less happy with how the whole thing was proceeding. But the *'-ish'* inspired doubt, and when added to the proceeding *'um'* introduced fear. I'd always felt that Ray's *'Bucket Club'* idea was odd, but had gone along with it because, well because I'm his wife and support was a wifely thing to do, but in my heart of hearts I had always thought that the whole thing was not only bonkers but fraught with disaster. First there was the chance that he would fail to complete his own bizarre ambition. That would be bad enough, although I think I could handle it. Much worse was his mad wish to aid the perverse ambitions of the club's future members. The advert was like a clarion call to the City's unhinged. God knows what weirdoes were this minute lolloping their way towards Walthamstow.

I got off the Overground at St. James' and began my walk up the High Street.

Three people were not a lot, rubbish in fact. It was not going to please Ray, especially if none of them fitted his entry criteria. And then there was Ed's text. *'Fine –ish'* could mean that he did not rate any of them. Three stark staring mad people was three too many. But then again, *Fine'* could mean that at least one of them was passible, which would then mean I was not about to waste my evening playing nursemaid a bunch of nutters, because me, Ray, Ed and the one possibly sane person would outnumber the remaining possible nutters four to two.

I checked the time. It was 7.15pm; there was still time for others to arrive. Instantly my fingers began tapping out a new text to Ed.

'I'm almost there. Meet me outside. X'

I saw Ed lighting up on the corner of Buxton Road and hurried towards him trying to read what I could from his delicious, crumpled face.

'Darling is it that bad?'

We gave each other an ambiguous peck and squeeze.

'It's the waiting, Angie. Raymondo won't get down and dirty until 7.30 has come and gone, so he's hardly said anything. He's just sat there smiling. I'd have had to come out even if you hadn't text.'

'Oh darling,' I said, clutching his forearm. 'And are they – you know, a bit?'

He scrunched his face up. It was a difficult question, I knew. But by scrunching his face I knew that they were 'a bit'. And I also appreciated his difficult position. He couldn't just come right out and say they were odd because he knew that that would reinforce my view that the whole thing was bonkers, and he couldn't say everything was hunky-dory, either, because that would then put my nose out of joint because as he would then be openly siding with Ray against me. My poor darling, he was yet again facing *'The Filling in the Sandwich Dilemma':* When you are stuck like a slice of ham between two competing but equal forces you can't take sides. He was my lover and Ray's best friend, which meant that he was stymied. There was only one thing he could do and that was to fudge the issue and keep a balance by saying something anodyne, which he did.

'More or less what we thought. Still, there's five minutes to go.'

I tried not to look too worried. He took a strong pull on his fag to avoid any more speech and turned away to exhale, as he did so we saw walking quickly towards us an attractive, purposeful young woman in her twenties whose long auburn hair hung almost to her waist. She was wearing jeans and a couple of contrasting bright vests whose spaghetti straps formed a trio with those of a black bra. She was all smiles, her face open and expectant.

She was eyeing the shop fronts.

'Hey up, love,' said Ed, dogging his fag. 'Are you looking for *Fin Aquatics?'*

'*The One-Stop Bucket Shop'*,' she said brightly.

He had done wonders with the inside of the old lock-up; what had been cluttered and dull had been recreated as a cheerful, welcoming space.

I smiled at Ray, and led by Ed, the girl and I took our seats on one of the dozen or so salvaged chairs that Ray had formed into a small circle. As we did so, Ray, who had been staring ahead with a vacuous smile on his face, suddenly became animated.

'Welcome everyone to the first meeting of the *'One-Stop-Bucket-Shop'*. I know,' he said as if frightened that even its title might stir up discontent, 'it is a bit of a mouthful, so let's just call it *'The Shop'*. Welcome to *'The Shop'*.'

Smiles broke across all of the faces.

'I'm Ray, I'm a retired cartographer, and I'm fifty-nine. I think we all know what a bucket-list is, and we all know that those things that we write on our list are important things we wish to achieve before we pop our clogs. What we don't know is when that is going to be. But we are here because we treat Life seriously. We don't want to be jumped before we're pushed.'

He smiled, and they laughed nervously, partly at his joke and partly I think because he'd hinted at the elephant in the room, the presence of Death, the great eraser. Now there was no need to pretend that they were there for a cup of tea and a biscuit. Death was no respecter of lists of any kind, and they knew that, and that's why they were there, to do something about it.

'Important is the key word here. We are not going to be a club for sensation seekers, unless the sensation achieved is secondary to the real object. So if you didn't read the advert properly: we're not here to help each other go bungee jumping.'

There was more nervous laughter, not just because what he had said was true, but because they knew that soon they would have to admit what their secret ambitions were. What had been nurtured in the darkness of their breasts would be out in the light and wriggling for all to see. A nervous laugh was totally appropriate.

'I want to find an appropriate place to die.' Ray's statement was bold, outright and in your face. It also sounded slightly mad. The secrets that each of them nursed suddenly felt more normal and less bizarre. 'I need help to do that, a back-up team, people around me to discuss what has and hasn't been achieved. That's why I conceived of *'The Shop'* as a place where serious ambitions harboured by serious people could be aided in their fulfilment by other serious people.'

Ray looked around at all of their faces. He had come out with it. His idea was in the hands of others. It felt hugely liberating, and his face was flushed with radiance.

'Who will be the first to share with us their unfulfilled ambition?'

While Ray sat back like a contented Buddha, I examined the faces of the others. The most comfortable was a man in his forties with a full hipster beard and hollow cheeks. He was looking at Ray with the same serious brown eyes that Geordie used when checking out the possibility of being fed.

On his right was a slightly older woman with a wide mouth and terrible skin. She was constantly looking from one face to the other, as if she had weighed us up and found us wanting. Her flowery, High Street frock looked summery, and on someone with less of a middle would probably have looked pretty, but she was too fleshy and too fidgety so that every time she squirmed in her chair the hem of her frock rose to reveal more of her ample thighs.

The young woman who had entered with Ed and I was a complete contrast. She looked extremely confident for a start. The young man next to her was as knock-kneed and gawky as a schoolboy. I guessed if she was a student of some kind, the gawky youth was probably still at school. He wore jeans and a black t-shirt crudely overwritten in white with a witless request to *'Just Do It'*.

'I'm Justine Cook.' The fidgety fifty-year old had taken the plunge. 'I came here tonight because I've realized that nothing is forever and that unless I get a grip of myself I'm going to end up surrounded by cats and not much else.'

'Thank you Justine. And your ambition is?'

'To change who I am before it's too late.'

Ray nodded wisely, but I could tell he had no idea what she had meant.

'Ok, let's just hold that for a moment, until we've all introduced ourselves.' He looked up, raised his eyebrows invitingly and looked around.

'I'm Toby Slight.' It was the gawky youth. 'I'm nineteen and a student. My ambition is to connect the wild in me with Nature so that I can exist as frugally and as simply as I can.' He nodded a few times to confirm the truth of what he had said.

'Great Toby, thank you.'

Without saying a word, Ray turned his gaze upon the girl, and she, without hesitation, introduced herself.

'I'm Lauren Makin. I'm a trainee barista.'

'Am I hearing coffee or the law?'

'Coffee. I work in a café on Upper Street.'

'So what brings you here then, Lauren? What's the secret desire that you need help with?'

I could see that Ray was quite taken by her open face and direct gaze. He certainly seemed more relaxed.

'I need to become a man, not I think forever, maybe just a month.'

Even Ray was taken aback. She was beautiful and her hair was magnificent. As a girl I would have given my right arm to have grown such a mane. To pass herself off as a man she would surely have to cut it off.

'Couldn't you do it on your own? Simply dress as a man and conduct yourself accordingly? I mean this is London, no one's going to say anything.'

'I've thought about that, and yes, I could, but I need other eyes to check me out and to offer feedback. I don't just want to wear drag. I need to become immersed in the man I'm to become.'

Ray's bottom lip was protruding, which was a sure sign that he was thinking hard, but then, suddenly, he simply nodded.

'Yes, well, why not? All of us could become your advisors and your eyes and ears. It would be a wonderful challenge. Welcome aboard, Lauren.'

'I want to be called Josh.'

'Oh, then welcome aboard, Josh.'

We all laughed and smiled awkwardly. I mean it was odd, but also fairly easy to accommodate, and it could be fun. Who hasn't wondered what life would be like if we'd been re-gendered.

As Ray smiled he turned to Josh's left, to the man with the beard.

'I am Peter Rock. I'm forty-five and I am a follower of the Risen Christ. I'm also a computer programmer. My ambition is to identify as close as possible with my lord and saviour. To that end I have given up many things, and have attempted to lead a life not too dissimilar from the lives of those living two thousand years ago in the Holy land. For example, I do not shop at supermarkets but at Farmers' Markets. I would like help to achieve the crowning act of correspondence – crucifixion.'

Peter lifted his dark, bearded chin and looked from one awe-struck embarrassed face to another as if measuring their responses. 'I should add that it would only be a simulation. I would not be looking for the Full-Monty; there would be no nails, simply bindings.'

Pleased that he had cleared up what he felt was an ambiguity; he sat back and beamed at the others.

'Oh god!' I said to myself, 'he is Ed's -ish, a bona fide religious nutter.'

Without being summoned, Ed spoke and did his best to blast the last revelation out of our minds.

'I'm Ed, I'm an artist and I want a good London gallery to offer me a retrospective.'

He had barked rather than spoken. The effect was immediate and everyone was pleased to move on. Unfortunately, they moved on to me.

'No, not me! I'm Ray's wife. I'm Angie. I don't have any secret ambitions. I'm here to act as secretary, to make sure that nothing that is said is forgotten. I'm also a qualified British sign-language interpreter, so if any of you are deaf-.' Oh god! I stopped in mid-sentence, feeling sick with stupidity. 'Which of course you aren't. But if you were – well.'

Their smothered laughter stifled the words in my throat. All I could do was to turn to Ray and look expectant.

'Wonderful. It's great to have you all here,' he said. 'But I must be honest. Final ambitions are too important to treat casually. In fact I must be brutal, because only that way can I really judge the strength of your desires and the rightness or wrongness of your being here.'

He beamed at us, and then, like a thunder clap from a cloudless sky he spoke to Justine.

'So tell me then, who the fuck are you?'

My stomach wrenched and I felt immediately worse. Ray is usually such a considerate person and rarely given to outright rudeness. I wasn't alone in feeling shocked. Everyone had blanched and they were staring at the hapless woman desperate to investigate her response and to avoid his gimlet eyes.

Justine's skin had turned to the texture of porridge; the only colour left was a faint pink blush around the base of her stubby nose. But then, unexpectedly, she smiled. I couldn't believe it. She grinned at Ray and he was grinning back.

'Thank you, Ray. You saw me and the way I can be. No room for whinging here. No wallowing. Yes. We're here to work. I'll tell who I am not – I am not a loser. I can be whoever I want to be, within reason. But I need help to make Justine shine again.'

Ray looked like an evangelical pastor who had just filched a soul from the Devil.

'Yes. And we can help, Justine; the Bucket Shop can help you to achieve that. You are in. This is the place for you.'

The tension and the fear evaporated. She laughed, stood up and punched the air like an athlete. There was a sense of joy in the air. Even Ed was grinning.

'The risen Christ? That's a tall order Peter,' said Ray, cutting through the chatter, 'we are told that he was perfect. But surely it's not the crucifixion that matters most but the rising from the dead, the ascension to heaven? Avoiding supermarket shopping won't affect that.'

Our moment of delight vanished completely. Ray had replied to the nutter in the room.

'It would be blasphemous to suggest that my crucifixion would result in my resurrection, but you are right. I wish to suffer enough to feel something of what my lord felt, and to understand the stresses and strains of his passion. Once I have achieved that I can measure my progress through life with a greater accuracy.'

'Another one who wishes to change their life, then? That is a laudable ambition. Although your desire to suffer a little is not my desire, I have no right to consider that odd, because each of us must find the route to that change on their own. However, I think that between us we could easily help you to fulfil your ambition. Welcome to the 'Shop', Peter.'

This time there was even more clapping. I found myself grinning, whether that was because I was moving further and further into fairyland or because Ray seemed so pleased, I didn't know. But when I looked across at Ed, he was not being carried along by the euphoria. He looked vaguely worried. Ray looked at him too.

'This man is my friend. I know his ambition and I know his value. He has been instrumental in helping me to set this whole thing up. He's *in* regardless. Ladies and gentlemen, I give you Ed Farrow.'

More clapping and an isolated whoop from Toby Slight. It was the whoop that refocused Ray's attention. Toby had almost been accepted without having been interrogated at all.

Ray laughed. 'Slight by nature and Slight by name, eh, Toby? You nearly slipped passed me, then.'

'I was wondering when you'd ask me. As a point of information, although we *are* in fact a tall family and given to being very slim, and Slight could mean being slender or slim, it could also mean cunning.'

'Slight we can see, but cunning?'

'I like to think that I'm sharp enough.'

'And while we are on meanings, what did you mean when you used that word – wild? *'Connect the wild in me with Nature'* is more or less what I think you said.'

Toby, despite his spindly appearance, became for a moment grave, and looked much like a heron does when staring fixedly into the murky edges of a river for its supper. Gravitas on such a frame engendered a feeling of pity. How could such a gawky person summon enough strength for anything requiring determination and perseverance? I felt that even I could have snapped him in half like a twig.

'We are kin to the beasts of the fields, although human, we are the same. We are all animals.'

There was a strange poetic quality to what he was saying quite out of keeping with his age.

'For too long we have treated our wild brothers and sisters as subjects, not as equals. I believe that the time has come for the human imperium to be shattered, and to do that I think we urban simpletons need to recognize our wild ancestry and reconnect with nature. As the great Henry David Thoreau has said in *'Walden, or Life in the Woods'*: *"I went to the woods because I wished to live deliberately, to front only the essential facts of life, and see if I could not learn what it had to teach, and not, when I came to die, discover that I had not lived."* That's what I want to do.'

Ray looked slightly aghast, as if he had not expected so much from so slight a frame.

'And *'urban simpletons'* means what?'

'I have been spoon fed from birth. In cities that is how we live. Everything is on hand for us. Everything is prepacked and all we have to do is reach out and receive. We have become Life's simpletons unable to recognize what lies around us and unable to cope without support.'

Ray was nodding sagely. 'Food for thought. Well – well we must not stand in the way of such an ambition, Toby. If you could list the sort of things that you consider necessary for your rewilding, before our next meeting, then we can see what we can *all* do.' Ray then turned from the beaming boy to open his arms to the others. 'We can *all* do! We can *all* do, ladies and gentlemen. Together we will make *all* our dreams come true.'

Even I got carried away by the clapping and let out a couple of infant whoops. Ed, although smiling and responding adequately to sudden hugs from both Toby and Justine, did not let go.

CHAPTER 7

ED

I lay in my bed after the *'Shop'* had disbanded and couldn't sleep. I tried starting again. I got up had a wee, lit a fag, opened the window, looked out onto the dull backyards of the street and sighed out loud.

'Bloody hell!'

What had I got myself involved in? It had been a new Ray. I had hardly recognized him. He had been a man on a mission and somehow I had sleep-walked right into going along with it. Whichever way you cut it, the group were a bunch of – I couldn't say losers, that would have been far too judgemental, and I didn't like that American way of labelling supposedly unsuccessful people. They weren't even out and out loonies, although maybe that Peter Rock was. Crucifixion? Yet Ray had agreed, which meant as a member of the *'Shop'* I had agreed to it too. Madness!

'Bloody hell!'

I flicked the fag away into the night. My throat felt dry and tasted like rope.

The next morning, I slumped down stairs, unwashed and unshaved, coffee in hand, and went into the shop to start my morning circuit of the tanks. It is always cosy and warm, and the dozens of air pumps burbling away in the background are just about the only level of sound that my head can cope with in the morning. Unlike other pets, fish create few surprises. They don't leave muddy prints over the work surfaces like cats, nor pee on the carpets or gnaw chunks off furniture like dogs. They simply exist. The worse that can happen is that they die, and even then, if I'm honest, the upset is essentially financial; a dead exotic is a hiccup in my cash-flow.

I stopped by my favourite tank; it's not for sale. It's my *Fin Aquatics* come on, my *'see what your tank could look like if you spent a bit of cash'*. I've taken a lot of care with its lighting and have filled it with just the right background plants and materials to show off the array of affordable and colourful fish to their best advantage. Aquariums are miniature live theatres and with the right cast can provide endless intrigue and drama. It takes a real understanding of colour and form to combine fish, vegetation and surroundings, and so there's no place for miniature divers, treasure chests and sunken galleons in any of my tanks, although I sell them to the punters; there is always a compromise when you are dealing with art.

I stood for a while staring at the fish although my real attention was deeper in my head. I was thinking about Angie. I knew that she was off in the morning to the Bristol Old Vic or somewhere for the next few days. But I needed to talk to her before the whole bucket thing got out of control. We hadn't planned for this trip to be one of our discrete 'away days', and so she wouldn't be expecting me to follow her, but I had to see her face to face, a phone call just wouldn't do it. A fish swirled, and in that moment I was resolved. I spun on my heels, left the fish to their gormless activities and went back upstairs. I would follow her west and see what we could salvage between us.

To save money, Angie often stays with friends when she's off on one of her gigs. This job just paid board and lodging, and I knew she'd secured a bed in a friend's flat somewhere off The Horse Fair.

Mind clear, washed and shaved, I text her of my intentions, but not my reasons; she was delighted, but less so when I phoned later and told her that I'd booked a double room in a Premier Inn.

'It *was* last minute, darling!'

'Yes, well,' she said, before hanging up.

The hotel was a massive up-ended rectangle, which fitted in perfectly with the other charmless buildings in the area. Bristol was a city I knew only as an inadequate memory. The one or two brief visits I had made there as a student had not impressed me. The sixties architectural scourge had passed over the city centre and had laid it waste, and for that reason I had crossed it off my list of places to revisit.

The train left on time, and I'd settled back with a coffee ready to enjoy the journey when Ray called. As it wasn't a quiet coach, I got up and went out to the exit.

'You're not in the shop,' he said. 'I've just been there.'

I've lied so often to him over the years that adding more lies no longer give me any qualms.

'Mum's a bit groggy, mate, and my sister's busy, so just a swift visit; check that she's ok.'

'Yeah, of course. Well give her my love. I thought Carla was on holiday?'

'That's what I meant – too busy as in on holiday.'

'Last night, eh? Wonderful or what? I think we've hit gold.'

'Ray, I'm on a train so I can't speak easily. If it's ok, I'll call you back when I arrive.'

'You know the crucifixion idea of Peter Rock's, the bearded guy?'

'We need to talk about that, Ray. Perhaps it's not what we had in mind.'

'Yes, but I had this amazing idea on the way over. I was walking across Millfields on the way to you, and you know in the left hand bit of the park there's a circle of giant plane trees?'

'Yes.'

'There's thirteen of them, I counted them twice.'

'And?'

'The twelve disciples and one for Christ – thirteen. It's prefect.'

'What's perfect?'

'Symbolically it's perfect: the number and the fact that it's a circle. People get off on the mystical nature of circles. Hey! And even better, just inside the circle there's the stump of a different tree. It's about ten foot tall. You can't see it clearly because the foliage of the big trees means it's always in shadow.'

'Yes.'

'Round about the solstice or Easter or something someone added a cross piece and decorated the whole thing with vegetation. Do you remember?'

I did, and as I did so I knew exactly what he was going to say.'

'Let's crucify him there in the circle tied to the crosspiece. We can nail up something for his feet. What do you think?'

Someone came out of the toilet and I turned my head to the window in the door. He'd gone further than I'd thought. I felt sick.

'Sorry mate, only got a bit of that,' I said, holding the phone into the noise of the exit. 'The line is breaking. Look, I'll call when I get to Bris– Br- Br- Braford Water, Lincoln, ok?'

Brayford Water was a huge great canal basin in the middle of Lincoln. Why would I be going down to Brayford, for fuck sake? No, no; it would work. It was close to the station. Having coffee and cakes in one of the cafes would make sense. I turned off the phone and trailed back to my seat aware that I had said absolutely nothing about my deep reservations about the fucking shop! I was hurtling off to Angie to try and stop him and it was too late; he'd already taken off and was planning the first- the first whatever it was - first enterprise. My trip was doomed before it had begun. I put in some nicotine gum, slumped into my seat and chewed, thoroughly depressed.

'Braford fucking Water!'

Angie continued to be sniffy when she at last entered my hotel room. You've have thought I'd lured her to a doss house the way she gave everything the once over. It was a perfectly fine room and its bed was big enough for two, what else did she want?

'This is not a romantic visit, for fuck's sake. I'm here on business.'

She gave me an old fashioned look.

'Oh come on, you know that would be the case wherever we were.' I scrunched my face alluringly. '*"Needs must when the devil..."* darling,' I said, flourishing my index finger into the spaces where the missing words should have been.

She arched her eyebrows. 'And spoken by a clown, I seem to remember,' she added for good measure.

'I don't care who fucking said it. The point is that this is a perfectly acceptable room. So stop being so poncey and come here and give us a hug.'

We were only playing. This was all part of our usual mating ritual. Monkeys pick off each other's fleas to get each other going, and we enjoy a bit of sparring, and we are good lovers and always have been. The years haven't dulled our desires, and the continual if interrupted practice has not blunted our interest. We like making love because we love each other. It's as simple as that. Ray might have lost interest, but we hadn't. This time though we were fairly quick. There was business to be done.

'He's got to be stopped.'

I had no need to indicate who 'he' was.

'Why, darling? It's what he wanted, and I think it could be fun.'

'Aiding and abetting crucifixion has got to be a crime.'

'God! Sometimes Ed you can be too – provincial for words. It's only acting. No one is going to get the hammers out. What's the harm in it? Come on, we both like a little rough and tumble, this is only slightly different. And some people would think what we get up to is a bit odd, which of course it isn't; it only sounds like it is when you say it out loud.'

'A loving spank on the arse is not the same as masquerading as Jesus Christ in a public park.'

'What park?'

'That, my darling, is why I've hot footed it up here. He wants to perform the bloody thing in Millfields, inside that ring of huge plane trees.'

'Marvellous! Inspired. The perfect place.'

'No darling, not the perfect place. Supposing it all goes wrong and something happens to him, what then? There's some pretty rum characters lurking on the marsh.'

Her face became more serious; there were and she knew it.

'So what are we going to do?'

'Talk to him, get him to see sense. And then get him to ditch the maddest of them. Yes,' I said when she raised her eyebrows, 'Peter bloody Rock.'

'Have you ever met someone called Rock before, darling?'

I frowned. She was given to sudden tangential flights and I had no idea what she meant.

'Funny name, don't you think?'

'Well, maybe he's foreign.'

'Meaning?'

'He's got a big black beard like Jesus, so maybe he's Jewish.'

'Don't be racist, darling.'

'I'm not being fucking racist, Angie.'

Suddenly she started laughing. 'No, that's it, darling. It *is* unusual because it's not *his* name.'

I was totally confused.

'Oh come on, Ed, what is he?'

'A nutter?'

'No, he's a believer. He identifies with Jesus, and who did Jesus say was the rock upon which he would build his church?'

She waited eyes ablaze like a circus ring master waiting for me to cough up the answer on demand. I pulled a face and shook my head.

'Peter. Peter, Saint Peter as in Rome? He was the *rock* upon which the church was built. Our Peter has simply taken the name in his efforts at identification. Peter Rock. Good eh?'

'Farfetched,' I said, finally understanding.

She didn't think so; in fact, she got quite agitated and was grinning like a loon, excited that she had smoked him out. I didn't care; I was interpreting another set of more basic clues: she was waggling her toes, and when Angie gets sexually excited the toes are a dead give-away.

'So I suppose you want a reward for being a super sleuth, then?'

'Well, we'd better make good use of the bed now that we've got it.'

She threw back the covers and turned over so that I got a clear view of her delicious arse, beside which all of my hesitations seemed somehow petty, or at least deferrable.

CHAPTER 8

RAY

E d did not phone back, not that it mattered, because my mind was totally centred on the crucifixion. I had the whole thing worked out in my head, and later that evening I went back to the circle of trees for a final inspection.

It was a warm night, not as brilliantly lit as some of the more recent ones, but pleasant enough despite the cloud. Groups of twenty-somethings were scattered here and there in groups chatting and drinking. Somewhere someone was cooking on a portable barbeque. A couple of elderly foreign men were sitting on a bench talking and spitting out the husks of sunflower seeds; in other words - nothing unusual.

I released Geordie to his own devises and sauntered down the left hand side of the main path, my eyes scanning to either side looking for anyone who might be a witness to what I intended to do. I tracked the barbeque stink to a small cluster of bodies sitting way off to the side near the canal. There was no one near enough to bother me, so I immediately cut across the grass to the circle of trees.

Once inside the ring I was practically invisible in the gloom. During the day meditators and body stretchers were drawn into the circle, but thankfully it was empty. I went straight across to the isolated tree stump, looked quickly around to check that no one had popped out from behind a tree, and yanked at the cross piece. It came away in my hand and dangled uselessly from the end of an electric cable that had been used to tie it on; so much for New Age technology, it now looked more like an old fashioned railway signal than a cross.

Message to self: pre-drill two screw holes in a piece of wood and bring a battery operated screw driver to fix it.

No one that I was aware of had seen my sudden lunge at the beam. I turned slowly around and walked off towards where the dog was head down amongst some rubbish. I was pleased with myself. To have turned up on the day with everyone else and tried to get our man onto the bar would have been a disaster, even more so if he had expected to do the whole thing in Old Testament drag.

'Geordie!'

Once the dog was trotting along behind me, again, I ignored him. My head was elsewhere going through the organizational details of the whole thing.

Essentially there needed to be two cross-pieces: a stout one for the arms and a lighter one to carry his feet. The bindings were easy, washing line would do, or even, come to think of it, Velcro, especially if there was a need to get him down quickly.

Once I had settled the outlines I began to think about Ed. What had he said on the train: 'not what we had in mind'? I realized that it had been niggling me. Did he mean the crucifixion or the whole bucket shop thing? He hadn't been exactly brimming with enthusiasm during the meeting, a bit pained in fact. Then I remembered his mum. Durr! Not surprising that he'd looked a bit glum if the old dear was having a turn; who wouldn't be, especially when all of our parents were getting closer to the departure lounge? Or then again, maybe it wasn't Helen; maybe it was the religious element of the undertaking that was narking him. He was no lover of any kind of hocus-pocus, and for us to aid someone in pursuit of fairyland would absolutely cause him to look grumpy.

Undoubtedly, Peter Rock's wish to experience Christ's passion was different, eccentric even, but then, you could say the same about my own bucket list desire. But so what? Belief itself is less about words, more an assumption based on feelings. I assumed that if I found my mystical place to die it would settle my head, and hopefully that other even less definable thing – my heart. It was a belief. Angie and Ed thought it was bonkers, but that was just their opinion, and opinions were thoughts and therefore had no actual weight.

Importantly, if we as a team could bring off the crucifixion, then without doubt we could bring off the other wishes too. We should treat it as a test, as time to get the logistics and organization right. To succeed would be to set up 'The Shop' once and for all, and once it was running smoothly then my own use of the members could begin, after all, finding an elusive spot on the map was a damn site harder than strapping someone to a tree or dressing a woman as a man.

I'd gone upstairs to the study when I'd got back to carry on with my work on the River Lea's tributaries, but because my head was still buzzing with Angie's and Ed's implied opposition, I couldn't settle. We were either all in this or we were not. There was no room for havering; the club had been formed; our new members expected results. I therefore decided I would confront them head on when they got back, and to do so I would soften them both up with a meal. Angie would half expect a meal, and I knew Ed would jump at it because otherwise it was his usual Pot-Noodles.

Most dwellers on river banks hardly ever think about the river as anything other than a wet boundary between where they are and where they might like to be. They don't see it as a system with its own life and with its own very graphic history. From its rising in the Chiltons to its outlet into the Thames at Bow Creek, the river Lee has been central to the lives of the people whose towns and villages crowd its banks. It was once also an international boundary between England and Denmark, or rather England and the Dane Law, the kingdom that was created in the east from the scattered remnants of the Danish Great Army that had settled on the lands boarding the North Sea in the ninth century.

I've lived near to it for years, and I've even wondered if my hankering to find my place of extinction is in some weird way intimately connected to its proximity, because everything east of the river always feels like home, and everything west like the lands of strangers. I have what feels like an internal magnet that draws me ever east, even to the very edge of the sea. This compulsion, this hankering to look east, is what I want to explore. I've mentioned it to some of our friends and they've tried to explain it away as echoes from former lives that I've lived somewhere within the heart of East Anglia, or, if they are less romantic, the result of being taken to the beaches near Yarmouth as a young child and wanting to re-experience the joys I felt then. I don't know; all that I'm sure of is that I want to die within the boundaries of the Dane Law.

As a cartographer, you constantly come up against alternative spellings of the names you are adding to the map. The pronunciation of names changes over time, and without an approved reference book, maps would soon degenerate into gibberish if we went with every localized pronunciation and spelling. What gazetteer writers choose as the correct spelling is what eventually stops the written name from further mutation. London is London whether you live in John O'Groats or the Scilly Isles. It is only *Londinium* or *Lundenburh*, if you look up its history, but the River Lea, or the River Lee, is an example of a name that hasn't fully been brought to heel, and so can be rendered in either way.

I've been working on it for years, especially trying to make more obvious the dozens of tributaries that feed it. A rule of thumb helps a little. From Hertford west, that's up stream, the spelling: Lea predominates; downstream from Hertford to the Thames it's both Lea and Lee.

An interesting fact about place names in England is how few have Celtic roots. To the west of the island's imagined spine Celtic names increase; east of that imaginary line they become considerably rarer. Why is the big question? Was the pre-English population slaughtered or driven west, or was it that the original inhabitants did not in fact speak a Celtic language, but spoke a more Germanic tongue like that suggested for the Belgae, and therefore named their rivers, towns and villages in much the same way as the incoming English?

There is much to commend that theory, but my research into the Lea suggests that a Celtic admixture does exist to influence topographic names. Lee itself probably comes from a Celtic root word, which meant 'bright' or 'light', or even, as some people have suggested, comes from the name of an ancient Celtic deity called 'Lug'.

Apart from sorting out the dinner that's where my head was for much of the day, I was looking over my list of tributaries and trying to discover what percentage could perhaps be called Celtic. For that reason I almost forgot to turn the gas on underneath the stew pot before Angie arrived home.

'Stroganoff! Wonderful, darling.'

I'm guessing that Angie knew that I had something on my mind, because when I told her that Ed was coming over for dinner, she seemed startled.

'Been away, dear; got back about the same time as you.'

'Oh! Interesting,' she said fussing with her bag. 'Everything all right, is it?'

'Went up to see his mum; been a bit out of sorts.'

Angie brightened considerably, which was a bit heartless. I'd always thought that she'd got on with Helen.

When we'd all finished and finally pushed our plates away, slightly worse for the considerable amount of red wine we'd drunk, we were in what I thought was a receptive mood.

'Bit of good that, mate,' said a very red faced Ed.

'One of my favourites,' said Angie, 'pure comfort food. Oh and Ed, so pleased everything's all right. I dread those unexpected phone calls.'

His face turned as two-dimensional as one of his self-portraits.

'Helen,' said Angie, vigorously nodding her head and squeezing his wrist.

It was a lovely gesture, and brought his memory flooding back.

'She's a game old bird.'

'Let's have one of your continental chocolates to celebrate,' I said, reaching for the box of Thornton's he'd brought, and reckoning that a face full of chocolate was the perfect time to strike. 'Listen you two. I'm not as blind as you both think I am.'

Ed coughed his chocolate out into his hand. 'Wrong way,' he said, looking for his napkin.

'I reckon there's something you've got to tell me. Yes?'

They went from animated and convivial companions to blank faced simpletons without a pause in the middle. I laughed. 'This crucifixion thing has been giving you second thoughts. Am I right?'

'Not me, darling, no,' said Angie, almost tripping over herself. 'I think it would be great fun.'

'Ed?'

'Crucifixion?' he repeated, gormlessly.

I threw my hands out to encourage him to say more.

'Is this - is this what you expected – a crucifixion?'

'No, of course not!' I said brightly. 'And?'

He frowned. 'Is it legal?'

I pulled a face; this wasn't like Ed. 'Is that it? Is that what's bugging you; you of all people?'

Angie reached across and squeezed his bicep encouragingly.

'He's a tosser, Ray.'

'Aren't we all tossers in the cold light of day? When we were walking through Stokey cemetery you said it was like an urban wilderness, yes; that Nature reclaims everyone and makes no distinction between the good, the bad and the moderately beastly? How the trees had toppled the expensive tombstones and smashed their marble whatnots?'

'Yeah.'

'Well it was staring us in the face. There were hundreds of people under our feet and every one of them had a different view of the world. But now all of their cherished beliefs had vanished. Everything they once believed in had evaporated and every thought they'd had, or every good or bad deed they'd ever done had been obliterated. All that was left of them was the mud shitted out by earthworms. Have another chocolate.'

He popped one in his mouth and jiggled his head around as if talking and eating had become too complex to do together. Angie smiled encouragingly.

'The sooner the better, then,' he said, swallowing. 'String him up.'

I felt a surge of love for my two oldest friends and in a spontaneous gesture laid my arms on their shoulders. 'I'll get the emails sent out.'

CHAPTER 9

GEORDIE

---

he night before this one, I really thought that Ray had caught my fleas. All night he'd been jiggling about in bed. Not that that would have surprised me, because Angie had given me a bath the day before and I was truly, unpleasantly clean. In my experience that's when the little bastards jump off onto whatever more aromatic creature is lying nearby. I was sleeping where I usually sleep on the floor down the side of their bed, so the noise was just above my head. It was like having lodgers. His intermittent twitching and snoring eventually woke Angie, and from then on sleep was out of the question.

When she stays with Ed bedroom activity is predictable. They go hard at it when they first get into bed and then, once the grunting and moaning are over, there's a blessed, if fuggy, silence, which means that I can get a good night's sleep until the morning session, which thankfully is not as common as it once was. Ray on the other hand doesn't spend his time with Angie in quite the same way. They mate occasionally, but not predictably. Normally this would mean that going to bed had become less stressful and that I would get plenty of rest and recuperation, but not always. Once a year there are the fireworks, when despite shivering under the table with fear, I am at my most dangerous. It is a time when the wolf is upon me and the desire to kill is strong. In between the bangs and the whimpers, I have glorious fantasies about grabbing the neck of who or whatever it is that's causing my distress, ripping out their windpipe and shaking the bastards to death. Last night was merely annoying.

It turned out that the *'Shop'* meeting had gone well, but Ray couldn't settle. He'd organized the 'shoppers', allocated roles and had told them all to assemble the next evening at the trees for a run through, but as Angie discovered, it was praying on his mind. 'You're over excited, darling' is what she said, and in situations like this she did what she often did to quieten him down, and that was to spend some time playing with his genitals, which seemed a tad unfair, since he'd made all the fuss in the first place, while I had been as good as gold and had got nothing but a restless night.

This evening though was different. I was more or less left to my own devices and allowed free reign.

'Geordie will act as our outer defences. He'll spot intruders before we do.'

'Some hopes, Ray baby,' I thought to myself. 'I'll bark, if that's what you mean, but there's no way I'm doing anything more taxing. Some people round hear carry Zombie knives.'

It's not that I mind acting as their 'watchdog'; it's just that in the dark humans can be totally pathetic, and their nocturnal incompetence does me no favours, because we get identified with the activities of our owners. With that in mind I mooched off and more or less left them to get on with it, while I spent my time trying to track down an elusive but incredibly attractive scent of what the apes call a fox, and we know as a *roscher*, and Ray put the *'shoppers'*, as he'd started to call them, into their start positions.

Ed, being the most practical, had been given the role of woodworker. He had the drilled cross-pieces and the support itself, and was loitering conspicuously in the deeper shadow of a nearby plane tree. To my eyes he stood out as clearly as a hedgehog at twilight.

There was a noticeably different scent in the air, slightly sweet and sour, which I couldn't place at first until I realized that it came from the where Angie and the other women were seated incognito on one of the benches, and then it all made sense. It was that rare human aroma - fear. I quite like it in a rather disturbing way because it rouses in me the sort of feelings I get when I come across a kitten or a distracted cat, which is a delicious mixture of excitement and blood lust.

The bearded ape and the skinny one were clustered with Ray more or less in line with the tree circle but inside the park railings alongside Chatsworth Road.

And then, glory be, I found the elusive source of the *roscher's* scent. You have no idea how evocative and how attractive *roscher* piss can be, especially after you've just been bathed. With the falling of the wind, the scent had stayed close to the grass and had snaked only a short distance from where it had been pissed. Where a *roscher* pees there's usually some shit nearby. Normally I would hunt that down, but this time the pee almost overwhelmed me with desire and I dropped my shoulder and went down on my back and wriggled and wriggled in pure ecstasy. I can't imagine a better way to make use of a mild evening than to wonder around caked in something so sexy. I felt irresistible, and turned towards the women and trotted jauntily passed them.

'Jesus, Geordie!' A badly aimed kick reminded me of the difference between our two sensitivities. 'You stinking hound!'

This was followed by a general, 'Woo!'

I didn't hang around for the rest of their outbursts, but beetled off sharpish into the shadows and lay down in the grass. From where I was lying I watched the tableaux suddenly come to life. I saw Ed appear from his hiding place and cross quickly to the tree stump. The moment he moved Ray and the other two ran towards the circle. There's nothing I like better than a lot of bustle and activity so I got up and took off, swinging wide to avoid the women, who were now standing up, and headed into the circle.

'The stepladder? Who's got the fucking ladder?' said Ed.

'Damn, it's still in the house.'

'I can't reach the spot without it.'

'No! Yes! Look, I'll bend down, climb on my back,' said Ray. 'Toby will give you a hand.'

Ed clambered onto Ray's back while holding one of the pieces of wood and began frantically screwing it into place.

'Shift your foot a bit to the right, mate.'

As soon as the foot bar was in place they hoisted Ed carefully upwards so that he could stand on top of it to reach where the cross piece was to be fixed.

'That's it. Done!' Help me down.'

Immediately he'd touched down, they all grabbed the bearded ape and manhandled him up onto the foot bar and left him clinging dangerously from the top bar.

'This is not what I imagined.'

'You're up that's the main thing.' said Ray. 'Just hang on there for a minute while I take a picture.'

There was a flash.

I kept well out of the way as they brought the bearded one down, and Ed was lifted up to begin the unscrewing. It was then that my intruder alarm went off. I could smell a bitch somewhere behind me, and as they gathered their things I trotted off to investigate. Sure enough, just outside the circle, there was a rather attractive curly haired little number sniffing about.

'Out late,' I said.

'She likes the dark,' she said, cocking her head in the direction of her invisible owner.

'New around here?'

'We normally hang about in Springfield Park.'

I popped my nose up her arse and she stood long enough for me to get a good whiff of all her details, and then allowed her space to return the favour.

'I'm Skrart.'

'Naarn.'

'Always nice to meet someone new.'

'What's going on, then? She's been watching you lot for ages.'

I followed her glance and saw for the first time a human lurking a little way off in the shadows. I should have picked her up long ago because as soon as I saw her I became aware of her scent. That's what comes of ignoring nature and getting caught up in the mad affairs of the apes. The scent was very particular, familiar and earthy, a bit like wet soil. I'd smelt it lots of times, especially along the towpath coming from some of the boats, and I guess its familiarity is what caused me to ignore it. This presented me with a dilemma. My role, according to Ray, was to act as their watchdog. I should have barked immediately and galloped off to the shady figure, but I rather liked Naarn and didn't want her to think I was just a run-of-the-mill ape-snitch.

She gave a little snort and smiled. 'Not got your mind on the job, have you?'

I skipped a little in front of her. 'I like you.'

'Go on; give them all a thrill – bark.' She gave me an encouraging look.

That was all I needed, I threw my head back and gave voice in a true and dog-full way. Naarn was impressed, I could tell, so I ran off to the shadow figure and began running around her trying to corral her and prevent her slipping away. It worked, not only did she stand still, but the others came over to see what all the fuss was about.

'Nice smell,' said Naarn, smiling as she skipped passed to stand beside her owner.

I didn't have time to bask in her admiration, too much was happening. First, Naarn gave a series of threatening, theatrical growls, very sweet, and more for my ears than for theirs, I guessed; she had a lovely resonance. I took my cue and barked back, showing just enough of my fangs to excite her interest.

'Geordie leave it!' Ray's bark of command.

I trotted back and bristled enough to make them think that I was on the case. Naarn let her hackles rise in response and for a brief moment, for their benefit, we posed aggressively before each other.

'Love it,' she said, jinking away.

'Dogs eh?' said the dark figure, cooing winningly. 'Sorry about that, I didn't realize you were filming.'

'Difficult in the dark,' said Ray obliquely.

'They're always filming round here,' she said. 'What's it about?'

They all fell silent and looked towards Ray for an explanation. He nodded vigorously as if convincing himself that he was right and then produced one of the 'Shop's' flyers.

'It's not a film. Look, this will explain it all. Nice to have met you. Let's go everyone.'

As they headed off smartish, I was aware that the woman found whatever was on the paper interesting, because she also nodded, looked up and then smiled at their retreating backs.

'Come on Queenie.'

Queenie! I looked towards Naarn and grinned. She looked towards me and shrugged her shoulders.

'Oh yes!'

Roscher piss works every time: a good night's business, my son.

CHAPTER 10

RAY

'She's contacted you! When?' Angie's eyes protruded alarmingly.

'This morning.'

I've learned not to look into her eyes when she stares, and never to look surprised.

'Why didn't you tell me? I'm the secretary.'

'I just did.'

'But she phoned hours ago.'

'You were in the shower, and I've only just remembered.'

'What did she want?'

'To join. She thought it all sounded wonderful.'

'She can't just join, so what did you say?'

'I asked her what her secret desire was.'

'And?'

'She wants to cover Hackney Central railway bridge in graffiti.'

'Oh no, darling, not another fucking artist! Did you tell her to get lost?'

I couldn't understand why a woman we'd seen only once in the murky light of evening was giving Angie so much grief. On the phone she had sounded relatively normal, or at least she had sounded like an artist. I thought she was very nice.

'We must always remember, darling, it's not whether we think someone's ideas are barmy or not, it's whether we can help them.'

'Graffiti – ugh! It's like encouraging a dog to piss on a wall. It's been done too often to be interesting anymore.'

'Well, I'm meeting her for a coffee this afternoon, just to make sure.'

'Why not tomorrow? I don't finish work until five.'

'I know, but she's busy. Don't worry; I'll text you what happens.'

Although I was interested in finding out more about our potential new shopper: Izzie Capricious, I didn't want to finalize my decision as to whether she was in or out until we'd all met her at the next meeting. The coffee would be my chance to sound her out, and as far as I was concerned the meeting was more important than the admission of one more member. The crucifixion had been, to say the least, less than it could have been. Although we had succeeded in getting Peter up onto the cross, it had been a close run thing, and could easily have ended in disaster. I blame myself for the missing stepladder; I should have delegated the role to someone else. And as for Ms Capricious' sudden appearance out of the dark! It just proved we could not really rely on Geordie; we had to have security. If someone turned up unexpectedly on the actual night there had to be time to get Peter down or for all of us to freeze and blend into the background.

Once I had typed up my report on the night's proceedings, I shot off up the road to meet Izzie in one of Chatsworth's Roads many cafes. I was early and so was she. She was sitting outside *'L'épicerie'* supping a flat white. After last night the last thing I wanted was for her to think that she was in the company of nutters, so I was wearing a black and white stripped t-shirt, blue jeans and canvas sided white shoes without socks; signs enough for the prescient, I thought, to lull her fears and for her to see that we too were essentially creatives and not from another planet.

In the light of day she seemed darker, and sat on the chair as if she was astride a saddle.

'Great,' I said and we shook hands. 'I'll just grab a coffee.'

While I waited for my coffee, I was able to observe her through the window and examine her more closely. She was dark, but it was mostly her clothing, and although she looked British, her hair was a glowing, raven black, so black in fact that it left her skin looking wan and papery. The only colour came from her bright, plastic broach, which was about the size of a small cup cake.

'Another great day,' I said as I sat down.

'I'm not a great fan of the sun,' she said, looking me straight in the face.

My usual response to someone I don't know, who has just voiced a conflicting opinion, is to alter what I am going to say next enough to blur any possible differences between us, but she didn't give me time to reply.

'I'm a creature of the night.'

My alarm rang, but I nodded, smiled and looked away only to become unpleasantly aware that she was one of those women who appeared not to have been trained in childhood to keep their legs closed when sitting. I instantly turned back at her face and found myself staring at her diamond nose stud. To avoid any suggestion that I was being critical, I looked away and inadvertently back to her legs. Horror! The gapping void!

'How much did you see? Last night,' I added quickly. 'All a bit hectic; our first run through.'

'Brilliant. I saw you took some pictures.'

I took out my phone and fumbled the picture in front of her.

'Your thumb doesn't help. You could do with a decent photographer.'

'What? Oh yes, no,' I said, pointlessly holding up the phone before putting it away.

'If I joined could I also be your archivist?'

She suddenly swivelled to the side of her chair and leaned towards me. Despite *my* childhood training never to look up a woman's skirt, in the blink of an eye I'd taken in every aspect of her movement.

'Look'. She opened her bag and took out a camera. 'I'll show you some of my stuff.'

I leaned further in as she flicked photo after photo in front of me.

'You know that bridge along the Hertford Union Canal where the A 12 crosses? Up from the Olympic Park near Wick Road?'

'Yes, by the lock gates.'

'That's mine.'

A huge colourful nostril in a giant head filled the screen. She made it smaller until I could see the whole of a swirling portrait sprayed on the wall by the lock side.

'Wow! I've seen it. So that's one of yours.'

'I was pissed off by the bloody amateurs. They'd had that space to themselves long enough, so I repossessed it in the name of art. Won't last, of course, they'll fuck all over it, but then why shouldn't they? It's not my wall.'

And then there was a picture of her in a mask, signing the picture with a spray-can: *'Capricious'*. In the next shot she was smiling at the camera with the mask up on her forehead.

'Capricious!' I said laughing. 'I thought it was unusual. It's a tag.'

'Sometimes I'm Mayola Rhodes or just MR.'

I frowned knowingly and wagged my finger in front of her like a metronome. 'Rhodes Road. Love it. Mayola Road's near us.'

'I know.'

Her eyes I noticed were blue. I'd assumed they were brown.

When she had left, I stayed on a bit longer to text Angie. But what to say? We'd gone on to talk about the other 'shoppers', about the crucifixion and about the forthcoming meeting. All very civilized. Beyond seeing more examples of her work, I'd learned her main studio was in an old railway arch off London Fields, which was not far from 'E9', my favourite bakers, and that she lived in Stoke Newington. She also gave be an open invitation to pop in for a coffee anytime I was passing.

'Hi sweetheart. Saw Izzie. All well, she'll come to the next meeting so you can see for yourself. Hope the job went ok. X.'

'I know who she is,' said Ed, as we journeyed into Islington on the 38 bus. 'Graffiti's just one of her things. When you said Izzie Capricious, I checked my magazines. There's an article about her in here.' He handed me the magazine.

'I'll look at it properly later. I get sick reading on a bus. She ok then?'

'Eclectic. Multi-media; bit of everything really. Refuses to be typecast.' He took back the magazine and read. '*I do whatever it needs, and whatever it needs, I'll use it.*''

'Any good?'

Ed did his usual side to side head nod as if answering demanded a lot of thought. 'Popular.'

I laughed. 'But as far as we're concerned – ok?'

'No worse than anyone else.'

We got off at Angel and crossed the road to the Oxfam bookshop. According to Ed, he'd seen an art book upstairs of famous paintings of the crucifixion, and that considering the subject matter and the nature of Islington's book reading public, he guessed it would still be there.

It was: a battered but presentable volume with a great big Velazquez Christ on the front cover. I bought it, and immediately felt uncomfortable parading the saviour's tortured portrait around the streets. It's not something you do anymore, unless you are selling '*The Watch Tower*'.

We bought our coffees in '*Pret-A-Manger*', and I laid the book down so that its title: '*The Crucifixion as Art*' was obscured.

'It's not bloody pornography, for god's sake. Give it here.'

Ed opened the cover and flicked the pages. 'That one,' he said, pointing at a painting by Matthias Grunewald. The Giotto. Even Gauguin's '*The Yellow Christ*', and this one by Thomas Eakins.'

'Who?'

'It doesn't matter, mate. You see how they've depicted it.' He flicked forward and back between the four images. 'There's often a board with words on, usually though just the letters INRI, and there's sometimes more of a stand than a bar for the feet.'

'Or just nails.'

'Yes, but unless you've changed your mind, we're using Velcro. The point is - we need to get a better idea from Peter of how he sees the whole thing. Straight up and down feels a bit furtive. There's more to the whole thing than that. See on here, there's often onlookers gathered around the bottom of the cross. It's a bit of artistic theatre, but we could do that, there's enough of us.'

'What? You mean see the whole thing as a tableaux based on these?' I said, pointing at the book.

'We could make it an art work. If Izzie Capricious is on-board and taking pictures, she'll want to see more than a fucking scarecrow on a pole.'

I looked again at the paintings. I hadn't really thought about it much beyond answering his desire and getting him up and hung.

'I reckon Peter bloody Rock's image of his crucifixion owes more to Hollywood than to the traditions of Western Art, so we need to widen his prospective and get him to think about making it a bit more dramatic, less bloodless and more cutting edge.'

'This Tintoretto,' I said, pointing to the foot of the cross, 'there's a dozen people there at least.'

'And more behind.'

'We could allot roles, but we'd need to read the Bible first and check for names.'

'Angela as one of the Marys?'

For the first time in ages, there was a light in Ed's eyes. I thought he had begun to see what 'The Shop' could be, but then again, maybe it was professional jealousy and he wanted to get in before Izzie put her spoke in. I liked it, because he'd also opened my eyes too.

CHAPTER 11

ANGIE

One thing I hate about the university office off Bedford Square is that there's no real room for me to sit anywhere comfortably. It's too small for a start and not designed for more than a desk and a filing cabinet; as a so called 'lab' it's rubbish. To do my job well I need to have good sight of my client: the deaf person, and adequate light. You'd be surprised how often these two essentials are overlooked. In the 'lab' there isn't even a proper seat! I perch on the table most of the time, which means I'm twisting my spine. It's excruciating after a while.

Sonia, my deaf client, is great. She's doing a Ph.D. and I've worked with her a few times before. At least with her I get to see what it is I'm likely to interpret before I arrive; rocking up without any prep is an interpreter's nightmare, especially if it's some deeply boring, jargon rich, academic meeting or, as in this case – a series of psychology experiments.

As soon as it was over, I couldn't wait to be out and walking. I half thought of going round the corner to the British Museum and grabbing something to eat there, but in the end I decided to walk down Tottenham Court Road to a brilliant Middle-Eastern eatery I knew behind Warren Street Station.

There's something about walking that really lifts my soul. I just love the sense of movement and the knowledge that the body is working well and that under my feet the miles are slipping by unnoticed. It also opens up my head to all the wonders of speculation and memory. It wasn't much of a schlep to the café, but long enough to bring to the surface a delicious memory of a holiday in Iceland with Ed.

Strictly speaking, it wasn't a holiday; it was a short-break or to be even more precise: a work related jolly. Ed had been invited by the *ASÍ Art Museum* in Reykjavik to give a talk about his paintings. In the UK art world he may struggle for recognition, but in that great fishing nation off the edge of the polar ice, his work was much appreciated. Was it the fish or was it his style? I've tormented him for ages, suggesting that they only wanted him there so that they could use him to promote fish fingers.

Sometimes I believe in divine intervention, because a month after his invite I was also offered a job in Iceland; it was to take part in an international conference on *'Deaf health & accessibility'*.

The conference was in the stark, modern splendour of the Reykjavik University, which wasn't too far from Ed's gallery, so it meant that we could share a hotel room. Thank heavens for cod, say I!

As I passed Heals on Tottenham Court Road I was in a romantic reverie, remembering Ed standing on a grey volcanic headland facing out across the sea. Despite his stature, his jutting bearded chin, gnarled face and windswept hair was much as l imagined Leif Erikson must have looked before he set off from Iceland on his epic voyage to the west and eventual landfall on the shores of North America.

Don't for a minute think that I am in any sense a beardist, by which I mean a vocal propagandist for hair on men's faces, I've seen too many disasters, but somewhere inside of me the sight of a full bearded man reaches deep down to where the forces of attraction lurk. I once got Ray to grow one. It was fine while ever it was just corn coloured stubble. The chin framed by a soft ruddy-blond halo sort of matched the peasant style theme of our soft furnishings at the time, but once it got longer it began to eat his face, and waking up in the night next to a werewolf could be quite scary.

I guess in a way that the two chins most dear to me, the one bearded, the other naked, could be seen as reflecting a split in my personality, because I can be both very romantic and hideously pragmatic. Being kissed by Ed is a different sensation to being kissed by Ray. Ray has a good strong, nineteenth-century jaw; it is the jaw of a resolute man, the sort of man who would die on the end of a native spear and not whimper. I could imagine him during a last stand in some far flung corner of the Empire, pistol in hand, straddling me as I lay prone on the ground awaiting death. That's the romantic side of me, and a picture totally at odds with my political beliefs which are resolutely anti-imperialist. Ed's beard, on the other hand, fits his character; he'd be the one the rebels caught in a brothel as they rushed through the city gates. He's also less fastidious, not unclean, but less attentive to detail. I'm sure that if he were beardless it would never enter his head to shave before we climbed into bed. But Ray will shave twice a day if he thinks I might come across, and since I am touched by his concern, he sometimes *does* get his leg-over. What a clean chin doesn't do for me, alas, is to make a difference when it comes to more intimate nuzzling. Ed's chin wins every time. It is very, very erotic.

The next meeting of *'the Shop'* was more businesslike than the first. I'd decided that if I was going to act as a secretary I'd better actually do something, so I had produced an agenda. There were only four points to cover: Ray's report, matters arising, Izzie Capricious' application to join, and AO.B.

Everyone was there, on time and ready to rock. Now that they had vaunted their secret desires in public, and nobody had rushed screaming from the room as a result, they were much more relaxed and open, and were chatting away as though they had known each other for ages. I was most impressed. I think the crucifixion run-through had proved to everyone that *'The Shop'* was a serious endeavour, and that their wishes would actually be met.

I sat next to Ed, who surreptitiously nipped my thigh with his fingers. I love those little secret gestures. His smile was surprisingly fulsome, and he looked much more relaxed than last time. I was going to say something about it, but Ray called the meeting to order, and got right down to business.

'Crucifixion or shambles – discuss.' He laughed, and so did we. 'Sounds like an essay title doesn't it?' More laughter. 'But it's not a laughing matter, actually. Philip has a desire, and we'd pledged to bring it to fruition, but we nearly cocked the whole thing up. I raise my hand as one of those guilty for not being as organized as I thought I was. If we are to succeed in achieving our various aims then we must be sharper and better prepared. So – first, the step ladder must be the responsibility of one person alone.' His eyes scanned the room. 'We'll return to that in Matters Arising. Secondly, security based on a dog, even one as trustworthy as Geordie, is no security.' More nervous laughter. 'Someone needs to take that on board. Lastly, we need to be in radio or telephone contact throughout - forewarned is forearmed. If we had a chairperson, this is where I would take a step back, but as I am the chairperson and also the main speaker, let's move on to Matters Arising, by asking Peter for his feed-back.'

A Christ simulacrum is not a role ideally suited for the twenty-first century, and I could see that he was trying to love us and not to be too critical.

'I don't mind admitting that I experienced fear, anxiety and dread.'

We could believe that, and until he suddenly smiled, everyone looked upset and slightly ashamed.

'But that was good. For even in those circumstances, I was able to get closer to my saviour's pain. My main concern though is that being bunked up onto the crossbar took away something of the solemnity of the occasion. I'd hoped to be spending my time contemplating his passion rather than fearing for my life. A ladder would have given it dignity.'

'A point we will be coming to,' said Ray.

'I was holding on to the tree for grim death.'

'*Mea maxima culpa.*' said Ray. 'But the proper bindings should solve that problem.'

'Just want to thank everyone for their help.'

Toby let out a spontaneous gibbon like whoop of delight and everyone started clapping.

Ed turned to me with a big smile on his face, and tapped my thigh.

'Thank you Peter. Stepladder then?'

The only other matters-arising were the allocation of roles: the stepladder went to Justine Cook, and Toby Slight volunteered to act as Security coordinator, and the fixing of the date for the actual crucifixion, which was to be in June.

The next item on the agenda was the one that interested us most of all, the new applicant: Izzie Capricious. Throughout the discussions she had been sat off to the side quietly secure in a heavy parka and black beanie. Although she hadn't spoken, I was conscious of her presence because of a faint chemical aroma emanating from where she sat.

Instead of speaking from there, when Ray addressed her, she rose and came to the front, carrying with her an artist's black portfolio. As she passed I realized that what I could smell came from spray stains on her parka.

Instead of simply telling us her secret desire, she began ceremonially removing her parka and beanie. The effect was like the opening of a chrysalis. She had coloured part of her fringe crimson, and above her black leggings, and under the drab, spray stained coat, she was dressed in a matching red top and red cropped shorts. I was in awe; she looked like an exotic moth.

'I am an artist. My desire is to create a masterpiece in Hackney.' She spoke slowly, and I was aware that her words were directed mainly to Ray, who was nodding foolishly. 'I'm not impressed when I hear over and over again, like some kind of mantra, that the borough has more artists to the acre than almost anywhere else on earth, because unless one of us creates something outstanding, which will have lasting value, then that statistic amounts to nothing more interesting than having a quirky collection of tradesmen.

'My art encompasses all media. I will not define myself. But I need help to find the right vehicle for my masterpiece. I need you. But here, look.

She unzipped her portfolio and drew out four A2 sized photographs which she displayed against the walls.

'Come closer and look.'

We all came to the front and gazed down at the black and white photographs of Peter's crucifixion. They had been altered and cropped from her original shots. They were brilliant, amazing even. She had cropped Peter's face and then enlarged it so much that you could almost read his fear in the searing white light that played along the lines on his skin. The other cuts and enlargements caught the anxiety on the faces of those of us had been gathered at the foot of the tree stump looking up at him. They were hauntingly beautiful.

'Bloody hell.'

Ed was impressed. He was wide-eyed and desperately trying to attract Ray's attention by pointing at the animated faces.

'If you will have me as one of your number, I would also love to use my skills to authenticate your desires and to archive them for posterity. One comrade amongst others.'

When we had taken our seats again, everyone looked both amazed and delighted. And when Ray called for a vote, the result was unanimous. She was in. I was equally enthusiastic, but conscious also of a slight unease, almost a feeling of repulsion, which I put down to having awoken in the morning feeling a little bloated.

Later, in bed, the feeling returned, and it dawned on me that although she had said what her wish was, she hadn't actually said what her 'masterpiece' would be. It was more of a general wish; the sort of thing that anyone might say. There was no detail and no real focus. And masterpiece! That was a bit over the top. Maybe her huge ego was behind my unease.

I put my book down and pushed my specs up on to my forehead. 'Darling. Didn't you say that Izzie wanted to cover Hackney Central station in graffiti?'

Ray peered at me from above his glasses. 'Yes, something like that.'

'She didn't actually say that at the meeting.'

'No,' he smiled. 'Lot more inside that head than her graffiti.'

'Shouldn't you have teased it out a bit; let us know a bit more before letting her in?'

'I've a hunch that she'll come up with something sensational if we give her time.'

'Not quite what you imagined at the start though, is it?

'Better. Evolution, darling. The same thing but slightly different.'

Ray has a habit of citing evolution whenever something he likes seems threatened. But I was too tired to make anything more of it, and put my book down and turned over.

Before we'd come away from the meeting, I had been stopped at the door by Justine Cook. When we'd been all girls together sitting in the dark prior to the crucifixion, I'd been at one end of the bench and she'd been at the other, and so we had hardly exchanged a word.

'What do you think, then?' I said, glancing in Izzie's direction.

'Fabulous! So confident. Makes me feel quite dowdy.'

I laughed. 'Yes, bit in your face.'

'I'd love to be like that: wear what you like, say what you like and do what you like.'

'What's stopping you?'

As soon as I said it I recalled her secret desire: to change who she was. Not my most tactful comment. 'Artists like to show off.'

'But not estate agents,' she said.

'Is that what you do?'

'Yes, in Stamford Hill. Must say I like your husband. He's very dynamic, isn't he?'

I looked across to where Ray and Ed were still in conversation. I'd have said pedantic, but I suppose he was, in his own fastidious way.

'You married?'

'No – although I've got a friend I see reasonably often. Basically for sex,' she said lowering her voice and giggling. 'We're fuck-buddies'.

I held my mouth tight and tried desperately not to show any surprise. She just didn't look, well, didn't look – what? Like me? Because in a sense that was what Ed and I were: fuck-buddies. It sounded a bit blunt, and the words didn't have much room for the word love, but you could say if you didn't know everything, that we provided each other with modest sexual services. I grimaced. No, no, we didn't, we weren't like that, not anything like that. I loved Ed – and Ray, and our sex was always essentially an upwelling of mutual love, or at least a loving release of sexual tension. It confirmed our commitment to each other. She might have a 'fuck-buddy', but I had a lover.

'Nice. How does that work?'

'Well, I have known Stuart for ages, used to work at the same branch of Stretton's, until he got married. But we meet now and again when we both feel the need.'

'I thought you said you wanted to change who you are? Sounds like a nice arrangement – sex without strings. What's to change?'

I tried to make light of her circumstances and laugh it off, but I was too curious to let it go.

'I would like someone special, not necessarily all to myself, but someone to come home to – a husband, or a wife.'

She'd done it again, totally floored me just as I had begun to get an idea of who she was.

'Oh.'

Before I could say anything else she turned her large, mottled face towards me and wrinkled her nose.

'I know we're all working on Peter's desire, but I would love to get my one up and running as soon as possible. I can't see why they couldn't run in tandem. I don't need many props. Do you think we could meet some time and talk it through, perhaps over coffee or a meal? I'm a good cook.'

Well, I couldn't say no, not after hearing all that I'd heard; it would have been rude. So I agreed to pop over to her place in Dalston, once I had checked my diary.

I didn't tell Ray; somehow I felt that Justine had confided in me, and that what she had said was for my ears only.

CHAPTER 12

ED

Over the years, I've bought so many fish from Mehmet, my Turkish fishmonger, that when anything interesting comes in he allows me to preview his morning's slab before it goes public. He's not just a businessman. He values fish for their intrinsic beauty, a rare trait, and he has an innate sense of style, so that the display is always worth a look. Thanks to the new demographics, there is now a wider colour range of the fish from the warmer seas. Traditional British fish are less prevalent in Walthamstow than some Caribbean or African varieties. You get mackerel often enough, even skate wings, but a good sized cod or haddock is a rarity, and I've never seen a Hake.

He had text me at some god-awful hour in the morning that if I was quick I could inspect a rarity: a king-sized haddock. And by god, it was a monster, well over three feet, with a head on it like the nose cone of a rocket. He'd set it amongst the parsley so that its back was bent into the sensuous shape of a sine curve. On either side of its body above the pectoral fins, were two bold, black patches, the traditional ' *devil's thumbprint'*, which made it look as though the fisherman had leant out of the boat and simply pinched the fish from the cold Atlantic waters with his fingers.

'Special order,' said Mehmet.

'Amazing eyes; they're almost square.'

While we were talking, I was snapping away with my camera collecting all of the detail I could before he took the fish away. Haddocks have remarkably soft faces for fish, and their pale, fleshy lips and wide, soulful eyes seem to reflect a distant kinship with us.

One of the reasons I'd responded to his text so promptly was because of Izzie-fucking-Capricious. Her images had stung me. I had been pissed off that someone with such a huge ego could be as sensitive as she so bloody obviously was, and goaded by what she had said about Hackney. I may not have lived in the borough, but Walthamstow was only across the water in the Danelaw, so close enough to be tarred with her same fucking brush. I was an artist. On my tax returns I claimed for artists' materials. I was one of those she had dismissed as a *'quirky collection of tradesmen'.* That was too close, because it was true; I did trade – in bloody aquarium fish!

My morning haddock lay on the slab in a state of grace. It was beautiful. There was no ego, it just was; perfect in every detail, but unless I could make it into something greater then it was, a work of art, I was exactly as Ms. Capricious had almost described me – a glorified fishmonger.

I couldn't use it for one of my gyotaku prints since it was spoken for, and in any case I could never have afforded such a colossus. My visual memory and photographs would have to do. I had decided that I could only answer Izzie C's challenge by taking a fish, and in this case – the haddock, and advancing it into the realms of fine art. Despite what snooty people said, artists battled with beauty and meaning, not identity. We have nothing to say outside of what we make. The haddock and I would go forward together and meet her challenge.

'What sex is it, Mem?'

'Female.'

Mehmet went into his cold store, and before I left I looked again into her sightless eyes, so large and so dark.

'Right then, we're in this together, so from now on you will no longer be an anonymous haddock; you, you lovely creature, will be known as Daisy-May.'

When I got back to the Shop and opened up for the day, my enthusiasm had waned a bit. The enormity of the task daunted me. I would be going against the whole trend of contemporary, identity based art, and I would be attempting to do something that I hadn't the first idea of how to achieve. I felt like Sisyphus as he took his first gander at the boulder. And on top of that there was the bloody crucifixion. Getting the religious half-wit up onto the cross was the easy bit. It was what I'd got Ray into: the idea of making the whole enterprise into an artwork, which was the problem. Two masterpieces in one go was a bit optimistic.

I made myself a coffee and went out into the yard for a smoke. I sat with my back to the garage desperate to catch the fleeting morning sun before it vanished for the day behind the buildings.

I wasn't exactly despondent, more perplexed. I'd let myself be cajoled into Ray's crazy *Bucket Shop* when everything inside of me had said have nothing to do with it, and now I'd got myself into a state over a fantasy. Masterpiece – fuck off! What sort of twat talk was that? Once, as a callow, empty headed student, I might have dreamed of becoming a famous painter, but I was fifty-fucking-eight. That was wishful thinking; a shopkeeper couldn't afford such ideas. And yet, and yet - I really wanted to make something beyond myself instead of quietly chuffing down the track on a branch line that ended in death, and where the scenery wasn't startling, but ok; the service was adequate and the food acceptable, but it was still only one of life's lesser branch lines. Carrying on the way I was would not end in fame, but at least I would have done what I had wanted to do and would die - ordinary.

'You asleep?'

Angie had stepped into the yard followed by Geordie, who came straight to me and stuffed his head between my legs.

'I thought you were working today?'

'Cancelled,' she said, as I shielded my balls from the dog's jabbing snout, 'so a whole day to myself,' she said, kissing me on the forehead.

I got up and took her in my arms. 'Sorry, I was quietly maundering. That bloody Izzie Capricious has got to me.'

She laughed. 'You mean the moth!'

I laughed too. 'Bloody vampire more like.'

I kissed her hungrily; deliberately chewing her ear and nipping the back of her neck to let her know that I was more than pleased to see her. When we parted her eyes had softened.

'I let what she said get to me; all that stuff about Hackney artists. One part of me wants to give her an artistic slap and the other wants to give in and let her trample my simple endeavours beneath her fucking boots.'

She kissed my cheek.

'Trouble is - I think she's right. I am too comfortable. When Ray asked me what my dream was all I could come up with was to be recognized as worthwhile.'

'A retrospective is more than that, sweetheart. It's an affirmation.'

'But wrong. That's not what I really want. I really want to paint something great, not comfortable. That's where she's right. My aspirations are too low. I've lost my drive, darling. I need to step up and get back into the fight.'

Her face brightened. 'Yes, darling, yes, and why not? I was just as unsure about her when she turned up, but maybe that's going to be her contribution, maybe that's what she has to offer; she's the goad you need to get you going. She certainly seems to have invigorated Ray. He's been talking nonstop about making *the Shop* into some kind of art work.'

I winced. 'Yeah, I know.' I looked at my watch. 'Fancy a quick one before I open up?'

I know that some couples get very tetchy when one wants sex and the other doesn't, but we've never been like that; thanks to our years of living apart we take our chances when we can; even if our urges don't always overlap, we oblige.

Ray had gone off to one of his beloved streamlets somewhere north of Ware, so instead of opening the shop after we'd made love, we decided we'd walk the dog and have a second breakfast in Stoke Newington. I was an artist first and a fucking ornamental fishmonger a long way second.

I couldn't help blathering on about Daisy-May and the masterpiece-to-order. But instead of treating the whole thing as a joke and laughing at my love-affair with a haddock, Angie almost exploded with delight and support, waxing lyrical about seizing the moment and there being something or other in the affairs of men, which I should grab.

'Everything leads to this moment, darling, everything. All you need is the focus, and I think I've got an idea that could do just that. But first – ditch Daisy May, not the fish, but the silly name; it's demeaning. It harks of mimsy. Fame is a serious business.'

'I'm not doing this for fame, sweetheart.'

'Fame will follow if the intent and execution are sincere.'

I pulled a face. Suddenly the whole idea began to look threadbare and ridiculous. You don't set out to create a masterpiece; it was a crazy idea.

'Don't go wet on me, Edward. You can do this and I can tell you how. God! Sometimes you want a bloody good shake.'

I smiled. I love it when she gets belligerent.

'The haddock is still the key, so hold that. Think fish and think of the Bible. What do you come up with?'

We passed in front of the first of the reservoirs down Copper Mill Lane and I let my eyes sweep across the geese and ducks for inspiration. I'd never been to Sunday school or church, except for the usual weddings and the odd funeral. Bible stuff was a big hole in my knowledge.

'Jonah and the whale!' I said as an unbidden memory flashed into my head.

'Whales are cetaceans, darling, not fish.'

I rolled my eyes.

'Jesus and the two miracles?' she said, more ferociously. I looked bewildered, so she elaborated with all the love of an exasperated Sunday school teacher. 'The apostles were fishing on the Sea of Galilee and getting nowhere, so Christ, either shouting from the shore or actually in the boat with them, told them to try once more and all would be well. They dropped their nets, and – voila! They came up teeming with fish. A miracle!'

'And?'

'*I will make you fishers of men, fishers of men, fishers of men. I will make you fishers of men, if you follow me.*' Angie sang at me as though I were a cretin.

I pulled a face.

'Oh God, you can be dense, sometimes.'

'Ignorance is not a crime.'

'Right, sorry, I forgot your impoverished childhood. There was either one miracle or two involving Jesus, a fishing boat and those disciples who were originally fishermen.'

'And?'

'And I give in. I don't know why I bother, Edward. Go on, paint what you bloody like.'

She walked on ahead, which meant I had to think quickly. As we came to the carpark she stopped and turned back to me.

'Well?'

'I've been thinking about what you said.'

'And?'

'You mean – paint the disciples' fish?'

'Glory be and alleluia. The two miracles have been painted by some of the greatest artists in Europe. It's the perfect subject for you, darling; you understand fish. And more to the point, you have Peter Rock, a latter day Jesus, on hand to sketch and photograph. When we crucify him, he's not going to go anywhere, so you get him to model free gratis and for nothing.'

God, I was being dull. She was right, it was perfect, and so was he.

CHAPTER 13

RAY

O ld Father Thames starts its life as the River Isis. You can't help being aware off this process of name mutation when you've worked at the Ordinance Survey for as long as I have. Sometimes the river's name alters within only a few miles of its source, and sometimes it changes when the 'original' name is swapped for the name of some settlement that it flows beside. Not far from where I grew up in Lincolnshire, the River Lymn does exactly that; half way towards its exit into the North Sea it pinches the name of a nearby village and morphs into the River Steeping. In Lincoln, the river that flows through the centre of the city is called the Witham, but by the time it's crossed the fens and has passed beyond Ed's home town of Boston, it has become The Haven. What gets me annoyed is when toponymists are so tied to their books that they can't entertain any other explanations for the origins of a river's name other than their ancient texts.

I was stumbling through a thicket alongside the River Stort, a tributary of the Lea, thinking about the linguistic origins of nearby Bishops Stortford. You'd think that the ford in the name referred to a crossing of that river, but according to the literature it was the town which named the river: Stort stemming from an Anglo-Saxon word for *'the tongue of land'*. Wonderful, a linguistic puzzle sorted; but is it? What makes sense in a book doesn't always make sense on the ground when you take into consideration the actual topography. I grant you that the *'tongue of land'* meaning could easily refer to the historically boggy land around the town, because the Stort twists, turns, separates and then re-joins across the whole of its flood plain, and crossing that morass would have been difficult. But there could be another explanation for the name, and it was this thought that was buzzing in my brain as I made my way through the undergrowth along the river's bank.

Now, I'm a Celt, not a chippy professional Celt, but a deep vein Celt, one of those originating in England in the lands over which the various post-Bronze Age invasions passed, and what I'm trying to do is to see the landscape around the Lee's tributaries as it was in those pre-literate times, and to get a feel for how it might have looked to those people. Early spellings of names discovered in ancient records and books are important, but they take you only so far, for they were first written down centuries after the name's origin and by foreign clerks whose native languages were not the same as those spoken by the Britons or others amongst whom they lived.

The first people to name our rivers probably lived in the Stone Age. Some river names like the Ouse and Ex are so ancient that they probably pre-date our present Indo-European languages, which means that what they actually mean is no more than an educated guess. What drives my interest in the Lee and its tributaries is the thought that the landscape and its uses named the rivers all those years ago.

Rivers sustained the tribes that lived along their banks. They marked off their various territories, and their fishing and hunting grounds. Getting about in marshy wooded land was difficult, but moving about on rivers was easier. What was needed to help competing tribes know who was who, and where one tribe's hunting lands started and ended, were signs, and the easiest sign to see from a distance in difficult country was smoke. Fires and beacons must have had an important place in the landscape. Ancient peoples also needed to know where game was plentiful, and the best places to land their canoes or to butcher the deer or aurochs that they had killed. I think things like this could well have influenced river names.

Sadly, I'm not a linguist, I'm a cartographer, but I did read that the Stort and related river names like the Stor and the Stour could all refer to hunting related terms if you gloss them using ancient Gaelic. I'm testing this idea during my rambles along the Lee and its tributaries, and so far it seems to be making more and more sense, because sometimes I can almost see the prehistoric herds of deer galloping across the hill sides

Walking frees up my head and allows my speculations to flow unhindered, but you can't always predict what your head will throw up for rumination. Before I'd reached the pub I was hoping to have lunch in, Bishop Stortford and its origins vanished from my consciousness to be replaced by the delightful face of Izzie Capricious. I did not generate her from my imaginings. She sent me an I-phone image of herself holding up a sign upon which was written in large, black, Gothic looking script: HELLO. There was nothing else.

For some reason seeing her made my stomach churn, and I felt a strong desire to sit down, so I made my way back onto the gravelled path and walked on until I found a river side bench. As I had a packed lunch with me I decided to eat it while I pondered upon her sudden arrival in my pocket.

I bit into my wholemeal, seeded, mini-baguette and chomped on the chorizo and manchego filling. While my jaws worked overtime on the tough crust I enlarged the photograph and investigated the background more closely. From everything around her, I guessed it was her studio. Then I investigated her. She was sitting on a stool and wearing an orange boiler suit and a pork pie hat. Her written sign covered her chest and the index finger of her left hand was pointing at it. Her face looked remarkably friendly, welcoming in fact, and her rather full lips were smiling. There was a mischievous look in her eyes that in a different age would have been called coquettish. I realized with some dismay that I was smiling back at her.

We hadn't been in communication directly since we'd met at the café. My only contact had been my *Bucket Shop* texts addressed to everyone.

She had a sense of humour that was obvious, playfulness, even. But why had she texted me, and did that mean that I should reply, and if so, should it be in like manner? I did have my note book with me, but a biro sign wouldn't quite hack it. Then I had an idea. I would create a sign on the ground out of twigs, photograph it and send it to her.

When I came to look, the river bank was surprisingly short of letter making material, the only stuff that was available in any quantity was goose poo. The question was: if I used that would she see the funny side of it? It was a gamble, but then she was a bit of a tease.

Canada geese crap a lot. At its worst their crap consists of green and white moist rolls of grass residues. At its best, it is friable, but it was all I had. Unfortunately I started my message being too verbose and ended up with nothing on the ground but an illegible dungy mess and fingers covered in shit. I cleared it all away and started again. 'Hi Iz'. The moderately firm turds held their shape long enough to produce a good image and I sent it to her at once.

I was so pleased by my audacity that it was only after I had chomped into my roll that I remembered my shitty fingers. I could only smell chorizo, but just in case, I rubbed my fingers vigorously on the grass before taking another bite. As I chewed I magnified my sent image. You couldn't miss that the letters were of animal origin. Whether she would recognize what animal that was, I had no idea.

Almost immediately there came a text in reply.

'hi ray, honk, honk! loved the letters! where are you?'

'On the banks of the Stort.' I was chuffed and quickly added another text just in case she was unfamiliar with the local river systems. *'It's a tributary of the River Lee.'*

'great, lovely day for it. fancy calling in for a coffee on your way back?'

'Yes! Where?'

I surprised myself with the speed of my answer. To have coffee would mean curtailing the river work and turning back immediately to Dobbs Weir, crossing the bridge to the Lee and heading down the river to the station at Broxbourne. I was getting quite excited.

'*come to the house. 2A spring building, lordship road. off church street. text when you are near X*

'*Will do. See you there.*'

Her kiss had been a capital letter; that was deliberate, but should I add a kiss or not, especially as I hardly knew her? But then she was different.

'*X*'

A simple capital *X*; I felt sick. I'm not the most forward person I know, but I had just done what I had done, just gone with the moment. I felt instantly guilty. Going to see another woman was a new experience. I'd always been careful not to cultivate women friends, not because I thought Angie would be jealous, well a bit, but because I've never been very good alone with women. I wasn't by nature a ladies' man or a man's man, come to that. My circle of friends was very small, but now, suddenly and on a whim, I was enlarging it.

All the way back to Hackney Downs station my sickness grew, and I began to work out ways of not going through with it. What would be the point of the whole thing? What on earth had we to say to each other, unless, of course, she wanted to talk about her *Bucket Shop* 'desire' and how it was to be achieved? That seemed like the most obvious reason for her text. Whatever I was thinking was just nervousness, after all, she was an odd bod, and being alone with an odd bod carried risks. That was it. It was *Shop* talk.

Smiling to myself at my own witticism, I sat back and watched the Walthamstow Marshes vanish below us as the train began its crossing of the last rail bridge over the Lee.

I approached Lordship Road from Church Street, which even on a Friday afternoon was crowded with educated young mums and their noisy offspring. I scoffed to myself where they clustered outside a popular eatery like dung beetles around a cowpat. I've never understood this desire to queue for food. There were plenty of other places to eat.

Lordship Road had the undeniable good fortune of being close to Clissold Park. I'd often walked down it, but this time I looked at the buildings with new interest. The houses reflected the aspiring social ambitions of the emerging Victorian and Edwardian diligent classes, and were comfortable rather than grand. Despite its rather modern sounding name, Spring Building was actually a rather rectangular Edwardian structure that might well once have housed a business of some kind, since it incorporated an attractive wagon-sized arch, off to the side, complete with its original wooden double-doors.

I composed my face and rang the bell. Nothing happened. I rang again with the same result. Just as I was beginning to feel awkward, I noticed that the bell system did not include 2A. A small painted arrow pointed towards the archway.

'God what a twat!'

I hurried down to the double-doors and a very obvious illuminated entry system. Before I had time to press the button a disembodied voice spoke to me from the box.

'Doors open, Ray, come on in.'

I stepped though the inset door and into a totally concealed yard filled with artistic junk. But there was no time to look around, somewhere above me Izzie spoke.

'The iron steps to your right.'

Like a prisoner mounting the scaffold, I had a crude sense of doom as I approached the orange figure.

'Lovely to see you, Ray.'

She kissed me warmly on both cheeks and I tried to match her kiss for kiss.

'Amazing place.'

'Isn't it. Come inside.'

It was a warm fine day and every window in what I assumed was her studio was open, and the cool draught that blew through carried with it a hint of white spirit or glue; whatever it was it was definitely chemical.

'Great space.'

'Let's go through here.'

She led me out of the studio and into a very cosy room that was a cross between a dining room and a junk room.

'How do you like your coffee? No don't tell me,' she said, holding her hand up imperiously. 'I'm good at this. Let me guess.'

Rather disconcertingly you stepped back and looked me up and down like a judge at Crufts.

'Um? Good figure, square jaw, clear eyes.' It was Crufts! 'Direct and strong minded. Um? Black and strong. Am I right?'

Instantly, I became every adjective she had uttered, and felt ridiculously excited.

'Spot on.'

We both chuckled and she began the coffee making.

'I'm guessing you also like something sweet to go with it?'

I threw my hands apart to show that once again she was on target. 'What are you offering?'

'Ah! When I knew you were coming I went out and got something special.' She raised her eyebrows suggestively and once again deployed her index finger to indicate in what direction I should look to where her goodies lay.

'Doughnuts!'

I knew where she had got them. They were the best doughnuts on Church Street: fat, succulent and loaded with jam.

'My favourite.'

'And mine. But not too often. The watchwords are – a little of what you fancy.'

Again our mutual chuckling.

We took our coffees and sat across from each other at a table covered in what looked like a very old Victorian curtain.

She observed me again, smiling and nodding. 'When I first saw you in the moon light in Millfields Park I knew you were special, Ray.'

I made the usual visual objections.

'No. It's true. There was a phrase that entered my head: *'Cometh the hour, cometh the man.'* You, Ray, have that sense of ordained time. You have a vision of life that I find particularly attractive. When I look at you I can see it at the back of your eyes.' She leant across the table and stared fixedly at me.

I couldn't have turned away even if I had wanted to because to do so would have meant that she was wrong and the hour and I had not cometh together, and I rather liked what she was saying, whether it was true or not.

'To set up something as noble as *'the Shop'*, which has only one purpose – the satisfaction of *other* people's greatest desires, is an inspired and selfless act. That reaches me here.'

She slipped her fingers between the pop studs of her boiler suit to where her heart lay.

'I have great desires, Ray, and you can satisfy them.'

She got up so quickly that her hips ruckled the table cloth as she came round the top towards me. I steadied my coffee and pushed it away from the edge before standing up. She stopped in front of me and stared into my face as though she were reading something written upon the skin.

'You feel it too, don't you - that tightness in the chest, that coursing of the blood?' As she spoke her hand came up and gripped the front of the boiler suit.

My throat contracted. I forced a cough and managed a constrained, 'Yes.'

'Yes! Of course you do, for we are two of a kind, Ray.'

She stepped towards me with such force that I sank back against the table. As I reached out for support, she stepped between my splayed arms and pushed me so hard against the crumpled curtain table-cloth that it and my coffee went sliding off dramatically along the surface. The instant that her mouth smothered mine I felt something hot and wet seeping into my hair and along the back of my neck.

'Ah! Ah!' I cried, lifting my head to avoid the pain.

Mistaking my cries for an excess of passion, she pushed me back into the puddle so that tidal waves of coffee swept down my spine until my shirt and back were soaked. Ignoring the strong aroma of coffee she lifted me bodily onto the table and climbed up beside me. The Victorian curtain gave up the struggle and fell to the floor taking our coffee mugs with it.

She kissed me like a fury. Her lips were never still. They flitted across my face from one side to the other and back again. I heard myself panting and then, like the snapping of an elastic band, something broke inside me and I found myself consumed by the same wild desire and began smothering her in kisses, rolling from side to side and jiggling my body in time with hers.

'Ray, Ray, Ray!

'Izzie, Izzie, Izzie!'

As we screamed at each other like rival football supporters, my hand went down her chest ripping open the poppers of her boiler suit from neck to crutch like a butcher's knife. She sat up, wrenched apart the last catch and sloughed off the suit like a snake skin, revealing beneath it a naked skin swirling with exotic tattoos. I was spellbound until I remembered with dismay that I was still wearing my walking boots; they would be impossible to get off easily. I dived down to the laces, but she had got there before me and had begun scrabbling at them with her finger ends. I sat up and felt the cold sodden shirt cling to my back. I pulled it off, careless of the buttons, and in the joy of liberation twirled it around my head before letting it fly. Where it landed I had no idea and cared less for at that moment she yanked off the left boot and hurled it carelessly across the room. Ignoring the sound of breaking crocks she gave a final wrench to the right boot and it came off too. She held it before me like the spoils of a victorious wrestler and then tossed it nonchalantly over her shoulder. In the onslaught that followed the last of our clothing followed the boots. For one brief moment we were still, eyeing each other's flesh like hungry raptors. I saw her ribs rising and falling beneath her purple inked curlicues, her full breasts and a narrow shaved coppice of black virginal hair. She saw my erect penis, dark against my sickly white flesh. It was enough. My face burned; hers was flushed. She laid herself upon the table top, opened her legs and I climbed on top of her. Then with a few deft slippery movements we were coupled and heaving enough to make the table groan.

With a wild shriek she came and as she did so I felt the bite of her nails in my buttocks.

'More! Harder!'

She attacked my cheeks with relish and drove her nails into the flesh until I squealed. It was the jolt I needed. I pressed harder, pushing my forehead onto the table and heaving my tingling buttocks until with a violent spasm the end of my penis seemed to explode.

'Ah! Ooh!'

I stared goggle eyed at her. Her skin was rubicund and her nostrils were flaring aggressively.

'How delicious, darling, your skin smells like a cappuccino.'

I left much later in a charity shop man's shirt, which she used for work. It was not identical to the one she had ruined, but it was the same colour more or less and clean. I doubted that Angie would notice the difference.

We had parted in a very businesslike manner. We were not in love that was for sure. What happened between us had been good, very good, but it was not the overture to romance, about that we had both been clear.

'Sex, Raymondo,' she said, annoyingly using Ed's nickname for me, 'is always better when unexpected. The next time we mate we will already have that secret carnal knowledge of each other, so it must be unforeseen and surprising.'

Before I had gone far up the road towards Church Street my phone buzzed. I smiled. I half expected that she might send departing words of endearment.

'I'm with you, Ray – let's get Peter Rock nailed up sooner rather than later.'

There were no kisses, not even a reference to what we had just done. I might have bridled at their blandness had it not occurred to me that to the best of my remembrance, at no time had we discussed the crucifixion. But she was right. The thought had occurred to me too. Peter needed to see the culmination of his desires before we lost the good weather. I glanced at my phone. Monday would be the summer solstice. It would be perfect, unless, that is, pagans in the neighbourhood decided to use the same venue.

CHAPTER 14

ANGIE

'Hello Boundary One, this is Base. Come in please.'

I was the coordinator of the whole proceedings and despite my best efforts I couldn't help feeling truly excited, after all this was the real thing: the conclusion of our first 'desire'.

'Boundary One reporting. All quite. Earlier movement down to fox. Over. Oh, and Angie, is there any coffee left?'

'Please keep to protocol, Boundary One. No names. And yes.'

'You must be wondering why I'm doing this,' said Peter, who was sat beside me dressed for the occasion in a pair of white pants and a singlet.

'Doing it? What? Oh yes. Hold that a minute, Peter, while I check with Boundary Two. Hello Boundary Two, this is Base. Report please.'

There was nothing but a slight hiss from the hand piece.

'We're in their thrall, aren't we?' said Peter, pointing to the intercom. 'They'll be taking over the world soon, what with fridges and kettles that talk to each other.'

'Maybe it's the beginning of Armageddon,' I said sympathetically.

'Well, I'll be prepared, won't I?'

'Sorry Base, someone was walking nearby.'

'All clear now?' I said, ignoring Lauren's procedural lapse.

'All clear.'

'Thank you Boundary Two. Out.'

'I'm not a nutter, Angie. I want you to know that. I realize that to other people my desires might seem strange, but my wish to identify with our lord's suffering is a genuine desire to *know* what he went through. Because only by *knowing* can we understand fully the depth of his love for us.'

'No, I s'pose you're right. But it is odd, Peter. It's not something that most twenty-first century people would want to do.'

'Christ is my hero. I try to model my whole life upon his. You wouldn't think it was strange if I was identifying with someone more contemporary, would you? Someone say like Gandhi or Einstein.'

'Or Che Guevara. Even David Bowie.'

'Jesus of Nazareth died for our sins, Angie. Che Guevara and the other one died sinners. Hardly icons to emulate.'

'No, no. I see what you're saying, not if you're looking beyond the temporal.'

Sitting beside a man in his underwear in the delayed darkness of a warm June night debating his philosophical underpinnings seemed almost normal – just two friends chatting.

'Tell me, though, Peter, you're name isn't really Peter Rock is it, because it would be too much of a coincidence if it were?' I smiled, winningly. I wasn't wishing to expose him, simply to clear my own head from doubt, and to get one over on Ed.

He returned my smile. 'And Guevara wasn't called Che; he was christened Ernesto and Bowie was originally named David Jones. No. I woke one day and decided that I could no longer inhabit the name that my parents bestowed upon me. I was a born again human being and needed to reflect that in my everyday life.'

'And what was your name, if you don't mind me asking?'

'Michael Yates.'

'No relation to William Butler, I suppose?' I said, but I could see he had no idea who I was referring to. 'The Irish poet? *'And what rough beast, its hour come round at last,*

Slouches towards Bethlehem to be born?'

The mention of Bethlehem both caught his attention and induced confusion, but before I could extricate myself the handset sprang to life.

'Base. Centre here. Send over the package. I repeat, send over the package.'

'This is it, time Peter. Good luck.'

I watched him as he scampered off from the shadows towards the darker circle of trees and the small torch light that showed where Ray and Ed were waiting for him, and then collected my things and went to my new station in the ley of one of the plain trees that formed the main circle, where Justine was already ensconced in her capacity as First Aid Officer. From there I would be able to signal more quickly to the cross-party if either Toby or Lauren spotted any intruders.

'All ok?' she said.

'Like clockwork.'

'That offers still open,' she said quietly.

For a moment I had no idea what she was on about, and then I remembered. Oh God – lunch! I'd never phoned her back. I rolled my eyes wearily, as if just being alive had taken all of my strength and all of my memory.

'Sorry, Justine, just not been possible.' I threw my hands out to indicate what was happening around us. 'As soon as this is over, yes, let's do it. I would like that.'

She smiled, totally unfazed by my pathetic miming and we both continued staring vacantly into the darkness.

Compared to the last effort, Peter's assent seemed very quick. He was up the ladder and Velcro-ed remarkably fast. I could already see Ed collapsing the ladder and running across with it to another tree.

'Base, tune to package, please.'

I checked my phone and put in an ear piece. Ray had decided that we couldn't leave Peter up on the cross and just disappear into the shadows and wait. We needed to be in contact in case anything went wrong or he got so desperate that he needed to come down. With that in mind he had attached Peter's phone to his chest and wired him up with a microphone and ear piece.

I could hear Peter's breathing and what sounded like a very quiet conversation.

'I think he's praying.'

There was movement around the foot of the cross and then we saw two sudden bursts of light.

'Izzie about her business,' I said.

'Very confident, isn't she?'

I was going to say overbearing, but remembered that maybe Justine needed to hear something a little more positive.

'Strong woman, Justine, bit like you.' I said, smiling and hoping she would catch the implied memory of her restrained vocal support for those who at the last meeting had thought that Peter should be allowed to suffer for as long as he thought sufficient.'

She smiled; pleased I think that I'd remembered. 'Well, it's not for us to judge anyone else's desires.'

'Maybe he likes a bit of pain,' I said, smirking.

Her smile was almost bashful. 'He doesn't strike me as someone who enjoys too much – excitement.'

'No, perhaps not. But didn't it surprise you that Izzie was the main one who wanted to curtail his time on the cross? She had struck me as someone for whom a little controlled suffering would have appealed.'

'Maybe you're confusing pain and suffering.'

In the darkness it was difficult to say if she was smiling. I said nothing, but it triggered a memory of the discussion she and Ray had had at the last meeting just before the final vote.

'We all suffer in different ways. I think Peter's wish should be honoured.'

'I sort of agree with you, Justine, but at the same time I half agree with Izzie. Of course, in principal, we should honour each of our wishes in full, but Millfields Park *is* a public place, it is not licensed for theatrical productions, which is what it could easily become if we pushed it too far.'

I think that Ray's opinion persuaded most of the group to vote for limiting Peter's time to one hour. And then I remembered how after the count I had caught Izzie giving Ray a strange, rather patronizing look, such as you'd give to a clever pet, but before I could pursue the memory further, Toby called in.

'*Hello Base. Boundary One. No alarm, but group of people in outer paddock. Over.*'

'*Thank you, Boundary One. Keep me posted.*'

'Where's that?' said Justine.

'Across the Lea Bridge Road, that bit that runs down passed the flats; near the playground.'

I checked my phone. Peter still had half an hour to go. It was now deep dark, so we settled down to wait, which wasn't a great deal of fun because although Ray and Ed were across on the other side of the trees ready to assist in Peter's descent, we were all too far apart to chat.

'Can I have a listen?' said Justine, pointing to my phone.

She moved closer and I gave her one of the ear-pieces.

'He's singing.'

'Jesus bids us shine with a clear, pure light,
Like a little candle burning in the night;
In this world of darkness, we must shine,
You in your small corner, and I in mine.

We looked at each other in dismay.

'That's lovely.'

'It's a children's hymn,' I said.

'*Base, Boundary One. Come in please.*'

'*Go ahead Boundary One.*'

'*Party has crossed road. Heading your way. Over.*'

'*Keep track Boundary One. Hello Centre. Visitors on the way. Out.*'

'Now what?' said Justine.

'We keep our eyes peeled.'

'*Base. Boundary Two. Visitors here too. Entering via bottom of Chats. At least ten. Over.*'

'*Centre here, Base. Get ready to abort. I repeat. Prepare for lift down.*'

Just as I relayed the message to Lauren and Toby, Justine, who had started to pack away all of her medical stuff, gave an excited yelp.

'Oh my God!'

'What?'

'Look. We're surrounded.'

Out of the darkness, and approaching us from all directions like the army of the dead, came a slow moving ring of people.

'Centre, get him down. We're discovered.'

There was a sudden metal clatter and a loud curse as Ray or Ed tripped over the ladder and fell sprawling onto the grass. I ran towards them.

'Would someone tell me what's going on?'

Peter's panicky voice sounded shrill in my ear.

By the time Justine and I got to the cross, Ray and Ed had got the ladder in position, but it was too late to get Peter down without a fuss because the first of the strangers had arrived at the foot of the cross.

'What the fuck's going on? Who are you? This is our tree.'

Ray, with remarkable presence of mind, mounted the aluminium ladder so that he rose above the mob.

'Listen, listen. We're only here for another half hour, and then we're off. Is that a problem?'

There was a rumbling roar of discontent.

'Well, we could go now, if it's easier.'

I noticed that on the fringes of the melee Izzie's camera was flashing away again.

'Are you part of the East London Pagan Alliance?'

The voice from the crowd came from a large, bushy bearded man sporting what appeared to be deer antlers attached to a small cap.

'Could somebody get me down please?'

Ed tried to climb up beside Ray, but the ladder yawed dangerously on the soft ground and he had to jump off. I rushed forward to give a hand.

'We're making a film,' said Ray.

'Not here you're not,' said a loud, angry voice.

'This is the summer solstice; it is our holy time and this is where we celebrate the blessings conferred upon us by mother earth. It is a holy place not a film location.'

'Yeah, fuck off.'

'Media tossers!'

'Wait, wait. Look, we're just about to go. If you would like to retire a little to give us some space, we'll get him down and be off.' Ray was trying to smile, but Ed was looking dangerously tense.

'Ok, ok, fair enough. You weren't to know, I s'pose. We'll step away.' He nodded his horned head towards the others. 'Back off, people. Give them some space.' The circle expanded slightly. 'Nice idea that though, the bloke in the underpants. Great image. Big movie is it? Would I have heard of the stars?'

'No, sadly, low budget. It's an art house movie. Could you just step back a bit further? Great, great, thank you.'

Ed climbed up the ladder and balanced precariously on the crosspiece fumbling with the Velcro.

'Shall we take our cross piece with us or would you like it? Not a problem, few screws.'

'Take it,' said a red haired woman buzzing about checking on what was going on. 'Christ was the enemy of Wicca.'

'Not really a cross, though, is it? More of a T,' said the man. 'You could get more garlands around it than just on the trunk.'

Peter was shaking quite violently and was able to come down the ladder only with Ed's help. Justine ran forward with the aluminized emergency blanket that we'd bought for the occasion and wrapped it around him, and then the two of us escorted him through the crowd of gawking, curious pagans, many of whom had painted faces or things platted into their hair, to where the car was parked.

'Well, that's that. We'll be off then,' said Ray, stepping out the way of Ed and the ladder and shaking the antlered man's hand. 'Hope you have a brilliant solstice.'

'Before you go, mate. You got the time on you?'

'Eleven forty-five,' said Ray.

CHAPTER 15

RAY

I wasted no time in calling the next meeting because there was so much to discuss. The crucifixion had been our test run for the whole enterprise, on it rested the whole future of the *Bucket Shop* concept.

It was Angie who suggested that we hold it at our house. At first I wasn't too sure. The house was moderately central, which made it sensible, and I liked the idea of a more relaxed atmosphere, but although I agreed that we all needed be free to open up and voice our opinions, the thought of so many 'others' in the house unnerved me, for it forced me to confront my own unvoiced opinion, which was that I actually considered most of my fellow *Shoppers* to be a collection of nutters. Inviting instability into my inner sanctum sent my head into a spin. If anything went wrong further down the line then they would know where I lived and could easily come round and besiege the place carrying placards and staves. I would be exposed. There would be disorder in the streets, which at the very least could lead to our being ostracized by outraged neighbours.

Only after I confessed these fears to Angie was I able to let them go and do as she suggested which was to go with the flow and stop being a total tosspot. The clincher was when she pointed out that they already knew where I lived, so it was too late to have any ideas about anonymity.

'And what about poor old Ed? He's your oldest friend. He's even more exposed. We meet in his garage, for god's sake.'

'Well, yes, all right, but I don't want anybody going into my study, then.'

'Why would anybody in their right mind want to ferret about in all of your maps and river stuff?'

I was taken aback by her sarky vehemence.

'Meaning what exactly?'

'They will be coming here to talk about their own desires, not burgle the bloody house.'

I frowned.

'Darling, I'm sorry I shouted, and when I said 'stuff' I absolutely didn't mean – rubbish; I meant that your research, when laid out on the table, is not attractive to the acquisitive eye, that's all. The moment you walk into the study you can tell that there's nothing inside worth pinching. No electronics!'

'No, I s'ppose not. They are not cartographers, are they?' I said, smiling at the thought.

'And your Apple Mac is hardly new, is it?'

Then I remembered my collection cabinet. 'Ah, but wait a minute. What about my stuff in the front room, the remains of my smoking paraphernalia, that *is* worth something? You'd only need to nick the Vietnam Zippo and you'd we quids in.'

'Darling, darling – shut up! You are being paranoid. The cabinet is locked and you have the key upstairs in your desk. So no one is going to nick the Zippo, the Zig Zag or your saucy collection of meerschaum pipes.'

I sniggered, pretending that I knew all along that I was being stupid. But Angie had made me realize something else, by inviting them inside the castle, as it were, I would be exposing my treasures to different eyes, eyes that could easily misunderstood what they were looking at. The meerschaum pipes were only vaguely saucy, and they had come into my possession by happenstance. But to someone else, with a different mind-set, the fact that two or three of them had been fashioned around the torsos of amply bosomed women could well be interpreted salaciously. I kept them for their craftsmanship not for their over ripe breasts.

'Don't worry, darling, one day I'll get shot of the lot,' I said cheerily, at the same time reminding myself to hide the pipes once Angie was out of the house.

Ed and I had gone for a walk the day after the Millfields confrontation. We'd met outside John Lewis's in the new Westfield Centre in Stratford, where I'd been sent by Angie to buy some summer shorts. Unlike Ed, shorts are not something I wear with ease, and to get me into a shop or into the seductive confines of Westfield is difficult at the best of times. I need a lot of cajoling before I will buy anything.

'Oh my god!' I said under my breath as we rose up the escalator towards the heavenly embrace of John Lewis' cafe. 'Look at the slap on that one.'

Two heavily made up young women passed us on the way down, their faces as inanimate and as sharply defined as Sindy Dolls.

'Reality imitating art.'

Feeling decidedly superior, we stepped off the final escalator and into the warm, calm atmosphere of the café.

'Bit less of the Gadarene Swine in here,' I said, taking our tray towards the comfortable arm chairs.

Once we'd settled down, Ed opened his back pack and pulled out a large sketchpad and laid it before me with a silent fanfare.

'Is this the Christ?' I said, moving my Americano and shortbread to the side.

He flipped open the cover. Filling the page was a full face charcoal drawing of Peter, his eyes strained and his mouth half open in apparent agony.

'Wow! That is powerful. God, he fits the part, doesn't he?'

On other pages there were quick attitude sketches and drawings done from slightly further away so that the whole of the cross complex could be seen. As sketches they were highly competent, but the most important bit, the bit that revealed his true skill, was that Ed had caught Peter's highly individual facial gestures. They may not have been produced by actual physical pain, but the grimaces looked enough real to me.

'Brilliant mate. I was right, wasn't I? He is the perfect subject for your 'masterpiece.'

He winced at the word. 'You know what, though? He may be out to lunch, but you can't tell that, can you, not from looking at his face, not up there like he was?'

'No, no, true. He's got the eyes of a believer.'

He reached into his bag and pulled out another smaller sketch book. 'I worked these up at home from some of the pictures I took while you were both fiddling about.'

He handed me the book. 'Fuck me, these are good, Ed. These are the real deal. That could be the face of Christ talking to the fishermen.'

'Yeah, that's what I thought. And look at the way he held his head, those eyes again, it was like he was saying – listen, just do it, cos what I'm saying is true.'

'Totally, totally, it does; it really does. Wow, brilliant.'

'Look, I just need to remind you, Ray, not that I'd think you'd forget, that this is a work in progress, just between you and me. OK?'

'Absolutely, absolutely. Not a word. Not even to Angie.'

I was feeling pretty good and moderately relaxed when we entered the men's department. Ed set off like a ferret and in no time at all had selected three pairs of shorts for me to try on, one dark blue, one khaki and one slightly yellow. In the privacy of the changing room I tried on the yellow one first. I couldn't remember if I had ever in my whole life worn yellow, and seeing myself semi naked in the mirror I could see why. Yellow! I could never walk through Hackney's mean streets wearing yellow, everyone wears black. And if I was worried about what the *Shoppers* would misinterpret about my house, seeing me in yellow shorts might set all sorts of unnecessary hares running. I slipped out of them, put on the khaki ones and returned to Ed and the brazen stares of the milling shoppers.

His going 'da-Da-da-Da', as I stepped out of the changing room did not help my confidence.

'Give us a twirl.'

Reluctantly, I rotated, pretending to be light hearted and unabashed about where I was and who was looking.

'You know why it's called khaki?' he said, looking unimpressed.

'No, why?'

'It's Urdu for dust coloured.'

'Ah, wonderful, one of the better legacies of Empire - like curry and jodhpurs.'

Ed was not laughing. 'In that colour you will be totally anonymous.'

'Perfect, then they're just the ones.'

'Oh no. Angie said I've got to move you along the spectrum a bit and introduce some colour. *Put* the yellowy ones on.'

'No, I have. I look ridiculous.'

'Show me.'

I put them on, peeped out of the changing room, and then came out. He laughed, which immediately attracted glances from other shoppers.

'Brown legs, maybe, but your legs? They look like two straws in a pina colada.'

I went home with the blue ones. It was a compromise.

My first outing in the new shorts came the same day. Angie had been delighted with my purchase and had suggested taking Geordie for a walk so that my legs could 'catch the sun'.

'Hang on darling, just before you leave,' she said, coming behind me with a pair of scissors. 'Let me just snip off the price tag.'

I felt strangely naked being outside, and the unaccustomed breeze around my knees was not at first very pleasant. But once I got going, and had noticed that most men seemed to be in shorts, I felt more able to strut, and be less conscious of the actual colour of my legs.

I walked down the main path through Millfields carefully searching for clues to the wild goings-on of the previous night. The pagan swags were still there, and although they had wilted a little they were still very obvious, even from a distance. But the only visible references to Peter's elevation were the cross pieces themselves, around which the pagan garlands had been draped. Apart from that the space within the trees remained the same; there had been something and now there was nothing. What had happened was as unknowable as the amorphous goddess herself.

I turned along the canal towards the Walthamstow marshes and the first iron bridge. At all times this bridge was a significant crossing point for me: on one side was London and on the other Essex, which was that romantic thing – a county. And as long as I was careful not to look at the horizon and the industrial estate nuzzling the fringes of the railway line, I could almost convince myself that these few coarse, ancient Lammas pastures with their rampant bramble patches and unkempt hedges, were in fact remnants of Merry England.

On the bridge I peered down upon a heron padding cautiously through the thick alien mat of floating pennywort intent upon movements beneath the surface. It ignored me. Its life and mine had no connection. It pursued the watery shadows instinctively, it's head filled with intimations of food. It stalked and I passed; my head filled with abstract ruminations.

Beyond my rather fuzzy early expectations, and Ed's warnings, the *Bucket Shop* was up and running. It was a success. Fact. It now had a life of its own, which meant that there were expectations, and I knew that with Peter out the way the *Shoppers* would be queuing up expecting to get started on their own dodgy quests, but where did that leave me and mine? Was I still as keen to pursue my own less than tangible desire? Death is a tricky subject. By comparison, Peter's ridiculous crucifixion was solid. It was even theatrical, which as far as participants were concerned was a plus. It was something that could be shared. Mine was in essence more solitary, more like wanking, and yet by creating *the Shop* I had sent out invitations to what should have been a very private activity.

After the first meeting, Angie had said: 'The trouble with you is that your dad brought you up to believe you should say *nowt-to-nobody. Keep it to thee sen* could have been your family's motto. I'm impressed that you've shared your idea with the others, darling. I'm proud of you.'

She was right; it could have been, and he did say all that folksy Yorkshire nonsense, even though he was actually born in Surrey.

Once I was across, and with my eyes focused only on the gravel road that topped the river bank, I ambled along trying to reconcile my *Bucket Shop* aspiration with those of the others: with Toby's wish to become some sort of medieval green man, Lauren's tentative gender swop, and Justine's re-orientation. In the light of the mood I was in, they all sounded rather wet, little more than play acting, dressing up in other peoples' borrowed clothes. I believed my desire was far more instinctual and therefore closer to the heron's unvoiced needs. It ate or it died. It didn't shop around for looks or gender. It just was.

A narrow boat passed heading south to the Olympic Park crewed by young, laid-back boozers. They were having fun, maybe even finding a brief moment of inebriated happiness. But my desire was nothing to do with fun. It was more serious than that because I really did believe that out there, somewhere far beyond Walthamstow, further out towards the sea, I should and would die. I knew it like you know a truth, and it tugged upon my inner self as strongly as if I had been standing next to the heron and feeling the drag of the current against my legs.

By the time I'd reached the boardwalk that took me across the boggy bit, walking had worked its calming magic and I was no longer grumpy. I had also decided that of all of the others' desires, Lauren's wish to try out masculinity for size was the easiest to set in motion, but could in fact be more or less run as a troika with Toby's and Justine's'. None of them required the sort of planning and props we'd put together for Peter. The two 'desires' that did not fit the troika were Ed's 'masterpiece' and Izzie's desire to turn the whole *Bucket Shop* experience into a work of art. Ed wasn't a problem; I could see from his sketching that he was on his way and was committed. Izzie had been active around the crucifixion but what had she achieved?

The only way to discover that was to see her. But what she would make of a man in blue shorts? For some reason I felt incredibly vulnerable. Ed had laughed. Although she'd seen my legs naked as participants in a sexual frenzy, she had not witnessed them as distinct actors in a peripatetic happening. If I turned up at her studio just as I was, she might well reject me and consider me to be uncool. Not of course that it mattered. We weren't lovers. Well, we were lovers, or rather had been lovers, although even coupling the word 'love' with what we'd done felt a bit too romantic; about that we'd both been very clear, or rather, almost clear, since she had actually said something about 'the next time we mate'. There was no way to interpret that other than it might happen again, or even, probably would happen, and going to her flat could actually make it happen, or did at least invite the possibility of it happening.

I was feeling so good about having cleared the fug from my head, and the prospect of sex with Izzie, that while Geordie vanished into the thick of a bramble clump, I stood in the ley of a hedgerow, unzipped, popped out a slightly energized Percy and pissed nonchalantly into the vegetation, relying upon his weak tumescence rather than my hands to sustain the direction of the flow.

'Raymondo! '

Izzie's voice startled me. I was caught so unprepared that I jerked forward in confusion; causing my already dwindling stream to weave about like a demented snake, which sent the last trickle dribbling down the front of my shorts.

Izzie! Oh no! She had seen it all, but I couldn't just ignore her and speak over my shoulder, nor could I turn and face her with a wet patch the size of Africa around my flies. I made elaborate reshuffling gestures as though I was forcing a beast back into a cage, pulled out my shirt flaps to shield the stain and turned around.

'Izzie,' I said, laughing.

'Nothing better than doing it out in the open, eh?'

She didn't wait for an answer but stepped up and kissed me on both cheeks.

'When you've got to go,' I said lamely. She laughed. 'So, where did you pop out from, then?'

She pointed back over her shoulder. 'I wanted to cut you off at the gulch,' she said gnomically, holding up a pair of binoculars.

'Bird watching?'

'No – *man* watching,' she said, rolling her eyes.

'Me?'

'Not your micturition, my darling - alas. I spied you from my eyrie upon the far crags of Springfield Park.'

I looked past her to where the park rose up gently beyond the river and the marina. She'd moved quickly.

'Come, let's walk back together, there is something I want to show you.'

It was then, as though she had suddenly had caught up with herself, that she seemed to see me clearly for the first time.

'Legs – um! May I?'

She pointed towards them with an open palm, and then, without waiting for an answer, she dived down and ran her hand from my ankles to my knees.

'Lovely skin. Do you moisturize?'

Her sally was so sudden that the rush of testosterone it produced left my mouth inactive and the front of my shorts straining.

'So rare to find a man with good skin.'

I smiled as if positive comments about my skin were common place.

'I sometimes put a few drops of Angie's baby oil in the bath.'

'Your secret is out,' she said laughing. 'But it's safe with me, Ray. I shall treasure it and I shall build upon it, because, as Mae West once said: *You are never too old to become young again.* I'm going to introduce you to unguents that you've never even heard of. Your skin will glow.' She laughed again, slightly higher. 'I won't be able to leave you alone. Come!'

'Wait a minute, Iz; I need to call the dog.' I waved the whistle at her.

'Oh, I had forgotten the dog. I'll tell you what, my dear, take the mutt home and *then* hurry over to me. If you are quick I might even run a bath for you. Skin care waits for no man.'

She turned away chortling to herself, and then walked swiftly off towards the marina. Geordie galloped up behind me his face fringed with grime. 'Well and wow,' was all I was able to say. I was too excited to even think straight. 'A bath!' What could be more exotic then that? The last time I had had a meaningful bath with Angie was years ago, probably even before the birth of Max.

'You are very red,' Angie said, popping her head out from the sitting room as I unleashed the hell hound into the hallway.

'I've caught the sun.'

'Well, I should put some calamine lotion on your legs. They look roasted.'

I was just going to say I was going out again to see Ed, when she stepped into the hall leading Max by the hand.

'Look what has arrived on our door step, darling - our lovely son.'

I was gobsmacked and then distraught. There would be no easy exit if Max was here. His visits were so rare that Angie recorded them in the diary. My introduction to pampering was not going to be. I couldn't just fly out, linger in Izzie's bath, make love, see her work and return within an acceptable time frame. I was stymied.

'Brilliant, what a wonderful surprise.'

We man hugged, or rather he crushed me to his chest, making me very aware how incredibly fit he was. His biceps positively bulged out of his blindingly white t-shirt. He didn't get muscles like that from being a Geography teacher.

Angie was laughing when he released me. 'It's only when Max is here that I can see just how slight you really are.'

I toothed back a sarcastic grin.

You'd imagine that a good looking, well-honed and financially stable man of thirty-five, who owned his own flat in Brighton, would be a catch for any woman, that is until you also asked yourself why he wasn't married and never seemed to have too many women friends. Nothing was ever said, but Angie was convinced that he was gay.

'He's got such a way with draperies.'

Well he hasn't. He is a bearded man of the mountains, and that's not a hipster beard either, but one that devours his whole face. After our man hug my cheeks were on fire with beard rash, which considering what Izzie had said about my colour was not a good thing.

I think Angie desperately wanted him to be gay, since it would have increased her standing amongst her more trendy friends. It wouldn't have surprised me if he was, but he never talked much about his private life: a true scion of the Brook family. Granddad David would have been proud of him.

I was desperate to speak to Izzie and dreading it at the same time. She had such a mercurial temperament, and I couldn't work out how she would react. I feared for our intimacy, so I made sure that when we spoke I laid on the Max thing pretty heavily.

'God if only, darling, if only, but with Max you have to take him when he's ready - a bird of passage, always off somewhere exotic.'

'Where?'

'Oh, I think the last trip was to North Wales. So you can see, I obviously don't have much choice. Can't have a son and not act like a dad, can I?'

'We all make choices, Raymondo. The sainted JMW Turner never acknowledged his two illegitimate daughters. Gustav Klimt is rumoured to have fathered anywhere between six and fourteen children to four different women, and Paul Gauguin smacked his wife in the chops before leaving her with five children and buggering off to Tahiti to father a few more.'

'Yes, I know, some artists have been domestic bastards, but I'm not an artist, am I; I'm a cartographer.'

'I have something for you, something you must see.' There was a wheedling tone to her voice which was not very pleasant.

'Absolutely, I can't wait to see what you've been up to. Although, I suspect,' I said, greatly daring, 'after today, my skin care might have to wait.'

'It all depends.'

'On what?'

'Your true desires – and mine.'

'Pardon?'

'Speed Raymondo, speed. Text me.'

I wasn't being spurned, the bath was still on, but only if I was quick.

We dined out in Islington, *en famille*, which was nice, although short, since Max was meeting a friend later in town. He is not by any stretch of the imagination an animated talker unless you get him on geographical subjects and mountain climbing. Angie sat with us desperate to investigate what he did when he wasn't climbing or teaching, but every time she intervened the conversation went flat, and I was forced, being reasonably knowledgeable about geography, to intervene. He was especially interested in how my Celtic river system work was proceeding. I would have been happy to give him more detail, but Angie pinched my thigh and gave me a withering look.

'Much more to do, son, but it keeps me busy.'

Not long after that he caught a 38 bus and disappeared.

'Honestly, Ray, did you have to go on and on about your bloody rivers?'

CHAPTER 16

GEORDIE

E very dog has a big dog moment. I come half way up Ray's shin, which means I'm on the short side. Now I know that this all depends upon who you are judging me by. They say, or at least Ed said, that the great ancestor wolf, *peace be upon him*, would more or less have reached the top of his thigh. Compared to our origins, then, I'm a short arse, but compared to a measly Chihuahua, I stand tall. But, and it's a big but, most other dogs I run into are head and shoulders above me. I see them standing out on the fields looking awesome and terrible, but as long as they stay where they are, I know that they will pass on and eventually disappear from sight, if not from smell.

My big dog moment came many moons ago when I was little more than a pup. It was a time of playfulness and wonders when every scent excited and all apes bent down to fondle and caress. It was also spring and the light in the evening now lingered longer. I was head down following unfamiliar odours in the churchyard unaware of anything else save for the presence of Angie, my new minder, who was stood off to the side tapping on her phone. That's when it happened. Crashing through the shrubbery and leaping the low retaining wall near the war memorial, a huge great hound headed straight towards me mouth open and giving it some.

'Come here you scruffy little bastard!'

I cowed submissively, but the ignorant black beast didn't stop. It came on fangs bared, showing every intention of grabbing me by the scruff of the neck. I closed my eyes and waited to die. But instead of the crack as it broke my neck, the brute started to howl in pain. I opened my eyes and saw Angie slashing at it with the heavy end of my lead.

'Oy, that's my dog.'

A scruffy ape, smelling powerfully of pee, came shambling out of the shrubbery and headed towards her.

'It should be on a fucking lead.'

'He ain't done nothing.'

'Only nearly killed my dog.'

The man had no chance, I could see that. Angie stood before him lead in hand and would have thrashed him had he come any closer. I was well impressed, and so was the man's cur, which was now snivelling well out of range behind him. After a lot of back chat the two of them disappeared leaving the glorious Angie in command of the turf. I knew then that not only was Angie one alpha bitch, but that I would be her slave for life. It happened when I was very impressionable, but sadly has continued to affect me ever since. I still live in fear of being jumped. I can't pass a dodgy looking hedge without a lot of preliminary sniffing and listening, and if I see a huge silhouette coming across the fields, or even a bin bag, I'm very, very, cautious. Being harassed by a big dog is one of my recurring nightmares.

Talking of dodgy experiences, that son of theirs, that Max, am I pleased he's gone; he *is* odd. When he arrived, I wiggled my arse at him like you do, and nothing, he looked right through me, didn't even bend to scratch my ear. It was as though I didn't exist. I thought, be charitable, benefit of the doubt, he's tall, he might have missed me, so I rubbed my body against his legs, which as everyone knows is the usual the signal for a bit of ape fondling. But did he? Did he heck? I got a sneaky back-hander, which bloody hurt. He doesn't know how lucky he was because I was all on to give him one.

Thankfully, when he had gone and everything had returned to normal, I was sprawled out in the front room happily dreaming, when, for no apparent reason, that black dog muscled into my dream again, slavering all over me. I woke up in a panic only to find Angie grinning at me with her phone stuck to her ear.

'You dreaming, you daft dog?'

I refrained from any reaction. Sometimes apes are so stupid I wonder how on earth they ever came to be the ones on the other end of the lead. What did she think I was doing? Of course I was dreaming.

'Geordie's been dreaming,' she said into the phone. 'His little legs galloping away and sweet little yelping noises.' She laughed.

Oh yes, advertise it why don't you! Really!

'Ha ha, yes of course, darling, I'm always dreaming of you. No, that's not fair, I do not twitch. Well, if I do yelp,' she said laughing, 'you should know.' She walked towards the door. 'No, Ray's popped out. Said he's gone to see Izzie. She's got some more pictures.'

'Ok, darling, I'll be over in about an hour. See you then.'

The one they call Izzie, now she *is* an interesting one. There's a smell to her, all right, very pungent, but not unpleasant; memorable, I'd say. Angie gets a bit that way herself, especially when she's near Ed. I more or less think it's when apes come into season.

Talking of pungent, a *roscher* came over the fence in the garden the other day while I was dozing in the sun. By god, it won't do that again in a hurry. I was up and on it almost before it reached the far wall. Damn nearly had its big bushy tail in my jaws. I let out a huge warning cry so that every dog up the gardens would know that the red bugger was about.

'Heading your way!'

'Thanks Skrart – got it!'

'Me too!'

'Too late. He's over the wall and gone!'

That last one was Trekk, the little pug who lives near the top of the road. If any one of us was never going to get their teeth into old red, it was him: too small and too toothy: plenty of throat, but no bite, as we say.

In my case I'm definitely more tooth than bark. It's just the way we Border Terriers are. If you were being kind you'd say we're very focused; if you were being a bit sarky you might change that to being obsessed. Both descriptions are true, since I know in the deepest depths of my being that I only really exist to kill foxes, which means that when we are heads down and on the job we rarely give tongue unless the sneaky red bastard has evaded us and has done a runner.

Later in the day, as Angie had indicated, we were off across the marsh heading for Ed's. What I hadn't expected was that Ed would meet us half way towards the café near the boat club. He'd been painting, or something, because the smell of whatever he had been doing was clinging to him like an invisible skin. Far too acrid for pleasant, so to avoid it I kept walking more or less abreast of them, that way our movement kept the worst of the stench wafting behind me.

They were linked together, arm in arm.

'I'm off to see Justine tomorrow for lunch,' said Angie.

'You remembered then?'

'Just. She's cooking me something special.'

'What do you think?'

'About what?'

'Changing her to something else.'

'I think it's going to be a bit more to do with revamping her than changing her.'

'Not easy.'

'Oh I don't know; there's a lot going on under that - oh I don't know, I just find her interesting.'

Having registered that what they were twittering about was nonthreatening, I happily ignored it. Ape speak can be reasonably pleasant on the ear when it's directed to someone else, but too much of their constant blather can give me a headache. The up side of it all was that while they were head to head jabbering quietly to each other, I was off into the rough searching for anything edible.

CHAPTER 17

ANGIE

I had walked Geordie early because, despite certain trepidation, I was off to Dalston to lunch with Justine Cook.

'Brilliant. Have a nice time,' said Ray, kissing me on the cheek. 'One less for me to deal with.'

That was that, a quick peck and he was off. I was sorely tempted to slap him, and might have done so had I not just done my nails. I was off to lunch with one of *his* collection of odds and sods, and all he could say was – brilliant! I was a martyr to his cause and he should have acknowledged that. Peck on the cheek! The sodding *Bucket Shop* was his idea and yet I was the one doing the running around.

By the time I had marched up Powerscroft Road and had reached the Round Chapel, I had worked off my annoyance and was feeling very mellow. It's something to do with the streets; they're very encouraging. We've lived around here more or less since the millennium and it's strange how more homely and village like it feels now, considering that when we first moved here we were only a stone's throw from Clapton Road, the notorious *'Murder Mile'* as the press called it. My out of town friends were horrified. 'Hackney! You must be mad.' I can smile now, but at first it was a bit scary. You had to keep your eyes open coming home at night, especially if you were crossing the open area around Saint Augustine's tower; in those days it was full of druggies and other lowlifes, and the lighting was appalling. But when it came to Turkish or West Indian drug dealers killing each other we weren't that bothered. It was one less hoodlum to worry about as far as I was concerned. Not that I'd say that in front of some of my trendy new neighbours, but it's true. They got what they deserved. Oh I know everyone goes on about how terrible gentrification is, how it's driving ordinary people out of the borough, but secretly, we're all more than thankful it's happening. If we wanted a good night out in the past we had to go to Islington, but now Hackney's got plenty of decent cafés, restaurants, organic food shops and, wonder of wonders, brilliant artisanal bakers. All we need now is for Waitrose to open a branch on Mare Street and we're home and dry. But at least we've got a Marks and Sparks.

I use 'village' in the estate agent sense of the word, which means that the housing stock is worth doing up but it's a bit of a walk to get to the shops and the station. If you think of Powerscroft Road as the area's spine, then the 'village' is more or less centred in those streets that radiate from it, and from the streets that do the same from Chatsworth Road, which forms one arm of a ninety degree turn at the bottom. Our little enclave around Mayola Road feels like a village within a village. Being on an incline helps to give it a little character. Most of the houses have already been done up and their smart, trendy paintwork and trim front yards give the road an almost continental gaiety. Such a contrast to how it was when we first came here. It was very run down, but now the houses fetch a bomb and are full of lots of lovely middle class professionals and creative types. It suits Ray and me perfectly.

The back gardens are compact, and at first I felt a bit exposed. I'm all for being neighbourly, but I do like my privacy, so thanks to clever planting it's no longer quite so open and so obviously elbows-on-the-garden-fence. Ray did the garden design; he loves nothing more than fiddling around with shapes and drawing up plans, but I chose the plants. He managed to fit in a fabulous York stone patio, which makes a fantastic, cosy outdoor dining space and, best of all, there's room for my beautiful, Italian chimenea. Toasting beside it in the evening supping wine is one of my all-time favourite things to do.

They say that fifty is the new forty, well I'm fifty-five, which means that theoretically I'm still up for it; and where 'it' is, if you are young, is Dalston, which is still Hackney, but scruffy enough for entrepreneurs to open clubs, pubs and eats geared to the needs of the groovy. Justine lives on Richmond Road, an elegant street that leans more to neighbouring Islington than to shabby Hackney.

I had walked all the way and was hot, as was the day; summer at its best. I was more than thankful to have decided upon a simple vest and three-quarter length light trousers. I just hoped that she had a garden. She didn't.

'I was looking for a garden flat, but when I discovered that there was a small roof terrace, I took it. Come on out.'

She was wearing a thin cotton top and a colourful wrap. The imagined body that I had created for her should have looked – fuller, but in fact, despite being ample, her body was well proportioned, although height wise perhaps too short to be called Junoesque.

I could see at a glance that what I assumed was a Victorian extension was shielded from its neighbours by a modest brick wall, which would have easily hidden anybody lying down on the cushions and beach towels that lay strewn upon the ancient asphalt.

'My *terrazza*!

I walked up to the balcony and peered over. 'Wow!'

'Prosecco?'

'Oh yes, lovely, thanks.'

She disappeared into the kitchen.

'My god! Is that the Shard I can see?'

'Yeah.'

I took the proffered bubbles and she stood beside me pointing out various landmarks. As she did so it was very obvious that she was not wearing a bra.

'Let's enjoy the sun.'

I followed her example and sat down on one of the cushions. The world disappeared, we were totally obscured.

'No prying neighbours, then,' I said, but my smile turned quickly to alarm as she removed her wrap and began unbuttoning her shirt.

'Such a blessing.' She turned to the light like a liberated sunflower. 'Go on, no one can see us up here.'

Stripping off with a comparative stranger had not been how I had imagined the day would go. Tentative conversation, a bit of digging for information and then the bus back. Chatting in the buff was a bit further than I was prepared to go, so I just took off my vest and pretended to examine the brickwork, being thankful that at least I was wearing one of my better bras. When I looked back, smiling sheepishly, her eyes were focused on my bra, and so pretending that I'd simply been pausing, I unhooked the damned thing and dropped it nonchalantly on top of the vest.

'That's better,' I said, but when her eyes moved to my trousers, I glanced again at the brickwork.

She had obviously been making the most of the recent fine spell, for compared to her my chest looked rather pallid and insignificant.

'Cheers!

'Cheers.'

'You've got a lovely body. I envy you.'

'Genes,' I said, taking a long sip at the Prosecco.

'Look at me. No really, it's ok, look at me. I'm too big to be considered interesting. People take one look and think that if I'm this big then I must be either thick or weak willed, or both.

I didn't know what to say so I squirmed sympathetically and sniffed dismissively. 'But your – um – friend, he likes you as you are, surely?

'My fuck buddy! Yes, he does, but I've an awful feeling that as long as I wasn't actually dead, it wouldn't make any difference to him.'

'No, come on. He can't be that unfeeling.'

'No, he's not, he's lovely, but I think like most men he's got two brains, and when it comes to sex, this one,' she said, tapping her forehead, 'doesn't get much of a look in.'

I laughed. 'Ed says that if men weren't randy none of us would be here. It's evolution's way of insuring our survival.'

'Oh, I'm not complaining.'

In the brief moment that she looked away her jollity vanished.

I couldn't bear the thought that she was becoming weepy, so I rattled on, regardless. 'How does that work, you know?' I didn't mean to be nosey, but I was curious, and it didn't seem quite so personal when we were both practically naked.

'Stuart?'

I nodded, putting my face in the bubbles.

'One of the unexpected benefits of the digital age: we text, not the details, just that we're up for it.'

'What like "want a fuck"?'

'Sort of, just one word – not fuck, but something innocuous like: Tottenham.'

I laughed, 'Why Tottenham?'

'Tottenham Hotspurs – *hots*!'

The penny dropped. I laughed. 'Why don't you just phone?'

'We're buddies, not lovers. He's got his life and I've got mine. It keeps it private.'

'Not tempted to make it permanent, then?'

'Oh God, no! Stuart's a useless bastard. It would be a complete disaster. He's good at sex but that's about it. And even that wouldn't last if he talked too much.'

'Is this one of the things about yourself that you want to change,' I said, remembering why I was there, 'you're looking for something a bit more permanent?'

She didn't answer the question, although her whole demeanour altered on account of it. I had reminded her of why I was there. We weren't just two girls together; she had come to the *Bucket Shop* for a purpose – to change.

'I said to your husband that I wanted to change who I was before it's too late. That's more than changing partners or even getting a partner, however desirable.'

She leaned forward cradling her breasts. Sitting beside me naked save for a pair of flesh coloured cotton pants, she looked abject, and her solidity seemed immaterial and meaningless. I felt an immediate desire to hold her, to embrace her.

'I'm a failure, Angie. I'm what the Americans unkindly call a loser, one of life's also-rans.'

I could see that she was near to tears, so I shuffled across to her side and put my arm around her. As she nestled against me I was aware of the heat of her skin.

'That just isn't true, Justine. You've got a job, somewhere to live and you are a lovely person, those are not the qualities of a - of an also-ran. If they were, then we'd all be also-rans. I'm not so different, apart from having Ray - and my son Max.' What I didn't add was that I was lying. I also had Ed.

'That's not the same then is it? I'm a wasted life. I'm even too old to have children. My creation didn't bear fruit. I'm a dud.'

'Darling.' She was crying and I held her close.

'It's hard being alone, having no one who gives a damn, no one to talk to.'

Oh god, this was awful! I'd half thought of myself as Lady Bountiful come to spread joy to a troubled soul: in for five minutes and out again. But I was a fraud. I was in no position to reply, since I was not alone, and had never been alone, not since the days when Ray and Ed had been students at Chelsea and I had been working in a pub on the Kings Road. Our friendship was ancient and our love almost as old. I had two men, and therefore more than my fair share of love. How could I give her advice? I had no idea how she felt.

She shuffled herself upright, her pudgy face looking even pudgier; her cheeks blotched and reddened by tears. She looked at me and tried to smile, and then, without warning, she kissed me full on the lips. I could feel the dampness of the tears on her cheek. And then I kissed her back. There was such an erotic tenderness in our embrace that I immediately started to giggle. She pulled back searching my face for rejection, but I was smiling, and so she came back into my arms and we sank onto the cushions. To say that there was no thought would have been a lie. I did think, but only in snatches that were too brief to carry meaning. All I knew was that at that moment I wanted her and what was happening.

It was different, not hugely, but different. For the first time the beauty of a woman's body became more than a visual reflection. She was fragrant. Even her size fell away as an impediment. She felt beautiful, tender and inviting, and her hands on my body were soft and soothing. Compared to Ray and Ed's stubbled faces her skin was like silk, of a texture I associated only with children.

My orgasm convulsed me and sent so many aftershocks rippling through my body that I started to giggle again. When she came she did so almost silently, it was only her body that reacted. I felt a huge powerful force grip me. I couldn't have removed my hand from between her thighs even if I had wanted to, and then it was over; she pulled away and turned on her back, her eyes closed and lay there gently rocking from side to side.

We both sat up, flushed and gawping. Two semi-strangers suddenly and unexpectedly united. I laughed out loud; it was ridiculous, but she didn't join in. She just sat there staring at me, her eyes wide and her mouth half open in a smile, as if my laughter was the most unlikely thing that she had ever heard.

Life gives you no preparation for what we had done. I had no real idea how to respond. As the heat of our passion was replaced by the heat of the sun, my brain kicked in and words began jumbling inside my head, but I did my best to resist them, to remain mute. I didn't know what to do other than to continue laughing or be silent.

'Your first time?' She said this looking straight at me. I nodded, and slowly like a flower, her lips opened into a beautiful smile.

What do you say when someone has given you something beautiful and unexpected? I had no idea, so I'm pleased to say I said nothing, letting my whole body answer her with its silence.

On the way home my scrambled brain did its best to reassert itself. I was walking along the same streets. I was dressed for the day. I was returning to my home. When people passed me I looked at them half expecting that they would know, but nothing about me said anything different than it had said earlier. There was a sense of unreality. If Justine said nothing; if what we had done remained entirely between the two of us, then as far as the world was concerned nothing had happened. And yet it had.

'My god, Ange – you're a lesbian!' What a thought; one of *'the other persuasion'*, as my aunt used to say. If I told my mother she would have dropped her tea in shock. 'A lezzie – me? A dyke!' I tried walking with a bit of attitude, but sandals just aren't that sassy. Without meaning to I had stepped into the world of sexual ambiguity. I could fly the rainbow flag with pride, and being lesbian would have gone down well with some of my right-on women friends.

By the time I reached London Fields I was no longer a lesbian, which left me only with bi-sexual, but I doubted that too. There was Ed and Ray, and then there was the whole history of my sexual preferences before that. Nowhere had I ever shown any sign of a preference for sex with women, or interest in them. So what had I just done? I had had sex with a woman – that was all. It was and then again - it wasn't.

Having resolved my new sexual preference issues I was then able to think more clearly about my – my what? What did I call Justine? My lover? No, no, no, I already had a lover, and there was no love, and nor was she my fuck buddy that was too gross. It was a one off. So, therefore what on earth was she? I needed a name. She was – actually – she was nothing. It was a horrid thing to realize, so fresh from her arms, but she meant absolutely nothing to me. I had enjoyed our sex, but that had been enough. It was done. It was over. We had nothing in common apart from the damned *Bucket* nonsense. I was what I had always been, a woman split down the middle, torn forever between two men, both loved and both ridiculous.

CHAPTER 18

RAY

I had left the shorts behind; I wasn't taking any chances. I knew too little about Izzie to be sure of her response. She wanted to show me something; it could only be her work. I was sure it was not some barely concealed invitation to sex, and am totally aware that my sexual expectations are generated entirely in my head. Perhaps, had I had more sex in the past, then maybe I wouldn't have been so needy now. But I was who I was and that was down to my shared history with Angie. Ours had not been a life of riotous rutting. It had very quickly settled into a less hormonal relationship. We still had sex of course, sort of, but that was mainly a holiday and special day thing, which meant that on April 4th, my birthday, I could more or less guarantee we'd have it. Beyond that we co-existed happily, but without the spontaneity that had brought Max into the world.

I'd been left in the studio while Izzie got ready whatever it was that I was there to see. One wall was covered with all of the usual artist's junk – work in progress, frames, natural objects, photographs and paintings. The most interesting one, and the one I spent some time peering at, was a small scruffy looking picture of a crumpled female nude on her back revealing her vagina, and whose head had been partially obliterated in biro fuzz. Above the sketch, like a newspaper headline, were the crudely written words: *'This is not love'*. Down on the right was a squiggly signature.

'Before you ask, yes, it's one of Tracey's. A gift.'

'Is that you?'

'It's a sketch.'

'But you?'

'No. I am here, standing beside you. That,' she said, stabbing her finger to the wall, 'is a page torn from history.'

I had no idea what she was on about; in fact I found the whole exchange a bit more aggressive than I had hoped for, and my excitement was quelled considerably.

'Come, things to see.'

She linked her arm in mine and propelled me into the next room. Arranged around the wall were a new series of large photographs of Peter Rock's crucifixion. The impact was immediate. They were extraordinary, haunting, and created, as far as I could tell, with absolutely no hint of irony. The original display in Ed's store had been brilliant, but these were qualitatively different. Maybe she'd used *Photoshop*, I couldn't say, but the images had been utterly distressed. The surface of the prints was grained and pooled with obscuring, bright spots of light. Most drastic of all, though, and echoing the Tracey sketch on the wall, they had been scratched all over. It was as though she had caught the anguish of a real crucifixion, not a mockery. The contemporary details of his binding made no difference to the reality of it. Her handling of the colour, light and texture transformed the modernity of these materials. He could have been bound with straw.

At my open mouthed wonder, she released me with a smile.

'Now you really know what I can do.'

I nodded. I did.

'This is not all, Ray. You saw Peter there, but Peter transformed. He *was* the Christ. I saw it in your eyes. But when you looked at that sketch of Tracey's, you thought you saw me, didn't you? A younger me. All a bit sneaky isn't it, a bit like perving?'

'Rubbish! I was just curious.'

'I only keep it because it's worth a bit. It's a reminder that all portraiture is dangerous. We should be on our guard at what faces we surround ourselves with. These,' she wafted her arm to her work, 'are only moments in time. I've sliced reality so thinly that they have become less real than dreams. That is not Peter. It is a beautiful creation born out of my head.'

'Don't you have pictures of yourself when young, then?'

'None. All that has gone is gone.'

'No family pictures?'

'Raymond, what are you, some kind of archaeologist? The only me that you will ever be allowed to see is this one.'

She took my hand and held it against her chest. It was not a sexual gesture, but my body didn't know that and so I felt a rekindling of my desire.

'What I was is all in here.' She almost chuckled as she touched her head. 'I am only what you can see in front of you.'

My alarms were ringing. This wasn't true. 'Only flesh and blood?'

'What you see is what you get.'

'You're on the web. I Googled you. There's enough of it. Doesn't that count?'

'*They* can do what they want. *They* are beyond me. But here, in my domain, there is no history. I start each day afresh.' She grinned, staring at me with her icy blue eyes. 'You, on the other hand, are history in the making. I know you, Raymondo, more than you know yourself, and of all the people in *the Shop*, I am the one who can help you to the resolution of your desire.'

I tried to look arch, hoping she meant that the bath was back on the agenda, but she was looking at me more like a headmistress admonishing a recalcitrant pupil than as a potential voluptuary.

'Oh Raymond,' she scoffed dismissively, 'were you thinking about the bath?'

'No – course not.'

'We mustn't let sex neutralize our ambitions. You will get your bath, all in good time, but first, my love, I need to give you something else.'

'What?'

'A kick up your tight little arse!'

I tried to step back but she caught hold of my arm.

'You have been sitting on your talents for far too long. I can sense the power of your dreams. *The Bucket Shop* is a brilliant idea, but you must take your share of it – first. Don't let others dominate your future. You have the vison and I am the one to get you there.'

'Where – the future?'

'Absolutely. You and I together, Raymondo, will make it happen. No past, no memories, just now – the two of us on the quest, your quest.'

She was looking at me so adoringly that I felt quite fired up. She was right. That was the purpose of the whole thing. I was not a branch of Social Services. The others could wait a bit. I believed her. It was a fact. She and I could work together to make it happen.

'Now I think it's time for your bath.'

I was putty in her hands, or rather, willing flesh. She led me into a large, newly refurbished bathroom, tiled throughout in gleaming white. The bath was large and central to the space. She turned on the taps, reached for a bottle from the side and squeezed into the fall of the water a rich stream of pearly coloured drops. As they dissolved the room filled with delicious scents.

'I shall return when you are *in* the water,' she said, touching my shoulder fleetingly with her finger tips before leaving me to my undressing.

As I hovered on the edge of the bath swirling the waters with my hand, the room filled with the unexpected sound of a beautiful woman's voice singing what I took to be some kind of medieval religious chant. I was so surprised that I stopped myself from stepping in; it seemed almost sacrilegious to climb into the tub while being accompanied by such a pure and heavenly voice. But I did, sinking up to my ears in the slippery, sweetly scented suds. Nothing of me rose above the water save for my head and the angelic voice.

I reached between my legs and gave myself a good soaping, just to make sure all was equally and sweetly scented before she returned. My penis stiffened delightfully.

'Hildegard von Bingen.'

I pulled my hands away and skittered over awkwardly onto my elbow so that I could look back over my shoulder. Izzie stood there looking down at me with the concentrated stare of a hunting eagle. She was naked.

'*The Sibyl of the Rhine.*'

Without further ado she stepped into the bath and sat down opposite me, forcing both of our legs to rise like volcanic islands above the bubbles.

'I'm not familiar with her.'

Her imperious descent had actually made me feel quite vulnerable. The bath was like a wet prison. There was no easy escape. I had never been in the presence of such a theatrical woman before, and didn't know how to handle her.

'Few men know anything of woman's spirituality. She was a nun, a medieval mystic. *The Voice of the living light.* Some also say that Hildegard had an acute understanding of the anatomy of female desire.

Despite the word desire, and all that I hoped it might foretell, when she had finished talking there was nothing left to the superstructure of my penis. It had lost all form, all desire and all size. I sat before her neutered, my knees pale and insipid outcrops compared to her darker skin with its swirling patches of inked colour.

'Don't look so scared, Raymondo. It's only a short track.' She leaned forward and kissed my knees. 'Um – you smell like a Bakewell tart.'

My penis liked the sound of that and gave a tweak. I sniffed the back of my hands. 'Almond?'

'And avocado and jojobas oils. Your skin will be reborn.' And so saying, she seized my arm and began vigorously kneading the muscles as if they had been dough. 'Do you work out, Ray?'

'I lift a few weights,' I said with mock modesty. And then I saw the inquisitor lurking behind her eyes, and retracted, suddenly feeling the need to be totally honest. 'Not, you know, bar bells, usually a couple of packs of Geordie's dog food. Although not easy to hold both at the same time.'

'Well, it shows.'

She reached for my other hand, and while she kneaded away I felt convinced enough of where this was leading to let my newly released hand rest on her thigh. Suddenly, she pulled me to her so that our eyes were level and our lips almost touching. The effect on my hydraulics was immediate. I reached that level of desire where I was no longer embarrassed by the sudden emergence of my dick from beneath a halo of suds like the periscope of a lost U-boat.

'Why the east, Raymond, why do you believe that your destiny lies there?'

I wasn't expecting to be cross-examined, and refused to listen, letting my wandering hand inch further up her thigh, and moving my lips closer to her cheek.

'I think you must have a transcendental soul.'

That was it. Trumped! Sexual excitement can't beat detached speculation. The kraken went back to sleep and I withdrew my hand to the safety of my own thighs.

'Meaning what exactly?'

She seemed to notice nothing about my changed demeanour and smiling insouciantly she bent my head towards her so that it was pressed against the heavenly smoothness of her damp breasts, and proceeded to drip more bath oil on the back of my neck and shoulders.

'Your death has a location; it's not a very rational thing to say.'

My voice was muffled by her skin, so I almost shouted. 'Intuition!'

She laughed. 'And what pray is that?'

I was rankled by her attitude; I didn't expect her to be so personal, nor that I would be taking part in some ridiculous dictionary quiz, so I pulled away and sat up. She was still smiling.

'It's a sense, just less easy to locate than the other senses.'

'Like non-sense?'

'That's just not fair. It is not nonsense. You could say the same about a bird's ability to fly south to its winter quarters, or a Monarch butterflies ability to travel from the south of the Americas to the north and back again.'

We sat facing each other like two boxers. The room was warm but now that the water had dried on me my flesh I was feeling slightly chilled. This was not what I had been expecting and I was almost inclined to get out, get dressed and call it a day. I would have done had she not leant across and kissed me.

'I'm not denying it, Ray, I'm confirming it but in a different way. Most people who talk like you eventually lean towards voices in the head, fairies and mystical Chinamen, but that is only because they do not have the physical skills to use intuition.'

I frowned. 'I'm feeling cold.'

'Poor dear, I'm so sorry, let me turn on the hot tap.'

The tab burbled into the space between us and I felt the flood of warmth climb up my legs.

'Here.' She took a sponge and drizzled hot water and dripping suds on my exposed skin.

'That feels good.'

'Intuition in the right hands becomes art. You have an artist's soul and I have the skills to release it. I'm a photographer, although I like to think of myself as a light engineer. I mediate thin slivers of reality into art. Nothing more. Daubing paint or bashing stone and wood is one degree removed from the essence of art. I've tried them. The intellect always intervenes. Sadly, I'm not a musician, because music is the highest of the arts. Although that's not to say it inspires purity, because both the good and the evil can be moved by it. And that's because you don't need words. It is pure intuition,' she said, pointing into the void where Saint Hildegard's words continued to float.

'She's using words.'

'But sound is what counts. Words are even less precise than paint. Literature is the intellect's whore.'

I thought: 'says who?', but because she was so animated, and her skin so infused with colour I was unable to maintain my doubts. Her passion was catching; I felt totally alive in her presence, my skirt of tepid water totally forgotten. At that moment I would have done anything she asked of me.

Then she collapsed. The tension left her shoulders and her back crumpled, and she was as still and as lifeless as a slot machine automaton that had come to an end of its act. And just as quickly she returned and her body was reanimated. She looked deep into my eyes. I was overwhelmed. It was a cruelly penetrating stare.

'We are going to create wonders, you and I.'

I believed her.

'But first, let's meld our bodies into one.'

At last! I was out of the bath as quick as a flash, and had grabbed her proffered towel and had begun vigorously drying myself off. I was so keen to be ready that I hadn't watched what she was doing. When I took my face from the towel I saw that she had picked up a camera that had been on the floor and was taking pictures of me. I was a bit taken aback. I wasn't sure I wanted to be trapped inside one of her future art works, so I danced about theatrically and covered my mouth with the towel.

She ignored me and began looking through the images. 'This is the best.' She handed the camera to me. I was caught one leg up, cock up and my arms wafting the towel over my body.

'Looks like I'm dancing,' I said, handing the camera back.

'Drop the towel, darling. Imagine you are in a cave dancing around a fire.'

I pulled a face, dancing to a medieval chant wasn't easy, but I did what she said.

'Move about, that's it. Keep going. Good.'

When I stopped, we stood together and I watched the images appear one by one.

'There. That's the closest.'

'To what?'

'A prehistoric shaman.'

She had caught me both legs bent, my arms crooked and reaching forward, my face to the camera. As we stared at it the singing stopped.

'Hilda approves,' she said. 'All you need is a beard and pair of antlers and it would be perfect.' Seeing my frown, she added, 'There's a famous prehistoric cave painting in France just like this. They call it *The Sorcerer*.' She rolled her eyes salaciously.

'Yes, I know it,' I said, remembering the image from my art history.

'Wonderful, then let's see what *you* can conjure.' She pursed her lips, took my hand and both giggling wildly, she led me out of the bathroom.

CHAPTER 19

ED

I'm aware that many people find my love of fish odd or at least perplexing, a sign perhaps of something missing in my personality. I accept that, although it continues to rankle, and I have tried to understand it, because I'm well aware that dealing in fish is a quantum leap beyond keeping a few tiddlers in a jar. The best answer I've come up with is that we humans are so up our own arses when it comes to understanding the world around us, that we can only see fish from a *'what's-in-it-for-us'* perspective. As far as we're concerned fish don't cut it; they are too other to warrant consideration. We put up monuments to the wartime sacrifice of warm blooded mammals, and remember fondly how valuable they can be in times of danger and stress, but when it comes to fish, we ask the simple question: what contribution have they ever made to our emotional or psychological well-being? On a pair of scales fish would weigh next to nothing when compared to a domestic dog or cat. And it's not because they exist in a water-world, because cetaceans are drooled over as if they were only a couple of chromosomes off from being our brothers and sisters. Maybe it's simpler: fish don't give a damn about us; they're totally self-contained.

I've no idea where my love of fish came from. For me it's just not strange, and certainly no odder than many of the weird things other people get off on. My cousin Stephen has a drawer full of women's gloves. I hate to think what he does with them; although, actually, I know what he does with them, and that is weird.

Watching a tank full of fish has a calming effect on some people. I sell lots of fish to old peoples' homes. It's this, and their beauty that are, in my opinion, the main contributions fish make to their side of the balance. When I come down in the morning or take a last look around at night before heading up stairs to bed the shop is a magical place. It's almost silent, there's just the whir of the pumps and the gentle pop popping of the aerators. Sometimes, while I'm just standing there taking the last few drags of my fag, I know that I want for nothing. I'm at peace. That, in my book, is a huge contribution to *my* personal wellbeing.

If things are going wrong in the tanks I can always tell. The moment I walk in I can sense a change in the atmosphere. It could be just a variation in the sounds, especially if a pump has crashed, or it might be a subtle change in the smell, whatever it is, I'll know. People who've never kept fish find it hard to believe that fish smell, and healthy fish generally don't, but their tanks do. They don't just float about, they also eat and excrete, and not all of that gets recycled by the plants and the snails, some of it sinks into the gravel and stays there until it gets stirred up by conscientious aquarists. Then, by God, it does smell. Cleaning tanks is not my favourite job.

I think my being super sensitive to atmospheres and people's moods comes from working with fish. Angie says I can always tell when someone at work has pissed her off or when she and Ray have had a row, like they did this Wednesday night, when we were assembled for the a meeting of 'The Shop'. Although Angie wasn't there, she was off in Middlesbrough, doing what she does; I knew something was up immediately, because Ray was a lot more buoyant than usual, and being amazingly tolerant of Izzie's loopy interjections.

I've tried to give that woman the benefit of the doubt, but I still find her decidedly strange; talented for sure, but as far as I'm concerned - travelling on a different compass. She's one of those artists who are not content with just doing the work; they have to make an exhibit of themselves. All those pseudonyms, and Izzie Capricious, what's all that about? I know for a fact that her real name is the perfectly acceptable Isabel Mc Ketterick; it's on her website.

Before Angie went, she told me that Ray wanted Izzie to reveal the final presentation suit of crucifix portraits at the end of the Wednesday session, as a sort of dramatic finale, and that he had been *'blown away'* by them. I got all that, what I didn't get was why she then rolled her eyes dismissively. Something was bugging her. After a little probing I discovered what.

'Honestly, darling, sometimes he treats me like his bloody messenger. I mean Justine is a nice woman and we had a pleasant enough lunch, but why me, why not him?'

'Coz you're a woman?'

She frowned as though what I had said was incomprehensible.

'It wasn't as though we were talking about anything serious. It was only women's magazine stuff, really.'

But the Justine who had walked into the meeting on Wednesday night was a woman changed. She looked quite different, actually quite attractive, and certainly more colourful. Whether that was all down to Angie's 'magazine stuff' or something else, I couldn't say. The others noticed it too, and she smiled at everyone with the confidence of a woman who was used to the plaudits of others. When Izzie began clicking away with her camera, she didn't blanch and turn away; she gave her a full frontal smile.

Stranger still, in her transformation she was not alone. Lauren was almost unrecognizable, and to some extent so was Toby. I looked at Ray and he looked at me and winked. He was beaming.

Lauren did not sit down straight away. She knew the effect she had made, so while Toby stood by the door, she strode into the centre of our small circle and struck a pose, daring us to give her the once over, which we happily did.

Her beautiful, long, auburn hair had gone. In its place was a cropped skull topped with a blond coconut tuft. It altered her completely. I was looking at a funky young man with chest architecture to match. God knows where she had hidden her breasts.

When she sat down, we all applauded, and as we did so Toby took his place in the ring. He had foregone his silly t-shirt and was wearing a green plaid shirt. Although without Lauren's natural poise, he too stood motionless for a moment courting our attention. There was little he could do to alter his essentially lankiness, the change was in his demeanour and head. He stood up straight, his shoulders relaxed and his arms hanging free. His hair was if anything slightly longer than before, but had now been complimented by a gingery beard, which bulked out his narrow features and highlighted the blue of his eyes.

Being the bloke he was, he couldn't hold the pose for long without laughing, which immediately set everybody off clapping again. They had obviously got together on this, but their entry had Ray's choreography all over it. I suspected that while Angie had been acting as an Agony Aunt to Justine, he had been sorting out the other two, and one glance at his smug face told me I was right.

'Yes, yes. And all three of you deserve that. Brilliant, brilliant. Well done to Justine, to Toby and to-?' He held out his hand to Lauren like an expectant ringmaster.

'Josh,' she said on cue.

'To Josh.'

There was more applause.

'Who we are and who we want to be matters to us, to all of us. That's why we're here – to support each other and to help each other achieve that one thing that we feel will make our lives meaningful.' He turned to Peter. 'You told me that thanks to everyone here you now felt complete, is that still so?'

Peter's face shone. 'Absolutely.'

Ray allowed the applause to run its course. 'And you are going to like this, Peter. At the end of the meeting Izzie is going to show us the final version of the crucifixion. ' Izzie gave a queenly bob of her head.

'Each of us has a responsibility to achieve our desires by our own efforts. Josh, Toby and Justine have shown us that it starts at home, away from everyone's eyes, with a change in ourselves. It is now our turn to help them go further. I'm going to ask you all to split into smaller groups and to help refine the process that they have started. Talk, act, point out and suggest: anything that might help. These are the groupings I would like to start with: Ed would you go with Toby; Peter and Izzie would you help Justine, and Josh, you'll be with me. Ok? Let's assemble again in, say - thirty minutes.'

'Toby! Bloody hell, what on earth could I say to him?' I smiled affably, but at that moment I could have bloody swung for Ray.

'Like the shirt, mate.'

'It's genuine.'

'What?'

'It's a genuine tartan.'

'Great. All you need now is a felling axe and you'll be the real deal.' I was struggling. He was a nature lover, not a bloody lumberjack.

'The boots are leather. I thought that to get closer to nature you needed to experience materials that actually come from nature, so I didn't go for Gortex.'

'Good choice. I like leather boots.'

'I'm preparing for my first foray.' He was excited, but seeing my lack of understanding he added. 'I'm planning to live in the woods for a bit. Perhaps just the summer. Depends really on finding the time.'

'You're a student aren't you?'

'Yes, well, almost, I've just finished A levels. Might take a gap year if this goes all right.'

'Living in the woods?' He nodded. 'Have you done any camping before?'

'Not really, not real camping. I've camped in the back garden a few times.'

I had less than thirty minutes to help him refine his ambition of getting closer to what he had called *'the wild in me'* and the poor sod hadn't even been camping before. The whole exercise was ridiculous. The whole fucking *Bucket Shop* was ridiculous. I could have been in Middlesbrough with Angie sporting the night away and yet here I was wasting my time with a bunch of -. It was with some difficulty that I stopped myself saying that word; it was forbidden. Fuck it – losers!

'You know what, mate. My suggestion is get yourself a tent, a small one, and start just by going away for the weekend. Epping Forest would do. And make sure that the tent is green or camouflaged, just so you don't stick out and attract unwanted attention from wondering loonies and axe wielding psychopaths.'

Despite my smile, he seemed to take what I said to be a real possibility, and for a moment or two went quiet and thoughtful.

'Damn!' I said. 'Bloody clock. We'd better finish there, Toby, for the time being. Great shirt, though.'

Although Ray had said he would spend time at the end to hear from each of the groups, in actual fact he cut the whole thing short so that there was time for Izzie to get her presentation up and running.

He was right; she was good, better than good for a photographer. She'd done what she'd set out to do. Everyone was enraptured. They couldn't get enough of it. But I boiled. That she was using us didn't bother me, what bothered me was the speed of our response. It was almost instant; the pictures and our experience coalesced. They were, despite the mutilation and the distress, the reality we had already seen. My fucking marks can't do that; they approximate; they suggest. My struggle was between reality and mere illustration, and it made me feel sick, because while they fawned in front of her pictures I felt inadequate to the task I had set myself.

I inspected the images calmly, my face frozen into a mask of interest, but inside my stomach churned. I felt ill with ineptitude, and had the meeting finished then I would have gone to bed in a real state, but thankfully I was saved from despair by overhearing a conversation she was having with Peter.

'These are post card facsimiles of the images, Peter; I printed them myself. I would love you to have one, any one.'

She fanned the small number of cards in front of him as though she was performing a magic trick.

'They're all wonderful. It's hard to choose. I like them all.'

She laughed. 'Choose.'

'Could I have two?'

The magician's face hardened. 'They maybe postcards, Peter, but they're still art works. I have signed them. They have monetary value. You'd not say to a plumber who had come to fix your tap, could you also fix the toilet flush while you're about it, and then expect him to work for nothing. Choose.'

He did, and shame-faced scuttled away clutching it to his chest like a holy relic. I looked at her face. She knew what she had done - the bitch. But it cheered me up no end, because now I knew that my perception of her was right, and that despite Ray's regard, I could now actively dislike her with a clear conscience.

I didn't say much to Ray when we'd finished, I was too worked up, but as soon as they'd all gone, I went straight into the workshop and stood before my 'Miracle of the Fishes'.

'I did that. It's my work,' I said, talking out loud so that I could hear my thoughts. 'Everything on that canvas I did. Nothing came between me and the marks but the brushes. It comes out of my head, flows down my arm, guides my hand and makes the fucking marks. That's a febrile process. All she does is look, hold the fucking camera, calibrate it and press the fucking trigger. The rest is mechanical. *It* produces the image; all she has to do then is to play with it.

The picture glared at me. I had painted a fucking good fish; the one held before the Christ to show the bounty of the catch, but the apostles weren't nearly as good. I hated them. They were insipid, second-rate human forms, more or less like every other second-rate contemporary, figurative image that I'd ever seen. I just did not have the ability or the creativity to take up photography's challenge. And it was Ray's fault. He'd got me to do the bloody thing. If he had not said what he said I would have carried on happily painting fish and doing my Japanese gyotaku prints. He'd had exposed me.

I was half inclined to take a knife and rip the canvas to shreds. I didn't; I took up my brushes and worked my anger out through the paint.

CHAPTER 20

RAY

I t took a surprising amount of chivvying from me, prior to last Wednesday night's meeting, to get Lauren started on her month long 'gender holiday', and have her mass of auburn hair cut and restyled. Not that I put it quite like that, of course, I'm totally aware of the sensitivities over the issue, but I had assumed, after her declaration of intent, that she would be raring to go. Her sartorial transformation I left entirely to her, since she was far more aware of contemporary male fashions than I was. It would only be after she had altered the externals that I would step in as a sympathetic, but critical friend, and offer advice, because she might look like a Josh, but could she walk like a Josh?

Her first full outing was to take place at the next meeting, hence the chivvying. If the rest of the '*Shoppers*' liked what they saw, then the next day she would walk through town in drag, while I followed her surreptitiously making pertinent observations.

The *Shoppers* loved her. And because stage one had been so successful, we agreed to move straight on to stage two – the walk on the wild side. The next day I arrived at the top of the Narrow Way nice and early so that I could get a good look at her as she was arriving. Obviously, I didn't just stand on the corner and gawk at her like some gormless half-wit; I used that classic spy technique of watching the road by looking at its reflection in a shop window.

'Well, what do you think?'

I nearly jumped out of my skin when she taped my shoulder. I'd missed her completely. She was totally transformed, almost anonymous.

'What? Oh yes! Like it, like it. Spot on. The real deal.'

'Were you watching me?' she said, glancing at the window.

'*They seek him here, they seek him there,*' I said, laughing. What I said meant nothing to her so I added, '*The Scarlet Pimpernel?*' but she was none the wiser. 'Right then - Josh, let's do this thing. I want you to walk all the way down the street, take your time, look in the shop windows, anything you like, and we'll meet again: '*Don't know where, don't know when,*' Her face was immobile. 'Well, actually I do - outside the Town Hall on Mare Street. Then we can compare notes. OK?'

'Yes mate,' she said, lowering her voice effectively.

Dark jeans, a hoody and a beanie are fairly standard issue amongst young men, so she fitted in and drew no adverse looks. The only inconsistency that I could see was her tendency to move between the walk of a middle class youth and a street youth; there was a bit too much intermittent shoulder rocking for me. But that aside, I thought she looked really convincing, and so half way down the Narrow Way I slipped off down a side street and rushed around to get in front of her so that I could watch her approach from the corner of the Empire Theatre. Front and back views are crucial. They don't necessarily match.

From my vantage point tucked into the Empire's entrance, I saw her cross over at the lights and head up Mare Street towards me. At the last minute, I left my hiding place and came towards her smiling, not just because I was pleased with her performance, but because I wanted to trick her into responding as Lauren.

'How was that then?'

She gave a surprised laugh and immediately let her shoulders drop as if relieved of a great burden.

'Ha ha! Got yeah!' I said, pointing out the sudden change in her demeanour.

She wasn't upset by what I'd done. She laughed and resumed her stiffer male persona with a theatrical flourish.

'This is harder than I thought. My shoulders are aching.'

'You were good. I'm impressed. Only a few things we need to talk about, but nothing desperate. If you like, we could pop across the road to the cinema and talk there? Let go of Josh for a bit, if you like? It's up to you. I don't mind.'

'No, I don't have a choice. I've gone too far. Josh would love a coffee, mate.'

Her intensity surprised me, but I liked her hutzpah, and we crossed Mare Street laughing and went into the Picture House café. Before I could volunteer to do the honours she was at the counter.

'My shout, mate. What do you want?'

She was good. 'Cheers, Josh, I'll have an expresso and a brownie.'

I found a space on one of the long tables where I could watch her. I've never looked at men's bottoms very much, but I was looking at hers, which was rather disturbing, considering that she wasn't Lauren, she was Josh.

'You're grinning,' she said, handing me my cake.

'Well, it's fun, isn't it, dressing up. Make-believe?'

She smiled tolerantly. 'It is amusing, but it's not a laugh. I'm deadly serious.'

'No, I'm not being facetious - Josh. I'm absolutely behind you in this. Just wondering whether it might have been easier just to study us a bit first – like a bird watcher. Make notes, that sort of thing?'

'I've done that already. I've even made a special study of you at the meetings.'

I laughed, but not because it was amusing. 'Me? And what did you learn, perchance.'

'About you or about men?'

'Both.'

'You are very controlling.'

I was going to say something, but she hadn't finished.

'A bit picky, pedantic even; this makes you a bit purblind.'

'That's not a word you hear every day.'

'I like old words. I like their music. We read *'Love's Labour's Lost'* in my last year at school, and I think it fits. You think you see everything that goes on in front of you, but I don't think you do.'

'In what way?'

'You make sure that we all go in one direction, which is fine, because that's why we're there – the realization of our dreams. But that means you can be a bit one dimensional. You only see what you want to see. Our other interactions pass you by.'

'Meaning?'

'You either don't see or don't want to see who interacts with whom.'

'And you do?'

Seeing my high speed processing of what she had said, she added. 'If you want to get to know someone, you need to try on their bodies for size, creep around inside their skin; feel the fit. When I was walking down Mare Street, it became painfully obvious that when men and women move through life, their locomotion is different.'

'But not that different, and that's something I was going to say.'

'I think it is.' She placed her hands on her hips. 'The difference here is enough to alter how we walk. If we both had a compass and mine was fractionally different from yours we could end up miles apart. It's the little things upon which other things are raised. Men seem very stiff and unwieldy. At our best we're suppler, less resisting.'

'Ah, your walk,' I said, taking my chance. 'I think it's to do with your feet; they were coming down too close to an imaginary central line. A man's gait is usually more widespread, and our shoulders tend to move to and fro a lot more. But not too much!' I nodded forcefully trying to knock my observation home, in an effort to shut her up. She was a lot cleverer than I had thought, and I wasn't too sure I could help her.

'I get all that Ray, but today was special. The hair cut was dramatic, I know, but because I was actually going to walk out as a man, it meant that when I got up this morning I had to decide what to wear.'

'What you've got on is fine. I think you look good.'

'It was not this, not what you can see. It was what pants to put on!'

We both laughed, although my laugh was slightly overexcited. I hadn't expected to be discussing her underwear.

'If I'd slipped on my usual knickers then the whole new edifice would have been built on the wrong foundations. I couldn't be Josh while wearing fancy knickers.'

'Oh I don't know,' I said smirking. 'Wouldn't be the first man to wander the streets in frilly panties.' I didn't mean to be salacious, but I was embarrassed.

'It's important, Ray, it is the little things. It wouldn't feel right. Identity is based on subtlety. Josh has to be built from the base up, from the foundations. So the knickers had to go. I'm wearing M&S small men's slips. Everything else is new or bought from a charity shop.'

I nodded vigorously, my usual response when I'm confused. I was out of my depth. I'd never met such a single-minded person before. To be honest, I was in awe of her. She was a wonder. I was captivated by her animation and her appearance. She was lovely.

'If gender was just down to this,' she said, pinching her jeans, 'we'd be in and out of each other's pants all the time. But this is the hard bit.' She drummed her forefinger on her skull. 'This is where it has to change.'

'This is important to you, I know that, Lauren, sorry Josh, but why take it so far? Why a month? You could be a weekend Josh. I mean, when the door's shut no one knows what we all get up to.'

She gave me a piercing stare, as if assessing the worth or otherwise of my soul.

'I am a twin. My brother was called Josh. He died when he was six, run down by a complete twat who had no licence and no insurance. Something in me also died then. Recently I've been acutely conscious of his presence. I think he's trying to come through to me. Tell me something I need to know. Only when I become him will I know what it is, and until that happens I must bear his presence like a permanent headache.'

She ground her knuckles so hard into her forehead that they left a mark.

'I need to get everything perfect so that it can happen. One thing out of place and I'm frightened that it won't work. And if that happened I'm not sure I could cope.' She stared at me again, but this time her eyes were softer.

'Wow! Well! Thank you for telling me - Josh. Not easy, not at all. I can see why you hadn't told me before.'

'Now that you know, I don't mind if the others know. But nothing must get in the way of my channelling, Ray. It's too dangerous.'

'But, um, he died a long time ago, when you were both children, won't that affect how you think he is? You know - what you wear and your hair?'

She smiled. 'Yes, but I have an image in my head, a very strong image. I don't know where it comes from, but I know what he wants. Trust me, I know.'

When she had gone, I stayed on a while longer, trying to get my head around all that she had said. I thought it was all going to be a bit of fun, an exercise in gender assignment or something; this was different, it was like being part of some sort of physic experiment. To tell the truth, she unnerved me. There was too much going on below the surface.

We both agreed to meet again later when she had had a little longer at being Josh in public, but I desperately needed to talk to someone else about it. I didn't want to talk to Angie because I didn't want her to assume there was some underlying sexual monkey business. I didn't want her to feel threatened. Not that I desired her/him, I didn't. Josh/Lauren was attractive but I didn't want either of them, especially now that I knew she was bonkers. So I went to see Ed.

For a change, and because I was a bit stirred up, I took the train to Walthamstow. It felt like an indulgence, but once in a while I enjoyed travelling over my usual walking route and seeing it from above, since the railway was raised over the river and the surrounding floodplain on a brick viaduct. Dogs ran about, lovers nested in the outlying corners of the meadows and all along the east side of the Lea boats were moored end to end.

It was hardly the world that Izaak Walton would have known when he had fished the Lea in the seventeenth century, but from my vantage point it was still very pleasurable. The bucolic idyll was long gone, of course. Bleak Hall, an *'honest ale house'*, where he and his companion had stayed was now a fiction buried way down beneath the Edmonton Solid Waste Incineration Plant. But I'd travelled the river banks to long and too often to be deterred by present and past despoliations. The river Lea below me was the river I actually knew, and had come to love. All the rest was history.

I had to wait for a while before Ed was customer-free, so I went upstairs to his kitchen and put on the coffee. I didn't have to wait long, because he came up the stairs at full tilt.

'Are you shagging that woman, Ray? Is that what all this is about? All this bloody - let's dance about in front of her fucking photos like a bunch of tosspots. You set me up, didn't you? You wanted me to fail just so that she would shine and you could get into her knickers.'

'Fuck me, are you on something?'

'*You* are a selfish bastard.'

'Let's stop there, mate.' I held up my hands up before him and did an imaginary press up on his chest. 'No, I am not shagging her, if her means Izzie Whatnot. No. As if! And as for the rest, I've no idea what you are on about.'

'*Jesus and the fucking Fishermen*'.

He stared into my face like a lunatic, but I was still none the wiser. 'What about them?'

'I can't do it, Ray. I fucking can't do it.'

He was breathing hard and close to tears, but his anger had evaporated. He just stood where he was red faced and gently wheezing.

'Ed. Ed,' I took him in my arms, and gripped him tight. His cheek felt bristly and rough and his clothes smelt unpleasantly of old tobacco smoke. 'Let's go and have a look.'

The fight had left him completely. We stood in the studio, and he turned the easel around showing no emotion whatsoever.

Christ was on the left seated in a boat. In front of him were the disciples: Peter, John and the other one, whose name I'd temporarily forgotten. I guessed it was based on the famous painting of Raphael's – '*The Miraculous Draught of Fishes*'. The boat was drawn in outline heaving with sketches of fish, and Peter was on his knees looking up at the Saviour, but unlike the original, he didn't have his hands together in prayer, he was holding up a magnificent fish in homage to his master. That's where the similarity ended. The whole arrangement and concept was different, and apart from the big fish, which was outstanding, nearly everything else was rudimentary.

I gave it the once over and critic's frown. 'That is an incredible fish, Ed. Fact, it's brilliant.'

'And Christ?'

It was a loaded question, but I couldn't avoid it.

'You've got the position and proportions bang on.'

'But he looks deader than the fucking fish, doesn't he?'

'Um.' I looked extremely thoughtful, trying desperately to think of what to say. 'You know what mate; you know what I think it is? Your figures have a touch of the Modigliani's? That's the problem; they are clashing with the fish. Different styles. Yes. That's it.'

He squinted at the picture. 'They're fucking insipid, I'll tell you that.'

'Because you've been looking at fish too long, mate,' I tried laughing. 'You need to look at some nudes. Get some sketching time in, again; see how it all works.'

He stepped back as if considering what I had said, took out one of his own roll-ups and lit it. He then looked at me through a cloud of smoke, but this time without any obvious dislike.

'Yeah. Well, you got my into this, so you can get me out. Get your fucking kit off. We'll start now.'

'Me? What about the customers?'

'Art first. Isn't that what we used to say? Yes – commitment. Hang your stuff on the chair while I close the shop.'

We sat in semi-silence for the first part of the sitting; I was meant to be Christ and sat on a stool with one arm forward. I did my best to remain still, but then I just couldn't help myself, I desperately wanted to talk to him about Lauren.

'She's absolutely solid on doing it. Really hard core. Impressive woman.'

'Oh yeah.' He gave me an old fashioned look.

This time we both laughed. That was all I'd needed. 'Difficult though, mate, when she's dressed as a man. Feels a bit, you know - weird.'

'Exciting hidden passions, eh? The love that cannot speak its name.'

'Come on, nothing like that. She's a woman, and in any case-.'

'Slippery slope, Raymondo,' he said, puckering his lips and making kissing noises.

I raised my arm to remonstrate.

'Keep still, for fuck's sake!'

'She's trying to become her dead brother,' I said out of the corner of my mouth.

He stopped what he was doing and turned to face me. 'What?'

All pretence at sitting went, and I squirmed around to face him.

'They were twins, died when he was a kid.'

He rolled his eyes and then snorted. 'You certainly pick them, mate.'

'What are we going to do? It's all a bit-

'Yes – weird,' he said cutting in. 'But as to the 'we', I think this is your problem, mate, not mine.'

All the way back I pondered on what he'd said: the sexual attraction bit. It was bollocks of course, I was not attracted to men, never had been, never would be, but it was disturbing, because I wasn't sexually attracted to Lauren either. It wasn't like that. I liked looking at her, but I didn't want her, certainly not after what she'd told me. I didn't want anyone, well, that wasn't exactly true. Since I'd met Izzie I wanted her, not permanently. I wouldn't want to share more time with her than it took to do the business. She was too unstable, too likely to do something that I hadn't thought of. I'd be a nervous wreck. No, occasional sex would be lovely, but nothing more, nothing that invoked commitment.

As for Ed and his masterpiece, that was something else. The fish was without doubt brilliant, but he hadn't been able to cross from the cold blooded to the hot blooded. If he couldn't do that then the picture would never get done. I knew him. Too many reverses and the canvas would end up in the yard blocking a hole in the fence.

I'd cooked my standard spag-bol for Angie's return. It was a something of a tradition. If she stayed away for more than one night, on her return I would give her a lovely meal, a good wine, and all things being well – a good seeing to once we got to bed. The last bit was the bit that wasn't actually stable. There were times when she came home so bushed that all she wanted to do was crash, drink and fall asleep. But that was fine; it was a totally normal response to absence and hard work, not to want sex.

'I don't know how many times I've told bloody Carlos that deaf people need to see the interpreter and that he should get a proper light on us. It was rubbish. Not only was the light inadequate, the cast kept crossing in front of me. He's the bloody director, he should think of these things.'

'Why doesn't he get you in earlier?'

'God knows.'

'Saw Ed this morning, not in a good way, darling. Having trouble with his 'picture'.'

She perked-up. 'I thought he was feeling good about it.'

'He's doubting his abilities – again. Says he can't paint people. I told him to do some life drawing, even volunteered to sit for him there and then – in the nude. Seemed like the least I could do.'

She laughed. 'When was the last time you did that, darling?'

'Back in Chelsea.'

'Actually, I think that was later, when I said I fancied taking up painting. You couldn't get your kit off quick enough.'

We laughed. I remembered. It had been fun. That's when the three of us had first met. I was in my last year at Chelsea, Ed was in his first year and Angie was doing part time bar work in a pub on the Kings Road.

'You thought painters were so romantic. Didn't last though, did it? You soon clocked that there was no money in Art.'

'Certainly earnt more as a barmaid than you two scruffy buggers put together'

'God, I remember now. They'd done the pub out like a Bavarian beer hall.'

'We all had wear dirndl skirts.'

'And Ed tried to copy their leg slapping dance, completely off his face. When he did the knees bend bit, he just stayed there, never got up; I don't think I've ever seen him so drunk. '

'Tell you what, darling, I'll pop over and see how he's doing; might help. I can take Geordie; he could do with a run.'

'Brilliant. You are about the one person he talks to.'

CHAPTER 21

ANGIE

S ometimes a bed is just a bed, a rectangle of modest comfort drifting across the calm seas of sleep. Rarely, in my experience, is it such a placid place that nothing happens. After Ed and I had made love, his bed looked as dishevelled as Robinson Crusoe's raft and, thanks to his tardiness when it came to changing his sheets, smelt like it too.

Love conquers everything, but when it comes to stale bed sheets it's a close call. Ed's not malodorous in the *'Oh my-god-you-stink*, sort of way, so I don't rush gagging to the window for a breath of fresh air. He smells like an absent minded man who lives alone, but with rather peculiar fish food base notes. Had I not felt particularly randy, I don't think we would have made love at all. As it was, it was fast and furious and over quickly, and we didn't linger afterwards. There's ripe and there's ripe. I retired to the kitchen table for a cup of tea, while he, at my suggestion, bundled up the bedding and put it in the washer.

'So what's all this 'I can't paint' nonsense, then?' I said when he came back.

He looked hurt. 'He's got a big mouth. I never said that. I said I was having a problem, that's all. He exaggerates.'

'And are you?'

His body made small, awkward undulations, as if he had forgotten how to stand up straight.

'A bit.'

After my admonition about his bedding, he was easy meat, and seeing my look of disbelief went into the studio and returned with his canvas, which he leant up against the microwave.

'It's the figures. They seem to die in front of me.'

'Well, what are you trying to say? What's the essence of the whole thing, then?'

'I don't fucking know, that's just it. I don't know what's going on. What it's all about.'

'Look, I know I suggested this, but maybe it would be better to forget Jesus and the whole son of God thing and concentrate upon fishermen today. Narrow the focus.'

I knew he wasn't convinced, because he stood in front of the canvas nodding at it like a nitwit. He can be such a negative bugger sometimes that I just want to shake him.

While he took the canvas back I had a good look through his fridge and cupboard. The only option for lunch was crisp bread and sardines in tomato sauce. Fine, if I was dieting, but I wasn't; all the exercise had made me ravenous, so I suggested that we went to the William Morris Gallery; they usually had plenty of good stuff to chow down on, and Geordie was always happy enough to be left alone in the kitchen.

We didn't say much as we walked towards Forest Road, which suited me fine, because I enjoyed staring into the windows of all the foreign cafes and cake shops, and it was only when we got close to the Gallery that I realized that not only was Ed holding my left arm, he was absentmindedly kneading my bicep.

'You all right, love?'

He shrugged, and waited until we were huddled over our spicy lentil soup before he really opened out.

'This bloody *Bucket Shop* is bugging me, Angie. Ray's so far into it that he can't see how weird it really is. I mean that Izzie woman is a total fruit cake, but he thinks that the sun shines out of her arse.'

'Not professional jealousy, this?'

'Come on, sweetheart, she's just a technician with a good eye.' I love it when his prejudice comes out, and smiled. 'But this thing with Lauren or whatever her bloody name is – it's bonkers. I don't think he can see that. He thinks that we're all part of some sort of glorious democratic self-help group, but as far as I can see, apart from thee and me, everyone else is a nutter.'

A few heads turned towards us as the word exploded from his lips.

'Channelling her fucking brother! Come on Angie, if I said that to you, you'd have me locked up.'

Seated as we were in the temple of the Arts and Crafts movement being so loud and intense felt almost blasphemous, and Ed had annoyed me. He had forced me to admit to myself that what we'd all been engaged in was a bit odd. I should have challenged Ray more, but when you live your life between two men it doesn't pay to be too critical of either one. It's easier to accept what's what and flee to the arms of the other if it all gets too much. Then I felt suddenly sick, in the wake of these thoughts I remembered Justine's huge lips and the sweet smell of her flesh.

I was my turn to nod inanely as I tried desperately to force her memory down into the deeper recesses of my brain. When I spoke my voice sound very small, 'What can we do though?'

He didn't know and I didn't know, so that left us with nothing to do but chomp on our Italian bread and sop up the soup. In the end we went back to his place, made love a bit more slowly on the sofa, made the bed between us and had another coffee. The sex and caffeine worked wonders, and for a short space of time we felt both sane and normal. But on my way back across the marsh Ed's fears rose again and continued to niggle inside my head.

Although I'd calmed down by the evening, it wasn't until I'd finished yoga and was packing up to go that I felt in control enough to carry on with my own life. It was lovely just to hang out with Greta and a couple of the others and chat about nothing remotely connected to either Ray or Ed. I loved them both, but sometimes I wanted my head free of any commitment or relationship. I wanted to be me and freewheeling; one of the girls.

Greta and I walked home together. The one thing you could be sure of with her was that she would always say what was on her mind. There was no politeness or shilly-shallying. With Greta you got what you could see. She was always direct and in your face.

'Your shoulders were like wood tonight, darling. Too stiff by halves. You must loosen up or you'll get one of your migraines.'

'That obvious was it?'

'The body is like a book, but you have to learn to read first if you are going to understand it. So, *liebling* – what's in your head? What's knotting these neck muscles?'

She lent her bike against a hedge, and with the speed of a practised strangler had her hands around my neck.

'Ooh! That hurt.'

Saying that didn't make any difference, her fingers kept ferreting into the centre of the pain.

'So – what is it then? These are telling me something.'

'Nothing special, well, just everything; you know - life. Ow!'

'Life, eh? Tell you what, darling. You need a good massage and a bit of relaxation. Relationships have solutions, but Life is the hard one, but at least it's terminal.'

I adjusted my neck and laughed. 'Thanks Greta. Feels better all ready.'

'I don't think. Seriously Angie – listen to your body. It knows you.'

We kissed and I went inside in a happier frame of mind than when I had left.

On Thursday night, after dinner, I was happily curled up on the sofa, wrapped in a throw and munching on After Eights. I knew it was sinful, I knew that what I was watching would warp the mind of a child, but I was happy, mindless and content. Ray, as far as I knew, was upstairs in his study doing whatever he did. What more could one ask for after a strenuous day at work.

I'd had two jobs, one before lunch and one after, which was great. It meant that I could lunch somewhere nice, look in a few shops and get two cheques instead of one. The first job had been relatively straight forward and not particularly taxing, but the second was interpreting at a group meeting. My client was one of the participants. If the topic that's being discussed is boring, then the job is hard graft and tedious. This meeting was both, since it was primarily about finance and organization.

Suffice it to say that after a good long soak in scented suds, and dressed in my onesie, I was half way between attention and sleep, and feeling quietly content, when my phone buzzed. I was half inclined to let it go, but as most of my jobs come to me by text or email, I picked it up and looked. It was a message from Max, which woke me up immediately. He wanted to Skype. Goodie!

'Hi mum.'

We went through the usual greetings, questions and answers until we got to where he wanted to tell me something.

'I want you to meet someone, my friend.'

Ding! The alarm bell in the head that every mother has on standby jingled for the first time in ages.

'That's nice.'

My heart was in my mouth. Who would appear from the side of the screen? What monster was I about to be introduced to?

'Hello Mrs. Brook, I'm Gwen. I've heard so much about you.'

It was the face of a beautiful young woman, although maybe not that young. She had well styled shinny dark hair and wonderful cheek bones. She was gorgeous. I lightened up instantly.

'Mum,' said Max, bending his grinning face into the screen, 'Gwen and I are engaged.'

I felt sick.

My face set itself immediately to 'receptively neutral' as they batted anodyne expressions of joy from one side of the screen to the other. I was the umpire to this game of emotional ping-pong, turning my eyes this way and that as I tried to score their sincerity.

'That sounds wonderful, I'm so happy for you both. Sadly, your dad isn't here at the moment,' I said, not wanting to bring Ray down before I had had time to process the information myself, 'but perhaps we can all Skype again later?'

'You must both come down to Brighton so that we can all get to know each other.'

The screens closed on our smiles and arcades of white teeth, but my smile vanished the moment they went blank, because something I had noticed as they had talked, but had chosen to ignore, suddenly filled my head with alarm. Once, when Gwen had laughed and her head had rocked back into the light of a hidden table lamp, I had seen what looked like fine stubble growing on her chin. The stubble in my imagination now grew into a thick dark forest. She was hairy. Not as hairy probably as the Japanese Ainu, but decidedly hirsute. Images of bearded babies and strange hairy children flooded unwished into my head. A grandmother to mutants! I felt lightheaded with anxiety. I was being foolish of course, silly, phobic even, but I did see what I saw.

'I sometimes wonder, darling whether some archaeologists are serious scientists or just fanciful story tellers?' said Ray, waving a magazine at me when he came down later. 'A few cuts on a human bone and we're either off amongst the cannibals or into ritual dismemberment. They get off on nothing.'

I very rarely pay attention to the content of whatever he's been reading or looking at. I just listen to the tone of his voice and adjust my face accordingly.

'Would you open another bottle, darling?' I said, feeling the need for alcohol.

A few drinks later, and after a mind-numbing tour of what was on offer on the television, I felt able to reinterpret Max's news.

'How old is Max?'

'Coming up thirty-five, I think. Yes, that's it. Why?'

'What were we doing when we were his age?'

He gave what passed as an amused out breathe, as if being asked to recall the past was to recall a time when only real things happened, unlike today, when nothing of interest happened. My father had had a similar snort.

'Me, well, I know where I was, down in bloody Southampton with the OS, but you, my darling, if I remember rightly, were doing your degree in Bristol; the start of your new career.'

'Yes, and Max was being looked after by ma and pa.'

'Thank god for amenable grandparents, even mad ones.'

'Ed had got divorced a couple of years earlier.'

'Best thing he ever did, apart from leaving Boston.'

'Max tells me he's engaged – to a beautiful looking woman called Gwen.' I wanted to say: beautiful hairy woman', but I held back. 'He Skyped me while you were upstairs.'

'Blood hell! At last! Look all right does she, nothing odd? You never know with Max. To tell you the truth, Angie, I'm a bit surprised it's a woman.'

We chuckled, but I suddenly recalled the hairy chin again, and a cold shiver ran down my back. Was it a woman? Not that it mattered, god, no, that sort of thing was not a problem, no way. We would never make a fuss. What Max did was absolutely fine by us.

'Yes, well, I didn't get to see much of her, just her face. Very strong. Good cheek bones.'

It was a fairly busy week, and I was more often on the train than walking across the marsh to see Ed. On Tuesday I'd been booked to interpret a show at the Battersea Arts Centre, which had been great, and I'd met lots of old friends, amongst them Martin, who had trained with me in Bristol, and with whom I had had a long term confessional relationship. After a few drinks at the bar we went off to eat in one of the local Italian restaurants on Lavender Hill.

'So, how's your love life then,' I said 'still being pissed about by Roger?'

'Honestly, sweetie, that man is a complete mess. He ran me ragged. And to think I nearly moved in with him. He's living proof that beauty is just skin deep.'

'I did try to warn you.'

'I should have listened. I mean he had the body and profile of a Greek statue but a heart of marble to match. I'm just pleased he wasn't violent. Feels like a weight's been lifted. Now I'm free to stretch my wings, but sadly I haven't found anywhere new to perch. And you, Cassandra, darling, are you still flitting between your beaus like a weaver's shuttle?'

'All that is good.'

'Don't think I could do it. I'd be too jealous.'

'I've had years of practise.'

'And how's that handsome son of yours?'

'He's just told me he's getting engaged.'

Martin cocked his head with a knowing look.

'That's just it. I'm not sure if it *is* to a woman or a man.'

He looked surprised. 'I thought you said he was gay?'

'Well, I think she might be-'

'-Trans? Oh my god,' he said, smiling excitedly. 'There are some beautiful trans in Brighton.'

'She looked lovely, you know, stylish but?'

'For goodness sake, girlfriend, but what? Stop being so evasive. Just tell me.'

'I think that I saw stubble on her chin.'

Saying it out loud it sounded silly. I'd seen Gwen only for moments and then only on Skype. PC cameras always made you look crap. He laughed.

'Sweetie, I know lots of women with five o'clock shadows. You are such worrier. Skype for god's sake! And what if she is? Not like you to be prejudiced.'

He had uttered the one word capable of straightening out any liberal's wavering conscience.

I laughed. 'Course not, Martin, you know me. Just curious. No, wonderful. Looking forward to meeting her.'

'And there's always face creams. As her mother-in-law you could recommend some. I'm told Estee Lauder is expensive, but does the trick.'

We both laughed now. Martin was good for me. I liked him and leant over and kissed him on the lips.

'I love you.'

'Likewise, darling. Likewise.'

Chapter Twenty-Two - Angie

Ray disappeared on Friday morning and I forgot to ask him when he would be back. I assumed he was either off searching the undergrowth for his elusive destiny or upstream following some river to its source through the jungles of Essex.

I hadn't forgotten Ed's anxiety about what Ray had got us all into, and being alone in the house I was more than happy to ignore everything and get on with the weekly wash. I'm away so often or at least out of the house for long periods that I quite enjoy being domestic for awhile. Ray does his best to be helpful, but his mind is so often elsewhere that between us it's possible for the house to get a little wayward. It was a glorious sunny day and ideal for drying.

When the first loads were in and out on the line I went into the front room to straighten things up. It's not a big room, and ever since we got rid of the carpets easy enough to keep clean with a broom. I whisked a desultory duster over the cast iron fireplace and flicked the surrounds of the TV, while singing scrambled versions of Abba favourites.

'They are closer now Fernando
And every hour seemed to last eternally'

As I crossed the bay window preparing to run the duster over the windowsill, a face suddenly appeared through the glass. It was such a surprise that I gasped and stepped back shaking. The initial surprise produced the shock, but the real surprise was recognising whose face it was. Smiling like mad and waving to me was Justine. As I recovered myself she left the window and went to the door. There was no escape; I would have to let her in. I was feeling so unsteady that I needed to touch the hall wall momentarily for support.

'Come in, come in. How lovely to see you.

'So pleased you're in.'

We had embraced, because you do, and had given each other the customary buzz on both cheeks, and so by the time we had moved into the kitchen I had stripped off my yellow Marigolds, had put the coffee on and was more or less emotionally back in control.

'How's it going, then? The change,' I said, making my face contort in sympathetic collusion.

She scrunched up her nose, 'All right – sort of. No, not well really, not at all.'

'Oh Justine, I thought you were feeling better.'

'It's better in one way. Now, I know what I want.'

'Well that's brilliant. It's a start.'

She smiled at me, her face still and open. 'I want you.'

Squirts of electricity or sickness zoomed all over me. I was suddenly hyper alert and on tenterhooks. She saw my alarm.

'Is that so bad?'

'Ooh Justine, no, not bad – just, well – I don't really know. Surprising.'

We were both leaning against the wall. I went across to the stove and stood by the Italian coffee maker to encourage it to bubble.

'It was good wasn't it, you and me?' I nodded, adding words would have complicated things. 'Look, I'm not going to take you away from Ray. I know how things are. I've had a lot of experience.'

Her fuck buddy, Stuart. Yes, of course. I nodded. She came across and stood beside me.

'Couldn't we be the same – lovers for the moment, friends. I'm discrete. I would never be a nuisance.'

The coffee started burbling so I turned off the gas, and as I did so she laid her hand on my shoulder. It was a gesture; she was telling me she could be trusted, but it felt highly charged, because she was right. I did want her, but I didn't know why I wanted her. I picked up her hand and kissed it, shrugging my shoulders incoherently.

'It was good,' I said, hardly daring to look her in the eyes. 'It was beautiful, and I do want you, but this is all so unexpected, new, weird. I'm hardly sure of myself. I don't know if I can do it.'

We turned to each other and she placed her hands either side of my face. 'We could try.'

I was on fire. I felt a sick craving for stimulation, adoration and touch. It had been good. I kept telling myself that; unnerving but exciting and different. Difference is a huge come on when you've been in a relationship for as long as I have. Ray and Ed were different, they loved differently. Their expectations were different, and I responded to them differently. Ray was predictable, caring and gentle. He never demanded. He never held grudges if I said no. Above all he was amenable, and for that I sometimes disliked him. I hated my ability to control his wishes. I felt mean and conniving. Ed you couldn't control. He had his own problems and he assumed, rightly, that he and I would always be available to each other whatever the reason and whenever the time. He was also less predictable and had a depth of passion that could verge on the wild. This I liked too, not always, but mostly. He brought my lust to the surface. With Ed I felt able to pursue my fantasies as and when they arose. But Justine was another country, and like all explorers I had my misgivings. She would be troubling, unsettling and threatening, but rich with possibilities and new discoveries.

I kissed her and held her close.

'We could.'

'We will.'

So much for the Marigolds and shapeless joggy-bottoms; in Justine's arms none of that seemed to matter. We went upstairs and made love wildly, passionately and blindly. At the end, as I lay on my back with her head nestled on my shoulder, I felt beautifully exhausted and emotionally drained.

'Thank you, Angie.'

'No, don't thank me, darling. You were right, we can do this.' I kissed her forehead and lay back mindless, my skin tingling and my loins still fluttering sporadically.

I've always felt that sex is dangerous, because it inevitably dismisses the guard and leaves us vulnerable. Our animal mind takes over and reconditions everything we see and hear around us. Idiocy appears like sense and stupidity like reason. The first time I slept with Ed I had been overwhelmed, but every reason I had to say no was as resilient as a snow flake falling on my fevered brow. We coupled hard and long, neither of us using our heads or memories to adjudicate what we were doing. All that we wanted and all that we were was concentrated where our genitals were locked together.

I didn't regret it, and I don't regret it. I love Ed and I also love Ray, but differently, and so when we make love it is not the same. Take Ed, he loves rugby, but when I've watched it with him I don't see the difference between Rugby Union and Rugby League. He's tried to teach me, but all I see is men running and falling over in pursuit of the same oddly shaped ball. It looks like the same game, but to those in the know the differences are blindingly obvious. So it is when I make love to either of them: it seems like the same thing, but to me the differences are equally, blindingly obvious.

Now I had played another version of the two games that I had been playing most of my life. It was also different. The dangerous and fickle nature of sex is that it doesn't give a damn about who you are coupling with, because if you do it often enough any mistakes you make with your choice of partner will work themselves out.

All these thoughts floated through my head, because the animal brain doesn't hang around for the aftermath. Only after you climax does it quit the scene and leave the space available for speculation.

We were lying back arms entwined, warm, toasty, flushed and replete, but in my case with a supercharged brain that couldn't be made to think in straight lines. My answer to all of these complexities was, in the end, to be practical.

'We can't do this too often, sweetheart. I just don't have room for a more demanding relationship, and I'm often out and away working.'

She wriggled herself upright against the pillows. Once she had moved I did the same. Sitting upright is a more productive way to think straight. From her neck to the fall of her breasts her skin was suffused in pink.

'I know, Angie. It's not a problem. You have all this and Ray to think off. And I'm not demanding. Now and again would be wonderful, and if we can't, well, there's always Stuart if I'm feeling randy. '

Although we both smiled, to me what she had said sounded almost insensitive, as if I was nothing more to her than an interlude in her ongoing shenanigans with her equally callous sex mechanic. But then what was I? We'd never mentioned love; In fact we'd hardly mentioned anything, certainly not exclusivity. And I wasn't in love with her, and realising that made me smile, because I'd never imagined that I would have sex without love. I don't know why that should have made me happy, but it did. I leant over and kissed her again, recalling what we had said before we went upstairs.

'Well, we've tried.

'We have.'

When Justine had gone I didn't hang around and mope. I didn't even think much about it, not then at least; I got on and finished the cleaning. Despite its short lived intensity and physical excitement it didn't interfere with my routine. It had come and gone like a storm, and after storms there are often periods of calm. I think, in retrospect, that I was echoing Justine's suggestion that we become 'lovers for the moment'. Perhaps I felt I had become a 'fuck buddy' like Stuart with all of the emotional distance that that entailed, and was in fact not so different from her, from anyone if given the chance; we were all creatures of sensation, and now that I was no longer in the breeding herd there was no need for commitment.

Ed phoned in the afternoon and he and Ray agreed that we should all get together and eat out. We did this on a regular basis. Ed would come round in the early evening and then we would all troll off up the road to the nearest acceptable eatery, in this case, a modern Turkish restaurant on Chatsworth Road.

Two bottles into the meal, we'd begun to glow. I'm usually moderate in my drinking, but what had happened during the day had released an inner, less inhibited me. I was having fun. Fun is usually in short supply as you get older, and in the mood that I was in I was determined to have it when I could.

'We're like the three musketeers,' I said unoriginally, but then what do you expect when you've been drinking – sense? To seal the illusion I laid my hands on each of their shoulders. 'This must be our almost thirty odd something or other anniversary?'

'Really?' said Ray, starting to count. 'Well, Max was born in 82.'

'Yes, so it is; it's thirty five.'

'Yeah, but we all met during my first year at Chelsea and that was in 77,' said Ed.

'All anniversaries have a name or something,' said Ray. 'Look it up, sweetheart.

'You'd dyed your hair blond, hadn't you, to be like Hockney. Although you looked more like Elton John. '

'It was an homage, actually,' said Ray.

'Look,' I said, waving my phone in front of them. 'It's either our Coral or Jade anniversary. Jade's the modern name. Wow, when you read the list there's some really odd ones: the seventh was called the Copper or Wool, but, oh no, this is weird. It says that the modern version is – wait for it - a Desk Set?'

'A desk set anniversary?'

'What is a desk set?'

Once we got to the baklava we were well oiled, red faced and overly sentimental. I was full of love for these two men in my life, and throughout the meal had given both of them little touches and tweaks, and being well cut was on the verge now and again of blurting out the actual secrets of my abiding love for them both. This was not the first time that I had felt that urge, but thankfully, through constant practice, I had learnt to control it.

'Do you think we'll still all be together when we're old and crumbly?' said Ray.

'Horrible thought,' said Ed.

'Oh I don't know,' I said, 'we could all move into together and pool our pensions.'

'And where would that be, because there's no way I'm living on the south coast waiting die?'

'What about Brighton, Ed, that's not quite so bad, is it?'

'Hang on, hang on,' said Ray, 'nearly forgot. Max wants us all to come down on Saturday and meet Gwen.'

My alcoholic haze vanished. 'Saturday?'

'Meet the daughter-in-law,' said Ed, tittering.

'It's not funny, Ed. It's serious. What did you say darling?'

'I said yes. You too Ed. He wants you to meet her too.'

I've always liked Brighton; it's a proper resort with more to it than fish and chips and a tawdry seafront. Thanks to the quality of the light and the colour range of the sea it can even feel vaguely continental, especially when the sun is shining, which it was when we went down on Saturday. The plan was to meet in town, wander about and then eat somewhere nice, and our meeting place was what the guides referred to pretentiously as the Cultural Quarter, a title that immediately riled Ed.

'Fucking nonsense.'

And more precisely, outside the Royal Pavilion, near the India Gate, which also did not go down well with Mr Farrow.

'It looks like something out of a bloody funfair.'

'Shut up, you grumpy bastard. It's a lovely day, you can smell the sea and any minute now Max and Gwen are going to appear. Ignore it.'

'I'm only saying.'

'Well don't.'

The last thing I wanted was for my attention to be anywhere but on the approaching happy couple. I wanted to check her out as she walked towards me. I needed to know where I was and where he was, after all, I was his mother. That gave me certain rights.

Then they appeared, ambling hand in hand innocently into the narrow approach like beasts into a trap. Max's grin was so wide that his beard had been pushed out to his ears. Gwen was equally fulsome, but without the beard, or at least as far as I could see.

I got the first bear hug, and as soon as he moved on to grapple his father, I faced Gwen, who kept her distance and simply offered me her hand, which was a pity, because to have held her would have told me so much about her upper body strength and physical makeup. When the introductions were over we all stood back, eyed each other up and carried on freestyle grinning a bit longer before being led away by Max to a favoured restaurant. Gwen got to walk beside me, and considering how narrow and crowded the streets were we spent a great deal of the way bumping into each other, which I used constructively to feel the tone and texture of her body where it pressed against me. All felt pliable enough and, as far as I could judge, her body felt soft.

As we turned into The Lanes, the sun, which had been obscured by the narrowness of the entrance, sent a blinding shaft of light straight between the buildings down upon Gwen's upturned face. It was brutal, flattening all facets of her bone structure and illuminating her makeup in cruel detail. My eyes followed the ray to her chin. It was hairless! Yeehaa! There was nothing of note to be seen but the bland tones of her foundation cream. Glory be! She was a woman. I was so relieved that I beamed at her with a sun's intensity. So what if she had a rather sharp, masculine jaw, women came in all shapes and sizes, and a strong jaw suggested a strong character. If my son found her delectable, then who was I to suggest anything different?

But, oh my unrelenting, prying mind; despite having allayed my fears I just wanted to get a look at her legs, just to make absolutely sure, because thinking of all the transvestites that I'd ever known, it was the legs that let them down. They were always too bony and too defined to pass as feminine.

I hated myself for being so prurient. It really didn't matter to me if she was or was not what I thought she might be. Love is what mattered; love obliterates barriers, but not gender! I heard myself say in my head, and closed my eyes in disgust at the thought, and tried to summon up the willpower not to look down.

'Is your mum all right, darling?'

I sprang back, jaunty and smiling to find Gwen was holding my arm.

'Just got something in my eyes.' I blinked a few times for affect. 'That's better. Thank you Gwen, that was kind.' I tapped the back of her hand like a wrestler to make her let go. She didn't, well not straight away, not in fact until we'd entered the restaurant.

'What do you think?' said Max, whispering in my ear and nodding towards Gwen's retreating back.

'Lovely, darling, absolutely lovely.'

'Isn't she.'

At the table I had Ed on one side and Ray on the other. Max sat next to Ed and Gwen sat next to Ray. Max looked very handsome and animated. Thanks to his beard and maturity it was easier to compare his features with those of Ray and Ed, and to recognize the underlying Brook family characteristics. I had no doubt at that moment that he was Ray's, despite the Ed like beard.

There had been no chance to look at Gwen's legs as she had sat down, but I couldn't dismiss the idea that one glance would be enough to settle everything. I had to know, so while everyone was talking about the menu I turned towards Ed on my left while at the same time letting my napkin fall to the ground on my right, then, pretending to become suddenly aware of my loss, I turned back, ducked down below the table, grabbed the napkin and looked quickly across at her stockinged legs. Her knees were pressed chastely together and her feet were turned sideways, all very proper, but, more importantly, both knees and lower legs were softly rounded.

I was so relieved that I popped back up too fast and caught my forehead a crack on the table top. 'Aha!' I said, stifling a cry and waving the napkin. 'Got it!'

It was either the copious amount of wine I had drunk or my feeling of relief, but whatever it was I felt myself overwhelmed with good humour and motherly love. Marriage – such an adventure - and my boy. I chuckled on demand, laughed out loud at the men's jokes and was, in my estimation, projecting an image of the perfect mother-in-law to be. How could Gwen not warm to me and thank her lucky stars at having found not just a wonderful partner, but one who came from such a liberal and switched on family.

When Gwen left the table for the toilet, I decided to accompany her. There are few places as conducive to female intimacy.

'Your husband is such a laugh,' she said as we disappeared inside.

'It's Ed, he brings out the worst in him,' I said laughing.

Thanks to a quick turned around, I was checking my face in the mirror when she came out of the cubicle to wash her hands.

'I'm so pleased to have met you Angela.'

'Likewise, dear, likewise. And please – Angie.'

We embraced.

'Now that we're alone perhaps you'd like to have a good look at the ring?'

She offered her hand to me, and because I was so intent on the diamond I didn't really take particular note of the hand itself.

'That is amazing. Hope he hasn't bankrupted himself.'

'It was Max's idea. I told him I'd have been happy with a curtain ring.'

We laughed and returned still giggling to the table, much to the delight of Max, who had obviously been keenly aware how we would both get on.

Later that evening, back in Mayola Road before bed, I was removing my make-up and gently processing everything that had happened during the day. It had gone better than I'd expected. No, I could be more fulsome than that; it had gone brilliantly. And what a relief! Meeting the future in-laws is one of Life's dodgier details, and I was proud of Max, he had handled it well, in fact, couldn't be better. God, when I first met Dennis and Peggy, Ray's parents, I was dreading it. They lived in Lincoln, for god's sake, which was a place I'd never been to and would have found difficult to point to on a map. But we met, got on and have still got on, although Dennis has recently died and gone to some B&Q heaven in the sky. Ray, I think, has always found my mother and father difficult, not because they've ever been unpleasant. I think it's the classic provincial's sense of inferiority when confronting anyone born into what they assume is the affluent South East. You either join them and merge, or hate them and become even more provincial, peppering your speech with resurrected dialect words and adopting a sense of injured belligerence. Ray merged. He was happy to leave all of his Yellow Belly Lincolnshire nonsense to memories of fat laden sausage products and family reunions.

All of this was going through my mind when the man himself came in ready for bed.

'What do you make of *Gwen*, then?' He pronounced her name with an exaggerated quaver, accompanied with a little shake of his head.

'Meaning what? I thought you liked her?'

'Her or him?'

I snorted. 'I thought I'd told you that she *is* a woman. Darling, I checked her legs.'

'You maybe a woman, and I know it takes one to find one, but believe me, I've been watching women long enough to know that Gwen is a man.'

'God, you are so prejudiced.'

'Oh no, just observant. Remember, I've been following the transformation of Lauren Makin over the last few days. It's the little things. Oh, I'll give you her legs; they are unisex, but not her hands. They are male.'

You are at a disadvantage when arguing behind a thin mask of anti-wrinkle, night cream, especially with someone like Ray, who poo-poos anything applied to the skin that is more drastic than soap, so I just froze and ignored him.

What he said flushed all thoughts of sleep from my system; while he snored away I was left brooding from irritation and from the possibility that he was right. An hour or so later this evolved into an internal analysis of 'So what?', and my understanding of gender and my philosophical stance on freedom of choice. Like most people I had read next to nothing more taxing on the subjects than Sunday Magazine articles, or seen anything deeper than the occasional TV documentary, so my thoughts were essential vague and probably circular, for despite Ray's snores, my fruitless disquisition ended very quickly in sleep.

CHAPTER 23

ED

I was so fired up after the Brighton trip that I got up early and went straight into the loft to dig out my old photograph albums. This was not nostalgia, this was archaeology. They were in a ruinous state. Apart from a thick pelt of dust, generations of mice had mined their contents for bedding, and had shat and peed all over the pages in the process. The mouse shit didn't bother me, but the condition of the photographs did. Many of the early colour photos were so faded and tarnished, or had been so badly gnawed, that the images were unrecognizable. I wasn't emotionally bothered by their loss; all I wanted from the dead people who gawped back up at me from the pages was a clear look at their faces.

It was not some artistic flight of fancy that had sent me into the loft, and there was nothing in the albums that could be considered even vaguely aesthetically pleasing, but in the end I did find what I was looking for, which was plenty of snaps of my dad, Frank, and the rest of the Farrow family. Most of the early photographs in the album had been taken on box Brownies and were too small to be useful, but I couldn't help noticing that in nearly all of them my dad had a fag between his lips, which was fitting, since it was the fags that eventually gave him the cancer that killed him.

My sister Carla and my mother share the same blunt jaws and rather long noses, which I could see from the photographs, had also graced the gnarled old face of grannie Sturman. I was struck by how much the older Carla now looked like my mother at the same age, not that she would have thanked me for that observation. The two of them went at each other like ferrets in a box, and as soon as Carla was old enough she buggered off to Nottingham too work in the Player's cigarette factory.

You could say, but never to her face if you valued your manhood, that she was instrumental in the old man's death, because she not only produced his favourite Navy Cut fags, but used to bring him a couple of cartons every time she came by for a visit.

After a quick flick through it was only too clear that we were not a handsome lot, but we did have certain features in common, like good heads of dark hair, thick eyebrows and surprisingly high foreheads. It suggested intelligence, but as our history showed, it had never been more than a suggestion.

When I had pulled out enough pictures I descended to the kitchen to examine my hoard. I was desperate for a smoke, but just before I lit up I caught a whiff of my fingers. They were almost as grey as the mice that had soiled them.

Washed and smelling sweeter, I covered the kitchen table with old newspaper and dealt out the images like a game of Happy Families: Mr. Sod the Farmer, we'd got lots of them; Mr. Cod the Fisherman, likewise, and, looking at their faces, we'd also had plenty of doings with Mr. Bung the Brewer. There they all were grinning at me – my kinfolk: the darker, dock working Farrows, and a fair few of the lighter headed and more agricultural Sturmans. If it had been a game of Happy Families and you'd asked for Mr. Gormless, the Simpleton, both sides of the family would have competed for the trick. There was a complete lack of physical beauty and an overwhelming look of ordinariness, but this was not a game; I was not studying my family's features for fun; I was trying to see if any of them looked like Max.

When I'd seen him in the Brighton restaurant the change in his appearance had staggered me. Although Angie had told me long ago that he wasn't my son, I'd never totally believed her, because she was quite capable of a little subterfuge to ease the obvious complications. That was the nice explanation, the one if pressed she might have admitted too; alternatively, her denial could have been seen as a nicely calculated response to my total unsuitability as a father. But Max had looked like me.

It had always been a long shot, but in the end all I got from scanning my family's mug shots was a head ache. Max was a twenty-first century, urban living, geography teacher, which was a state of being totally beyond the understanding of my twentieth century, Bostonian family, most of whom had never advanced educationally beyond adding up and taking away. But Max had looked like me, especially with the beard.

I had a reasonable photo of him on my computer, so I scanned in a picture of myself at his age and brought the two images together. I went further; I photo-shopped them into a composite face. By god, the likeness was scary; the fit was uncanny. I felt suddenly quite sick. My boy Max? But he couldn't be. I stopped to think and stare. He could be. But how would I ever know without taking a paternity test, which I was never going to do? The only available line of enquiry therefore was Angie, and that was not going to be easy.

I let a week go by and did my best to forget the whole thing, because what did it matter? If I was his father, so what, how would that knowledge change anything for the better? There could never be a public admission of paternity without destroying everything that Angie and I had created between us. There would be an almighty melt down and I would end up spurned by my two best friends, just a sad old bastard living alone with his fish. I may not have been married to Angie, but I loved her, and couldn't bear the thought of living my life without her. If I didn't rock the boat and kept it as it was, it would mean that I could carry on as before and watch over Max from a distance, admire his career and his family, and perhaps help out occasionally with money or whatever it was that a special uncle-ish sort of bloke did, and still remain with Angie.

When my head cleared, I got this sudden rush of creativity, and went into the studio, stripped off the cover and went to work on the painting. I worked my rubbish head of Peter, the fisherman, into a passing likeness of my uncle Jo, who really was a fisherman. His naturally large jaw, low brow and look of bewilderment were perfect. Peter was now rock solid, and sound enough to build any church upon. It worked so well that I thought about using daft Uncle Walter's head for the next disciple; trouble was, he did look a bit loopy, but in the end, despite my hesitation, down he went too. It was only when his lazy eye and startled expression began to annoy me that I scrubbed him out and started again using a photograph of my mum's father, grandad Harry. Despite being a man who had spent most of his life toiling in the cabbage fields of Boston, he had just the sort of gormless face you'd expect to see on someone too dense to comprehend the wonder of the Lord's fishy benevolence.

The upshot of it all was that by the time I had finished grappling with the canvas I had overcome my block and had moved the whole damn thing on far enough to be confident of eventually nailing it. I was excited, and say what you like, the fish were bloody brilliant. I was in a much better frame of mind by the time I heard Ray calling from the shop, and more than happy that he had called.

'What do you think of that then?'

I continued to clean my brushes while watching his face. I wanted to see his initial reaction. He did not bluster, which was good. He did not make wriggly body movements to appease my disappointment, which was better. He kept his mouth shut and remained concentrated, inspecting the work like an artist, so I knew that I had been right; the day's work had been a break through.

'Those fucking marks, man – wow!' he said, turning to me. 'Put it there, mate. Brilliant.' We shook hands.

'Works doesn't it?'

'Fucking does. This is the one, Ed. This is what the whole fucking *Bucket Shop* thing is about. I'm so thrilled for you.' He was; I could tell when he hugged me that he meant it.

We celebrated by shooting off onto the marsh and walking down the Lea towards our favourite watering hole, The Anchor and Hope, not far Springfield Park. In celebration Ray did the honours and I sat outside amongst the fag ends with Geordie enjoying the sun and the river traffic.

'Cheers, Ed, to you and *The Fishermen.*'

I gave a snort and we chinked glasses.

'And you mate,' I said. 'If you hadn't badgered me like you did, then maybe – who knows?'

'What a day, eh?' he said, embarrassed by my compliment and stretching himself in the sun like a cat. 'Ah, something else before I forget, are you up for a bit of hide-and-seek on Thursday evening? I've fixed for Jungle Jim to start his 'wilding'.

'What, Toby?'

'Yeah. I thought we could all go to Epping Forest. There's plenty of room for us all in Izzie's car.'

'What's she got to do with it?'

'The car mate; difficult to do on the train at night, especially if we run on a bit. And in any case, she *is* the official recorder.'

He smiled as though what he had said was not only perfectly logical but would provoke nothing in me but acceptance. I frowned, since when had she gained that title? Maybe it was the way he just dropped the thing on me, or maybe it was because I was feeling good about myself, but I felt strong enough to openly challenge him.

'Look, I'm up for it, of course, but her? To be honest, mate, I don't like her. Actually, I don't trust her. She's using you.'

'Of course she's fucking using me, you plonker. The whole purpose of *the Shop* is for us *all* to use each other.'

A pair of mallard landed on the river and skied to a halt in front of us.

'Well, your funeral then if it all goes belly up.'

'No chance of that, mate. I'm on to her; she's just another self-publicist – typical Hackney type. Don't look so long faced, you bastard, drink up. You've cracked it.' He lifted up his glass and seeing his beaming face I did the same.

'Cheers.'

'Hey, and what about our Max, eh? What do you think of his paramour, quite the *lady* isn't she?'

There was an odd nasal tone to his voice when he said 'lady', which I noticed but ignored.

'Well, she's got a good man there. You must be proud.'

'Ok, ok, so you didn't notice. Nothing struck you as odd about her, then?'

'Like what?'

'You're meant to see things, Ed. Artists don't just look, do they? They see.' He stared hard at me, but I hadn't the faintest idea what he was on about.

'See what, for fuck's sake?'

'You and Angie see a woman, but I reckon Gwen is or was – a man.'

He sat back very pleased with himself and waited for my reply.

'You're bonkers, mate. That is one good looking woman. Bit angular for my taste, maybe, but then I'm not the one marrying her, am I? No, you're wrong. And don't come the 'artists don't look thing' with me, that's bollocks and you know it.'

'So you say Edward, so you say, but hands, mate, hands. Everything else is female, fine, but the hands aren't. They are men's hands. Fact. Remember Michelangelo's sculpture of *'Night'*, meant to be a nude woman but it is obvious he just stuck breasts on a male model? We're primed to pick out the incongruities. It's evolution's way of guiding us to the right.'

He didn't complete the sentence, he just nodded suggestively.

'Honestly, you talk some shit sometimes, mate. If that was the case, where do gays fit in? Is that evolution's way too, a sort of reward for those who aren't alpha males and can't find the right hole to it stick in?'

He laughed. 'That's got nothing to do with it.' He took out his phone. 'Look at her hands and tell me that is not a man.'

I glanced across at an image of Gwen and Max holding hands. 'That's just one picture,' I said evasively, bringing out my own phone and flicking through the pictures. 'There,' I enlarged a close up of Gwen holding up a glass of wine. '*That's* a woman's hand. Go on look. You tell me *that* isn't.'

'Um, not clear there, I'll give you that. But believe me – she is a man, or rather, was a man. Not that it matters, I'm not saying that. I'm just trying to get to the actual truth of the whole thing. He, she, can be anything they like, but I just need to know the facts as they are. I'll still welcome her into the family. God, yes, that's not a problem. No grandchildren, of course, unless they adopt, but that's not a problem either. Interesting eh?

When Ray had gone and I was walking back, I went over what he had said. I didn't remember at the time, but in retrospect, and after all of that talk about Michelangelo's nude, there had been one incident that had stuck in my mind when we'd all been together. It wasn't strictly a gender thing, but I did think, only in passing, that she had rather a strong looking back. It was nothing, just an observation. I was 'looking', as Ray would say. I like women with strong bodies, so it wasn't a criticism, but now that he had raised doubts as to what I had been looking at, I was less sure of what I had actually seen.

Angie had always joked about Max being gay, and had tried to explain her closeness to him in terms of his sexuality, but if he was *my* son, then that raised questions as to where his gayness had come from. Not that I minded. I didn't actually know all that much about being gay, apart from it being the result of something in the genes. The question now though was whose genes? My head was still filled with the grim faces of my Bostonian clan, and to imagine that any of them could have produced anyone remotely gay was hard to believe. To have liked flowers would have been as close as any of my forebears would have come to being gay, and in the Fens that would have been enough to get you drowned in the nearest swamp. So if it wasn't my side of the family, whose side was it: Ray's or Angie's?

The evening that had been decided upon for Toby's first aided introduction to the wild started off mild and calm. Toby, who lived in Leighton, had been told to come over to me and wait at the shop, and then we would both be picked up by Izzie and Ray and carted off to the woods. Everyone else had agreed to make their own way to the meeting point, which was the car park next to Chingford Plain, a short walk away from the Chingford station. The thought of sharing a car with 'art-mouth' was daunting; an hour or so of her twaddle wasn't something I was looking forward to, but as impecunious buggers can't be choosers, and doing an enormous never ending favour for a friend, I would just have to bite my lip and choke slowly on my bile.

Toby and I sat side by side supping tea amongst the fish tanks; it was the second occasion that we had actually spent time alone together. Despite an initial wide-eyed response to being given free access to the shop, he was hard going. Mehmet's dead haddock had been easier to commune with, but at least he never mentioned art. Close up he was also much frailer than I'd realized; weedy rather than willowy, as though his body had grown tall in a desperate struggle for sunlight. As a consequence it had left him with narrow almost feminine shoulders. He was what would have been called in the days when people grew their own veg: a bean pole, although that suggests a stiffer backbone than was apparent. But what he lacked in physical robustness he made up for in keen naiveté, and I soon discovered that what he understood about the world stemmed largely from the meagre doings of those with whom he communicated on social media.

Epping Forest, the venue for our evening's fun, *is* a forest, but despite its origins, it is not the elemental wild wood of urban man's imagination; it has man made paths and tracks, and is divided in various places by busy roads. One of the advantages of going to Epping was that if Toby funked it, and gave it all up as a bad job, he had only to follow one of these roads and it would lead him out of the trees to civilization. That's not to belittle the wood; it is tricky, and very easy to get lost in. There are twists and turns, and ancient dips and dells that are very confusing, and for someone brought up on the one dimensional world of the electronic media their complexity is almost unfathomable, and I soon realized that his *Bucket Shop* dream had rather whimsical foundations.

This was to be the first of a few planned introductions to this other world. Ray had said that our night time visit was to be similar to what Guides and Scouts call 'a wide game'. Toby was going to be dropped off somewhere in the wood and then told to make his way back undetected through the trees to where a base camp would be set up. It would be considered a success if he got through undetected and an outstanding victory if he was able to sneak into the centre of the camp and capture a specially set up flag on a pole. The whole thing was meant to last for no more than a couple of hours; after which we would all celebrate with a pint in a nearby pub.

'Big backpack, that?' I said, clutching at straws. 'You'll only be gone a couple of hours.'

'Few basics; you know: waterproof matches, bottle of water, few biscuits and an apple. Oh - and a knife.'

'You aiming to kill a muntjac or something?' I said, humorously. He looked blank.

'If it was desperate, I reckon I could probably knock one out of a tree with a stone; I was quite good at cricket?'

'They're not squirrels, Toby; they're a sort of deer with weird vampire teeth. But if you are thinking of killing one, you'd better keep your eyes open for the Rangers.'

'I've been watching a bloke on YouTube gutting a deer. I think I've more or less got the hang of it.'

I looked at the earnest face that peeped out at me from his gingery beard. He meant it. He really believed that he would be playing Robin Hood and consulting YouTube when he needed help.'

'I should stick to actual squirrels,' I said, trying to bring his ambitions down to something almost manageable.

'This American bloke on YouTube barbeques them. Puts a stick up their arse and turns them on a spit.'

'Let's have a look at the knife.'

What came out of his backpack was an enormous, nine-inch, Bowie knife with an antler handle.

'Bloody hell, Toby, that's a fucking Zombie killer!'

He laughed, unsheathed it and made a few balletic passes in the air before handing it to me. 'Protection against those vampires.'

It was too heavy to be useful, but the edge of the blade felt keen to the touch and would have sliced a Zombie in half.

'Have you ever been on a wide game?'

'No, first time, this.'

I handed it back. 'You might think of leaving this behind in the car.'

CHAPTER 24

GEORDIE

My keepers, my human custodians, call them what you will, have voices ill-adapted to conveying depths of emotion. When Ray is angry, for instance, and lashes out at me, his voice comes from the back of his throat with all the force of a startled blackbird. There's no edge. It's totally one dimensional. He might still chase me around the room while he's cursing, but his voice conveys no real menace, not when compared to the deep growl that wells up from an angry dog's throat. Angie's no better. She once tried to snatch a chicken bone from my mouth, never a wise thing to do, but what came out of her mouth was just a lot of shrill ape babble.

'Leave it, leave it, you silly dog, it'll kill you!'

My lips quivered and I was close to a second degree snarl, but I restrained myself. If she wanted to discuss property rights then I would teach her how to approach the subject from a dog's point of view, so I growled to let her know that when I made that particular noise, she'd be wise to let me be. The first lesson that puppies learn at the teat is what is mine is mine. But she didn't go: 'Of course, sorry Geordie, I apologize for my rudeness. Now I understand.' No, she gave me such a swift backhander that I almost choked on the damned bone.

How on earth do you get through to them that when a dog means business, it will let you know? You will be warned, so more fool you if you ignore the signs and hang around to argue the toss. It couldn't be simpler: listen to the tone of our voice and register the physical manifestations of our ire, then you'll know when the time has come for you to back off and yield the ground to the better dog. Does it work? No, it's as though they're deaf, dumb and daft; right over their heads, no comprehension whatsoever.

This is by way of an introduction to a subject that has long concerned me in my role as leashed guardian of their wellbeing, and by that I mean their respective hearths and homes. Both Ray and Ed are more than capable of looking after themselves when they get into aggressive situations with other apes, and Ray keeps the boundaries of his domestic space well patrolled. Cats are chased off, the bigger birds put to flight and all minor creatures watched for signs of delinquency. Ed, on the other hand, is hopeless at keeping his territory safe, especially from what they call rats, and we generally call *krass*; pronounced with a long, throat rolling r. No matter how many of these little grey bastards that I kill over the year, there's always more to fill the void. Patrolling their houses and gardens is a full time job. It takes a lot of wee to mark everything adequately. But *krass* are real chancers; you could wet every single inch of the borders until you were dehydrated and they wouldn't give your piss a second sniff, because they are so single-minded. Any source of food attracts them. In Ed's case, of course, its fish and fish food that gets them going, but he never puts enough energy into keeping all of the holes blocked up, so as far as they are concerned his shop is yet another of Walthamstow's fast food outlets. If Ed was better organized, he would box up everything that's edible and seal it solid, but he doesn't. He forgets, and into that memory lapse pops the nearest *krass*.

The night of our big expedition I'd been left at Ed's, and so when Toby came over and they were talking, I decided to go on my rounds, starting with the outer edges of the shop and then progressing to the spaces underneath the fish tanks, which are the favourite haunts of another of my *bêtes noires*: the nasty little *grits*, or mice. As far as I'm concerned *grits* are just *krass* without the attitude. If I catch one in the open they provide a bit of sport, but in reality they are too small and are essentially cat fodder, and therefore beneath contempt. I began my border patrol while at the same time keeping an ear out for what was going on between Ed and longshanks.

In the light of what I have been saying, one thing was obvious from the start: there was no real animosity between them. The smell was all wrong for that and their voices were quite low, which meant that I could safely ignore most of what they were doing. All this changed the moment that Ray arrived with Izzie.

A good, healthy bitch has a scent that engages you immediately. A swift nose around the arse and she cancels out every other emotion, and if she is in season then – wow! She blows your mind. You can't step outside the door without being consumed by two overriding wishes – find and mate. Sadly, thanks to my earlier cut, I don't really lose it in quite the same way as my entire friends, but I am moved enough to seek out the source of this olfactory loveliness.

You will recall *Narrick*, the Jack Russell we met earlier? Well, he was a bugger for the bitches. He lives in the same sort of area as I do, but maybe closer to the park.

According to him, the furthest he's gone off in search of 'love' has been Stamford Hill, which is some hike. I know Jack Russells have a tendency to exaggerate, but in my experience he's not one of those, so I have no reason to doubt him. Scent can do funny things to dogs.

Ray was sitting next to Izzie in the front of the car, and when he opened the back door to let us in, a much more familiar smell flooded out, which was odd, since Angie was nowhere to be seen.

'This is it, Toby, my old son. All ready?'

'Ready to rock 'n' roll, Ray. Can't wait.'

As we arrived and crunched over the gravel carpark, I saw a small cluster of familiar faces. I couldn't wait to get out. At this time of the year the day light lingers and the great field in front of the forest was bathed in a warm, dying light, and all of the trees fringing its sides were bathed in gold. As soon as the door was open I was off meeting and greeting. Thanks to a lot of knees in the chest and head slapping as a pup, I'd learned early that apes do not like us trying to lick their chops, so I had confined my welcoming to the usual pleasantries of tail wagging and arse wiggling, but despite my best attempts at being matey, I was rebuffed more times than I was petted.

'Right, welcome everyone to Toby's *'Bucket Shop'* sleep-over!' said Ray, hooting wildly.

Who knows what Ray said next, but it caused every ape to laugh or hoot in unison. When they get like this it's always best to keep well into the background, so I slunk off, which proved fortuitous, for beyond us, somewhere in the huge meadow, I caught a niff of something very special. It appeared to be arising out the distant gilded scrub. It was - cow! My nostrils went into overdrive. Um, the night promised riches. To anoint oneself in fox poo can be almost an erotic experience, but a roll in fresh cow slip is the acme of serendipitous scent acquisition, and a rare find so close to a city. I raised my head and relished the air's invisible, dancing odours.

'Geordie, come on!'

Like a brainless chicken, I instantly forgot what I was doing and scampered off in the direction of Ray's voice. Oh! It's so depressing when I respond as quickly as that. I feel abject. I know why: it's the hours and hours of coercion I underwent in puppyhood. All those treats I happily scoffed were not doled out as gifts; they were bribes and testaments to my sickening greed. In my alacrity they saw success and the creation of a safe and biddable beast; I saw oppression, servitude and a dog with no will of its own. But run I did, bottling my fleeting moment of contempt and storing the direction of the hidden cattle for later examination when darkness fell. And as that wise old lab I met in Millfields all those years ago might well have said: what the hell, you are running free, and it is a night out in the wild with food to follow.

Where Ray was heading turned out to be a small gravelly knoll in the middle of a clearing of widely spaced trees, interspersed with straggly holly bushes.

'Home base,' he said, addressing the others from the crown of the hillock, 'and this is the flag that Mr. Slight, here, must capture.' A limp piece of cloth daubed in red paint hung from the flag pole. He then turned to Toby, dinked his head in the flag's direction and shouted, 'We'll give you a good start and then we shall be after you like the hounds of Hell. Go Toby, go! Vanish!'

Toby did just that. His long legs went into overdrive and he was off through the trees and out of sight in no time at all accompanied by more excited hooting from those he'd left behind. Now there's nothing I like more than a good chase, and so I trotted along behind him.

The paths in the forest were so well trodden that a puppy could have traced them back to where we had started, so I just let him lead me on. When we were well out of sight of the others he broke away from the main track and disappeared noisily into the bracken and snatching curls of hidden brambles. It was all right for him with his long legs; he skipped over the obstacles with ease, but I found this bit hard going. Suddenly he stopped and turned to me.

'Fuck off Geordie! Go on, go back.'

I stopped in my tracks. Charming! I eyed him warily, but said nothing. I just stood stock still until he had set off again, and then followed; you always need to test their resolve.

He stopped suddenly and snatched something up from the ground. When he turned towards me he was brandishing a small branch.

'Go on clear off!'

'So weapons is it?' I stopped, took up a defensive position and gave him my baleful eye.

'Go back, go on. Clear off!'

Timing is everything when it comes to stand offs, but when it comes to weapons, a stick in the hand beats a baleful eye every time. I turned and skedaddled just as the stick came crashing down in front of me.

'Thanks for nothing,' I said to myself, stopping only once I was well out of his reach. I tracked his career through the bushes until the noise faded away to nothing. By now it was dark, and the advent of night had brought with it a whole host of wonderful, sharpened aromas. I was in no hurry to return to the others. I knew where they were, and I could hear plenty of movement in the surrounding trees as they spread out to try and forestall Toby's return. All I had to do now was to keep well out of their way and enjoy it. If Toby was even slightly able he should be able to outwit Ray's noisy mob, and if he hunkered down in the bushes right beside them, the apes with their pitiful senses would inevitably miss him. I cocked my leg against a particularly musky trunk and pissed.

'Free, free, free at last. The open road and a scent to guide me,' I said, trotting off in the direction of the cows.

On a warm, still night scent keeps low to the ground and it wasn't long before I found the beasts bedded down for the night in a lose group on the side of a gently sloping hill. The fresh piss and the strong flavours of their recent shit made my head spin; they were intoxicating, and the closer I got the more I was able to tease out the sweeter undertones of their breath.

I'm small; they are huge, and much bulkier than even the biggest of the apes. I'm quicker and sharper, but they are more belligerent and surprisingly agile. The sensible thing to do when approaching horned beasts is to be friendly; it is also the polite way of behaving, a fact understood by most animals but, sadly, not by all apes. There is a proper way to behave in all situations, and there are signs to exhibit that declare your intentions. In the half-light it was important not to appear threatening, especially as there could have been a bull hidden somewhere, so I approached openly.

'To you and yours,' I said, wagging my tail furiously to the left.

'Likewise,' said one of the cows, whose horns were even longer than I was.

'Nice night.'

'More or less as it usually is,' she said. 'You running wild or just out for the night?'

'No, out with some apes. Over there doing ape things,' I said, nodding towards the trees.

'We heard them hoot,' she added, ruminating slowly.

'Mind if I come a bit closer and sample your wonderful offerings?'

'Connoisseur eh?'

I stepped into the circle. 'I like to think so.'

'Nice to be appreciated.'

The intensity of the smell was mind blowing and full of delicious, herby notes. Bliss! But where to first? The choice was overwhelming; it was all good, so in the end I just went down where I was. Ah! Heaven! I was born to smell so good.'

Suitably anointed, I backed off, and left them to their ruminations. I didn't just retrace my steps, I wanted to enjoy every moment of my temporary freedom, so I bent towards a small stream and quenched my thirst. As there was a good moon and the going was easy, I was in no hurry, and so I trotted back in a wide circle to where I had left Ray and the gang.

The closer I got, the more I remembered how Ray had been in the car. Agitated, sexually agitated to be more specific. The other woman was equally excited, that was obvious. There was an expectation in the air, such as I had met with more often when Angie and Ed were together. Between Reg and Angie these smells arose less often.

My only interest in the matter was self-preservation. I knew only too well that coming between any creatures intent upon mating was bad news. You only did that if you wanted to be the one doing the humping, and were prepared to battle for the favour. My curiosity was defensive. I did not want to provoke any ructions from either of them; lust can generate all sorts of ancillary emotions, not all of them good, and Reg was inclined to hit out if annoyed.

The thing was, he was top dog, as it were. Whom he humped was nobody's business but his own. In the hierarchy of humping, Ed was not the alpha male, although he was the one doing most of the humping. This new woman was just another member of the pack, not a close member, but a member nevertheless, and as such I needed my wits about me.

As I got closer, I started to hear shouting, not all from one place, but spread around in an arc. I stopped and listened. It was a 'where are you call', directed, I guessed towards wherever Toby was hiding. That amused me. He had obviously outwitted them. Whatever next? I was half inclined to search him out myself, just for fun. The memory of his scent and his last position were fixed in my head, so it wouldn't be that difficult. But – what seems straight forward to us is rarely how a situation is viewed by apes, so I ignored the thought and trotted off to where I guessed Ray to be.

You always assume that your arrival amongst friends will be greeted with approval, lots of wriggling, sniffing and a bit of licking if you are lucky; apes may lack the protocol, but they make up for it with a mixture of back and head scuffling and the sort of garbled noises they reserve for children.

'Bloody hell, Geordie – you evil hound, where have you been, and what have you been rolling in? Go away, you nasty creature. Oh god, Ed, look at the bastard.'

I wriggled my arse like a maniac, but hung back just in case Ray kicked out.

'I'm not having him on my lap.'

The ruckus brought the car woman to investigate. She screamed out loud.

'Not in my car! Ray – do something or you all walk home.'

Ray stood mute before her, arms raised in supplication, the equivalent of skulking off with his tail between his legs. I didn't stay around to argue, and as soon as she buggered off to the other side of the clearing I turned to go, but got nowhere. I ran straight into another woman and the man who had been tied to a tree. They took one look at me and began laughing. Ray was not amused. I squirmed abjectly courting their sympathy, but every time I came near they skipped away hooting. I was totally confused.

'Right, right everyone, this is what we'll do,' said Ray flapping his arms. 'OK, OK then. Wherever Toby is he's not heading this way. And as he knows the time limit, he'll just have to stay where he is and make his own way back. '

'We can't just leave him, he might have hurt himself. He might be lying out there now unconscious,' said Justine.

'He's not, he's holed up somewhere, and if you like I'll pop off and find him for you.' That was what I was trying to tell them, but as usual, my input was ignored.

'Ed thinks he planned it this way.'

'His pack was full of survival stuff. I reckon he's here for the night,' said Ed, shrugging his shoulders. 'He's got a phone, so if he is in trouble he can always call.'

'Perhaps we should phone him,' said the boyish woman.

'No, no, no,' said Ed, 'let the bugger stew. He wants wild, he's got it. We're not the Samaritans.'

'Clean that bloody dog!' said a voice from the dark.

'I will Izzie, I will. There's a small stream back behind us. I'll take Geordie there and clean him up. The rest of you can go home if you like. Ed's right. If this is the way he wanted it, then we've done what he wanted, so – actually - another success.'

'If he's not dead,' said the boyish one. 'No only joking.'

I was half inclined to double back and find him, but just as I'd decided to do a bunk, Ray grabbed my collar.

'You come with me.'

Chapter Twenty-Five - Ray

When Toby hopped across the clearing and disappeared into the enveloping darkness of the surrounding trees, followed at a discrete distance by Geordie, I found myself smiling. It felt good to have sent yet another member of *the Shop* in pursuit of their deepest desires.

'Job well done people.'

'What do we do now?' said Peter, who since his elevation upon the cross had become remarkably forth coming and much easier to converse with. 'Do we just hang about and wait?'

'He's got to get the flag, remember,' said Lauren. 'We think we should spread out and be prepared.'

I was about to look beyond her to see who the 'we' was when I remembered that she was speaking for her brother too.

'Spot on, yes. Spread out everybody so that he can't flank us. Ed will you take the left flank? We'll give him a bit longer and then drift into the wood and try to flush him out. If you've brought any hot drinks now would be a good time to sup them.'

'How about you, Izzie, fancy a coffee?'

Now that she was out of the car, and had removed her coat, I could see that she was dressed totally in black: black trousers, black top and a black scarf tying back her hair.

'You have unleashed the hounds, Raymond, now let them go, let them hunt down our miserable, sneaking little nonentity, but not too soon,' she said, pursing her lips.

'Meaning?'

'Meaning, my darling, that the night is warm, the grass dry and I fancy more than a shot of caffeine. I want to explore the revolutions of the earth.'

Her eyes smouldered, she stepped forward and I braced myself for what was to happen next, but instead of sinking into each other's arms, she let out a startled yelp and sank into the ground. I stepped back horrified.

'Don't just stand there gawking, man, give me a hand.'

'It's a pot hole, darling; these glacial moraines are full of them,' I said leaning towards her with both arms.

'Forget the bloody geography Raymondo. Get me out!'

I yanked her onto the knoll, but instead of breaking off she pressed herself further into my arms.

'Listen to me, you foolish man. I'm on fire. My whole body aches for love, for contact with the earth and with you. Can't you smell the soil?' She breathed in deeply. 'The air is fecund. Pan is calling his people. Come, come, take my hand, my darling and let us disappear into the trees and fuck.'

As I took her hand I looked around. Ed had disappeared into the darkness and the others had already spread out and were too far away to have heard anything.

We ran together slightly back the way we had come and then on a hunch I turned left further into the trees until I came to a great thicket of highly aromatic bracken.

'Follow me darling. We'll build a nest in here.'

The fronds were shoulder high and parted with difficulty, but our lust was stronger than their simple fecundity, and although we didn't venture far into them I was sure we were far enough away from the track to be totally invisible.

'Watching your shoulders as you forced your will upon the fronds was like watching the pulse of nature; you fought, you pushed and you tore. You were the very essence of desire. Now my darling, you must treat me like you treated the bracken. Bend me, take me, violate me, and do it hard upon the crushed stalks of the ferns so that my body is fused with the spirit of Gaia. Come!'

As I grappled with her clothing, she grabbed my shirt and simply ripped it apart sending the buttons flying off into the undergrowth. I tried to see where they fell, but it was hopeless.

I took the waistband of her knickers in two hands and fell to my knees drawing the knickers down with me. With a slight kick of her toes she stepped free.

'I am naked before the world,' she said.

I still had one trainer stuck in the cuff of my jeans, and was feverishly trying to pull it out.

'And you, my stag, my Minotaur, my Pan. Off with those pants.'

'My foot's stuck!' I said, steadying myself as best I could.

She went back to her clothes, rummaged in her bag and came back towards me brandishing an open Stanley knife.

'Oh my god! No, no, Izzie, how will I explain the trousers?'

She made a sound that verged on laughter and came up close enough for me to cling on to her.

'You and I Ray are bound only by the customs of the Gods.'

Her eyes smoked, her lips parted and she grabbed my pants and began sawing at the waistband. I yelped and staggered back, Stanley knives are razor sharp, but she clung on tightly, slashing wildly at the elastic until with a final sharp yank the pants gave up the struggle and my loins were free save for two ragged cloth bands still held up around my thighs. I stared wide-eyed at the knife hovering inches from my shrinking penis and then into her gurning face as she pulled the two bands together, slashed them apart, yanked them free and thrust them into the air as triumphantly as a matador who had been awarded a dead bull's ears. I looked down fearfully at my trouser leg and its trapped shoe.

'Details, my darling, details,' she said, following my eyes. 'I am so hot Raymond that I am going to melt your cock.'

With that she sank to the ground, grabbed my dick and began jerking it up and down like a sink plunger. It was engaging but it wasn't passionate, this was mechanical engineering. She wanted me fully primed and operational.

I was now beside myself. Getting a hard on was not the problem, nor were my trousers, it was the speed. Despite a growing tenderness caused by the friction, I felt my climax mounting, and as the last thing I wanted was for it all to be over too quickly, I wriggled myself free and slid my mouth down her stomach, intent only on her satisfaction.

'Oh the moon on your skin!' I said between kisses. 'In the dark all I can see are flashes of white skin appearing and disappearing like semaphore: *England expects*.'

'I expect, Raymond, just suck and leave the travelogue for later.'

I was shattered when we'd finished, but euphoric, despite having a penis that felt it had been wrung like the neck of a chicken. My arse radiated heat from her continual slapping and nipping. Whoever Izzie truly was, she suited her nickname; she was capricious and governed by her own rules. She was so single minded and driven that she scared me. I was simply a means to that end and ordered about as if I had no will, which in fact had been true. What she wanted, I wanted. I simply followed her goading.

You don't engage in chit chat after such love making. We stood up purged of thought and gawped at the dark mass of our trampled ferny bed as if we had been witnesses to a massacre, and were eager to be gone. Only once we had regained the beaten clay path did we feel able to speak.

'Your hounds hunt the bush around us; the long boy quivers somewhere in his hidey-hole, and you have fired your seed into my firmament with all the energy of an exploding star,' she said, her eyes moving erratically across my face like a sensor.

I had rather liked hearing myself described in such cosmic terms and had held myself upright and tall right up until the moment she reached the bit about exploding, then my face crumpled as the enormity of my recklessness struck home.

'God! I came inside her. Oh my god, what if?'

I stared. Her face seemed to magnify so that I could read even the slightest movements of the muscles. I needn't have worried. I was transparent. She saw it all and read it all.

'I love your generosity, my darling. But have no fear; your blessed seed will not grow. You have ploughed a barren field, I am no longer fertile.' The laugh that followed was light, almost carefree. 'Now my creativity is centred only on what will enhance the here and now; in other words, my darling – you. Now, more than any other time, you must do your thing. I've seen your power and the creativity of your soul. You must be the next to move. That silly girl is masquerading happily as her brother. The long boy has gone to ground, Christ has risen, Ed is engaged and our estate agent is beginning to blossom. There are no excuses. Now, Raymond, now.'

Her hand reached forward and gripped my bollocks firmly. It was a gesture of support but carried with it a hint of menace. I nodded winsomely and was released.

Although the journey home was not long, having a sore arse made sitting in the car uncomfortable. I was in any case restless; all that Izzie had said kept bubbling up and would not leave me. She was right, of course. The whole point of the *'Bucket Shop'* had been to enable me to achieve my nagging desire for an end of term certainty. To anyone other than me my whole enterprise must have looked odd to say the least. Who in their right mind would want to find the place where their life would end? And who could possibly know that? As the ineffable Doris Day had once said: *'the future's not ours to see'*. And yet I felt I would; not point specific as yet, but I did believe that I would somehow know where it was to be once I had found it: death at first sight. She was right. As long as the others got on with their wishes, and did what we had suggested that they should do, I was more or less free to go walkabout somewhere east of the Lea, but where?

The river was the starting point, and as yet I hadn't quite conceived where the best route should be. I had poured over maps and tried to feel the names of places through my fingertips. Rightly or wrongly, I had passed over all the land encompassed by a line connecting Chelmsford, Braintree and Colchester with the sea. The hinterland as far as Sudbury and Haverhill had produced nothing, no tingling in the fingers and no sudden vison in my head, assuming that this is how I would know where my destination was going to be. I thought about dousing the map with a ring dangling on a thread of cotton, but so far had resisted the urge, feeling that this should be kept until I had discovered the area in which my final moments would come, and then I would use it as target refinement.

'You all right, mate?' said Ed, breaking into my reverie and seeing me squirm yet again.

I turned around smiling. 'All this walking's made my hams a bit tender. You ok at the back there with the hound?'

'Sure, he's fine. What about Toby, then? Are you going to phone him, tell him we've gone?'

'Could do, yeah, good idea, just to make sure. Too late to give him a lift, but that's his problem.' I took out my phone. 'Ah, looks like our Toby has left me a message. '*All well, made camp and bedding down for the night. Will keep in touch.*' That's ok then,' I said, putting the phone away.

Once Ed had been dropped off and we were alone, Izzie slowed down and eventually pulled in and stopped on the quiet street behind Clapton Pond. It seemed very strange to be there so late in the evening, especially as the street lights reflecting upon the water gave our shady parking place an almost romantic aura, as if the top of Murder Mile was somewhere other than Hackney, somewhere more rural, or that we were in some era other than the present.

'I would like to make love to you in the car, my precious, but,' she added, casting her eyes maliciously towards Geordie, and perhaps sensing my hesitation, 'much as my mind wants to be savaged, my body doesn't. You were such a beast in the woods that I'm not sure it would survive your wild passion.' Her eyes twinkled in the street lights. 'You have set a flame under my life, Raymond. What I took for normal now seems mundane; what I took for delight now seems hollow. I am so inspired by all that you have set in motion in the lives of these crazy people that I believe I too am being drawn to the verge of greatness. And that is entirely down to you.'

She pulled against the strap of her safety belt, leant across and began hungrily chewing my face with her lips, leaving it wet and flushed. My cock was too sore to be immediately overwhelmed by the excitement, but I felt myself beginning to engorge and my hesitancy diminish.

'It's you, Izzie, it's you! You are a magician,' I said, struggling to find the release button to my own safety belt.

She pulled away, laid her palms gently on my chest and held me back. 'I am so easily swayed by you, darling. My resolution falters when your body is so close.'

'Yes, yes, we must be strong, darling,' I said with relief, letting the car belt pull me upright. I really did not want to get into a clinch in the car. 'I will leave you *now*, when my desire is strong, then I can take my memories home whole and unsullied.'

She adjusted the strap across her chest. 'Go, my love, go, before you overwhelm me. And take - the creature.'

As I opened the door Geordie leapt between us and landed in my lap. 'Ah!' I said, gripping my balls in pain.

'Be gone!' she said.

Whether she meant me or the dog I wasn't sure, so I quickly followed him out, and then, before I had had time to close the door, she was off like a rocket, almost removing my arm in the process.

'By-,' I said. My voice died before I had finished the word.

Standing alone in the road in the shadow of the tall buildings that fringed the street no longer felt romantic; the silence and the isolation now seemed malevolent. It was certainly not the place to hang about. But before I could walk away easily I needed to adjust my foreskin which in all of the excitement had got itself painful inverted. Standing in the dark pulling at my penis just added to my sense of foreboding. Behind the blank windows I imagined a thousand peeping eyes and surreptitious calls to the police. In the end, I just walked off awkwardly down Millfields Road with Geordie in tow.

Angie was still away on a gig interpreting a show that her friends had taken to the Hull Truck Theatre, so the house was quiet, and the fridge was more or less empty. She'd been away since Wednesday and what with one thing and another, I'd sort of forgotten to do any real shopping. But there was a beer, so I sat down with that and let my head skip around the events of the evening.

All bar one of the important decisions in my life seem to have been made without any apparent thought. Marriage to Angie was the obvious exception. You could have said that I had a choice, but I didn't. I might have fancied myself as a free spirit, but I wasn't. Leaving her to carry the can just wasn't part of my moral upbringing, and besides, I loved her, and an imaginary baby was always at the back of my mind as the natural outcome of that love, just not quite so soon after graduating.

I responded to all of Izzie's ideas in much the same way. I'd been excited by them and turned on by her bullying, but I hadn't made up my mind, not completely. I was in intellectual neutral and happy to be pushed around by her, which essentially meant I was mentally all fluffed up. I had no will, especially after her outrageous inflation of my ego. The life of a cartographer leaves little room for heroics, spiteful revenge, perhaps, but not heroics. Back in the wood I had stood tall on legs of oak, and even now, alone in the bathroom with just a bottle of beer for company there was still a vestige of the heroic in my demeanour as I inspected my buttocks for signs of Izzie's handiwork.

My decision to actually grab Time by the forelock and do what she said came into my head fully formed: 'Go East and search', which wasn't exactly site specific, but for all of its oracular vagueness, it confirmed my initial instinctive urge that my destiny lay in that direction, and once I lodged that in my head my brain started to fire. Cartographers may not be heroic but we are tenacious. I had something to work on, and so my thinking became thinking-thinking and I began working on the how and where. The most obvious thing was that Izzie should be my means: she had a car and she was up for it. That was transport organized. Another of a map maker's qualities is truth to facts. You can't alter physical geography; what's there in front of you must go down on the map. How you illustrate that fact is the only area that allows a smidgen of artistic interpretation, hence my deft inclusion of my name into the hatching of the Isle of Arran's coast line.

With my brain freewheeling around the whole enterprise, and in the same spirit of intellectual honesty, I also questioned whether the purity of my search had been compromised by the availability of such energetic sex, because prior to Izzie's eruption into my life, I had always assumed that at my age I would come like the full moon, only once a month, and my lunar cycle coupling with Angie had seemed more or less how I imagined antique sex to be. The only single male I knew of a similar age to me was Ed, and on the rare occasions that he had had some sort of female hook-up it had all floundered so quickly that it had made my intermittent sex with Angie appear at lot better than no sex at all. When she and I had discussed his lack of partners, she always dismissed his enforced celibacy, saying that it didn't matter because like all artists he put his sexual energies into his work. Complete nonsense of course; artists are renowned for their prolific sex life and their compulsion to screw anyone and anything. He keeps sane because his sexual energies are dampened down by being constantly in the company of fish, probably the least obviously erotic creatures you could imagine. People mate with other mammals, but I've never heard of any one mating with a fish, or being turned on by the lustful antics of their bowl of goldfish. I think that if it wasn't for his friendship with Angie, Ed wouldn't have any real contact with women at all, and she's less a woman woman and more a sister.

When I phoned Izzie, I put on a husky voice, but it was as though she already knew what the call was about, for as soon as I'd whispered: 'Let the search begin', she let out a shriek of wild laughter.

'Oh my angel, my love, perfect, perfect. Early tomorrow then my darling we leave for the darkest corners of Essex – with a picnic and an overnight bag.'

CHAPTER 26

ED

'Oh!' said Angie, stepping back and pretending to recoil from the force of my passion. 'That was a remarkably fulsome *welcome home*, darling.'

In her rolling eyes and mock surprise I saw again how she had looked when we had held each other for the first time after my return to London all those years ago. It had been the first time I'd really smiled since Megan had fucked off.

We'd been lovers before we were both married. The three of us, Angie, Ray and me had lived our *'Jules et Jim'* life; nothing was too serious, nothing fixed and nothing withheld. There were no lines drawn around us. We weren't just young; Ray and I were fucking art students, so what did society's mores mean to us? We were *Heedless in Wonderland*, three kindred souls wondering raucously together along the aisles to Life like children heading to the sweeties in Woolworth's *'Pick and Mix'* counter: a bit of this, a bit of that and all mixed together in one big bag that cost next to nothing; or so we thought until Angie fell pregnant. That was the start of the great debate: was it him or was it me, who fathered Max? Ray certainly picked up the tab, and, unprotestingly, carried Angie into marriage and domestic bliss. My bill was delayed; it came later when my marriage didn't live up to the joys I had known as a student, and when my provincial soul got the better of me and I returned to the seedbeds of my forebears amongst the skull domed cabbages of the Fens.

After the divorce both Ray and Angie had encouraged me to head south and join them in Hackney, which from the flat fields of Boston seemed to glow on the horizon like the distant lights of Sodom. When I came back, Angie had been the first to call round to my grotty little studio in Finsbury Park to welcome me, and it was when I saw her smile and felt her in my arms again, that all of the intervening years of our separation fell away. The lost time and space became irrelevant.

It sounds implausible, but I knew straight away that nothing had changed, that our love had survived our separation, and that despite the heartache of being married to my lifelong friend, our situation was bearable and there was still room in our lives for each other.

And here she was in my arms again, in another grotty studio, in another equally scruffy part of London. She touched my face briefly with both hands, and I pulled her close and whispered into her ear.

'It is done, sweetie. The picture's done.'

She pulled away. 'Really?'

I cocked my head towards the studio.

'Oh my god! Show me.'

This time I had no reservations when I took off the cover, and although I wanted her to like it, it didn't matter anymore. I knew what it was, and I knew it was good.

At first I had got too caught up in the art history and biblical side of the story, which was a mistake. When you range history and renown against your own feeble attempts at creativity you may as well give up there and then. The past weighs upon the soul. So I got shot of the lot and decided to do nothing more than paint the fish and fishermen who caught them. I went down to Hastings and sketched the fishing boats, the fishermen and the tall black sheds where they stowed their gear. It worked a treat, after all I was not a believer and I was not illustrating the Bible.

'Sweetheart.'

I turned to look at her as soon as she spoke. There were tears streaming down her cheeks.

'It's all in there. All I've believed in and seen in you is there. I'm overwhelmed.'

'Fucking good isn't it,' I said, smirking, but touched by her tears. 'And if I'm honest – down to Raymondo and his fucking *Bucket Shop*.'

She smiled. 'Come here.' She held me and kissed me. 'I know what it took, darling.'

'Yeah, well, all that. But it was his prodding that got me going. He's always known what buttons to press, the bastard,' I said, smiling at the thought.

'So where is the old bugger, then?'

'Doing his own thing, *at last*.'

We went back out again to the kitchen.

'Oh god, what does that mean? He gets so carried away.'

'The creature of the night picked him up and whisked him away.'

'Izzie? Where?'

'Essex, I think.'

We both looked at each other trying to summon a good reason for going to Essex.

'I remember him saying something about her helping him.'

'Do you think he's all right,' she said.

'You mean in the head?'

161

'No – with her, stupid. She's not exactly on the same planet, is she? God knows what goes on in her head.'

'Look, sweetheart, the whole idea of trying to find the place where you are doomed to die is fucking bonkers, yeah? So she fits in perfectly. She's no more odd than he is, and don't forget, my love, he started all this. Justine, Peter and the others, they are all his creatures. And so, for that matter, am I. That bloody painting,' I said, hooking my thumb towards the studio, 'and everything else is down to him. Whatever he is or isn't, he has to finish what he's started, and finish it his way.'

'You're right, darling; I should be more charitable. Look, maybe when he comes back we can all go out for a meal and see what he's been up to.'

I scrunched up my face. 'I think they're staying over. He had a bag with him.'

At first she was silent, as though what I had said had been spoken in a foreign tongue, and then, as if confirming something to herself, she nodded and uttered with finality, 'Well'.

'Are you all right about it, then?'

She gave me an old fashioned look, and then grinned. 'It just felt odd, that's all. I mean, I sleep with him and I sleep with you, but he doesn't sleep, as far as I know, with anyone else. It's just the idea of someone else outside our–, not that I mind; I mean how could I? Although she is odd, isn't she? Interesting, of course, but odd.'

'Odd makes her sound quite reasonable, darling. We can't comment you and I. We've got nothing to add. Ray has–'

'Yes, he has,' she said, butting in. 'More than enough reasons to–' She didn't end the sentence. 'Yes. True. And do we, you and me, really care which creak at this particular moment he is heading up with the weird sister? No. That's how it is, that's how it has always been. Me and him, you and me, divided and yet together. Everything else doesn't matter.'

'Not a bit jealous, then?' I said, being deliberately provocative. She amuses me when she gets riled.

'Oh come on! Of her?'

'I get jealous sometimes.'

'Not of Ray, surely?' she said, eyes staring.

I humped my shoulders and pursed my lips; putting what I meant into words somehow over stated what I felt.

'Oh darling, there's nothing to be jealous about. I love you both. You know that. We're unique. We share everything.'

'Love's not a democracy, darling.'

'Sweetheart.'

'It's not a rip your head off jealous, nothing like that, but sometimes, when I need you, I can't have you. That's when it hurts, that's what I mean.'

She took me in her arms and showered kisses on my neck and face. Then we stepped back and stared at each other; she was right; she was always right. We were unique. What else was there to say? I held out my hand and she took it, and together we let Ray and Izzie vanish from our minds and went upstairs to celebrate her homecoming, the picture and the glorious possibility of a whole day and night together.

Angie got up early the next morning and after taking a quick turn around the yard came back to bed with our teas and said that she wanted to walk home across the marsh while the sun was still shining. I was still half asleep but out of politeness shaped my face into what I hoped was a smile. I had absolutely no desire to get up, although I knew that I should, the shop wouldn't open itself.

Sometime after she'd gone, I was feeding the tetra when I heard her ringtone. *'Toby Slight's been arrested in Epping Forest,'* was the gist of what she said, which was fine until she added, *'The police phoned me.'*

'Fuck!' I didn't say that to her, but I said it to the phone when she'd rung off. I'd always known that Ray's cock-eyed enterprise was fraught with danger. You don't advertise for loonies, but he had. Now my fears had been realized. The sunlit morning and the joys of the night vanished instantly, replaced in my stomach by a great, cold, dollop of funk.

For the rest of the day I couldn't concentrate, and despite what people say about the calming effects of fish they didn't help. Every time I looked at them swimming round and round their bloody tanks I thought of convicts endlessly pacing their cramped cells.

But why was I getting so upset, I hadn't done anything? I was an artist. And in any case, the whole idea had been Ray's. He'd set it up. We'd just followed, so if anyone was to blame for anything it was his nibs. You couldn't argue with that. That was the truth: one of Ray's bloody facts. I felt instantly better for recognising that until I remembered that the *actual* physical shop where we met was my shop, *Fin Aquatics*. Oh my God, guilt by association. All of our meetings had been in the shop. I was absolutely implicated; in their eyes I was part of the gang, and I'd been there in Epping when Toby, the daft fucker, had run away and vanished beneath the trees.

Ah! I had another burst of inspiration. I was only there because I'd promised to do the painting, and a promise is a promise, and my studio happened to be part of the shop, and in any case, painting isn't a crime. But how could I explain to them how Ray had used my fish paintings and the shop itself to provoke me? They wouldn't understand. It didn't make sense; not even if I told them how he kept badgering me by saying snide things about my Japanese *gyotaku* prints like: *Nice fish what about the painting?* Why would I then need a gang of disparate nutters to keep me at it, when he was nutter enough? Oh fuck! What would I say to the police if they called?

More to the point, if Toby was dead or badly beaten up, as an accessary I could go to prison. All my fish would bloody die! I'd be ruined as an aquarist. But then, but then, maybe Angie would keep schtum. After all, as her lover, it wouldn't do to blurt out too many facts and figures. The police might use them when interviewing Ray. *'Did you know that your wife and best friend had been having it off for umpteen bloody years?'* That was nonsense, total nonsense. My bloody head! I didn't even know yet what he'd been arrested for.

I closed the shop and sat down in the yard with a coffee and a fag. I knew nothing. I had had no idea that Toby was going to stay out in the forest all night. It had been a game, a Wide Game, a Scout game, and nothing is more wholesome than a boy scout. I could admit that, all the rest though was conjecture, odd perhaps to an outsider, but nothing dangerous, nothing for the police to worry about, unless, unless they thought we were a bunch of terrorists using the forest for training. No, no they wouldn't. We didn't look like usual religious nutters; apart that is from my beard. But then I could always shave off. This was stupid. I was an artist. Artists wear beards; they do odd things, it's expected. No it was fine, nothing serious. God, Megan was right; I'm such a bloody wuss.

I dogged the fag and phoned Angie. 'So they haven't arrested you then?'

'What? Arrested, who?'

'Toby, darling – Epping Forest.'

'No, of course not, silly. He wasn't arrested, after all. The rangers found him asleep and thought he might have been injured. He told them to phone me. Didn't I tell you? Sorry love, I should have phoned. No, he's fine. I think he's gone home to his mum's. How about you darling, how's the morning, been, busy?'

I was relieved to put it mildly. It wasn't as strong a relief as I'd felt when I split with Megan, nor as profoundly life restoring as I'd felt when Ray had put his hand up to claim Max as his son, but it was a relief.

By nature, I'm one of those people who prefer to be on the edge of things. At Chelsea Ray had a reputation for being a bit of a mouth, and was always saying stupid things to amuse the rest of us. I admired him; he could be very funny, and I laughed along with the rest of them, but at the first sign of trouble I'd be off. I knew my place. I was just one of the support cast, one of the crew who provide the backup laughter and the camaraderie, but fuck all else.

My love for Angie is the wildest and most extreme thing I have ever done, but because it evolved out of youth and the stew pot of delayed adolescence, I was not particularly aware that it was a bold thing to do. At art school we all bathed in the same sexual broth, coupling, uncoupling, testing and luxuriating in the same bodily sensations. Making love to the girlfriend of your mate was risky, but not totally taboo, because we didn't possess each other. We were free agents moving from stimulation to stimulation as and when the mood took us.

Max's arrival hardened our borders. Angie told me she was pregnant after a nice day mooching in Hyde Park. We were lying on my bed and I was fully expecting that we would eventually make love. Her lips were close to my ear when she whispered those three doom laden words: *I'm pregnant.* I was only twenty-four, remember, fatherhood was still an undiscovered country. She spoke quietly and without drama. I'd always half expected it, since the ghost of an unformed fetus follows every youthful fuck. I felt instantly sick. My future, my brain and any prospect of immediate sex fell into my stomach as surely as if they had been sucked into a black hole. I withdraw inside. Although paternity was still undecided, I didn't even want to touch her. Now that I knew, touch was too intimate. Being pregnant was as good as being a mother, and you don't fuck mothers. They are untouchable.

From that moment on, while my future was in the balance, I peeped around the corner of our relationship waiting for the cosh I knew could come. But it didn't. Ray claimed the fetus for them both. My sickness left. I smiled again, but I couldn't get too close to Angie anymore, not while she was pregnant. My love for her remained, that never changed, but my physical expression of it did. Sexual contact became unthinkable, although she herself was not averse to the idea. I'd like to think my stance was a moral thing, but it wasn't; it was a physical thing. Making love to her while a baby created by someone else grew inside her repelled me at a very basic level. It was as though my magnetic pole had been reversed.

Sadly, without Angie, also meant without Ray; they now had things to do as a couple, which were fine, but unsettling. Distance, sexual frustration and being alone more often meant I was able to look away, and look elsewhere, and it was that that brought me back to Megan, a woman I'd been out with in the past when we had both been students together at Lincoln Art College. So while Ray and Angie grew fat and plumptious like a couple of fat white mushrooms, Megan and I, bewitched by their change, opted to follow their example: we got married. But as there was none of the necessary history of love; we became two poisonous toadstools growing in a god awful compost of our own creation.

Most of the time all this is water under the bridge, but sadly the nearest bridge to where I live is over a fetid drain that leads into the Lea, so I remember more times than I would like.

The outcome of my mental harassment by my fantasy police was that I determined to be proactive for once, to seize the day and anything else that would stir me into activity. I contacted my gallerist. I would not let my painting die amongst the fish tanks.

Rose & Packard's second floor gallery off Cork Street is modest but tasteful, specializing *'in the best of contemporary British Figurative Art'*. They are a husband and wife double act: Minerva Rose and Hugo Packard. I refer to them collectively, but not to their faces, as the Packhorses. They are not by any stretch of the metaphor:

cutting-edge; they are not 'pioneering'. The hottest art they ever handle is whatever hangs closest to their radiators. Theirs is a lucrative niche market. They provide well-made modern art to the taste conscious rich, and in so doing provide an outlet for my fish works. This means that they supply a steady, but not exciting, flow of cash into my account. We are what you would call close financial friends.

Unlike some gallerists, the Packhorses will travel modest distances away from central London in pursuit of art. Green Park station is very close to Cork Street and the Victoria Line brings you to Walthamstow Central, which is a short hike from the studio. The whole experience can be achieved in what passes as a gallerist's lunch hour. Seeing me is also an attraction in itself, since along with the art they get time gawking at the fish, and are able to experience first-hand the life they read about in the Guardian that flows down the cosmopolitan waters of the High Street.

I had set the painting up in the room off the shop, which once all the stuff is shifted out doubles up as a reasonable display space. Getting it right is important, for nothing fucks up your chance of a sale more than manky walks and shitty lighting.

'Your coffee always tastes better than mine, Ed,' said Minnie. 'You must tell me the secret.'

Stepping east carries risk. Elegance has no place on the mean streets of Walthamstow, so she was dressed in tailored three-quarter length jeans, a smart shirt and fashionable, but not too obviously expensive soft shoes. Hugo had removed his tie and wore his usual red trousers and suede boots.

'Looking at the coffee maker I'd suggest it's that, darling. Old and trusted friend, eh Ed?'

'I take care never to wash it out properly. It adds flavour.' I said, rocking my head. It wasn't true, obviously, but I could see that they weren't quite sure.

'So, somewhere under there, I'm guessing, is this amazing new picture that we've come all this way to see. Your clues were somewhat enigmatic, to say the least.'

'Positively conspiratorial,' said Minnie. 'I can't wait.'

'I can see even now,' said Hugo, 'that it's a damn site bigger than your usual works. Need a wall to itself, I'd say.'

'Oh yes – definitely all to its self,' I said, moving beside the picture. 'I don't want a bloody scrum around this.' And then, like a conjurer, I pulled away the covering. *'Voila! The Miracle of the Fishes.'*

'Bloody hell, Ed!' Hugo was out of his seat at once, advancing head bent towards the canvas.

'Darling, this is awesome, truly awesome,' said Minnie, sotto voce, and gripping my bicep in passing.

They inspected the work from all angles, stepping forward and stepping back. They were so keen, it wouldn't have surprised me if they had got down and licked the paint. For once in their collective existence they were gob smacked, save that is for the occasional sucking sounds and releases of air.

I knew before they had arrived that it was good. Angie had cried, but seeing them fawning in front of it, calculating its worth with every glance, made me truly happy, and I smiled.

Chapter Twenty-Seven - Ray

'Do you know something Ray, when you sleep you have the face of a saint, one of those alabaster, whey-faced saints that smirk at you in Gothic Cathedrals. Totally adorable. When I see them I just want to rub them, and when I see you slumbering, my love, I get the same intense desire – to rub you until you glow.

I was not an alabaster saint, and she who was suggesting the rubbing was no penitent pilgrim. It was Izzie. Her rubicund cheeks hung over me like two rosy apples. It was six thirty in the morning, for God's sake! I hardly had the energy to open my eyes. At my age, one climax a night was all I was good for, but here she was ready to go again, despite two earlier, crepuscular and ear-splitting orgasms.

'You nipples are like wine gums,' she said, lowering her lips to my chest, and flicking her tongue from nipple to nipple like a frenzied adder.

'Oh my god,' I thought, and so before her mouth could clamp shut on the wine gum of her choice, I forced myself up onto my elbows and shuffled back on the pillows. 'Oh is it only that time? I thought it was later.'

She adjusted herself against me and nuzzled my shoulder.

'Still, thanks for waking me, darling. Cos you know what? I think today's going to be *the* day? Got a good feeling. Today I shall find that my P.O.D.' I'd begun reducing my enterprise to its initials for ease of conversation, since there was no existing one word for: Place of Death.

'Slow down, Raymondo,' she said, foraging across my chest with her lips. It was hopeless. She was unrelenting. 'One county at a time.'

I was putty in her hand, although, rather surprisingly in the circumstances, not for long. Thanks to her diligent moulding and an unexpected flair for filthy talk, I rose to the occasion, but not without certain trepidation. Her sexual fantasies had got me going, but I had difficulty banishing from my head that my intuition about the day might be true and I would die from a heart attack between Izzie's thighs in a Travel Lodge near Colchester, which was not the mystical union I was hoping for.

We ignored breakfast in the hotel and opted instead to drive further south to Wivenhoe and eat at the Rose and Crown overlooking the river Colne.

'Why Wivenhoe, my darling?' she said as we sat in hotel carpark. 'Why not Fing-ring-hoe, it sounds so much more – exciting ?' she said, trembling her index finger at me. 'And what on earth is a hoe?'

I was ready for her, because not content with simply asking questions, Izzie had earlier insisted on photographing my response to everything that she said.

'Sometimes your strength and your self-control drive me so wild, darling, that I just want to tear you apart and ravish you.'

Had it not been for the camera hanging round her neck, I think she would have done so.

'But, hard as it is, we must both remember that I'm not just your lover; I am an artist and you, my precious, are the glorious subject of my great work.' She had made her hand into a fist and gently knocked on my chest as if asking to come in. 'You can be as tightly shut as a Colchester oyster, but if I'm going to find the pearl inside: the true you, then my darling, I need to prize you open.' The knocking stopped. 'And you know what? It happens in those fleeting but intense moments when we open our hearts to each other, those tiny spaces between hearing and replying. It is then, if I'm quick, that my camera slips between your barnacle crusted shells.'

She had said that earlier while I was hopping around trying to get my pants on, which under her intense scrutiny had not been easy. So now, in the bright morning light of the carpark, I knew that: *what on earth is a hoe* did not reveal a sudden interest in the origins of Essex place names, but was part of her strategy to open me up. Whatever I said, however innocent, would in her mind be a clue. So I decided to keep the conversation to facts, since they would be less open to self-revelation.

'Ha ha! Yes, well, Fingring does come from finger. So your dirty mind was spot on. It means a settlement on a finger of land.'

'And Wivenhoe?'

The camera whirred wildly.

'A settlement on a spur of land owned by someone with a name that sounds something like Wiven.' I said, keeping my face as emotionless as possible. 'Whizz away, sweetheart, you'll find I'm more fly than you realize,' I said to myself, confident that if this was a game we were playing I'd given nothing away.

'So why are we going there, then?'

'Because it's close, and because it says on Google that the pub will serve us breakfast overlooking the water.'

'Breakfast is fine Raymondo, but we are not tourists. This is business. Pod delivery will only come if you find what you are looking for. East Anglia is a big place. It will take time. We can't dally indefinitely. This is a symbiotic relationship, darling. I have to pay my mortgage.'

'Well, all right, I'll tell you.' Too late I realized a slight edge had crept into my voice. The camera whirred away. 'Because it felt right,' I said, regaining the initiative by smiling. 'Yesterday, when we were in Colchester, wandering about near the castle, yes? Well you went off into Boots for something, and while you were gone I went into myself, turned slowly a full three-hundred and sixty degrees and then, when I was stationary, turned to where I felt I could detect an emanation. That was to the south, and not only to the south, for I sensed it was not far to the south. A quick look at the map told me that it was probably Wivenhoe. That's why.'

'It could have been Fingering, they're almost in line with each other.'

'Oh god, Izzie! It's not a science! It's not precise. The whole thing is done by intuition, by feel. Wivenhoe felt right, Fingringhoe did not. I, I can't say more than that.'

But I knew I had. Her bloody camera had been inside my head the whole time. I was cross. Despite myself, I had let her wind me up.

'Now, my love, let's go down to the water and have a good breakfast.'

I didn't think for a moment that my grin had fooled her, but it shut her up. She put down the bloody camera and drove out of the car park.

Wivenhoe on a fine day with a modest on shore breeze and the tide on the turn was idyllic. We sat on the Quay outside the pastel walls of the Rose and Crown with our breakfast and feasted on the sights before us.

'I love the sound of gulls,' I said, 'so atmospheric.'

'Not on my roof at four in the morning; they're not.'

I laughed. 'They remind me how close we all are to the sea.'

'Right, Raymond. We're here. We've eaten, drunk the coffee and seen the view. Now what? Are you receiving anything?'

This time I was ready. Finding the Pod was always the difficult bit. It was a crazy idea to everyone but me. I knew that. And as a consequence I had faced ridicule and disbelief ever since I first mooted it to Angie and Ed. Izzie's frustration was understandable, but I didn't let it get to me.

'Darling,' I said, laying my hand on her camera, 'I can only respond to what I feel, and before you say another thing, yes, I do feel something.'

'Great! Where? Pay the bill, let's go!' She stood up and gathered her bag.

'I will pay the bill, but first I need to go in,' I said, indicating my inner self and a need for patience and silence.'

'Right. You go in and I'll pay the bill.'

As soon as she was half way towards the entrance I walked closer to the water's edge, stood still, closed my eyes and sighed. After a few more deep sighs I clearly sensed a direction somewhere off to my right in what I guessed was the direction of the riverbank. I concentrated on my breathing and on the intense sensation of warmth I was getting on the right side of my forehead. I tried to target the emanation more closely and inched my way forward in what I imagined was its direction.

'Ray stop!' Izzie had grabbed my arm. 'You were going to walk into the river.'

For a moment I was dazed. She wasn't filming, which was good. I smiled. 'Very strong.'

'And?'

I pointed away to the right. 'Down there.'

She was so excited that she danced about pointing the camera at everything.

'My god, Ray, I so want to thank you for bringing me here. All this!' She swept her free arm out to embrace the marsh, the Colne and the distant mouth of the estuary. 'I've never seen such a place. The end of land and the beginning of sea! Bliss! The aesthetics, the setting, perfect, absolutely perfect. I want to celebrate. I want to make love to you. I want to strip and lie beneath you while sea birds carol in the skies above. God, I feel so good.'

'I feel the same, of course, but perhaps if I'm going to get this thing done, we need to wait, and I need to concentrate on the task in hand.'

'There you go again, my hero. You have strength enough for both of us.'

She stood to the side and allowed me to take the lead along Quay and out towards a springy path that ran close to the river's edge. I could feel my direction as a pressure in my forehead and let myself follow the direction of the walk without hesitation. It felt absolutely right.

I knew that Izzie was working hard with her camera, but it made no difference, my mind was settled on what I had to do. The path lead up to what appeared to be the embankment of an old railway line, and as soon as she had space to pass she was off, scampering ungainly ahead to waylay me and shoot the expressions on my face. Fine, I had no problem with that. That was why she was there. She had her own bucket-shop ambition. Her antics meant nothing now. I was so close that I could almost point to where the Pod might be.

A heron lifted off from the river's edge and turned slowly away across the water. Izzie shot it; she shot everything. I walked on until my head suddenly went fuzzy and I felt the need to stop. For a moment or two I just stood there feeling totally confused, trying to pick up the ethereal trail, again. The emanations were strong but were now coming from somewhere off to my left. They were leading me away from the high ground and down to the nibbled, tidal edge of the riverbank.

'This way.'

Once I was down, Izzie picked her way carefully over the tussocks and gullies so that she could see me from the side. Without a moment's hesitation I stepped off the last dirty outreaches of the land and onto the glistening mud flats. I was so sure of myself, and so in thrall to my feelings that I simply walked on oblivious, ignoring the increasing suck of the squelching black estuarine mud. And then, quite suddenly, I halted again. It as though my reasoning brain had suddenly broken out from beneath my more primitive, intuitive brain and taken back control.

'Is that it, darling? Is that the Pod?'

I heard Izzie but only faintly. And then my internal fog cleared, reason took over and I was back to my normal state.

'It's over there,' I said, pointing across the river like Dante's Vigil. 'On the other bank, somewhere.'

'We're stuck then. We can't get across.'

'It said on the map there was a ferry, but I think it's further along. Too far for today, maybe.'

'Bugger! So what are we going to do? Go back?'

I looked down at my feet. My shoes had sunk deep beneath the black ooze and the water had long since overflowed their top. Looking at the eddies in the water, I guessed that the tide was turning. I didn't care about the state of my shoes, they would wash, what worried me was that I couldn't shift them. They were held in the mud as if in concrete.

'Izzie, I'm stuck. I can't move my shoes. You'll have to help me.'

'I'm not going in the mud, I'm wearing my Doc Martin's; they'll be ruined.'

'Sweetheart – I know for a fact, that I'm not meant to die here. I know that. The Pod is somewhere over there on the far bank. So just give me a hand and pull me out.'

Although I could hear the camera chirring away, I tried to remain calm.

'Izzie – put the camera down. The tide's coming in. This is serious. This is not the time for snaps.'

'Wash your mouth out Raymondo! I do not take snaps. I am an artist.'

'And I'm going to drown if you don't give me a hand.'

The water had risen above my ankles. I tried rocking my feet but it was useless; they wouldn't move.

'I was joking, darling,' I said, trying to sound jolly. 'Of course you are an artist, but please could you just help me? I am well and truly stuck.'

Reluctantly, she placed her bag carefully on a tussock and then equally carefully laid her camera on it.

'Quick!'

Very gingerly, she leant out from the edge to reach me, all the time keeping her precious boots firmly on the bank. It was hopeless. I was too far into the water.

'Ah!' She let out a sudden desperate cry as the bank collapsed beneath her weight and she went tumbling forward into the flood. 'I'm soaked!'

'Grab my hand,' I said, leaning over to catch her.

She had struggled to her feet and stood beside me dripping like a demented water sprite, grabbed my hand and pulled. Although she was remarkably strong, it made no difference. My feet refused to move.

'Try again. Pull!'

'I am fucking pulling!'

And then I shifted. My feet came out of my shoes so quickly that I was unbalanced and fell towards her. The sudden release came without warning and caught Izzie when all of her weight was leaning in the wrong direction. She let go at once, screamed out loud and once more fell into the river, but this time with me on top of her. We struggled onto our knees snorting and burbling like two pigs in a wallow. We were not only soaked, we were besmirched all over with the thick black mud.

Izzie began laughing; it was so unlikely. I expected her to shout and scream but she didn't.

'You look ridiculous, Raymond. All that mud, ha ha! Poseidon rises.' And with that she began reaching beneath the surface and dragging up handfuls of mud to sling at me.

'Don't! Ah stop it. Izzie!' I caught one of her mud pies in mid-air and flung it back at her, hitting her on the side of the head. 'Ha ha, two can play at that game, madam.'

We frolicked in the rising waters until we were absolutely soaked to the skin and covered all over in stinking slime.

I pushed myself onto my feet and dragged her up beside me. She was glorious. I was hugely impressed by her response to the disaster. I held her shoulders and we both laughed hysterically.

'Raymond, if I was not so fastidious about my sexual health, I would expect you to mount me like an animal here and now on the river bank. You are magnificent. I feel so charged. Thank you, dear man, thank you.'

Somehow it all made sense. There was still time to dry off in the sun, and I was without my shoes, but what did it matter? It was Izzie's car, and she didn't mind.

CHAPTER 28

ANGIE

When anyone asks me what are the good things about working for yourself, I always start with the most obvious, which is that you can be flexible with time. What I don't say is that the concept of flexibility is in itself flexible. It exists in the same way that long lazy days in the summer exist: you've heard of them, you've even experienced the odd one or two, but they are few and far between. Working for yourself means that if you don't work there's no cash, and that means you are far less flexible than you'd like to think you are.

I enjoy being a British Sign Language interpreter, and it really does give me flexibility, and it's a flexibility that exists over more than time; it includes space as well. It is not a nine-to-five job and, although most of my jobs are within London and the South-East, they can, in theory, come from anywhere else within Britain.

For all our marital foibles, Ray has never once questioned my present peripatetic life. When I first met him, I'd already spent a year learning to act at the Poor School in Kings Cross, and after Max was born I could have gone back and finished my drama training, but although I'd loved it, with a baby it tow acting didn't quite have the same appeal. I went back to bar work for awhile, but what I really wanted was a career. It was then, in my thirties, and thanks again to Ray's support, that I went to Bristol University Centre for Deaf Studies and became what I am now - a BSL/English Interpreter.

Another of Ray's qualities is that he's not jealous. When I'm away doing the Labour Party conference or working in one of the bigger theatres, like the National, he's not awed by the famous people I sometimes meet. In fact I think he likes me going away every so often, because then gets more time to get on with his more esoteric pursuits, like the one he's just been on with Izzie.

Sometimes, I wish he'd go away a bit more, because not only does it make seeing Ed less fraught, it would give him more to talk about than his maps and research. That's why I was more than curious to find out what he had been up to with our self-confessed *'creature of the night'* – la Capricious. I was not being prurient, and I wasn't jealous, I was just curious. I know Ray, he's not a sexual adventurer, but she could be. She has that look, and if she came on to him, well – I had his interests at heart. She would terrify him, he's even a bit scared when I get a bit beside myself and attempt one of our rarer sexual intimacies.

When Izzie dropped him off and he came into the kitchen, I just stared at him. I was truly gob-smacked. He looked like one of those New Guinea *'mud-men'*. He was filthy; his skin had a grey tinge, and every time he scratched his head there was a shower of muddy scurf. I immediately sat him down and made him a cup of tea.

When he told me the reason, that they'd been chased into the river by a bunch of cows, I just laughed. I had no sympathy. I mean, really, he can be such a plonker sometimes. As soon as he'd gone upstairs to get bathed, I whipped his stinky clothes straight into the washer.

When he was suitable for company again, he told me the whole story, and no matter how much I teased him about his 'companion' I was pretty shore that he had escaped her more lethal ministrations.

'I bet she wore black even in bed, silky, exciting black lingerie that drove you wild with desire.'

'Yes, yes, she may have done, darling, but I didn't get to see it, thank you. I had had quite enough of her tittle-tattle during the day to want any more at night.'

'No cosy twosome, then?'

He looked up exasperatedly at the ceiling. 'Yes, if that means a pint in the snug, yes.'

Although I was pleased that he had almost found his crazy Pod, as he calls it; I was also slightly apprehensive. I did my best to hide it by smiling a lot, but inside I wasn't smiling. Up until then I'd thought of his quest in the same way that I'd thought about people searching for four-leafed clovers or lay-lines: bonkers but harmless, but now that he was convinced that he had almost found it, everything changed. What was unsettling was that I imagined that it might bring on some weird desire in him to test his theory. Obviously, there is 'a place of death' since we all have to die somewhere, but you can't find it; where you die isn't down to you unless you will it so, and not for the first time it made me wonder why he had this need, and whether there was something in his head that I should be worried about. Everyone is a stranger even if you've known them for years.

His success in almost resolving his own *Bucket Shop* wish seemed to change him. He became somehow less energetic in pursuit of everybody else's secret desires. *The Shop* had done well, that was true. Ed, obviously, at least only to me at that moment, had accomplished what I never believed he would, and that was thanks to Ray. Peter Rock had got close to his hero; Toby Slight had had his moment in the forest, although no one had actually seen him since that night. The only two who were still in an on-going state of incompletion were Justin Cook and Lauren Makin, and their quests were more general and less measureable than the others.

As far as Justin went, she was definitely happier and far less fidgety than she had been, or at least she was when I saw her the other day, and I'm sure, if we are apportioning success that was totally down to me. To tell the truth, I'd quite enjoyed my walk on the wild side. I rather liked pretending to myself, very gently, that I might be bi-sexual. It made my previously vocal support for LGBT causes more anchored, more authentic, and I wore the rainbow button with pride.

My relationship with her was still essentially physical; intellectually we didn't share much at all. We weren't sexually rampant. It was all rather gentle. She was testing the waters and so was I. There had been so much talk in the media about sexual fluidity and non-binary attachment that I didn't want to miss out, and to be considered past it. Nothing can be more distressing than good things happening to the young when you are still young enough yourself to believe you could join in. I'd always believed that I was a liberated woman and on the edge of wherever progressive curve was passing; after all I was lover to two men. But the sexual revolution had moved on, and so with Justin I imagined I was there again, surfing the wave with the best of them.

Lauren was a different matter. Her 'fluidity' was decidedly odd. She believed she was channelling her dead twin brother, Nat, who must have been all of two when he died, and was doing her best to accommodate his wishes by dressing up and acting how she imagined he would be had he lived. He was two, for god's sake! How could she possibly know how he would turn out? If Ed had been worried that *The Bucket Shop* would attract nutters, Lauren fitted the bill perfectly. Her whole idea was weird.

When she wasn't channelling Nat, which was deeply unsettling when you were standing beside her, she was very nice, very good company; after all, she wasn't thick. Until the whole Nathan thing got out of control and screwed her head up, she was only a year off a degree in Events Management at the Metropolitan University on Holloway Road. With her slight body and elfin features, she also made quite an attractive 'boy'. So attractive, in fact, that I wondered if Justin and I should arrange to meet her somewhere less Spartan than Ed's garage, she might find a little strong feminine company conducive to unravelling her problem. It might help her to gage the extent of her channelling, or show that it was actually a gender thing and that she wanted to pass herself off as a boy.

Justine had slimmed down since we first met and had started to look almost pretty. Sadly, her skin would never be without its undulations, but thanks to whatever new foundation she was using, it had a smoother appearance. It was more than just her looks though; it was that she was happier being herself, which after all had been one of her reasons for joining the group in the first place. So, if Ray was counting, I reckon that Justine could be considered, indirectly, one of his successes too.

When she and I discussed Lauren, it was very difficult to pick a pronoun that accurately implied the Lauren-Nathan split, and unlike Ray's Pod, there wasn't an easy acronym available either. Even combining the two names to make: *Laurat* or *Naten* seemed contrived, so in the end we both just referred to her as Lauren, and left it at that.

'Do you fancy her?' said Justine. 'Just a bit?' She was being deliberately provocative, but I played along.

'Well, she is quite good looking.'

'Is that as a girl or as Nat?'

In our new role as 'lovers', however tenuous, we were both trying to be open and honest about the girl. We genuinely wanted to help her, and one way we thought was to treat her as a desirable woman or man depending upon who actually turned up when next we all met.

'Nothing too heavy,' I said, 'or she might run a mile.'

'No, no, no, just a bit of mild flirting, just so she can see herself in a positive light,' said Justine.'

'Feel good about herself.'

'Or himself,' said Justine.

'That way she can work out if her 'channelling', I said, inclining my head to confirm our actual mutual suspicion about the whole idea, 'is what she thinks she's really doing, or that she has some deeper psychological need that is way beyond both us.'

'Exactly – like she may actually want to be a man.'

'In which case we can only go so far. Bit of support.'

'Unless, of course, you actually *do* fancy her?' said Justine, laughing.

I laughed, but said nothing.

I hadn't seen Justine for much more than coffee since our last liaison, and like now, when we did meet, sex somehow wasn't as likely as it had been. We were still physical, in that we cuddled and kissed, but we were no longer driven to go further. I think our first crossings of the barrier had been enough. They had been fun and surprising, but we were both essentially attracted to men. Steve, her 'fuck-buddy' was still around, so I knew she wasn't totally committed to swinging one way or the other.

'You made me see that it wasn't sex and it wasn't looks, it was in here that I needed to change,' she had said, pointing to her heart. 'Thanks to you, Angie, I've stopped obsessing and begun to live a little. We all have shit jobs, but the job isn't me. I'm Justine and I'm all right; I'm fun to be with and can be loved. You showed me that. So important, darling,' she said, gripping my forearm. 'Thanks.'

We fell into each other's arms with lots of tears, and although I was flattered to be considered her 'saviour', I also felt a bit of a phoney. I hadn't done much more than provide her with a sympathetic ear. Or maybe it really had been the sex? And our excitement and our naivety perhaps had been enough for her, when all she had ever needed had been affection and love. I don't know; I just know I found the whole thing a bit awkward.

'Coming out of my dark place has empowered me, Angie,' she said with undue emphasis. 'I'm stronger. I know how it feels to be lost, and to have found someone who has love in their heart and is willing to show it.' This last platitude was directed squarely to me, and I touched her hand with what I hoped would be understood as appreciation. She responded by taking my hand and squeezing it. 'I've got a feeling that that's where Lauren is now. I want to be there for her, like you were for me – give a little back.'

On the strength of that saccharine emotion, and a swift phone call, it was agreed. We would all meet up in the café on Upper Street in Islington where Lauren worked.

The Islington I had known in my youth was ugly and unloved; you passed through it rather than lingered. Now, as if touched by a fairy's wand, it sported more cafes and restaurants than you could shake a stick at. 'Lacuna', the café where Lauren was a barista, was one of the pioneering cafes that had begun to fill in the gap on Upper Street between the Underground stations of Angel and Highbury. She wasn't due to start work again for at least an hour, so there was plenty of time for what we had in mind.

'Wow!' I said, kissing her cheek and then stepping back to admire her top. 'That is so perfect.'

She moved to embrace Justine, who tried to outdo me in admiration. 'You look so good.'

I think she was unaware of our pincer movement, and accepted our compliments as nothing more than the usual overblown verbal gush which did for a simple 'hi'.

We settled into a corner of the room and she wangled us free coffees and cakes from her friend behind the counter. If we thought we were going to set the agenda, we were wrong. She had obviously been thinking about our meeting.

'I need to come clean about Nat, my brother Nathan,' she added just in case we'd forgotten what she was on about.

When she said that I was all ready to smile, because I thought she would then come out with something that would clarify our earlier speculations. She did, but not in the way we imagined.

'I said I was 'channelling' him. I wasn't. It was a lie, not a nasty lie, but a lie to cover what I was really doing.'

'This is it,' I thought. 'It's a gender thing.'

'I haven't got and have never had a brother.' She sat back watching the result of her bombshell. 'I made it up.'

'It's not a gender issue, then?' said Justine in a quiet, confiding voice. 'We do understand.'

'No you don't!' She was smiling unashamedly. 'But I know where you're coming from. It's the hair isn't it?' Her hands twinkled around her coconut tuft. 'Always been a bit boyish, but this was all part of the act.'

We must have looked totally gormless.

'It was my boyfriend; he's a bit of a twat. It was his idea, the whole thing. He's a journalist, sort of, works for a Walthamstow paper, and he saw *The Shop* ad before it came out: *Need help to achieve a secret aspiration before you die?* Yeah? It sounded so weird that he dared me to go along. He said he would do an article on it. We came up with the dead brother thing together. It was brilliant. It meant that whatever I said or did, I could blame someone who didn't exist. Perfect excuse.'

'And you don't want to change sex or anything?' said Justine, as if struggling to lay aside her trump card.

Lauren laughed out loud. It was as if the traveller in the Bible parable, the one who had been beaten, stripped and left for dead, had got to his feet as the Good Samaritan approached and said, 'No, only joking,' and had then legged it.

'You're not, you know,' said Justine, still struggling, 'not transitioning then? You're normal.'

'Well, as normal as the rest of you,' she said, laughing, which I didn't like. 'Oh I know we shouldn't have, but it was fun. I tell you what though; I think my boyfriend might be a bit gay. Got really turned on when I started dressing like Nathan – Nat!' she said, rolling her eyes. 'We had some good laughs, though, didn't we? Christ up the tree – well, I nearly wet myself, and that nutter Toby – the Wild Man! If he had died, we'd never have known. Oh, but I really like your husband, Angie, nice man, never got flustered. Tell him thanks from me will you, because I'll not be coming back to *The Shop* anymore?'

'And your twatish boyfriend's article,' I said, half wanting to slap her face. 'Is that going ahead?'

'No, he's all talk. He said no one would believe it. I think he's right. Still, I've got to get back to work. Lovely seeing you both,' she leant over and pecked us both on the cheek. 'If you want any more coffee or something, won't be free of course, just ask. Chou.'

She got up, waved her fingers towards us and disappeared towards the staff door. Justine's face was pinched with anger. Whatever prettiness I'd seen in her had totally vanished. She was lived.

'The scheming little bitch! Honestly!'

'Look, let's go. I don't want a scene when she comes back.' I stood up.

'I've a good mind to slap her face.'

'We'll form a queue.'

Once outside and walking she let it all out.

'I feel violated, I really do, Angie. I've opened my heart in front of her and she's trampled on it. Torn it apart.'

'She doesn't know anything Justine; she's never heard the real you. You gave nothing away in the meetings, well, nothing that could hurt you.'

'S'pposing her boyfriend holds us up to ridicule, says things that make it obvious who we are. I'll die. No one's going to buy a house from a weirdo, are they? That's my commission gone. That's my job gone.'

She had begun to cry. The whole of her body was convulsed.

'Sweetheart,' I said holding her gingerly. 'It won't happen. He hasn't written it. And if he had, most of the people who come into your agency will be from away, so they wouldn't have read it in any case.'

She broke away and stared at me wildly. I gave her a weak smile, but it did no good. She ran off to the bus stop just as a number 30 pulled up and got on board. The last thing I saw was her woeful, red face staring at me, and then the briefest of brief waves. I smiled winningly and waved back.

When the bus was far enough away I smiled again, this time with genuine relief.

'Oh my god, Ray, what have you got me into? That's the last bit of nonsense I do for you. From now on I'm having nothing more to do with your ridiculous project. My god, she's a silly cow. She should count herself lucky she's got a fuck-buddy.'

My laughter ended abruptly. I couldn't laugh and not remember how I had lain with her, how I had enjoyed her. She was no more of a silly cow than I was. We both wanted love and understanding, the only difference was that I already had it. I suddenly felt flat and desperately wanted the whole time with her to vanish, to be expunged from my memory. What had I been thinking of? I was a middle aged woman who was loved, really loved, and by two lovely men. I didn't need more sexual excitement. I had had more than my fair share. I was just like one of those awful sensation seekers that Ray had warned about. He knew. Sensation only takes you so far, that's why he had ruled against it. He wasn't as daft as I sometimes thought he was, and in any case, if he was a bit bonkers, then so was I.

CHAPTER 29

GEORDIE

I like the early morning best, especially those mornings closer to the backend of the year when the sun has slipped further around the horizon. Everything is plumptious. Fruit has ripened and fallen, and for us creatures there are mouthfuls of delight wherever you look. As a consequence, all of the small fry that live in the tussocks and deeper stands of grass are full and fat, and therefore slower on their feet. Nothing is more fun that giving them the run around. Their little squeaks go right through you. I'm trembling just thinking about it. You can eat the *rursh*: they're the tubby ones with the blunt noses and the short tails. One quick swallow and they're gone. But you don't want to eat the tiny ones, those with the long pointy snouts; *Oouts* taste absolutely foul, almost as foul as they smell. You don't ever bite them to death! The chase is the thing; it's brilliant. They squeak and squeak, and get so excited that their little hearts explode and they just keel over dead. Brilliant fun.

Of course, if we are talking food-on-the-paw, you can't beat a *thicker*, what Angie calls a bunny or rabbit, or some such. They are not common on the marsh itself, but they are thick around the nature reserve. The trouble is it *is* a reserve and dogs aren't allowed in unless chained and shackled. Thankfully, *thickers* aren't very bright, and they travel, so when we walk around the boundary path there's usually one or two lurking beneath the sloes. I've never caught one, eaten a few dead ones, yes; can be a bit high, but tasty. Angie hates me chasing them, but neither Ed nor Ray seem to worry over much, although I have to be quick for if I disappear for too long they get agitated and then the hooting starts. If it's Ray, he also blows his horrible high pitched whistle, which does my head in.

Recently, Angie's friend, Greta, the one with the funny voice, has acquired a dog, a young dog. It's what she calls a pug. There is no specific dog name for it that I've heard of. Ed calls it an *ugly-bugger*, but apparently you can't say that when you're out. She calls it Fritz, which is fine. Well, Fritz and me were out wandering over the marsh with Angie and Greta in tow on one of those delightful mornings I've been talking about. The sun was up, the early morning mist was lifting and the grass was shimmering. We had the whole space to race around in.

'Do you ever get itches on your muzzle?' said Fritz, as we paused to investigate a piece of ape trash.

'What near your ears?' I said, cocking me leg and pissing next to the rubbish.

'No – here,' he said, wrinkling his already wrinkly face. 'In the crevices.'

I came up close and peered at him. 'Give us a twitch.' He did, and when he did I could see what his problem was; he'd got little creatures living deep down along the bottom of his wrinkle. '*Schushas*, mate. You've got bugs.'

'Dangerous?'

'We all get'em. Itchy little bastards. Sometimes my back legs are going all night scratching. Drives Angie crazy. Drives me crazy; they're always just out of reach. She gives me a squirt on the back of the neck. Seems to do the trick.'

'But not dangerous?'

'Who knows? The bastards come the bastards go. That's all I know.'

'Think you could lick them out for me, my tongue's just too short?'

'Not just your tongue, either,' I said laughing. 'No offence, but you do have a compact little muzzle.'

'Fritzie, Fritzie. Fetch the ball!'

'Here we go.' I said, getting ready for some chasing.

'Not you, Geordie. Geordie heel! Come here. Sorry Greta.'

I outpaced the Pug by a mile, picked up the ball without pausing and brought it to Angie's feet. I looked up, tongue hanging, eyes glinting and awaited the plaudits.

'That wasn't for you. You little bugger.'

She gave the ball to Greta and they walked ahead, while Fritz and I trotted along behind.

'Got a bit of a wheeze you've got there, haven't you?' I said, hearing the rasping coming from his throat.

'All this bloody running about, not good for my chest.'

His snorting did not go unnoticed, but the two apes seemed to think it was amusing, and did nothing more than laugh before gently strolling on oblivious to all but their own gossiping.

'You know that fellow I told you about,' said Greta, 'the one who comes to my yoga class on Wednesdays? He's asked me if I would like to meet for a coffee, and I said yes.'

'Good news, Greta, good news. When?'

'Yesterday!'

'Oh you sly cat. Did you go?'

'Of course, he's very nice.'

'And?'

Her eyes widened and they both laughed.

'Result, then,' said Angie. 'He is rather nice.'

Who would keep to heel when all of this gibberish is going on? I dropped back. Apes make a big thing about talking, but what do they talk about: the iniquity of the balance of power between the species? No. The unlikeliness of God being made in the image of an ape? No, they use their so called evolutionary advantage to talk about sex. Not always of course, but as good as. We do the business, those of us still capable of it, that is, and we move on. For them a fuck is never over with, and if it isn't the fuck itself, it's all of the nonsense that leads to or from it. Their conversation is so boring. I'd sooner talk to the pigeons; at least all they talk about is food.

The other day, coming across the Walthamstow marsh with Ed and Angie, she never stopped going over the possibility of Ray and that Izzie having had or not having had a fuck. What sort of creatures are these? As you'd say to a pup that's vomited: suck it up and move on.

'I don't think he did sleep with her, Ed, but she's a devious woman. She's got those eyes that look at you but don't seem to see anything. It's as though she knows all about you without you saying anything. It's creepy.'

'Art school was full of them. But, even so, Ray's not daft. Izzie might seem exciting and suggest unnatural passions and desires, but he's got you. Why would he want someone else?'

'Are you saying I'm dull and unexciting, Edward Farrow?'

Ed's eyes widened. 'No, no, how could I say that, my love? You are more exciting and sexier than Izzie any day. Much more.'

They stopped for more face pressing and then walked on, still talking about Ray.

'Um, not sure that's always true, though is it, not for him? I don't give him much fun; the odd wank and that's it. It's not like us. I only do it then, if I'm honest, to stop him exploding.'

'I'll remember that when I'm feeling randy.'

'When have I ever said no?' She squeezed his balls and they laughed. 'But what if he did, though, sleep with her?' said Angie, suddenly looking serious.

They stopped, yet again, and looked deep into each other's eyes, which suited me fine, because now that the day was warming up, the delicious scents coming from the dikes needed some investigation, so I mooched off for a bit of questing.

'Do you think she's clean – you know? I'm not saying she isn't, but if her habits are a bit dubious and she does put it about a bit, I'd hate to think he might have got something off her.'

'And brought it back?' said Ed, gesturing between them with his hand.

'The last thing we want is to catch something awful. I've seen the queues outside the STD clinics; one of my clients used to go. It's all a bit hole-in-the-corner. I think this one was out the back of the hospital beyond the carpark.'

'Was it a man or a woman?'

'He was a man, someone about my own age.'

'Bit embarrassing wasn't it?'

'No not really. I looked away when the nurse did that thing with the miniature hockey stick.'

Whatever it was she mimed it made Ed wince, but I didn't care. It was hot, and not only was I bored with all of their jabbering, but my tongue was hanging out. I was thirsty and the dike was close. I hung back as they walked on and then slithered down the side of the dyke to get a drink, sadly, my short legs could not get much traction and I kept going until I was up to my chest in cooling water. Bliss!

'Geordie! That bloody dog! Get out of there!'

I was lapping away happily until I caught sight of Ed bearing down on me. Ed running is always a bad sign; he's not beyond giving me a flick with the lead. I was off, but thanks to my short legs again, and the copious amounts of water that I sloshed onto the muddy bank I couldn't scramble out, so that every time I tried I slithered back down and into the water. It was hopeless, so I just stood where I was, tongue lolling and what I hoped he would recognize as the dog equivalent of a smile.

'God! He'll stink.'

Taking that as a positive, and spurred on by their angry voices, I struggled up until I was within reach of Ed's extended arm. He grabbed my collar and hoicked me onto the gravel path, where, much relieved, I shook myself free of the surplus water.

'You bugger! I'm drenched.'

He ran at me swinging the lead, so I skipped away pronto, but he was only halfhearted and gave up quickly. When I came to the meadow I charged around it in ever decreasing circuits until I was dry.

Sometime after we got to Ed's I came in from sunbathing in the yard and sauntered in to where they were in the kitchen. Between our arrival and my return I could smell that they'd been at it. Ape jissom is not an unpleasant smell; it's sweeter and less pungent than ours. I mention this just in passing, for there was a much more interesting smell coming from the stove; Angie was cooking.

I sensed that they were excited, more excited than they were usually after copulation. This was odd. Ed is often quite taciturn, but he was beaming and sat on his chair like a red faced garden gnome. Something was up. I laid my head on my paws and took stock.

'It's absolutely finished, Angie. Everything's done, signed and sealed. Just need to wrap it.'

'And Ray's definitely coming?'

'He'll be here in about twenty minutes.'

'Can I have another look at it?'

'No you bloody can't! Control yourself woman. You'll have to wait.'

She leant across and kissed him. 'I'm so proud of you darling.'

Another kiss and a hug. I was totally bemused, and remained so until Ray arrived. You have to be warry when apes get agitated or you can end up on the wrong side of them. That old lab in the park used to say: 'Clues! Look for the clues and avoid the clouts,' so I'd shifted my position ready for anything.

'Lead on Mac Farrow!'

They all trooped off towards Ed's bloody picture. And? That was it. What's so interesting about a blob on a wall? I relaxed.

'Right, both of you,' said Ed, 'treat this as a serious event, no laughter, no sniggering, no anything but oohs and ahhs.' I was confused his voice sounded serious, but his face was smiling. They went into his hanging room, and I sauntered along and lay down by the door.

Ray had not seen the finished picture. He'd heard of it from Angie, I guessed, and while he stood in front of it staring, she grinned at Ed. When Ray turned around there were tears in his eyes. He came up to Ed and hugged him. Ed was overwhelmed, and his eyes started watering too, and then all three of them were hugging and sobbing. Roll on lunch.

'It's a one man show, no more sharing. I get to display it how I want, and the two of them and me get to choose a selection of my work, which will also include some of the Japanese stuff – that's the deal. According to Minnie Rose, they have already had huge interest, and expect the private view to be packed. One moment please.'

Ed went back to the kitchen and I shut my eyes, letting Ray and Angie's chatter wash over me.

'Brilliant!' Ray was still fighting his tears. Angie was smiling and nodding her head.

Ed returned with a bottle and glasses, and then there was a sudden explosion. I was on my feet and out of the room in an instant.

'To my longest and most loved friends,' he said pouring something from the bottle and handing a glass to each of them. 'I want to share this moment. It's been a long time coming. So, to the fucking fishes!' He said, raising his glass.

'The fucking fishes!' they said and began laughing.

I farted.

'What's that hideous smell?' said Ray, pulling a face.

It was time for me to leave and I slunk away back into the yard.

CHAPTER 30

RAY

I called a meeting of *the Shop* for Thursday night, and I knew when I sent out the e's that not many of the group would come. This didn't bother me particularly. Having witnessed Ed's success and having got as close as I had to resolving my own 'desire', I had lost interest in the rest. There had been solid achievements, but to achieve the remaining desires, which were essentially personality issues, was never going to be clear cut, and knowing how the mind works, could drag on for months. It was therefore my intention to wind the whole thing up.

Obviously, I had aired all this previously with Angie, and with Ed, since he was providing the venue. And while we waited for the meeting that probably wouldn't be a meeting, I went through our success one more time.

'Job done, you clever bugger,' said Angie, giving me a fulsome hug when I'd finished. 'In fact – you are both clever buggers, my clever buggers.' She was so excited by the outcome that she grabbed us both round the waist and spun us around in an attenuated highland reel.

'We must drink to this,' she said, her face flushed. 'Ed – booze.'

I didn't say this to them at the time, but I knew that closing down *the Shop* would not happen without incident while ever Izzie was still in the middle of her photographic thing. To stop suddenly and without warning would mean I'd stymied everything that she had done so far. She'd kill me! That wasn't going to happen, and in any case she was as excited as I was to get back on the marsh and finish the job. We just didn't need the others any more. We weren't a social club.

Thursday night was wet and surprisingly cold for early September. The meeting room was freezing.

'Where's the heating, Ed? You know what Angie's like,' I said, quiet enough not to be overheard in the kitchen.

'There is no heating, it's a bloody garage.'

'What about those heaters in the shop?'

'No, they're for the fish.'

'An hour or two without heating's not going to kill them is it?'

When seven-thirty arrived no one had come, but the room had developed a pleasant fug, thanks to a couple of fan heaters.

'Oh I nearly forgot,' said Angie, putting down her coffee. 'Peter Rock left a message. He's definitely not coming again. That's two then, since we know Lauren's not coming.'

'We'll give'em till eight,' I said.

At that point, Izzie arrived, or rather entered. She never simply opened doors and stepped in. The door opened, as if by its own volition, and then she appeared. She was swathed in a huge cape made of some dark waterproof material.

'So much for the dog days,' she said, shaking off the rain as she crossed the threshold. 'I'm chilled to the bone.' With a matador's flourish, she spun the cape from her shoulders and onto the back of a chair. 'Nobody here? I was worried that I was late. Well, how cosy,' she said, not waiting for a reply.

Beneath her cape she blazed. She wore a woollen, tight fitting dress. It was pillar-box red; the same colour as the silk scarf that swathed her neck and her outrageously bright Doc Martins. The only muted space on her body was her legs, which were veiled in thick black leggings. But beneath her dress something had happened to her breasts. There was a gothic prominence to them that was quite unsettling.

The four of us turned out to be the full complement for the night. As eight o'clock came and went, I looked for a reason to end the session, but Izzie wasn't finished with us yet. I rather think that she knew we would be the only ones and had dressed to impress.

Ed had told me that on no account was I to offer his picture up for inspection. As far as the group was concerned what he was engaged upon was still a matter for him alone. Although I understood, I had a strong desire to do exactly the opposite just to make Izzie's presence easier to endure, and I was frightened of what she was capable of saying. It wasn't that I thought she would blurt out anything about our stay in Colchester; it was that she had a way of making me do what I wasn't sure I wanted to do.

'What neither of you know, since I was the only witness, is how assiduous Raymond is. When we were on the marsh he was as fixed to his invisible trail as a gundog. I almost expected him to stop and point.' Izzie immediately froze in the serious attitude of a cocker spaniel. I smiled and the others laughed. She was very convincing.

'Didn't you find it all a bit weird – the two of you heading off blindly into the mire?' said Angie. 'You could have got stuck and drowned.'

'Do they have quick sands in Essex?' said Ed.

Izzie ignored him. 'Logic would suggest we should have been more cautious, that's true Angie, but this quest of his has nothing to do with logic and reason. Am I right, Ray? This is to do with feeling.' One hand went gently to the foothills of a breast.

'And a certain amount of research,' I said, miffed at the easy way with which she had edited out my studies.

'Of course, Raymond, dear, of course; the research is interesting, but what provoked it is something else. You proceeded by instinct. You can't reason that away.'

'You make him sound like an animal,' said Angie defensively.

Izzie laughed, totally unfazed by either of them. 'We're all animals, darling, we just don't always remember. Instinct exists, we all have it, but most of us ignore it. What use is instinct to get around a busy city if you can Google? But it's there, and Raymond has it in spades.'

I felt suddenly as if I wasn't there and had been made up in her head, and I could see that Angie was getting upset by Izzie's assumption that she knew more about me than she did.

'He's certainly driven. It's no good you pulling a face, darling, you are.'

I could see that Ed was enjoying all this. He'd never been happy with my quest in the first place. 'Ok then, Raymondo, what exactly are you going to do when you mysteriously find this elusive spot? I assume it is a spot?'

That was unkind; there was no need to join in the kicking.

'Spot, place, what does it matter what it is, Edward? That's just semantics.'

'Don't get touchy, darling. We only want to know, especially as you say you are so close.'

'Look, I don't actually know, or rather I do know that I will know. I'll be able to point at it.' I said, making my hand gestures big enough to encompass any modest sized plot of land that they could envisage.

'Then what? You come back for tea? What happens next?'

I didn't know. My attention had always been on the Pod's discovery. 'I will know what to do when I find it; I can say no more than that. Now let's call it a day and get off home.'

As we got ready, Izzie took me aside. 'Strike while the iron is hot, Ray. I am free all week, just let me know.'

I didn't reply, I just nodded.

'I'll pack a bag,' she said, squeezing my elbow and fluttering her eyes.

It was a busy week, but thankfully Angie made the choice of expedition days clearer by reminding me that she was away at the weekend working with a theatre company in Brighton, so I pencilled in Izzie and my trip to Wivenhoe for the same days. Angie also had a gig on Monday afternoon and one of Wednesday evening. The first at University Collage at the back of Euston, and the other one was working with a deaf actor in one of the National Theatre practise rooms. As I was off up town with Ed on Tuesday and we were all off together in the evening of Friday to Ed's one man show in Cork Street that was pretty well the week sown up.

I don't know anyone who flits across the country as often as Angie does, but that's the nature of her job. It's not the most well paid profession in the country, but that doesn't stop some of her clients trying to screw her for less than the going rate. I told her they'd never treat a plumber like they treat her, because a plumber would tell them where they could stick their pittance, and that's a fact.

There was just one particular bit of research that I wanted to complete before the weekend, and when Angie was out I retired to my study with the maps. Wivenhoe is on the River Colne and lies on a line between Colchester in the north and the junction of the Colne and the River Blackwater to the south. The whole of the area is low lying and criss-crossed with small rivers, lakes and drainage channels. It is seabird country, and the estuaries of the two rivers have been famed for oysters and salt workings since before Roman times. This I knew, what I didn't know was anything serious about the River Colne itself.

I'd always assumed that the Celtic underlay of England could be touched with diligence. Despite Colchester being the oldest city in Britain and, as a city, a foundation of the Romans, beneath it lay the ghostly footings of the onetime capital of the powerful ancient British tribe known as the Trinovantes. I was genetically a Celt, whatever that meant in reality, fact. My hunch, the *raison d'être* to my whole *Bucket Shop* enterprise was that somehow I could intuit that deeper strata of our island history and it was this that was calling me to my grave. Now, I was also absolutely clear that this was a mental construct, but considering that contemporary genetic maps have shown that the root population of the British isles was until the coming of the railways pretty stable, and that, amazingly, the present population's genetic makeup echoes that stability and fits almost exactly with the same tribal boundaries of our dim and distant forebears, you never know, maybe something was drawing me to the Colne that was deeper and stronger than I understood.

There was one problem to my Celtic underlay theory. Were the Trinovantes Celts? They were a hugely powerful British tribe but they were linked to the Belgic end of the tribal continuum? This was important because Caesar refers to them as like their neighbours the Germans. Added to the fact that I knew that present day self-defined Celts, no matter what they might believe, do not have an overarching DNA link that unites them with all the other self-proclaimed Celts, it meant that the historic continuum was very, very, muddy.

I tried breaking down the name of the river itself, but got nowhere. It was supposed to be of British origin, and in some roundabout way linked to another well-known river name: Clun, but even so, the meaning was obscure. Without a fact to hold on to I was left with only my theory and the strange, but real, pressure of my internal homing device. I was torn between fantasy and facts, which for someone like me was unbearable. No wonder that even my best friends thought I was bonkers. I thought I was bonkers! But bonkers or not, the pull was real and I could almost touch it since it came now from a feeling in my gut, and I knew I would not be free of it until alone or with Izzie I crossed the Colne and found my place-of-death.

There was something liberating about walking with Ed through the back streets of the West End later in the week. As a student, and for some time afterwards, Soho and the galleries situated in the streets within walking distance of it was where we all hung out. Every cellar seemed to be a club, and cafes and restaurants came and went with the seasons. It was our town. Tourists could swarm through it as much as they liked, but they knew nothing. You had to be there and in-the-know to know exactly where IT was happening, which, actually, often meant a trek out of the West End and into the seedy dives of Camden or the even seedier clubs south of the river in Chelsea and Battersea. It was not that we did anything different from the kids now, apart from the music and the moves, it's the same: we simply hung out, talked and talked and talked and got rat arsed.

Shambling down Berwick Street I caught a reflection of the two of us in the window of a remnants shop. Ed had recently let his hair grow; it was still dark, but the extra length had bulked up the silver highlights; it suited him, and made him look less like a disgruntled badger, especially as he was also wearing an Italian cashmere scarf and the sort of greyish, herringbone, tweedy looking sports jacket favoured by aging TV pundits. Long hair refined Ed; the same effect on me would have been disastrous. We Brooks are not known for the abundance of our hair. Apart from an underpowered, fairish quiff that I wore like a cockade, the rest of my head was shorn almost to the bone. I was too angular to be interesting. I looked like one of those slim, Peter Pan, gay men who drift around Old Compton Street, or, considering my idiotic quest, a spindle-shanked Don Quixote accompanied by a leaner and more handsome Sancho Panza, who was also full of equally dull peasant sayings.

'Nice shoes,' I said as we were passing some plate glass windows on Regent's Street, not because I liked them, but because the windows were bigger.

While Ed looked in, I regarded us both standing side by side. No, Don Quixote was another stupid idea. I wasn't that much taller than him, and nor was I lean and lanky, I was just slightly taller and trim enough for my age without being gaunt.

190

'They're bollocks!' he said, trying to work out what had happened to my aesthetic sense.

We walked on to a pub just behind Burlington Arcade and settled down over a couple of pints and two huge ploughman's lunches.

'Good cheese,' I said.

'Beer's good too.'

Happiness all round.

'This thing you've got with Izzie, are you, you know?' He clamped his mouth shut on the roll, ripped off a mouthful and then stared at me over the knob end.

I had half been expecting something, and wasn't that surprised that once we were stationary it would all come pouring out. I made a 'weird suggestion' face and leaned towards my beer. 'Come on, Ed,' I said, hoping that supping the ale would alter my features enough to look casual. 'You're right, it is good beer.'

'How long have I known you, Raymondo? I'll tell you: nearly forty fucking years. You're like a brother. I know you and you are fundamentally sly. Come on, I'm not going to tell Angie.'

I put my beer down. I didn't need props anymore. I was ready. I smiled as one brother to another. 'I thought about it. You know, as you do in passing. Despite everything, she's one sexy lady, and approachable, but I haven't. Not that she wouldn't, no, I'm pretty sure she would, given half a chance, but we haven't.'

'Spoken like a bloody geriatric,' he said, laughing. 'Come on! What, too hot to handle?'

'Ha ha. No. As if! I'm just not interested, strange as you might find that. I'm a happily married man. And I know how frustrating it must be for you single men, but no, Izzie and I are just partners; we're working this thing together, that's all.'

Ed's face changed. The mockery had left it. 'No, I don't think I would either. Is she ok? You know, I mean do you get on with her? Not totally off the planet is she? I'm only asking because, well, she *is* odd.'

'Yeah, she is odd, I'll give you that. But no, we get on fine. In some ways she's a bit like you.'

'God, I hope not!'

'She wants recognition for her work, and she believes that what she's been doing with us, and with me in particular, will bring her that. Just like you, she says this will be her masterpiece, so that afterwards everyone will know her name.'

'Fuck off! I'm not like that. I don't give a toss about that sort of recognition. That's fucking celebrity rubbish.'

I laughed. I was now in control. 'Yeah, well, maybe. We'll see when she's finished.'

Why didn't I tell him that we had slept together? He wouldn't have told Angie, I was sure of that. He'd understand. He wasn't a prude. But then again, it wasn't the sex. I knew why I'd never tell him; it was because I'd look silly. Izzie was larger than life, certainly more alive than either of us. We plodded towards our graves but she wasn't even moving in the same direction. She was still busting with the present, still committed to her world and not to the next. The idea of such a vibrant person shagging me just didn't match. He'd think that it was weird, that I was too far away from the pulse of life to make a showing. I was dull, and at that moment I felt it.

CHAPTER 31

ED

O n the morning of the show, Angie had slipped across the marsh to the shop with Geordie. The cold spell had gone and there was light and sun again in the morning, on occasions. This was one of them. In honour of the forth-coming show, and because I couldn't settle down, I had cleaned the place from top to bottom. It hadn't looked as organized and as sparkling since the estate agent had first handed me the keys. I'd also sorted myself out. I was leaving nothing to chance. It is one thing to look like a scruffy bugger in the studio, that was expected, but the show had to be a success, and so no matter what I thought about tarting about in front of the money, I had to look the part. I couldn't afford to blow it. It was my big chance. So when Angie arrived, I was showered, shaved and smelling good.

The early morning celebration had been her idea. She said that she didn't want me to be alone on such a memorable day, and she also wanted to show me what it all meant to her, which meant that as soon as Geordie was settled, we went upstairs and snuggled down beneath the newly laundered duvet.

'You've even ironed the sheets!' she said. 'Oh darling!'

I wasn't the only one to have made an effort. She lay beside me in a beautiful black camisole and matching French knickers. It was my turn to grin. She knew what I liked and her forethought touched me deeply. We may have known each other for years and years, but I never grew tired of her beauty. In fact, knowing her for so long and watching the changes in her face and body made our love making even more delicious. All those years, all of the frustrations and difficulties were as nothing. When we were together we remade ourselves and our world. I even grew to accept my own gnarled features and less than ideal physique. In her eyes I was beautiful, as she was in mine.

'You never gave up did you, darling?' she said, leaning on my chest.

I looked up into her eyes and Ray's brutal, but banal, *'Artists don't just look, they see,'* came into my head with delicious irony, because I saw in detail the beautiful rise of Angie's breasts above the lace of her camisole, magic, but I turned away and looked up into her eyes, which were embarrassingly full of love.

'Don't make me out to be some kind of artistic hero, darling. It's just what I do. Take away the painting and I'm just a bloody fishmonger. It's not a hard choice, is it? While ever I paint there's some point to my - existence.'

'You're also a twat. But my twat,' she said, kissing me.

I raised my eyebrows, not at being called a twat, which was bang on, but at the thought that I was hers.

'Don't make that face, darling, it makes you look stupid. I just want to say that we've survived all this time because we love each other. And I know I'm married to Ray, and I love him too; I do. The maths might be odd but the love isn't. I love you both but differently. You both answer needs in me, and they don't conflict. I'm not torn between you both. He and I are not you and me. The only person who is divided is me. It just is. I can no more explain it than you can. That's how it works. So like it or not: you *are* my twat and I am yours.'

We slumped back giggling like two teenagers. She'd once said that he and I were like two sides of a sandwich with her as the filling, and she was right. Take either side away and what would it become? A bloody smorgasbord. We weren't like that, because if we were it would imply that one of us was missing out, which wasn't true. I could no more explain how it worked than she could. It just happened and has kept on happening. And neither he nor I have suffered unduly. He may have had more physical time with her, but I had sufficient for whom I was, essentially a loner; what was there not to like? We gave each other what we both wanted and, as a bonus, we gave each other space to be ourselves.

The movement of her body beneath the warm silk was too delicious to ignore and we stopped each other's mouths with kisses and moved easily into our familiar routine of love making.

There was hardly time for coffee before Angie was off again over the marsh. When she had gone, I hung around in my dressing gown not wanting the memory of our time together to vanish too quickly. I can't count the times over the years that I have smelt my hands and arms after we've been together hunting for traces of her perfume.

I stepped into the yard and sat on one of the retired kitchen chairs and let the sun warm my thighs. At that moment my head was clear of everything. A lover can gift the loved one nothing more beautiful than the obliteration of self. All I was conscious of was my smile and the sun. I knew then what contentment meant. The experience lasted for all of five minutes before the delivery man arrived with next week's shop order.

I must say that the Packhorses' gallery looked stunning, and the lighting, which I had supervised, was perfect. I allowed myself a brief moment of pride as I stood in front of the '*The Miracle of the Fishes*'. I'd done that, just me, and yet looking at it I couldn't imagine how on earth I had. It looked far too complicated and too well executed to be my work, but it was. Look at the marks! I'd bloody done it, all right.

'You'll be amazed, Ed, just how many of our visitors this week have stood where you are standing and done just what you're doing – stopped and stared,' said Hugo Packard, coming silently to my side. 'Terrific, don't you think?'

'Bloody marvellous!'

'And have you seen what we've done to the gyotaku? They look outstanding.'

In a smaller side room the dozen or so Japanese styled fish prints were arranged in a flowing wavelike movement across one of the walls. I stepped back amazed.

'Wow.'

As I went from one image to the next, I heard the tap, tap, tap of Minerva's high heels as she came into the room behind us. The tailored jeans had gone, but not the tailoring. Her dark trouser suit was immaculate.

'Come and have a drink, Ed, while we're waiting.'

'Hey up! Someone's had one, then?' I said, checking the red spot on one of the prints.

'Chap came in during the week, loved them. Hoping to be here tonight.'

On the way to their office we passed the hospitality table lined with a regiment of Argentinian Malbec. Good, I liked Malbec. But if they were the infantry, on their desk next to them was the colonel: an opened bottle of Gevrey-Chambertin; Edward Farrow, my old son, you have arrived.

'Salut,' said Minerva,' raising her glass.

'Man to man, Ed,' said Hugo, delivering a light punch to my shoulder.

'And woman to man,' added Minerva coyly.

'We are convinced that this is the break we've all been working towards. That,' he said pointing out towards the gallery, 'is a truly remarkable painting; huge amount of interest.'

'And we want more,' said Minerva. 'We want lots more.' Her eyes flashed. 'This is your time, Edward, and together we must maximize it.'

I emptied my glass. 'Bloody 'ell! The paints hardly dry and you're on about an encore.'

'*Di preciso!*' said Hugo, pointing the bottle at my empty glass. 'To the future!'

We clinked again.

'Well,' I said cagily, 'Already got a few ideas. Early yet, but fermenting nicely.'

'Wonderful,' said Minerva, giving me a gentle hug and a peck on the cheek.

It wasn't strictly true; I had had one idea: to create a visual love letter to Angie inspired by Correggio's *Leda*, with the Walthamstow marshes replacing the sylvan backdrop. In Correggio's picture of the Greek myth, Leda is seduced by Zeus disguised as a very randy swan. Now I've nothing against swans, everyman to his own, but if I was to have an animal stand-in then I reckoned it had to be Geordie, since he'd shuttled between us like one of the Greek Fates.

I only started to relax once Angie and Ray had arrived. It seemed like I'd been talking ever since the doors had opened. I just didn't expect to see so many people that I knew, but I've got to hand it to them, the Packhorses had been busy, it was almost a *Who's Who* of the figurative art world. It was amazing. I was blown away.

'Hey Angie, in the corner,' I said, surreptitiously nudging her, 'that's Billy Walcott, big noise at the University of the Arts. And you know what he said to me just now? The finest piece of figurative art he'd seen since Lucian Freud.'

'Come here, mate,' said Ray, sweeping me into an awkward hug. I looked behind him at Angie, her eyes radiant.

I smiled too, basking in their happiness, or I did until I saw my *doppelgänger* coming towards me. For a fraction of a second, he *was* me. My stomach chilled. I felt sick. Then I realized that it was Max. As he embraced first Angie and then Ray, I blanched and stood to the side gurning at Gwen. He may have been taller, but his features were a spitting image. I had to be his father, there was no other explanation; the likeness was too strong.

'Ed, good to see you.'

I was hugged again. My son hugged his dad, and his dad, only briefly, held on to him.

'So impressed. We love it, don't we Gwen?'

My son's intended and I embraced, as family's do.

'So pleased we came. I have always loved that fish print that you gave Max. And this picture is absolutely beautiful; Jesus's face is stunning. And when I say it's beautiful,' she said, staring at me, becoming suddenly anxious about her choice of adjectives, 'I mean; it's brilliant.'

'Thank you,' I said, squinting modestly. 'I like beautiful.'

Seeing that her adjective had been well received, she stepped forward and kissed me.

'Pardon my intrusion, just a quick word, Ed.' Hugo slid in beside me; put his hand between my shoulders, and smiling broadly whispered into my ear. 'Sold!'

It was only after following his eyes to where the picture hung in all its glory that I understood what he had said.

'Well, fuck me!'

'Rather not, old boy. We'll talk later.' He punched my shoulder again, only harder, and slipped away into the throng.

For a moment I just stood frowning.

'Nothing wrong is there?' said Ray.

'Oh yeah, ten-thousand quid, fucking wrong, mate. They've only gone and sold it.' We all turned to the picture and at the well-heeled punters who stood before it. 'Bloody hell! I think I need a drink.'

Looking back, I've no idea what happened to Max and Gwen after that, or what happened to any of us, for that matter. We drank, I know that, and the drinking carried on way after the Malbec regiment had fallen and most of the punters had left. I vaguely remember travelling in a taxi and lolling in the back like a sozzled pasha. I couldn't sit up straight; I just swayed between my two equally pissed friends, ignoring everything except the bands of colour that streaked passed the windows.

I don't even remember getting to bed, probably because I didn't actually make it into my own bed. I woke up in the house in Mayola Road with Ray on one side of me, snoring his head off, and Angie, gawping at the ceiling, on the other. Our romantic sandwich had metamorphosed, and I was now the bit in the middle. Ray was well gone, and as far as I could see so had his trousers and jacket. He lay beside me in his shirt and shorts. Angie was spark out, lying beside me in a shimmering deep blue slip, her legs bared to the thighs and her arms splayed out like a comatose highland dancer. I looked down at myself; I was stripped to my T-shirt and new, M&S boxers.

I tried to wriggle upright, but the ceiling moved alarmingly and I lay back. I looked around instead. It was a novel view. I'd never been in this particular bed with Angie before; if we made love in the house, which wasn't that often, we went into the spare room. We maintained a sense of propriety even in our adultery.

The question was what to do? I didn't want to wake them, not yet, and being that close to Angie was too tempting to resist; I wanted to touch her. But to caress her while she lay sleeping next to Ray, my oldest and best loved friend, was so wrong and way beyond anything we'd ever done before that it was, as a consequence, totally irresistible. What an evil thought; I was such a bastard even to think it. I gawped at her with my mouth open; she looked so totally available and so glorious in the mottled light. I wanted very much to run my hand over her stomach and follow the silk to where it ended just above her knees. I knew it was stupid. If Ray woke up and found me rummaging his wife on the marital bed he would not be best pleased. He would go fucking bonkers!

But I was possessed, so much that my chest ached. Very gently I laid my hand on her hip. Oh god the silk was hot as skin and the temptation to explore even further was overwhelming. My hand slid higher, and then, with the lightning speed of a closing gin trap, she grabbed my wrist. She was awake.

In the half-darkness we stared into the wide black pits of each other's eyes. I had almost stopped breathing. Our faces were only a tongue's distance apart. I could have licked her nose. I did lick her nose. We slid closer until we touched from top to toe, but there was no question of making love. It was an antique bed; too much hammer and it would sing loud enough to raise Ray and the neighbours. So we kissed as quietly and as secretly as mice and let loose the fingers of fun, and all the time we played Ray slumbered, snorting away in oblivion. It was one of the most exciting and sensual experiences that I've ever had. Afterwards we were completely spent. There was nothing to say, so we simply lay apart and lost ourselves in sleep.

At breakfast the next day, we went over the opening in all its fine detail, but the fact that we'd all woken up together in the same bed was hardly mentioned. A few ribald comments at the start and it became of no more significance than all of the rest of the evening's events.

Angie had been the first one up. I'd felt her move and had heard her disappear downstairs, so after a swift douse in the bathroom I went down to join her. The memory of our love making was still very fresh, and we held each other in a long, passionate embrace.

'That was so beautiful, darling. I don't think I've had such a good sleep in ages,' she said chuckling. 'Thank you.'

'What a way to end the day.'

CHAPTER 32

RAY

'I shall miss you, darling,' said Angie, when I was standing by the door ready to go. 'But if you, you know – can't help yourself, I won't mind, you know that? I'd be jealous, but I don't own you. And she is sexy.'

I made a few feeble face contortions before answering. 'Thanks, I'll remember when we're getting down and dirty.'

'No, I mean it, darling, just lie back and enjoy it. Don't even think about me.'

'We are not going away for a dirty weekend, darling. This is research.'

I'd been really excited at the prospect of driving off to Essex as I waved Angie goodbye from the doorstep, but the road soon put an end to that. At some time, off to the south, the distant gleaming towers of Dagenham and the low edge of Essex disappeared as Izzie and I headed further east towards Chelmsford and Colchester. Although I had studied the area's maps many times before, and had delighted in its underlying topography, nothing ever prepared me for the horror of its present reality. As I stared out of the window of her car, I felt my earlier excitement leach away. London's expansion between the arms of the A12 and the A13 had wiped out out whatever charm the area had once known, and had replaced it with a landscape of grim despair.

The relentless ugliness sank me so far into my boots that I started to question what I was doing hunched up in the car in the first place. Even Izzie, who had been chirping away from the moment we set off, had become silent once we had passed Barking. When I had got up I'd felt really keen, because I knew that today was going to be a special day. Izzie had felt the same and we had both been expecting success. My POD was close; last time it had been almost close enough to touch, but now, as the wheels hissed in anguish, I had begun to rubbish the whole enterprise.

Ed had been right; the whole idea of finding my place-of-death had been stark staring mad. Friends are sanity's sounding boards and I should have listened, but instead I had heeded the feeling in my stomach, which was real, and even as my gloom grew I could still feel it nagging away. That wasn't make-believe that was a fact.

The tedious eastern suburbs had sapped my will to live and had teased away at everything I'd been working towards more thoroughly than all the arguments I had heard from my friends, leaving me with nothing but questions. Did I really believe that when we crossed over the river Colne and walked into the marsh there would be something to look at, some object, something solid that I would instantly recognise as it, my POD? Looking across the river last time there had been nothing taller than a dog, nothing obvious to see at all, not a tree, not a wreck, not even overblown weeds and vegetation. So how in a uniform world of vegetation would I know? Would I just stop and point to some spot on the ground and say: 'That's it, that's where I will die?'

It had been at that moment that I had remembered what Izzie had said about all the stuff I'd seen stuffed into the back of her car as we had left Hackney.

'Props, my darling. Today is an auspicious day and we need to make sure we've got things to enhance it with.'

'What like these posts and things?'

She'd laughed. 'It's a good job you gave up art, Raymond, and turned to cartography. The marsh is bleak, *n'est pas?* Curiously haunting, of course, but devoid of objects to enhance the scene. Supposing your POD turns out to be just a pool of stagnant water or a mildly interesting tussock? Where's the art in that? These,' she had inclined her finger to the rear, 'are my photographic aids, my travelling studio.'

As I wasn't going to be the one taking the photographs, I'd let it go at the time. But supposing she had been right, and where I thought the place was turned out to be completely featureless, what then? I might have started to think that the whole enterprise was looking threadbare, but not Izzie, especially as she was still engaged in her 'great work'. As an artist, she was not going to be satisfied with the photograph of a damp sod, even if it turned out to be me.

Everything I had worked for had begun to unravel. For months most of my energies had been centred on finding that one significant place, and yet in the end what was it based on: intellect, no, nothing more durable than a form of mental and spiritual dyspepsia? Why on earth had I imagined that it would make sense that I was going to die on a marsh in Essex, for god's sake? Even if my intuition had been right, and the nagging had stopped at a particular place on the marsh, what sane person would have ever gone near that place again? It's a marsh for god's sake, there's nothing there unless you are a birdwatcher or a fisherman, and I was neither of them. If I wished to cheat death then all I had to do was avoid going anywhere near Wiven-fucking-hoe again.

But the pull was still strong, even where we were on the charmless outskirts of Romford. It had to mean something. Maybe though, it wasn't about my death at all, maybe my interpretation of the feeling was skew-whiff; perhaps it was all to do with a sense of belonging, of identifying with a place? Perhaps I was connecting with the past in some way, to things that had happened on the marsh long, long, ago, things buried beneath the land; ancestral things; secrets that will out? But Izzie was right; artistically speaking the marsh was a blank canvas. Shorn of people, buildings and interruptions by the sea and the weather the marsh was a void. It was a space where the past was constantly wiped clean. In which case, I suppose, anyone with a strong enough desire to belong could claim it for their own, even me.

Ever since I had switched to map making I had become increasingly conscious of the deep history of our islands and the people who had named their features. It had thrilled me. All those ancient names sown onto a relatively unchanging topography were beautiful. I used to inscribe them with joy. I was connected to those people, even though my family and I were rootless metropolitans. There were no stories in my family of country villages where the churchyard heaved with the worm soil of my dead ancestors. Studying the landscape and talking to it through cartography had set me apart from those other luckier people, who knew their more precise origins, and had given me a broader connection to our island history. Maybe then, my POD was not a place of death, therefore, but a place of discovery? Perhaps the quest was an attempt to put down metaphorical roots?

My brain went into over drive; and not just metaphorical roots, because if I altered my will, I could physically put down roots at my POD by insisting that my ashes be buried or scattered there, so that from that time hence my life would have a focal point: Raymond Brook was scattered there.

It had all suddenly become sickeningly clear. I'd been too close to the outcome of the whole project, and had not spent enough time evaluating it. I felt completely foolish, and had begun to imagine how everyone else must have thought of me. How could I have been so one-tracked? I almost didn't want to go on, since an exact spot on the marsh was now hardly appropriate. And unless I took my executor to the actual spot before I popped my clogs, who would know where that spot was when the time came for the scattering? Izzie wouldn't be around to ask, and even if I had produced a beautiful and exact map of the place it wouldn't work either, because people don't read maps properly and no one is going to think that there's any difference between one anonymous spot and another. They'll just turn up with the plastic urn, be overawed by the bleakness of the landscape, look for an easy place to shed the load and then high tail it back to the marina for a swift half in the Rose and Crown.

'You know what, Izzie?' I said excitedly, 'I think I've found the POD already.'

'Excellent, darling, excellent – where?'

'It's the marsh itself. The whole place; there is no *one* spot.'

She did not smile at my revelation. Her face was still, her perpetually pale skin if anything paler.

'Oh no, no, no, Ray, not the whole marsh. That's absurd. You pointed out across the river to an actual place. I saw you. You did not sweep your arms out to embrace the wide blue yonder. It was specific. No, no, there is a place and *together* we will find it.' Her eyes were bright but steely as she laid her hand on my knee and gave it an encouraging squeeze. 'I too feel a compulsion. No faint hearts, *mio compagno*. We're in this together. One last trek and the job is almost done.'

'Almost?'

She gave a short hollow laugh. 'When I have caught all that is worth catching, when I have drained the fetid marsh of its soul, then I shall return home and exercise my magic and only after that, after I have transformed you, and the results are on the wall, will the job really be done.'

'Well, yes of course; I mean that–; it was only a thought.'

Again she laughed, and equally without humour. 'How hard we moderns try to argue away instinct. The rational brain just can't cope with intuition. Tell me, Ray, do you dream?'

'Ah well, yes, we all dream, don't we, and I'm no different.' She was beginning to worry me. 'That's what keeps us sane, isn't it?'

'And where do your dreams take you?'

'Nowhere, I mean, all over. They're dreams. There's never anything stronger than a hint of an actual place.'

'Last night I dreamt that you and I made love under a star lit sky.'

She turned to make sure I could see her face, but I was too concerned with her driving to take more than a cursory glance.

'Wishful thinking,' I added, and wished I hadn't.

'Dreams are gateways to the soul and to our true feelings,' she said, gripping my knee again. 'I have dreamed how this day will end, and have already experienced something of the emotion its conclusion will bring.' She seemed to gyrate slowly on her seat, while her hand slid a short distance up my thigh.

'And the work,' I said, feeling stirrings in my trousers, 'once it's up on the wall, I want to be first in line to look at it.'

'That will be after our own private celebrations, Raymondo.' Her hand slipped between my legs and gently squeezed my balls. 'When my work is shown, when all that you have gone through is viewed by others, I want it to be a testament to *feeling*, and to me, of course.' Her hand returned to the steering wheel. 'Edward has had his moment, mine is to come. My great work will finally announce *me* to the world; and *you*, my darling, will be hailed as the midwife to my birth.'

'Oh come on, Izzie,' I said, wriggling to get comfortable, 'that's a bit over the top, no one gives a toss about me, and people know who you are already. Remember, I've Googled you.'

'And *you* remember, dear man, that *that* is history. My own creation is still in process. It's not complete, and nor is our mission. We shall find the POD, and later I shall rise to the internet heaven on a cloud of glittering pixels. Now, do be a love, take a gander at the map and tell me: do we bypass Chelmsford *after* Margaretting?'

We had booked in at The Black Buoy, an ancient riverside pub in Wivenhoe, and after depositing our personal stuff, and admiring the beautiful view over the Colne, Izzie and I went back down to the car and started to unload her mobile studio.

'What on earth?' I said, seeing for the first time what lay underneath the baggage on the backseat. 'That's a sheep hurdle!'

'A *small* hurdle,' she replied, as if its size was explanation enough.

'But?'

'All in good time, Raymondo, all in good time. Could you grab that small carving on the floor, there's a dear.'

I leant into the foot well and brought out a wooden, very crudely sculpted human figure. It was primitive, little more than a casual whittling.

By the time we began our trudge out towards the ferry crossing, we were heavily laden. Apart from her props, Izzie had packed enough food to see us through the whole day, and, I noticed, bottles of beer.

As the mid-day sun gilded the water, the water threw the light back into the sky. Birds rose and fell, geese in bunches flew low towards the saltmarsh and hidden water birds piped and called. There was no sign of rain; everything suggested we would have no problems reaching our destination dry shod. The only hindrance was the weight of our burdens, which grew heavier with every step.

We had crossed the Colne by the ferry to the Rowhedge side of the river, and were going to eat our lunch once we'd trudged away from the outlying buildings and boat yards. I was a bit peeved that thanks to all of Izzie's tranklements, we had been charged at the going rate for bicycles and not foot passengers.

I didn't share my disgruntlement with Izzie, because, to tell the truth, I'd been so concerned with my own thoughts since we had left Hackney that I'd hardly been aware of her other than as a presence. On the path out from the village, where she had taken the lead, her position in front of me focused my attention to her back. I was so used to her dressing flamboyantly, that her present get up had gone more or less unnoticed. It was still bright, but not red, rather a mat bronze. There was a beautiful symmetry to her bottom, and its pleasant geography brought to mind the rolling contours of the South Downs, but before I could pursue the idea, she stumbled. As she flayed around trying to remain upright, her paint spattered old combat jacket flew open and I realized that the bronze trousers were in fact the bottom half of yet another of her habitual boiler suits. Nothing she wore was worn by chance; she was always a performance. So as I started to wonder at the choice of colour, I remembered something else. When I'd got into the car I had been struck by how surprisingly defined her breasts had appeared, which brought to mind the last night in Ed's garage, when she must have been wearing the same gothic brassiere. Izzie had obviously come in costume.

We set our loads down on a raised part of the river bank, and settled down side by side with our backs resting on a tiny eroded mud cliff covered in grey, dried river grass.

'Thank god! That was getting heavy.'

'You are still a fit man, my love. Well fit,' she added with a hint of street patois. 'I enjoy seeing your muscles work.'

'And I yours,' I said archly, feeling that if, as she had indicated, we had already had a dream fuck, then advancing the possibility of a real one forward an hour of two was no bad thing.

'I could feel your eyes on me,' she said, dipping into her bag and handing me a pork pie. 'I love to see a man eat pie.'

Happy to oblige, I rubbed the crust sensuously around my lips and then took an oversized bite at it. My noisy mastication seemed to confirm her interest and she rolled her eyes appreciatively.

'Good pie.'

'You can tell as much about a person by the way they eat as you can about what they eat.'

'Normally, I'm more refined, that was a *big* mouthful,' I replied, licking my lips lasciviously.

'You lunged at the pie with an almost animal passion.'

'I'm hungry,' I said, chewing the pie cud provocatively.

I knew she understood what I was doing, but instead of keeping the flirting at its present heat, she did what she often did, she came out with a completely bland, slightly authoritarian statement.

'I want to be at the POD before the light goes, my darling, so eat up and let's hoof it.'

The clinical tone of her voice removed the last vestiges of provocation from my mouthful and I swallowed.

Although I no longer really believed in the POD, I had to admit that I could still feel a pull, and it seemed to be pointing me towards a space no more than a few hundred yards off to the left of the path we were on.

As far as I could see, we were entirely alone. There was nothing between us and the distant estuary but low lying marsh and the self-interested activity of sea birds. Walking unencumbered would have been difficult, for what looked like a level surface at a distance was anything but. Lumbered as we were, we crossed the next few hundred yards haltingly, discovering hidden gullies and sea water creeks that had to be negotiated with extreme care. The further from the path we went, the springier the ground became, so that we appeared to be crossing the borderlands between land that was and land that might one day come to be.

I found the POD almost at once; I just stopped in my tracks. There was an actual spot. I was as surprised as Izzie. I couldn't stand over it because it was a small thin pool of brackish water, but it was there, my whole inside seemed to be pulled towards it. I was quite overwhelmed, because it was something beyond myself, and the me in my head no longer felt in command. I dropped my load, took a few steps beyond the pool, just to test it, but it was no good; I felt the pull to return. It was so precise and so strong that it made all of my previous speculations about the existence of the POD meaningless. It wasn't the whole marsh, it was *the* pool. I turned around and stared into the dark water hoping that its meaning would pop up from below like a gas bubble.

I heard Izzie drop her load and half saw her scurry around me. Then I heard her camera zizzing away. I turned to face her and the zizzing increased. There was no need to say anything, she knew, but in a sense, I didn't. What now? The pulling had ceased and had left me feeling empty. I looked around in a daze, hardly taking in the calling birds or the rest of the salt marsh. I was rooted to the spot in a state of quietude.

'Kneel down, darling. Kneel down. That's it. Just look into the pool, bend your head forward. That's it. Hold that.' She shot away. I had no will. I would look into the pool for ever if she asked.

'Right, Raymondo, up, come on. We've work to do.' I felt her arms around me as she hoisted me to my feet.

'I feel weird, Izzie.'

'Of course you do, of course you do. It's not every day we discover our POD!' The acronym resonated in my head like a small explosion. 'Now we must set the scene for posterity. This is the moment, Ray, the one we have been working for.' Her voice was very controlled, and very quiet. 'Take off you jacket and slip off your boots.'

I did as she commanded, happy to do anything that would kick start my brain again. The ground was warm and wet, and I felt the sun hot on my arms.

'Pop this on, my love,' she said, handing me a loose smock made of a coarse, plaid material. 'Perfect! You really look the part.'

'Of what?'

She didn't answer, instead she too began disrobing. I looked on wide eyed, barely understanding what I was watching. Underneath the trousers of her boiler suit she was wearing what looked like a pair of tie-dyed harem pants. But most dramatically,

I discovered the answer to puzzling shape of her breasts. She was wearing a moulded, conical bra framed to look like every decreasing circles of bronze.

She came towards me bearing a small drink in a vessel made from what appeared to be a cow horn.

'Drink this, darling. It is a love potion.'

I took the cup and drained it while she pressed herself against me. I remember the sun on my face, but not much more, nothing in fact until I became conscious of her face inches from mine.

'Oh Raymond! Under the sky and beneath the sun, soon, soon, my work will be done.'

Even though I was feeling both randy and incredibly woozy, the oddness of her words still struck me. 'What work?'

'*You* my darling, *you* are my work.' She took both of my hands in hers. 'Step into the pool!'

I had no will at all. Her voice echoed in my head and my legs seemed to move of their own volition. The water was warm and not unpleasant. For no reason at all it made me smile with delight.

'Lie down and let the water embrace you. Down you go, my darling, down.'

I was more than happy to oblige. I had no desire to do anything other than what she asked. Unfortunately, I couldn't lie down completely because my head would have disappeared beneath the water. I found my quandary unbearably amusing and sat with the water lapped around my waist giggling.

'Lie back, Raymond, back on to your elbows.'

The tepid water was wonderful, embracing and all surrounding. My head hung back like a heavy weight, and I stared into the sky grinning happily, while all the time the camera whirred.

Out of the corner of my eye, I saw her carrying the hurdle towards the pool's edge.

'Hold this on to top of you, my sweet.'

I did was she suggested, why not, why not do everything she said? And while I lay there with the hurdle on my chest she began scurrying around it pulling out the short cords which were attached to its chestnut poles. Then, using a mallet produced from her bag, she began banging in a lot of wooden pegs and tying the cords to them, so that I was eventually caught beneath the hurdle like a sardine on a griddle.

'Now what?'

She didn't answer, but worked silently at making the larger stakes we had lugged into a structure that stood upright near the pool's edge.

'There – the scene is set. How does it feel?'

'This hurdle makes it all a bit awkward. Couldn't we do without it?'

'Later, my little fuss pot. You can't have Yule without a tree, and you can't have a tree without trimmings.'

Her words sounded in my head like cracked bells, and made absolutely no sense until she started fetching things from her backpack. She carried a rough unglazed beaker and laid it reverentially beside me beneath the water. Then she leaned across me with what looked like a half-eaten leg of lamb and dropped it into the water.

'No chance of going hungry then,' I said, smiling up into the rings of her bronze bra where it pushed towards me through the lattice of the hurdle.

'No chance at all,' she said, emptying into the water what looked like a bag of hazelnuts in their shells.

When she returned next she brought with her the crudely carved manikin I'd seen in the car and gently laid it on top of the hurdle. And that was that. Satisfied that what she had arranged fitted the picture in her head, she began to set up a tripod and arrange her photographic stuff for the final pictures.

'Shall I smile?' I said, unable to do anything but grin inanely.

I was feeling totally relaxed and almost flippant. Whatever compulsion had brought me to this place was over. This was fun. The pull in my stomach had stopped, the day was bright and warm and soon I would clean up and we would return to the 'Dirty Dog' or whatever it was called and have the promised fuck.

'Oh Raymond, do look at this. I want you to imagine it blown up to life-size and printed on a perfect rag paper.'

She knelt down beside the pool and pointed her camera's viewer at me.

'Wow! That is impressive. You know what it reminds me of? One of those Bronze Age sacrifices our ancestors used to make. The bodies in the bog! Brilliant!'

'Well thank you for that, my darling. That's exactly what I was trying to achieve.' She put down the camera and brought out from her bag a bottle of beer, which she opened.

'At last – the celebration.'

'Strictly speaking, of course, it should be ale or better still mead; beer like this is rather too modern, but needs must. First the libation.' She sprinkled some of the beer into the pool. 'To your history and your destiny, my love.' Then she drank.

'I can't sit up with all of this stuff on me.'

'Of course not, darling. Here open your mouth.'

I opened wide, but no matter how hard I struggled to swallow, she took no notice and kept pouring until I almost choked.

'Thank you, Raymond. Thank you. And now - goodbye. We'll never meet again in life, although we'll be tied together in eternity.' She stood up, twinkled her right hand fingers at me and then began packing up the things she was taking back.

'Oh come on, Izzie, it's getting cold. Let's go back and *celebrate*.'

She turned round one last time and smiled. 'But I am celebrating. Bye bye.'

As she moved out of sight my horizon shrank. There was nothing to see now but a ring of blue sky surrounded by marsh grass. I was alone and so befuddled that I collapsed back into the water and nearly drowned myself. But the dunking seemed to bring back some of my senses and I struggled up onto my elbows spitting out the salty water. My eyes were stinging, and I waved my head from side to side desperately trying to avoid the sunlight. The pain was so great, and I was so desperate to rub them, that it brought my senses back.

'What the fuck?'

I pulled at my bonds, assuming that they were only lightly tied, but they were so tight that I couldn't get any real purchase. I was splayed out like a spatchcock.

'Izzie! Izzie!' My manic screams went unheeded into the wide Essex skies. 'Well bugger that!' I said, giving an exasperated wrench with my shoulders. 'Ah!' It hurt, but I felt a slight movement of the peg, and so I strained up again with my whole body. There was movement, but not a lot, so I tried rolling as far as I could from one side to the other. The movement increased. It was working. I knew that if I could loosen one bond then I would be able to slither out from beneath the hurdle and sort out the rest.

It was hard work; it took time, my bones and muscles ached, and then, after one enormous yank, I was so exhausted that I fell back without control and dunked my head under the water. The salt bit into my eyes, which angered me so much that I gave one almighty lunge and butted up against the hurdle with all my remaining strength. I was about to give in when there was a rude sucking noise and I felt a peg give. That was all I needed; I yanked with my arm and shoulder, and bucked up and down like a beached seal, until with a satisfying pop it came out. I lay back on my elbows, scrunched up my eyes and sobbed with relief.

From that moment on I knew that I would be free. I lay back and gathered my strength, no longer as desperate and no longer physically intimidated. I began to focus on Izzie, the treacherous cow. She had wanted to kill me. That was a fact; what other explanation was there? 'We'll never meet again in life.' That is what she had said. 'Well bitch, you are wrong. Whatever drug you gave me has worn off. And if your plan was to drown me under an incoming tide, you've failed. And as for your fame? We'll see about that, but I promise you this: it will be short lived.'

With my free arm I moved along the pegs one by one and soon there were enough of them out to allow me to wrench off the hurdle and climb unsteadily out from the pool. I stood up slowly in the gathering gloom of the early evening, my back bent and water streaming from my body, and reached up to the sky and roared like Grendel's grieving mother.

'Ahhhhhhhhhh!'

'Oh bloody hell!'

I was so shocked to hear another human voice that for a moment I was too scared to think; I just turned to the voice with wide eyes and gawked. Half obscured in the gloom someone was slowly approaching. 'Oh my god, she's got an accomplice?' I backed off unsteadily looking wildly around for a weapon, and stumbled over the hurdle and fell to the ground. The stranger came closer and loured over me. Through raw eyes I saw a man dressed in camouflage with a pair of binoculars hanging from his neck.

'You didn't half give me a shock popping out the ground like that,' he said, looking down at me as if unable to determine my species. 'You all right?

A bird watcher! Oh no! I laughed hysterically. 'Oh am I pleased to see you.'

'Not the best place to go camping, mate. It'll be under water in an hour. '

Meeting me put an end to my saviour's twilight birding and together we ambled back along the river tracks to the town. Despite the offer of a drink, he left me as soon as he was sure that the publican, who was a friend of his, recognized that I was who I said I was and had accepted me back into my room.

Thanks to a lingering fug in my head from Izzie's murderous 'love potion', I was happy to remain in the warmth of the shower mindlessly watching the swirl of residual marshland slime and scented hair wash swill around my feet. Only after I had toed the last vestiges of sand and gunk down the plughole did I come out, dressed in a bath towel kilt, and threw myself down onto the double bed, the venue for the fuck that never came. Not that I was interested in sex anymore; oh no, far from it. In fact I had identified that ridiculous craving as the source of my present predicament. How else could I explain what I was doing alone in a double bed in a pub in Essex?

What depressed me more than anything else was my age. I was as good as sixty and still being made a monkey off by sex. When I was a teen, I used to look at my parents' lives of quiet intimacy, and assume that once you got to their advanced age, they were both in their fifties, that sex was over and done with. I had imagined that only after I had reached that age would I too be able to break its strangle hold, and no longer have to dive into my underpants every few yards to wrestle my ridiculous dick into temporary submission.

Lying inert, in the cold after-shower equilibrium, at least I'd become honest enough to admit that I'd only gone along with Izzie's plans to accompany me on my search because she had promised sex. Sex! You buffoon! I'd nearly been murdered for that brief frenzy. Ugh! That's what hurt. It made a mockery of who I thought I was. And as for my ability to tell fact from fabrication – well! She called herself Izzie fucking Capricious, for God's sake; it should have been obvious she was untrustworthy; it was blatant enough.

I looked about the room. My overnight bag looked like an eviscerated sheep, its contents strewn across the floor when I'd searched for the washbag. Apart from that, there were was no other luggage to be seen. There had been nothing of Izzie's in the bathroom, either, which meant she had returned to the room, grabbed her gear and buggered off. I got dressed and went down to the bar; I needed a noisy background distraction and a drink.

I guessed she had imagined that by morning light I would be dead, and would have become a bog body in the making. It was possible of course, that thanks to the tide, my body would have been covered in the night by sand and silt; in which case I might actually have disappeared by the break of day and, as you couldn't see the little pond from any of the obvious tracks, remain undiscovered, perhaps forever.

'But why kill me? Most normal people shy away from anything drastic, especially murder. But then I was talking about Izzie. Normal? She was copper-bottom odd, everyone, or at least Ed and Angie, had even said as much. This meant that her 'great work', her artistic offering to the world, had always been based upon my death; that right from the start, when she had first appeared amongst us, she had envisaged a step by step progression to the grand finale – my demise. That was not odd, that was fucking madness!'

As I grimaced at the implications, I noticed the barman looking quizzically across at me. Perhaps he'd been warned by the innkeeper, who had obviously not been entirely convinced by my earlier explanation for arriving on his hearth drenched to the skin and looking like a marshland wraith. I nodded and half raised my glass in salutation.

'Bit warmer now!'

A thin smile settled unnaturally on his wan lips.

Izzie must have factored in what would happen once I was declared missing and that sooner or later someone would be banging on her door and asking questions. She'd have known that she had precious little time to finish my bit of the 'great work' and present it before the shit hit the fan. She could feign surprise and tell some cock and bull story about us rowing. She could admit going off in a huff and marooning me in Wivenhoe. She couldn't be arrested for that; she might be considered a selfish bitch, but not a murdering psychopath. Only if I failed to appear a few days later would suspicions grow and foul play be suspected.

Naturally, the first thing that the police would do, would be to search the marsh, but how efficiently? They were strapped for cash, so they probably wouldn't be able to afford more than a cursory glance, and the marsh was vast, with a surface that changed with every tide. Even with dogs trained to sniff out a corpse, where to start would always be a problem. All of which meant that Izzie only had a short time to do what had in mind to do, so the real question was: what on earth was that?

I supped at my pint, trying to suck inspiration from the bitter hops. I was her final subject, that was a fact, and her marshland tableau was, therefore, the last part of her extended study for *The Bucket Shop*, or whatever she was going to call it. I'd already seen the final prints of Peter Rock's *Risen Christ*; I'd seen some of the photographs she had taken of Toby and the others and, without exception, they had all been very good; she was talented - fact. Then there were her internet commendations: all positive. True again, she had form. The portraits of Ed were outstanding, really penetrating, some of the best I'd ever seen of him, but, I suddenly realized, there were none of the *Miracle of the Fishes* itself, which was odd. Then I recalled her initial response to the picture when we'd all gathered to see it. She had scanned it quickly like a professional, but instead of respect or admiration her eyes had told a different story. She had been shocked, I could see that, but at what: Ed's skill or something deeper, something personal? Then her eyes had gone cold. She had detached from the whole thing. Her face had gone blank. At the time I thought that she was jealous of him, but maybe it wasn't that, maybe it had been hostility, as if an old enemy had returned and that painting itself had angered her. I mean, she was a photographer. Figurative painting was meant to have been dealt the death blow by the advent of photography, and yet here we all were genuflecting before it again.

This was developing into a two pint problem, and although I would never normally have drunk a lot before going to bed, somehow weeing in the night was of lesser importance than working out what to do next.

Most parts of my body behave themselves unless I push them too hard. By the fourth pint, my bladder had taken over from my brain. I was hardly back at my seat before it ordered me out again and into the toilet. That's when I knew. As I stood in front of the basin half-heartedly washing my hands and staring at the gormless simpleton in the mirror, I understood what was happening. Izzie had to get me up on her walls, or someone's walls, as quickly as possible. Only then, when her oeuvre was up and visible, would the work be free to speak for itself. Police or no police, she would have done the business. If I was discovered dead, it wouldn't matter what happened to her, because if the critics had praised the work, her fame would be assured, and my death in her eyes would be a valuable publicity wheeze, and if it bombed, and she was accused of murder, she would still have a reputation, but not just as an artist, she would become a legend like Jack the Ripper: she would be the woman who had killed for art. Our faces would proceed through history and Wikipedia together, forever.

I was alive. Nobody knew anything of what happened, therefore, unless she confessed to attempted murder, no law had been broken, and as I was too poor and too reluctant to make out that it had, she was home and dry. But, and this was the thing, if I appeared at her show, what then: Lazarus rises from the dead? There would be no sad death to boost to her publicity. If I challenged her, she could deny everything I said had happened, but that wouldn't matter either, because I was not going to. The work would have to stand alone - fine, but she and I would no longer be careering through history yoked together, and I would become no more than a footnote in her catalogue.

I stood by the hand dryer smiling. I would find where she was planning to hang her work and appear at her opening like a bad fairy. It would be a shock. But I needn't say a thing, she would know; she would *always* know. But what she would never know was what I might do next, which meant that I would have the last laugh.

CHAPTER 33

RAY

I admit to brooding in the taxi from Wivenhoe to Colchester, not about the price, which was exorbitant, but about Izzie, and not just about Izzie Capricious, but also about Mayola Rhodes and Isabel Mc Ketterick, the last, I assumed, being her real name, although that was a huge assumption.

On the train to Liverpool Street, I wondered why Ed had taken such an immediate dislike to her and I hadn't. He'd been so adamant, even telling me, via Angie, that she was *'so far up her own arse that she'd forgotten the way out'*. I guess, he wanted to warn me and knew that Angie would pass the message on, which she did. He can be a contrary bugger, but it was not like him to take against someone so strongly after such a brief acquaintance, and what exactly did he mean: that she was just out on a limb and artistically lost, or totally self-regarding and dangerously unstable, or all of them?

By the outskirts of London I'd reached an introspective dead-end, and by the time the dark tunnels of Liverpool Street had hoved into view my mind had wondered off on to something else.

As I reached for the front door, it opened; Angie was off to work.

'I wish I'd known; I've just locked up,' she said.

We hugged and exchanged a quick kiss.

'Success?'

'Yes, yes, not quite what I expected, but yes, a success,' I said.

'Wonderful! Look, got to go darling. Tell me all about it when I'm back.'

'Have fun, sweetheart,' I said from the door.

'Oh, give Ed a bell and ask if he wants to come over for tea,' she said, turning back from the gate. 'Bye.'

I dumped my bag and went straight to my office and turned on the computer. If I was going to stymie Izzie I had no time to lose. What I wanted to know first was the likely venue for her *'great work'*, and so, once again, I Googled: *Izzie Capricious*; her website opened, but under what I was now sure was her real name: *Isabel Mc Ketterick*. Beneath the strapline was a picture of her in her Stoke Newington studio leaning over a large photographic print. She looked serious, every bit the committed artist. I recognized much of the background, but the image itself must have been taken before we'd all met, because the two mugs we had smashed in our wild love making were clearly visible on a table.

The rest of the website was much as I expected and not so dissimilar to Ed's. Below her name, but above the image, were the usual headings: Work, CV, Press, Contacts, News and Forthcoming shows. I flicked from one to the other, eventually stopping to read her CV, which was a brief essay that ended in an endorsement by a James Crosby, someone I'd never heard of before. He said: *'she was a ruthless observer of our common fate'*. She was certainly ruthless, all right; the rest of the piece was the usual hyperbolic art nonsense.

I clicked on Contacts. A simple well laid out window opened showing her foreign and domestic galleries. There was also a special text panel for anyone who wished to contact her directly. The temptation to do so was very strong. It was like finding a castle gate left open when you wished to sneak in. I could write anything I wished, but it had to be appropriate, something like: *'Guess who?'*, or *'The Essex Lazarus'*. It should be cryptic enough to keep her guessing, but not so dense that she couldn't make an educated guess that it was me: the unexpected voice from the grave. If I was going to do it, she needed to be discombobulated, scared even. Still undecided, I flicked on until I found what I wanted, news of her latest opening: *'Wild Desires – a photographic argument for authenticity.'* The opening was the day after today in Church Street, which was only a short walk from her studio.

I hadn't told Angie or Ed the truth about what had happened on the marsh. I wanted them to arrive at the show totally unprepared for whatever it was that I was going to say or do. Their surprise and subsequent outrage would then have the same quality as the other punters, and would add weight to the ensuing turmoil. After that we could leave, but Izzie couldn't. I would have spiked her heart. Exposure would lurk in her brain like a virus. She would become a queen bee in a suddenly hostile hive. Social media would buzz with the pernicious gossip of those who had witnessed the scene. Her integrity would be eroded. She would suffer but I wouldn't, because my revenge would be mild and sweet, and therefore not addictive.

Before leaving the website, I looked again at the text box. It would be fun to tease her. If I said something quirky it would make her apprehensive about the forthcoming opening. I clicked, and then I clicked a Quotation site for inspiration. I found more choices than I'd imagined, but some of the people quoted meant nothing to me. I wanted a bit of substance, and so I copied something from a Guy de Maupassant story and pasted it in.

"*A marsh is a whole world within a world, a different world, with a life of its own, with its own permanent denizens, its passing visitors, its voices, its sounds, its own strange MYSTERY.*" I put mystery in capitals, and then added: '*That is so true*'.

My email address: '*Mapmaker@*' would obviously be a clue as to my identity, but as I'd never emailed her, it would be unfamiliar. *Click* – away it went.

It wasn't entirely surprising that when Ed joined us for a meal that evening, I was the butt of various jokes and sallies about the whole POD enterprise. I deserved it. A penitent sometimes needs a friend or significant other to point out the error of their ways. They were right, I should have listened to them, and so I took my friendly drubbing as humbly as I could.

'Really, there was nothing there, not even a dead crab or bits of old fishing tackle?' said Ed.

'Nothing.'

'So how did you know that that was it?'

'The Ordinance Survey have sign for a POD,' said Angie, hugely enjoying my embarrassment.

'A coffin with a cross?' said Ed, laughing.

'No, no Edward, not a cross, that's far too Christocentric. Just a coffin.'

'Right, ha, ha, ok, so I should have listened; well, I know that now, but I had to do what I had to do, and that's a fact. But now it's over, apart, that is, from our visit to Izzie's show tomorrow. You are coming, I take it?'

'*Wild Desires*! I wouldn't miss it.'

'Me neither,' said Ed. 'You are not the only one she snapped, mate.'

'That's being a bit snooty, Ed,' said Angie. 'She's hardly a beach photographer; even you said her work was good.'

'Authentic *Wild Desires*, Raymondo. I can't wait.'

I didn't mind their good natured kicking, because, like all good flagellants, I was sure it was doing me good.

'Joking aside, Ray, I'm buggered if I can make that woman out? You've spent time away with her, so she can't be a complete nutter; unless, of course, it *was* the wild, authentic sex.' He and Angie found that totally amusing and laughed outrageously.

I smiled, not even bridling at the underlying assumption that sex and with me was intrinsically funny, because they were right, not that I would ever admit it; there's honesty and then there's bloody stupidity.

'You can laugh, but whatever you two may think, Izzie *is* an interesting person, although I admit, she can be a bit of handful.' This made them both laugh even more. 'No, no. God you two. Underneath her flamboyant artiness and the dressing up, she's as hard as nails, quite ruthless. There were times when I thought she's actually unstable,' I said, increasing the stress on 'unstable', and looking suitably concerned.

Ed pulled a grotesque face and tapped the side of his head.

'Ed!' said Angie, disapprovingly.

I felt uncomfortable mentioning my worries about Izzie's mental state, because I wasn't being honest. I was taking out an insurance policy. I was making sure that if things got out of hand at the opening, and the authorities were involved, then under questioning they would remember that I had expressed concern about her mental health. It would also help to diffuse their fantasies about 'wild sex'. Now they would imagine the stresses and strains of spending a weekend away with a screwball.

I reached across to them both and gave their hands a squeeze.

'I know I can be a twat sometimes, but you two, my two oldest and dearest friends, you stuck by me - despite thinking that I was out to lunch.' They laughed. 'But it was true, what I said. I did feel it here,' I touched my stomach, 'and here,' I said, touching my head. 'It was my interpretation of the feeling that was wrong.'

'It's your age, sunshine,' said Ed, smiling at me benignly.

'*Age can not wither her,*' said Angie, inappropriately.

'I'll drink to that,' said Ed, raising his glass. 'Seriously though, Ray, without you I'm not sure I would have done what I've done.'

'If that's true, mate, then it's all been worthwhile.'

Angie had tears in her eyes as Ed and I embraced.

'What was it all about though?' he said, close to my ear.

It was my turn to sigh, although it was more like a grown. 'Obviously, there *is* a place-of-death; we all have one of those, but I'll probably not know where it will be other than here, on this '*nook shotten isle of albion*', where our families have lived and died since the ice retreated.'

I saw tears well up in Angie's eyes, and she opened her arms for another group hug, but I knew that what I had said was only part of an explanation. My life was far too slippery to say anything truthful about it.

Geordie, always a sucker for sentimentality, began barking to be included.

'God you're a noisy bugger,' I said, signing for him to jump up on my lap. Being French kissed by a hairy mutt is antidote enough for mawkishness.

Never a great fan of being kissed by hairy faces, Angie got up to make coffee, and Ed and I trooped off into the sitting room.

'Hey, I forgot to tell you both,' he said, loud enough for Angie to hear in the kitchen, 'the Packhorses phoned this morning - the cheques in the bank.'

'Excellent!'

'We must celebrate,' said Angie.

'Why don't we all go out after this thing with Izzie tonight?' I said, shouting over the kettle. 'And as you're a rich man, Edward, we'll let you pay!'

'Was a rich man, mate, was a rich, man; don't forget the bloody gallery takes forty odd percent of my meagre earnings.'

'In that case, we'll have a take-away.'

I could have kept the news of Izzie's show just to the three of us, but because her photographs concerned everyone else in the *Bucket Shop*, I felt that my last act as its founder should be to text or email all its erstwhile members so that they could come and see themselves transformed into works of art. Not everyone replied, but most did, and most said they would come. From my point of view the more the merrier, I wanted an audience, even though I was still unsure what my performance would entail. I was torn between keeping it close and personal, like slipping a stiletto between her ribs, or going in hard and heavy and making a scene. Sadly, neither option suggested to me what I was actually going to say or do. The only thing I was sure about was not getting to the venue too early. There had to be an audience, and for my performance I was going to wear a costume – my 'bronze-age' smock.

Ed laughed when he saw it.

'It looks better without these trousers,' I said.

'You can't wear that thing, darling, you look ridiculous,' said Angie.

'Wait until you see the pictures.'

There was a brief thunder storm when we got to Stokey, and before we were half way up Church Street we were drenched. Having thought about their reaction to my smock, I'd already decided that I needed to give them a hint as to what had really happened out on the marsh.

'Just so you know,' I said, halting at a road junction, 'it was not all sweetness and light out there on the marsh. Izzie and I had a serious falling out, and there are still things I need to sort out with her. This might make the evening a bit more interesting than just looking at the work.'

'Oh my god! Why didn't you tell us?'

'I said he was being a bit cagey,' said Ed.'

'It's a question of timing, and I need this to be done in public. You'll find out soon enough.'

'There's not going to be a shouting match is there?' said Angie.

I smiled reassuringly. 'As if,' I said. 'Shall we?' I ushered them ahead towards the hall.

At the door I made my decision. I was not going to bang on it and enter like the Demon King. I would enter quietly, because I didn't want to be seen before I was well into the hall itself. I needed to occupy the centre.

'I'll go first, ok?'

I peeped through the two small windows of the swing door. The hall was the size of an average jumble sale, and there were more people in it than I'd expected.

'Peter and Toby are here.'

They were standing together in front of the image of Peter's crucifixion like two redundant imperial adventurers, their bushy beards, one dark and one red, giving their slight frames a certain Edwardian gravitas. It wasn't hard to spot Izzie. Dressed entirely in emerald, she stuck out like an exotic butterfly, and was standing with her back to me expatiating grandly to a group of arty looking folk. I pushed open the door, and slipped quietly inside. By the time I'd got to the middle, I'd decided that I would say nothing; I would rely on magic. If it's true that we can feel another's eyes on us, I would stare at her back until she turned to face me.

Her listeners became aware of me long before she did, and it was either their sidelong glances or my piercing stare which alerted her to my presence. She turned around as if expecting more admirers and blanched. The silent, staring figure in the sodden smock was supposed to be dead, and yet there I was. The gaudy butterfly became rigid, as though transfixed to the floor by a pin.

I kept shtum, inclining my head as if in in greeting, but still staring at her face with the fixed intensity of a movie corpse.

Beneath her skin I watched the finer muscles of her face moving, and the rise and fall of her lips, but I made no movements of my own. The dead have nothing to say physically, and I could see that my silence and stability were having their desired effect, because she suddenly turned, her eyes raked the hall behind and to the sides. She then took a step back. I couldn't resist it, so I stared even harder, as if I really did have the power to compel her backwards. She went; she staggered and then rushed into a small side room and slammed the door shut. The floor was mine. Her admirers were mine. The job was done. There was nothing else for me to do. I *had* the upper hand. She would forever be in my thrall. I turned to go. Angie and Ed were struggling to understand what they had just witnessed.

'I'll meet you at that Spanish restaurant we passed on the way here. Stay around awhile and tell me what happens.'

That was all I said in explanation. They were speechless. I could see that they were completely at a loss, so I smiled to calm them, and left, very satisfied with my charade.

I knew that as soon as they came to the restaurant I would be severely questioned, so I was ready when they eventually arrived.

'Hola.'

'What on earth was that all about? She looked like she'd seen a ghost.'

'She had,' I said laughing. 'Did she come out after I'd gone?'

'She was ranting; we could hear her through the door. She only came out once her friends had talked to her. She was deathly white; they had to support her.'

'Good job they did,' said Ed, 'because when she saw the wet ring on the floor where you'd been standing, she collapsed again.'

I laughed, 'Perfect!'

'That weren't the end though,' he added. 'A bit later, she started screaming the bloody house down, telling everyone to get out; wouldn't allow anyone to stay. That's when we buggered off.'

'No one had a clue what had happened. Although some woman said you were the figure in the bog or something.'

'That was a weird photograph,' said Ed.

'Ok. I'll explain, but only after we've ordered. And don't worry about the wine, Ed,' I said filling their glasses, 'it's not a Rioja.'

I told them more or less the whole story. They were shocked. Angie was all for going back and sorting her out.

'She's a bloody psychopath.'

'She's certainly mental,' said Ed.

That was more or less where we all were in our understanding. None of us really knew anything about mental health, we fell back on the usual multi-syllable words, gossip, and half remembered articles we'd once read in the Sunday papers.

I noticed that they treated me a bit differently after that. Whatever they'd imagined I'd gone through at her hands transformed itself into them being more solicitous about my comfort and ease, which was great, because I got more of the pudding when it came; more importantly though, I was more at ease. I'd seen her abject terror. As far as I could tell she really believed I had returned from the dead. What better revenge could there be than that? Apart from being a part of her art work, I had severed any connection that my death might have forged. She was on her own, and that, as far as Izzie and I were concerned, was that. It was over.

I was upstairs in the study working on my rivers when I knew that it wasn't. The front door bell rang and I trotted down happily intent on making a coffee after fielding whoever was calling.

I had no idea who the two callers were. The woman spoke first. She was a gimlet eyed woman in her twenties. Her male colleague was older but equally cold eyed.

'Raymond Brook?'

I stiffened and prepared to close the door. 'What do you want?' I'd met enough door step hustlers in my time to take no prisoners. 'Quick, I'm busy.'

'Do you know Isabel Mc Ketterick?'

'No, yes,' I said, suddenly remembering Izzie's real name. 'Why?'

'Did she take pictures of you?'

'Look are you the police or something?'

'You know she tried to commit suicide, don't you?'

God knows what my face looked like, but I didn't have time to think about it before the man brought out a camera and fired away at me.

'What? Hey! Fuck off!' I said, closing the door. 'Fucking reporters.'

They rabbeted on through the door, but I'd backed off into the sitting room too shocked to think straight. 'Suicide? The bitch, the bastard.' I slumped against the wall and slid down. 'Oh god, if the press is here, then the police can't be far behind. Suicide! Was that still a crime? It was certainly publicity. God, it would be all over the national press. Damn, damn, damn. I wish she had died, at least that would have silenced the bitch, now she could weave whatever story she liked. Just when I thought I was free of her, now I was the one in thrall. She could play me like a fish.

It wasn't until the afternoon that the police arrived, and by then I had had time to calm down. My head was clear. I had done nothing more than participate in her *'great desire'*, for God's sake. She was the criminal, not me; she had tried to kill me. Not that I could ever prove that. It would always be my word against hers, which made the whole thing about revelation difficult, if not impossible. Should I tell them all that had gone on, or keep that crucial fact to myself?

'She swallowed toilet cleaner.'

That's what the policewoman told me. 'Nasty,' I said, and seeing as though I was not being accused of anything, I was more than happy to help them. They were simply trying to discover all that they could about the incident, the facts of the case, or in my case, those details I was willing to share. No one in their right mind gulps downs bleach, and since I knew something of its effects I doubted that la Capricious would be in any fit state to say anything meaningful for a long time, since her oesophagus and gullet must have been in a pretty parlous state. I therefore minimized my connections and painted her as nothing more than an enterprising photographer.

'She appeared out of the dark, one evening. It was the first time any of us had seen her.'

Printed in Great Britain
by Amazon